A Crown of Stars

ALSO BY SHANA ABÉ

The Second Mrs. Astor
An American Beauty

A Crown of Stars

SHANA ABÉ

KENSINGTON
PUBLISHING CORP.
kensingtonbooks.com

KENSINGTON BOOKS are published by

Kensington Publishing Corp.
900 Third Avenue
New York, NY 10022

All Kensington titles, imprints and distributed lines are available at special quantity discounts for bulk purchases for sales promotion, premiums, fund-raising, educational or institutional use. Special book excerpts or customized printings can also be created to fit specific needs. For details, write or phone the office of the Kensington Special Sales Manager: Kensington Publishing Corp., 900 Third Avenue, New York, NY, 10022. Attn. Special Sales Department. Phone: 1-800-221-2647.

KENSINGTON and the K with book logo Reg. US & Pat TM Off.

Library of Congress Control Number: On file

ISBN: 978-1-4967-5135-5

First Kensington Hardcover Edition: March 2026

ISBN: 978-1-4967-5136-2 (trade)

ISBN: 978-1-4967-5137-9 (ebook)

10 9 8 7 6 5 4 3 2 1

Printed in the United States of America

The authorized representative in the EU for product safety and compliance
is eucomply OU, Parnu mnt 139b-14, Apt 123
Tallinn, Berlin 11317, hello@eucompliancepartner.com

For all those who strive for peace,
even while battling the maelstrom.

Prologue

JULY, 1917
THE HUDSON RIVER, NEW YORK

The water was gray and thick, and the wind that skimmed it tasted of summer. What might have been a thousand panicked voices, but was actually only hundreds, screamed in an eerie sort of harmony: bass, treble, soprano. Lifting and falling. All around Rita Jolivet, frantic people swam or sank in the river, scattered along its bright surface.

She wasn't frantic, not yet, but her arms were tired, and her legs were tired, and the water closed over her head. The voices were snuffed. She heard only the pulse of the river in her eardrums then, stronger than even her own heartbeat.

She kicked back to the surface, hands finding the air first, then her head and arms. Her long skirts billowed behind her, tangling in her legs; her corset cinched every breath.

It was a messy way to die. An inelegant, undignified way.

The water swallowed her down again. She held her breath and closed her eyes, battling the weight of her dress, the tug of the current that whispered *Yes, come with me, deeper.*

Deeper.

She opened her eyes and found the sun overhead, a silvery pale glimmer that shifted and danced. A darker shadow just beside it, steadier, almond-shaped. A lifeboat.

She mustered her energy, fought her way up again. This time when she broke free, she took a deep, whooping breath. The lifeboat was overturned but still floating, so Rita—who had been raised alongside a river, in fact, a wide strong one with its own whispering currents, and so knew very well how to swim—sliced her way to it, gray water, white froth.

Her fingers dug into the ridges of the planking, and the boat gave an alarming tilt, but then a man with a walrus moustache grabbed hold of the prow, and the tilt leveled out.

The screaming wound on. Even the seagulls, gliding in their white-and-black lines, joined in.

Rita hitched her way higher up the boat. She met the man's eyes, lifted her chin, and managed a smile, a brave one, a beautiful one. One that would, eventually, make its way around the world in posters and promotional stills and postcards, and inspire thousands of women (in their more intimate moments) to arrange their hair in just the way hers looked right now, freed from its pins, swept dark and dramatic across her pale brow, dampened curls clinging sensually to her cheekbones and shoulders and back.

A man yelled, "Cut!"

Instantly, the screaming stopped. The people who had been drowning seconds before now only treaded in place, every face turned toward a nearby skiff holding a trio of dry, well-dressed men, one with a megaphone dangling from his fingers. Beyond them, at the edge of the shore, a tall wooden platform loomed over them all, loaded with more men and a moving-picture camera on a tripod.

Rita slipped off the lifeboat, swam the short distance to the skiff. She was plucked from the water and wrapped at once in a blanket, a tin mug of whiskey pressed into her hands.

Léonce Perret, director of *Lest We Forget*, Rita's film child, her dream child, her nightmare, sank into a squat beside her. The skiff rocked; water smacked against the hull. Although the humans had fallen quiet, the gulls had not, still cawing and cackling. Somewhere in the distance, a ship's bell clanged three metallic, minor notes.

Léonce ran a palm down his cheek. He gave her a sideways look, the oiled part in his hair gleaming under the sun.

"What do you think, love?" he asked. "*Cinéma vérité* enough for you?"

Rita clutched the blanket tighter around her. Over two hundred extras bobbing in the Hudson stared back at her, at her director, waiting for the signal for the next take.

She lifted the mug, her hand shaking. She downed the whiskey and cleared her throat.

"It's close," she said finally, flat. "Not as cold, not as many people, but close. And everyone here's still alive. So that's goddamned different, I guess."

Part 1

Chapter 1

19 July, 1915

Marguerite,

Forgive me.

It's been so hot these latter days. Sweltering, rancid, the sky bleached near to white like an old dog bone, the grass in Central Park faded to straw. I can tell that, while I was gone, my housekeeper did her best to salvage the bougainvilleas in their urns lining the balcony, but poor things. Early spring they promised a verdant bramble. I've come back to my apartment to find that even they have been sacrificed to the heat, pink leaves dried to dust, their tender edges crisped and dead.

Forgive me. I did not mean to dwell on the morose.

At night—oh, especially at night, when I'm abed and I hang, suspended, between my dreams—I take a deep breath of this stinking Manhattan air, and all I smell is the cool salt wind off the Celtic Sea.

Isn't that funny, sissy?

MEDMENHAM, ENGLAND

Most locals claimed that the misty, leafy estate known as Winter Queen was named after Charlotte of Mecklenburg-Strelitz, who might—or might not—have spent three snowbound nights in its manor house, and who might—or might not—have found three snowbound nights of respite from her mad husband, King George, in the warm arms of an unnamed courtier. Or perhaps a stable lad.

Nonsense, said others. The house and land were actually named for the fairy queen said to dwell in the surrounding woods, Mab or Old Moss or Gloriana, depending on who was telling the tale, and how many pints they'd enjoyed before starting in.

Whatever its origin, Winter Queen was indeed an impressive mess of a place, close enough to a wide bend of the Thames to attract errant seabirds blown inland, far enough to barely glimpse its ribbon of silver from the tallest hill. The original manor house was small, mysterious, and Tudor, cupped by trees and surrounded by deep purple bellflowers. Stained-glass windows sliced through dark-paneled rooms, so many windows that on bright days the house's walls and floors were bejeweled with color.

Subsequent owners kept the glass but expanded the rooms, generation by generation, adding two wings of gilt and marble, a conservatory. A library. A koi pond, also surrounded by bellflowers. By the time Charles Jolivet and his wife, Pauline, purchased the estate, the eldest fish in the pond were nearly thirty years old, and the imported turtles nestled along the shore much older.

The scent of ageless grandeur, the whiff of royalty that still lingered in the manor's corners and crevices, suited Pauline quite well.

She was tall, almost too tall for a man's comfort, but hand-some Charles never minded, so neither did she. Pauline had a blue-blooded inheritance and a flair for the piano, chestnut hair and an aristocratic nose. Yet her eyes were warm and brown, and her laughter so infectious she'd had her choice of suitors. Both she and Charles were native Parisians; Pauline was fond of mentioning to her guests that her great-grand-mother was the only one in her family to survive the Revolution's guillotine.

But France was not meant to contain them. Utilizing Paul-ine's lofty connections and his own grit, Charles proved a singular success as a businessman, so even though they had first met as teens, giddy in Paris, now as a married couple they owned vineyards in Provence, a flat in New York, and, of course, Winter Queen, the home where they had decided, mu-tually, to raise their three children.

Alfred, the youngest, blond, stubborn, and adventurous.

Inez, the middle child, blue-eyed, a dreamer who heard music in the woods no one else could, and who could replay it by memory (for the unbelieving) on her violin.

And Marguerite, the eldest, who had inherited her mother's glossy chestnut hair and vivacious laugh, but also an enthusiasm for independence and creativity that surpassed even Pauline's. Her spirit was not so much wild as it was gen-uinely unchained to convention. Of the three younger Jolivets, she was the natural leader.

Even before she'd mastered her alphabet, Marguerite in-vented feral dances and rambling plays, persuading her siblings to perform alongside her for their parents and the nanny and footmen and maids. In her plays, she was nearly always a princess, with Inez as her faithful handmaiden, which left Alfred (once he was old enough) to perform the role of either dragon or knight. He much preferred to be a dragon, roaring and stomping. So Pauline and Charles sat through a good many nursery performances about princesses slaying dragons, with Inez kneeling in terror—or awe, or joy—in the background.

It was an enchanted life for a child, even if the locals muttered under their breath about how *bohemian* the Jolivets were, with their Continental ways and rambunctious children tearing through the pastures and forests. One notorious story concerned the time the family had stopped by the Ruby Rabbit for supper. When six-year-old Marguerite had been offered a serving of the pub's famous cod and chips, perfectly golden and steaming hot, she'd turned up her nose and declined the plate, haughtily demanding *pot-au-feu* instead.

As the years passed, Marguerite heard echoes of the tale but honestly had no memory of it. The truth was, she adored fish and chips; she adored her English life and couldn't imagine that she'd ever disparage either. But, of course, she also loved France and the long, supple rows of grapevines composing their vineyards, the acres of fragrant soil and ancient crush houses scented of green and yeast. She loved New York, too, where she had been born. Their flat in Castleton was nice enough, but going into the city, walking along the streets and lanes of Manhattan, felt like visiting another world, under another sun, everything scintillating and glamorous and diamond-bright.

Broadway, with its luminous lights and theatres looming tall as castles, was especially enthralling. One the best evenings of her life was when her parents took her to see *The Shop Girl* at Palmer's Theater for her ninth birthday, and on that night, Marguerite's dreams swelled beyond the boundary of herself and overflowed. She didn't have to pretend to be only a princess. On a real stage, in front of a real audience, under flattering hot Fresnel lanterns, she could be anyone she wished.

THERE WERE OTHER luminous lights dotting her life, although it took her a while to realize it. Friends of her parents, men and women who moved through the parlors of Winter Queen with an almost uncannily similar elegance: ebony tailcoats, cravats pinned with rubies or pearls; silk dresses with hems that hissed along the floor or layers that rippled along the air; low heels, satin gloves, cultured voices.

There were formal dinners the children were not invited to, confined as they were to the nursery on the top floor. (*Someday*, Maman promised, when pressed by her eldest.) There were entertainments they were *sometimes* invited to, piano recitals by Pauline, arias sung by opera singers, lectures about oil painting or fan-making or botany. Once there came a rough bearded man who gave a talk about the perils of his voyage to the Antarctic and back. For a full three months afterward, Alfred insisted he was striking out soon to see it for himself, if only Mother and Father would lend him a ship.

Yet, by and large, these guests were simply *sir* or *ma'am* to the children, or *monsieur* or *madam*, or *signor* or *signora*. For years, very few really stood out, not even to the observant Marguerite. But one evening...

She was ten, and it was green April in Medmenham. The early, tender days of spring, when the cold fist of winter had finally loosened enough to allow yellow cowslips and delicate bluebells to uncurl from the earth, and the trees in the woods sparkled with rain instead of snow. Up in the nursery, Marguerite had been restless in her bed, her quilts pushed into a lump by her feet. Mother and Father were having another of their long, laughing dinner parties, and even through the floorboards, the company tonight seemed especially boisterous.

Both Inez and Alfred slept soundly, but Marguerite felt a prickling along her skin, a dryness to her eyes. She could not

relax; she could not sleep. She sat up, shoved her feet into her
slippers, found her robe, and crept out of the room.

She knew from experience how effortless it would be to
ease open the connecting door of the library to the west drawing room, where most of Winter Queen's guests lingered over
sherry and cigars after dinner. How she could press her face
against the seam of the opening—staying low, staying invisible—and observe the glitter of her parents' grand affairs.

She found her way on silent feet, freezing when she heard
servants nearby, pressing back into the shadows. The manor
was old, and she was young, but she'd already memorized its
quirks, which stairsteps would creak no matter how lightly she
trod; which corridors were dark or bright; the tucked-away
nooks where maids would pause to gossip in whispers. The
rhythms of the manor house were as familiar to Marguerite as
her own pulse.

Tonight, the library was illumed, but only barely. An elderly fire burned in the hearth, tarnished light dancing along
the bared teeth and scales of the wyverns carved into the man-
tlepiece. The tapers lining the chandelier above her were pale
slender ghosts, but a pair of oil lamps with cut-glass bases had
been lit in two corners, spreading a soft glow.

She lingered at the hallway entrance, listening, but heard
nothing beyond the sounds of the soirée bubbling on in the
drawing room, still a chamber away.

Marguerite crept forward; the air held its breath. Usually a
draft or two snaked across the room, chilling her ankles, but
tonight only the fire stirred, twisting and licking the logs piled
behind the fender, orange embers flashing patterns along the
charred wood.

The door to the drawing room was already cracked. She
fixed her attention on it, that chink of bright warmth that
arrowed through the opening, her heart already swelling over
the river of words and sultry laughter and perfume that

washed over her, promising her *someday*-future, promising en-
lightenment—when someone spoke.

Someone *behind* her.

"Child?" said an unfamiliar voice, soft and deep.

Marguerite turned so swiftly she bumped the door. It began
to swing closed. She only barely caught the knob in time to
stop it from slamming shut.

A gentleman sat in the dark, away from the fire and the
two lamps. He was in her father's favorite wingchair, the one
Papa used to read the papers early in the morning, when the
sun shone through the windows and lit the room to brilliance.

Marguerite dipped a hasty curtsy. "Oh! I'm sorry! Please
don't tell—"

She was already scurrying back toward the safety of the
hall, but the man in her father's chair only lifted an open
palm to her, somehow stopping her in place even though she
was nowhere near him.

She stared at him warily.

"Never fear," he said. A thin wash of starlight from the window beyond him brushed silver along his hair and beard. "I
know full well what it's like."

"What what's like?" she asked, still ready to bolt.

"To peer in from the outside. To be small and kept apart,
when all you want is to be included."

Marguerite straightened. She'd never had an adult speak
to her so, as if she were grown too. As if someone so old might
understand her heart.

"Well," was all she said . . . but she inched a step closer.

Her eyes were adjusting to the night. The man had not
moved, so it was easier now to pick out the precise leftward
sweep of his gray hair, the trimmed beard and moustache that
ended in waxed points. The dull gleam of a watch chain that
curved from one section of his coat to the other. His legs were

crossed at the ankle, and the buttons of his tailcoat were un-done, revealing a sizable belly covered in a satin waistcoat.

She remembered the image of Saint Nicholas on a card Inez had given her last Christmas, one of him seated on a throne with his red coat open to show his big belly, smiling almost just as this gentleman was smiling at her now, so kind, and before she could stop herself, Marguerite blurted, "Are you Kris Kringle?"

For an instant, he seemed affronted—or maybe just surprised; his bushy eyebrows lifted, his eyes on hers. Then his smile deepened. "Why, child? Do I resemble Santa?"

"Yes," she said, and added, "well, not your clothing, of course. But your beard, and your hair and face and"—she gestured to his torso, then hurried on. "He carries a gold pocket watch like yours, to keep time on Christmas Eve."

"Indeed," said the man.

"But," she went on, working out the logic, "why would you be here now? It's not even Christmas."

"Must I disappear after Christmastime?"

She tilted her head, thinking about it. "No. But...you should go back to the North Pole, shouldn't you? Isn't that your home?"

He made a small sound, not quite a sigh. "I suppose it must be."

Marguerite was ten, not six or seven or eight. In the cool hush of Winter Queen's library, she came back to herself, a girl more grown for her age than not.

"You're not him."

"I'm afraid not."

"Oh."

She waited, but the man added nothing more. She rubbed her left foot against her right ankle, stalling, then asked, "Who are you, then?"

He gave her another smile, but this one seemed weary. "No one nearly as important as Santa Claus, I'm afraid."

"But you're someone important."

"Some would say not."

"No," she replied, impatient. "Maman and Papa don't invite just anyone here, you know. You must be important to someone."

He looked up at her, still weary, still smiling. "I suppose you're right. I must be, mustn't I?"

He held out a hand to her, and after a second, she stepped forward and accepted it in both of hers. His skin was chilled; his fingers curled lightly around hers.

She felt it then, his fatigue, the sorrow that weighted his bones. On instinct, she bent her head, pressed a swift kiss to his knuckles.

"Don't be sad about it," she commanded, looking up again. "Whatever it may be, don't be so sad."

"No," the man said. He released her hands. This close to him, she could tell that his eyes were pale, his hair mostly silver, and the chain across his stomach more golden than the fire. "Thank you, dear. I won't be. I'm not."

For the rest of her life, Marguerite Lucile Jolivet would entertain her friends and the press with the tale of how she'd once informed the Prince of Wales that he must surely be important, and of how he had eventually, reluctantly, agreed.

THE POND HELD a particular fascination for Inez. She would spend hours draped along its shore, her head bent and her long, honied hair sometimes brushing the water as she followed the languid, orange-red-white turns of the koi. The pond wasn't overly wide, but it was deep—well over twelve feet—dug that way, perhaps, to ensure the survival of the fish through the winter. In the bitterest months, the surface would

thicken into ice, and all the beautiful koi would sink into a stu-
por at the bottom, still breathing, but oh so barely.

Inez told everyone they were dreaming and then, one afternoon over tea in the nursery, wondered what fish would
dream about.

"Juicy worms," said Alfred.

"July," said Marguerite.

"Their happiest selves," said Pauline, hugging her younger
daughter close. "They dream of waking up again in warmer
waters, surrounded by all their friends, their husbands or
wives."

Marguerite looked up from the lukewarm crumpet she was
smearing with jam; she respected Maman but didn't feel it appropriate to let the comment pass. "Fish don't have husbands
or wives."

Pauline smiled, reaching for her own crumpet. "Don't they?
Many creatures find their partners and bond for life, much as
we do. Fish, swans, rabbits, snails—all of nature, all of hidden
life—live nations apart from us. It would be foolish to pretend
they don't have their own secret realms. So turns the glorious
world."

"Mr. and Mrs. Fish!" said Alfred, and he fell into snorts of
laughter.

THE AUTUMN OF the year that Marguerite would come to consider the end of her childhood arrived when she was fourteen.
Too old for the nursery any longer, so she had her own room,
but still young enough to secretly miss the comradery of that
stuffy attic chamber, the soft snores of her little sister and
brother, the old familiar toys and apple-green curtains framing
a view of the rose garden three stories below. She'd kept a
handful of her favorite dolls to sit on a shelf by her bureau,
but the rest of the room was a harbinger of her future: gleaming furniture, crystal-prism lamps, dainty sparrows and wag-

tails hand-painted on butterscotch silk wallpaper, vases of fresh flowers. And, most significantly, a wardrobe of dresses with hems falling past her ankles.

But living rooms apart didn't mean living a roof apart, and Marguerite and Inez remained each other's devoted companions, with Alfred tagging along as he liked. On this fateful October day, the girls were returning from an early ramble through the woods. Inez had discovered a fairy ring the day before and was eager to show it to her sister, to ask her opinion whether it could be the work of Gloriana or Old Moss.

"Neither," Marguerite had announced, after squatting down to examine the circle of velvety gray toadstools. She shifted, and the leaves at her feet rustled and cracked. "This ring belongs to Mab, clear as could be. See how perfect it is? See how in the sunlight the caps turn to silver?"

"Yes," agreed Inez, solemn.

"Well, that's Mab, certainly. Well done! She wouldn't reveal this to just anyone, you know. You must be special."

"I do hear her music," Inez replied. In the dappled light, her face was heart-shaped and serious, but her eyes shone brilliant, a deeper blue than the heavens.

Marguerite stood up again, dusting off her hands. "Perhaps later on, after supper, we can steal back and leave some bread and milk for her and her court. She'd like that."

"Oh, yes, let's!"

So they were walking back to Winter Queen, following an olden path lined with rosebay and witches' butter, and emerald wood sorrel with broad, nodding leaves. The days were sneaking by, shorter and shorter; even the nuthatches above them chattered about the cold. It wouldn't be long before the first snow.

Every step they took along that forest path released a spiced scent of fallen leaves, of cinnamon and frost and dirt. Marguerite enjoyed that fragrance, the crunch of her boots against the earth, and when they left the woods behind them for the more formal grounds of Winter Queen, she lifted her face to the sky, to the sun, soaking up its meager warmth. She was lost in that moment, breathing in, breathing out, when Inez gave a sharp inhale and jerked to a stop.

Marguerite turned. Her sister had transformed into a pillar of salt, just like Lot's wife, pale and frozen.

"What is it?"

Inez lifted a hand to point ahead of them.

Marguerite turned back again.

They were near the koi pond, its dark waters throwing darts of light. Flashes of orange and white churned beneath its surface, the fish agitated, moving fast despite the cold. But above the koi, larger and very awful, was the shape of a person. A man in a tattered jumper, his arms out, his legs bent at the knees to fade into the deep. His hair—the color of silt, of the murky depths—swept lazily back and forth with the swish of the water. He lay against a fall of rocks; a strand of algae had got caught near his temple, lifting and swaying.

His face was puffy, upturned, the color of the toadstools, swollen lips opened to a slit around his tongue, glazed eyes staring.

One of the koi rose up and nudged the man's neck.

Marguerite spun back to Inez, clapped a hand over her eyes, and dragged her away, one step at a time.

"Don't look! Do *not* look!"

But as they staggered past the pond, Marguerite herself couldn't help but look, even though she didn't want to, even though she knew it was a mistake.

Bloated flesh, sodden clothes, hungry koi. Dead eyes fixed upon the eternity of the midday sky.

She realized that she knew him. That the horror of his face still resembled the gardener's son, known to drink and brawl as happily as he had tended the roses. A young man who whistled under his breath as he worked and always smelled of gin and sod.

She lowered her gaze again, still leading her sister, but it was too late. This particular mistake would sear itself in Marguerite's memory like an ember burning through sheets of paper, creating its own particular scorch mark in her mind, slowly dimming and cooling, but never fully erased.

Chapter 2

The voyage home seemed to stretch into forever. I know my time aboard the *Saint Paul* spun out into the same hours and minutes it usually does; I know that my dull mind was the problem. My vision was blurred. My body ached. Every moment felt like midnight.

But it gave me the opportunity to consider a good many things. During those midnight days and nights out there on the Atlantic, I found myself pondering the notion of courage. Of what it means to act boldly and fearlessly, even when confronted with death. As a girl, I used to believe that I was courageous. I would venture into the heart of the woods all alone. I would play my violin for Maman and Papa's ocean of humanity, for strangers and royalty, even when I was so sick with nerves I wanted only to hide.

I realize now that I was only pretending to be brave because you were. You were the girl in the sun and I was your shadow, and I swear I wanted nothing more than to be just like you.

Bold and fearless.

But shadows are what they are, fleeting shade that only exists in the presence of strong light.

AUGUST, 1901
MEDMENHAM, ENGLAND

Inez hardly recalled a time when her life was not saturated in song. Gentle music, sometimes like a breeze teasing a weeping birch into flutters, or the lapping of the Thames along a shore of shiny mud. Sometimes stronger, like rain pelting glass, or even violent, like a storm at sea, which, thank God, she'd only endured once in her life, on a crossing from Cherbourg to New York. A November gale had wrenched their steamship up and down, back and forth, a banshee that never stopped howling. For two days, it had been impossible to eat, impossible to drink; even Papa, usually so hale, kept to his berth. When, desperate, she'd tried to sip a mug of hot beef tea brought to her by a steward, her chin was left scalded and the front of her pinafore soaked.

Of course, all of that was the music of nature. Even in its most barbarous form, Inez adored it. She could transcribe it, transform it, stroke the notes of it from her cherished rosewood violin so that everyone could hear it, not just her. Wood and string, horsehair and rosin were her tools, and the otherworldly, fey pieces she produced (sometimes forgotten the moment the notes lifted from her bow) were her offering to the great mystery of life.

More difficult were the compositions of man. Paganini, Bach, Chevalier de Saint-Georges—all required more precision than passion, it seemed to her. Yet her mother, accomplished pianist that she was, insisted that Inez learn how to play not just from her heart but from sheets of paper printed with other people's notions of form and harmony.

"Learn the rules," Pauline had told her, "before deciding to shatter them. Don't leave room for anyone to claim your genius an accident."

It turned out to be excellent advice. By learning the rules, how others had handed their music to history, how dead men with fevered imaginations and grand reputations had created symphonies, composed scores that could spur crowds to weep, Inez gradually began to understand the truth of her own small magic. She *was* her music. She *was* her violin. She was the sonatas and concertos and the mysterious, half-hidden songs from the woods. When she stood, slender and alone, in the middle of Winter Queen's red salon and played for her parents' silk-and-satin guests, she was one of them, listening as they did, entranced as they were. When she played for the moon outside in her robe and bare feet, she was its alabaster light.

This was her world, and at sixteen, golden and slight, she was a spark ready to burn even more brightly.

Both she and Marguerite had long ago overcome their Medmenham reputations as Other, at least as far as the male population was concerned. The difference was that, although her older sister could flirt and charm and pull practically anyone along in her wake, willing hounds tethered to her leash . . . Inez was different. A friendly smile from a boy would either baffle her or embarrass her, depending.

A walk to the village on the most mundane of errands would end up with the two of them drawing a flock of interested fellows. The Jolivet girls were now considered fresh and lovely, local enough to matter, unusual enough to intrigue. And it certainly didn't hurt that their parents were intimates of the king. The good people of the parish were many things, fishermen and shopkeepers, doctors and gentry, but loyalty to the crown was the common thread that bound them tight.

Marguerite, of course, could manage them all. She would tilt back her head and pretend-laugh at a joke, and no one could look away. With her dark hair and eyes, her pale milky skin and bee-stung ruby lips—with that throaty, sultry voice— she was more goddess than girl, even at seventeen.

Inez could only stand awkwardly by as the boys (and a few older than boys) orbited her sister, wishing herself alone again, safe in her room at Winter Queen, safe in the solace of the music.

It was a miserable thing, to be so shy. But it was who she was, and the idea of trying to break free of it (beyond those transcendent moments when she played for an audience) seemed as impossible as swapping her soul for another's. Later in her life, years later, she would sometimes wonder if she might have ever left the grounds of Winter Queen at all if not for the irrepressible ambition of her sister.

Perhaps not. Inez found great comfort in the familiar, in respecting the boundaries of what was known.

But Marguerite was a *force majeure*, uncontained. She was determined to spread her wings and soar up to the stars, and she was determined to drag her sister along with her.

AT DUSK, AFTER the sun dimmed to pink or orange and sank away gently to warm the other side of the planet, the mists would rise from the woods. Thin tendrils slipped lovingly around the grounds, kissing the hedges and stone walls, smoothing all the rough spots, promising to hide any sort of secret. It usually lasted only around an hour. Then Mab would call it back to the trees, and all the tendrils would dissolve, revealing the earth again, revealing a sky that had transformed into something denser than before, darker, either glistening with galaxies or streaked with clouds, paled around the northeastern edge by London's eternal light.

Dinner the evening that everything changed took place after the mist had vanished. It was not a lucent sky that night but a cloudy one, a humid sigh of rain carried along with the breeze. By seven o'clock, the lone cracked pane in the glass dome of the conservatory had beaded with moisture. Tiny droplets gathered and trickled down the iron fretwork to spatter a palm tree below, a languid, muted rhythm against its fronds: *plink...plink...*

The palm was only one of several potted trees that fringed the chamber. There were also bay laurels and Spanish oranges and pomegranates, all with dense crowns that reached for the ceiling, along with the rows of orchids that grew thick between them. About six months past, a pair of wrens had stolen inside to take up permanent residence, and Inez ensured there were always bowls of seed and clean water set out for them. It was a bijou paradise, heady with perfume and birdsong.

When Winter Queen hosted no guests, the Jolivet family tended to take their meals there. A teak table was set up near the center, carved benches on either side. When he was younger, Alfred had complained about the benches—he'd been too short to reach his plate from them—so he'd been given his own chair at one end of the table. Even now, well out of short coats, he still claimed that chair. But everyone else sat side by side, elbow to elbow, knee to knee.

"What a right jolly peasant lot are we," Charles would announce in his most posh British accent, and his children would laugh.

Yet the footmen still served them with sterling spoons and forks and tongs. The fine bone china was painted with doves and olive leaves, a gleaming contrast to the plain table. Embossed flatware and crisp French linen napkins accompanied every meal; Pauline would have her children remember their court manners, passed down for generations through her line, no matter the location.

It happened over dessert, over the peach-and-blueberry trifle Inez was carefully exploring with her spoon, the custard a creamy smear along the glass sides of the dish. She had just lifted the spoon to her mouth when Marguerite spoke.

"I want to move to New York City. To the heart of it, Manhattan, Broadway. I want to perform on Broadway."

Inez's gaze slid up to her sister, the spoon frozen in front of her lips. Marguerite, sitting so close their skirts overlapped, was looking directly at Papa, across from her. Her cameo-pink silk was cut just below her neck, and her chin was lifted; this near to her, Inez could follow the telltale pounding of the pulse in her throat. Papa looked back at her with a slight, shocked peak to his eyebrows.

Maman, however... Maman was opposite Inez, and even though she sat perfectly straight and still, her hands on her lap, Inez saw at once that her mother was unsurprised by this announcement. That she had, in fact, maybe expected it, because although her eyes were cool and hooded, her lips curved upward, very faintly, into an expression that Inez could only call gratified.

"Broadway?" echoed Papa, sounding baffled.

"Yes. I'm good enough. You know that I am."

"I don't *know*—"

"Well, I am. *I* know that I am, and I've got to try, at least. I'll be eighteen soon, and I want to go."

"Now, listen—"

"I can stay at the flat in Castleton, can't I? It's not such a far distance away from the theatres, just a ferry ride over. And there's Mrs. Harris. She's still on as housekeeper, isn't she? She can find me a cook and a maid or a companion, what have you. It'll be absolutely proper, I swear. I'll never be alone."

"*Bien sûr*," said Charles, placing his napkin on the table, "you *won't* be alone, because you won't be there."

"Papa!"

"You cannot possibly imagine that I might send my daughter halfway around the world to play-act on *Broadway*." He slapped a hand hard against the table, an echoing clap; the wrens flitted in the trees. "*Ç'est ridicule.*"

Suddenly, everyone was speaking over each other in French.

"To travel across the ocean to chase a dream," Papa was saying, shaking his head. "A *fantasy*—"

Alfred was leaning forward, trying to cut in. "If *she* gets to go, then I—"

"*All* dreams are fantasy," Marguerite snapped, "until they are reality."

Inez put down her spoon. "What if, instead—"

"Nonsense!" Papa's cheeks were turning red. "It's unthinkable."

"You can't keep me here forever. I can't stay in this cage forever!"

"*Cage?* You think our home is a cage?"

"If I am trapped here, unable to leave, unable to be who I want to be—then, yes!"

Maman touched her napkin to a corner of her lips and gave a delicate cough; it was enough to silence the table.

"Actually," she murmured, "I don't believe the notion is *entirely* unthinkable."

Everyone stared.

"I've been pondering it anyway," she said, switching back to English. "Marguerite is correct. She can't stay here forever. She's nearly of age, and there are scant eligible gentlemen lingering nearby."

Marguerite looked ferocious. "I have *no* interest in—"

But Pauline only lifted a finger. "And so I've been thinking of renting something rather more central to the city—Bloomsbury, or South Kensington. A pied-à-terre, small but respectable. A hired chaperone, perhaps, for when I cannot be there. Marguerite is not the only one who cannot spend the rest of her days here. Inez is in need of a maestro to tutor her. She's grown far beyond anything I or this place could offer her."

Charles appeared flummoxed. "My dear..."

"Not Broadway, but the West End. I seem to recall that Enid Barrymore has a nephew managing one of the theatres there.

I'll write her for an introduction." Marguerite drew in a quick, happy breath, but Maman wasn't finished. "On the condition that you'll *also* attend any social events I deem suitable. Both of you, and no excuses. You'll be together, mind each other, and endure frequent visits from your beloved parents. Any hint of rebellion and we'll yank you right back here in shackles and chains, and you can live in this cage forever, slowly turning into mad spinsters who only venture out to howl at the moon. Yes?"

"I'd really prefer—" Inez began, alarmed.

"Yes!" interrupted Marguerite. Beneath the table, she seized Inez's hand—her bowing hand—and squeezed so hard it hurt.

"Yes," Inez agreed after a moment, much more softly. Her hand was released.

One of the wrens hopped down to a lower branch of a pomegranate tree to offer a single, treble note. Inez lifted her spoon again, but her fingers ached, and the trifle had lost its flavor.

LATER THAT NIGHT, after Winter Queen had settled into darkness and slumber, the rain began to fall, and Inez lay reading in her bed by lamplight. It was a slim volume of poems, or sonnets, or something. The words didn't matter; she wasn't really even reading it. She was supine beneath her flowered duvet, staring blindly up at the ceiling, tasting the damp night air as the shadows rippled and the rain pattered, and the thought circling round and round through her head, destroying her peace, was, *No, no, I can't.*

I can't go into the city. I can't live there. I can't study there, I can't be there, alone or nearly alone, I can't, I can't . . .

She knew it was unreasonable, this simmering panic that twisted her stomach and seared her lungs. She knew that London was only another place of streets and lanes and horses and buildings and people, rather an expanded version of the village, or a compounded one. It was smoke and palaces and cathedrals; it was the cacophony of millions of strangers, and how on earth was she to fit in there? How was she going to breathe there, much less hear her music? It seemed as impossible as going to live on the moon.

She blinked up at her ceiling, the cream-painted recesses, the heavy Tudor beams, and felt an ache in her heart so sharp it was like she'd been stabbed.

The door to her room opened. Marguerite slipped inside, dressed in a night rail of white lawn. She crossed silently to the bed and in the soft darkness, the hem flicked and flowed around her ankles; she might have been a ghost floating along the floor.

Inez turned her face away. Marguerite pulled back the duvet and crawled in beside her. Inez shifted to make room but still wouldn't look at her.

Her sister turned on her side and inched closer, enough so that they had to share the same pillow, then flipped her hair over her shoulder to drape warm and wavy along Inez's chest.

"Don't hate me," she whispered.

Inez said nothing, glaring at the ceiling.

"I have to do it," Marguerite said, almost pleading. "I have to go, I'm meant to go. I've read so much and researched so much and hoped so much, I'm ready to burst. But I planned to go alone, I swear."

Inez narrowed her eyes at the crossbeam above her, at the faint scar in the grain that always reminded her of an owl's face.

Marguerite stroked a finger down her sister's nose. "But this is going to be so much more fun. The two of us, together! We're going to have *such* a grand time."

Inez smacked her hand away. "You might. I won't."

"Maman was never going to let you hide away here forever. You know it's true."

"I certainly do not."

"Darling, think about it. Our blood has been blue, from one side of the blanket or the other, for centuries and centuries. Likely as far back as Charlemagne and Camelot, as far as Maman is concerned. She wasn't going to let all that glory end with us. You're her light and joy, but she was always going to land you in the king's court proper."

"I don't *want* to be in the king's court! All I want is to—to stay *here*, and live *here*, and be happy *here* with my music. I don't need diamonds or coronets. All I need..."

...*is to be left alone*, she almost said, but the words wouldn't come.

Please, please, everyone just leave me alone.

Marguerite's tone turned coaxing. "Isn't it better to come away now with me, than to be sent away on your own in a year or so?"

"They won't send me away! Papa would never."

"Papa," her sister said, "melts like butter in a frypan when Maman wants her way."

And Inez knew that was true enough.

"Why did you have to drag me into it?" she moaned anyway.

"*I* didn't! They did! It just turns out that you're the key. The key to unlocking my future. I'm sorry, I truly am. But this will be good for both of us. You'll see."

What Inez did see then, with a terrible sinking clarity, was that Marguerite was right. That her childhood here at Winter Queen had only been an enchantment, a prelude, no matter how fervently she wished otherwise. In the end, it didn't matter what she wanted, or what her parents' plans for her might have been. How she might have persuaded them to evolve. She was as small as a raindrop against the tempest of Marguerite's will.

"Maman's light and joy," she muttered, still upset anyway. "Hardly. That's you."

"Actually, I think it's Alfred."

"It's definitely Alfred."

Inez relented enough to allow a small smile. Marguerite rolled to her back and stretched her arms above her head.

"Well, she can have him, the stinky little darling. *We* are going to London, and I will act and you will compose, and we'll be the most gorgeous creatures ever to walk the streets."

"Walk the—"

"Grace the halls! Or trod the boards, or . . ."

"Carve our way?"

"Yes!" Marguerite laughed, that velvety laugh that could lure down the moon, stop the sun from rising and falling. "We'll carve out our own destinies there, I'm sure of it. You and I together!"

"Together," Inez echoed, capitulating as she always did, surrendering to her sister's spell as she and everyone else always did.

After all, Marguerite was the princess. Inez, the handmaiden, could only follow her.

Chapter 3

Every so often, I miss London. You'll laugh at that, no doubt, re-membering how nervous I was about it in the beginning, how hard you had to work to convince me that all would be well. When we first moved there I felt as if hobgoblins lurked around every corner, ready to devour me. So many people! So much noise. Colors were too bright or too dim; the air coated my tongue with the taste of coal. My eyes always burned. London hammered my body and battered my spirits until I could hardly think. In those early days I was such a timid country mouse, and the city such a wolf.

After a month of it, I was ready to bolt, did you know that? Per-haps you did. I was going to sneak back to Winter Queen and beg and weep and plead to stay—I think Papa might have listened, at least. I had a half-mad fantasy of marrying some local lad and hid-ing away forever.

But then you did the most clever thing. The most clever, unex-pected thing.

NOVEMBER, 1901
LONDON, ENGLAND

Backstage, the Catharine Theatre smelled of sawdust and
mice, and the pungent scent of horse and smoke whenever the
shop door was opened, inviting in spirals of snowflakes. Beyond the occasional gray flash of bright from that door, shadows upon shadows smothered the area, all the way up to the
curtains; the only steady illumination was a distant pool of yellow light from the rigging above the apron of the stage. The
lanterns in the rafters above Marguerite's head were dark, silent steel shapes clamped to long iron bars.

The snow had started last night, and the cold inside the
building was already crackling through her marrow. Perhaps
that was why the flock of young women waiting with her (thir-
teen of them; she'd counted) clustered so close together, dressed
in their best, pale chiffon and velvet, the brims of their hats
brushing, their whispers rising in slender frosted tendrils past
their rouged lips.

Who is she?

*No idea. She wasn't here for the first two calls, that's for bloody
certain.*

Someone's bit of fluff, is my guess. Jim or Harvey.

One of Jim's, I'd wager. He's an eye for them exotic types.

Marguerite lingered at their edge, observing her surroundings
with interest. It wasn't the first time she'd visited the labyrin-
thine corridors of a professional theatre, but it was her first time
in this one. The Catharine faced Shaftesbury Avenue with a façade of carved limestone and rails of wrought iron. It welcomed
its patrons with red-and-gold carpeting and red-and-gold curtains, red velveteen seats, but back here, where the craftspeople
sweated and worked and listened for their cues, it was as bare
bones as could be. No furniture, no candles, no lamps. No place
to sit. Everyone stood as they waited for their names to be called.

She met the eyes of the girl nearest her, a flaxen-haired blonde with a narrow gray gaze, and smiled. The other girl thinned her lips and turned away.

Someone's bit of fluff.

Well, Marguerite supposed she rather was, although not in the way the others thought. She was surely the only one here, for example, who had a hansom paid well enough to wait outside for her in the snow.

The play was called *Good Girls Stay Home*, a comedy by some American playwright she'd never heard of. It required three ingénue leads and was guaranteed a four-week run, minimum, and Marguerite was only here because her mother, that quiet force of tilt and change in her life, had made good on her connections and wrangled her daughter an invitation to the third, and final, call.

The initial two auditions had transpired over the past month, back when Marguerite and Inez had first arrived, lost in the wondrous chaos of the city, in the haze of unpacking their trunks and settling into their apartment in Bloomsbury. Pauline had traveled with them, inspected their newly leased lodgings—the quality of the locks, the cook who came with the kitchen, the maid who came with the cook, and the housekeeper who came with the entire flat—and announced herself moderately satisfied.

"A little compact," she observed, hands on her hips. "But it will do."

Compact or not, the flat felt like liberation to Marguerite. The tight back-and-forth stairways, the grape velvet curtains, the Aubusson rugs that covered the floors from the parlor to the living room to the dining room. The view from her bedroom behind clear glass panes: a wide, gracious street filled with horses and carriages and well-bundled people hurrying along through their days and nights, hurrying to conquer their next precious second, and the next, and the next.

I've done it. I'm here. At last, I'm here.

Maman had lingered a fortnight, then headed back to Winter Queen to tend to what was left of her flock. Papa needed to travel to Paris for business, and there was no room for Albert in this henhouse, as Maman had called it, so she would spend the next few weeks in Medmenham with her son. She'd written to various cousins, and then cousins of cousins, about the possibilities of chaperoning the London flat, but so far had heard nothing definitive in return.

"So it will be the two of you for now," she'd said sternly, kissing both girls goodbye on the cheek before climbing into the hired barouche. "Be good," she'd commanded from inside the carriage, and then paused, eyeing Inez. "Not *too* good. Be only just scandalous enough."

"Scandalous enough for what?" Marguerite asked.

Pauline gave a Gallic flick of her fingers, then smiled. "To... score a bull's-eye in all the fresh games to come. To win, no matter what."

THIS MORNING AT breakfast, Mrs. Corbyn, the housekeeper, had placed a folded note by Marguerite's plate. She was a tall, skeletal sort of woman, long-boned and silver-haired, someone who seemed almost too shaky for the heavy ring of keys dangling from her waist. The measuring way she took in the sisters when she thought they wouldn't notice told Marguerite that although Maman had approved of Mrs. Corbyn, Mrs. Corbyn had not yet quite approved of the Jolivets.

"Before she left, your mother instructed that I give this to you, miss. I was to hold onto it until today. Until this morning. For the audition, you see."

She managed the word *audition* with only the barest tinge of distaste.

"Thank you," Marguerite had replied and lifted her eyebrows at her sister.

In Maman's flowing, old-fashioned script, the note read:

I'm not ashamed to have lifted you this far, but now your fate is up to you. You wish to conquer Broadway? Go forth and shine.

Marguerite leaned across the table to hand it to Inez, who scanned it quickly in a splash of light from the window and then handed it back.

"You and Maman make a fine team," she'd said with smile, almost wistful, and returned to her porridge.

"MARGARET," BAWLED A voice, and then a pause. "Jo-livet? Hoo-ho! Margaret Jolivet, and hurry up, if you please."

Marguerite looked up, coming back to the cold and dark of the Catharine. The man calling her onstage had pronounced her surname Jaw-liv-it, spitting out all the syllables, even though she had introduced herself properly to the manager when she'd first arrived.

She'd not dressed in her very best—that would have been something from Lucile or House of Worth, and anyway was reserved for Maman's mandatory social schedule. Even so, she was in a gown of very fine melon organza, soft and feminine and bright, exactly the color of summer sunsets. Of banked ambitions and dreams, and maybe good girls who liked to stay at home.

Unlike everyone else, she'd only received the typed excerpts of the script twenty minutes past. From what she could tell, the play seemed to be about a trio of silly, predictable girlfriends flirting with the notion of careers before deciding to marry their silly, predictable beaux instead.

Marguerite lifted her skirts and swept forward with a smile, blinded for a moment by the lights above. She lowered her gaze to the planks of the stage and moved to its center. Her heart was racing faster than she wanted; she exhaled slowly, a silent release of air between her lips.

This is it, one chance, one reading, don't muck it up.

She lifted her lashes.

Compared to the spartan backstage area, the front of the Catharine opened up like a gaudy clam to a gilt-and-plastered ceiling and raked rows of seats that climbed toward the entrance of the theatre, well above her head. A single chandelier suspended above the house had been cinched in a balloon of linen, but for the prisms dangling from its base. They chimed with a draft, flashing darts of color, splintering the dark.

The assistant stage manager waved her forward impatiently.

"Downstage, luv, don't be shy."

"I'm not shy," Marguerite said, still smiling. "And my name is Marguerite, not Margaret." She paused and repeated it the proper way. "*Mar-gher-eet Sho-la-veh.*"

The man looked her up and down. He wore a plain brown shirt with a grease stain near the collar, and suspenders but no waistcoat; his chin was covered in stubble. As he bent closer, she caught the sour waft of ale surrounding him. "Yeah? You might want to change that. Foreign-sounding, it is. Do better with something homegrown."

"Do you think so?" She took another step forward, facing front. She made a show of removing the pins from her hat, all three of them one by one—arms curved above her head, fingers precise, chin lifted, neck stretched—before bending to place it all carefully upon the stage, pins in the hat, hat upside down, feathers brushing planks. In her splash of light, the melon dress gleamed like a flame.

The assistant scowled at her. He turned to the audience seats and shrugged with both palms up, a gesture of surrender. "Miss Mar-gar-*eet* Jo-liv-*eh.*"

The theatre's house was mostly empty. Only three seats were occupied near the center: the director, the producer, and the stage manager, although from here she couldn't tell who was who. All of them were half-lost in a dazzle of snowy light that poured in from the lobby behind them, solid silhouettes framed in silver.

"Experience?" called one of the men, the one in the middle, sounding bored already.

Go forth and shine.

"I'm new."

The silhouette to the left leaned toward the other, saying something too low to catch. The first man sat back, pushed a hand through his hair.

"Oh, lord. Her. Right." He raised his voice. "No experience, then? No formal training?"

"I spent two years at the Royal Dramatic Theatre in Stockholm," she said and waited a moment for that to sink in. "I played Kristin in *Miss Julie*, Irena in *Three Sisters*, and Hero in *Much Ado*. Mr. Strindberg spoke of putting me in his Part 3 of *Till Damaskus*, but I returned to England before he could finish it. My—my father recently passed away." She pressed two fingers to her heart and took a steadying breath. "Pardon me! It was rather sudden, and I found I wanted to be closer to my family. I arrived just last week."

The man leaned forward, rifled through some papers. "Quite a chronicle. Harvey, where's her—no?" He looked up again. "Why didn't you hand over your bona fides?"

"Because none of that was true." Marguerite dropped her hand. "But you believed me, didn't you?"

Someone in the wings gave a gasp, but otherwise only a ringing silence seemed to settle across the theatre. Plus those prisms, still tinkling, still swaying, flashing their rainbowed darts.

The man in the middle finally spoke.

"All right, Miss New, let's get this over with. Give me Bessie's monologue, top of page three."

Marguerite flipped the pages. She had nothing memorized—there had been no time for that—but she remembered the essence of the speech, and the character. Bessie, the flighty one, the prettiest one, the most ridiculous.

"*I don't think it's remarkable in the least—*"

"Louder," commanded the man.

"*—remarkable in the least that Alonzo should follow Nancy around like a puppy! He's quite besotted with her, you know, stardust in his eyes. Anyone could see it. And to think she'd toss him away to be a typist! I'd give anything, anything to hold Alonzo's heart, to bask in that smile—*"

"Thank you," interrupted the man. "The address you provided is real, at least?"

"Yes, I—"

"Stage left to the exit. Harv, who's next?"

She bent down, gathered her hat and pins. She walked off-stage and into a frosted cloud of soft, girlish snickering.

By the time the hansom made it back to Bloomsbury, the sky had roiled into a sullen slate, and the snow had thinned into needles. As soon as she stepped out of the cab, her face stung, and the needles lodged, cold and damp, under the collar and cuffs of her coat. Marguerite's mood was about as dour as that sky.

She was unused to failure. She was unused to men treating her as if she were an inconvenience—at least since she'd turned fourteen, when it'd seemed she'd walked across some magical, invisible threshold, and after that no one could look away from her.

Almost no one, apparently.

The steps leading to the front door of the flat were steep and handsomely carved, although right now they stood buried in about three inches of snow; apparently, the hired boy who was supposed to come by and sweep hadn't gotten to them yet. Marguerite minded her feet climbing them, one by one, all seven, her boots caked in white. Thanks to the unheated Catharine, it had been a while since she'd felt her toes, and she wondered at that, at the complete lack of sensation in her feet. Yet here she stood, still upright.

She fit her key into the lock and opened the door, releasing a waft of warm, stale air. She kicked the snow off her boots as best she could, then hurried inside.

There was just room enough in the entranceway for a vase of lilies in the nook and an embossed copper mirror mounted on the wall opposite. As she was shrugging out of her coat, she caught her reflection in the mirror. Her cheeks were chapped, her eyebrows lowered, her hat drooping. She stopped for a second, unsettled by this flinty stranger staring back at her, then plucked the pins from her hat, far more briskly than she had at the audition.

Mrs. Corbyn arrived to collect it all, her expression stoic.

"Welcome back, miss. I'll set this all out to dry downstairs."

"Sorry to track in the mess. It's heaps of snow out there."

"It's the time of year, miss, all this wet, nasty stuff. It'll get worse before it gets better."

"Ah."

"Shall I bring tea?"

"Yes, that would—"

"Marguerite?" Inez's voice floated out from the parlor. "Are you back already?"

"That would be lovely," Marguerite finished. "For us both, I'm sure. Thank you."

The housekeeper retreated. Marguerite threw a practiced smile at the mirror, smoothed her hands across her hair, and went to find her sister.

Inez sat wrapped in a pink-striped eiderdown before the hearth, only her head and feet visible, plus one pale hand clutching the ends of the quilt together over her chest. Her bun was coming loose in curls; her eyes were rimmed in red. She might have only just gotten out of bed. In the slippery light of the fire, with her tousled hair and delicate features, Marguerite thought she resembled a dryad or a sylph. Some tender wild thing out of place in the heavy Louis XVI splendor of the room, with its silver-gilt furniture and pewter satin cushions, and shadows scented of lemon polish.

Marguerite collapsed into the chair opposite hers, stretching her feet toward the hearth. Then she bent over, flipped back her sodden skirts, and began to unbutton her boots. Inez watched, unblinking.

"How was it?"

She kept working on the buttons. "Dazzling, *naturellement*. I dazzled them."

Inez seemed to rouse. "Oh, wonderful. Really?"

"No, not really."

"Oh," she said again, this time uncertain. And then, "I'm sure it wasn't as bad as that."

"It was."

Marguerite kicked off both boots, slumped back and held her feet as close to the iron fender as she dared. Inez settled deeper into her eiderdown.

"Well, it was only your first time. You'll become more used to it, figure out how it's all sorted here. If anyone can, it's you. You're on your way."

"I'm starting from nothing."

"You're *starting* from Maman. That's hardly nothing."

The fire crackled. From the lower bowels of the apartment, a door slammed. Marguerite closed her arms over her chest and fought a shiver. The cold soaked into her from the theatre wasn't yet banished; her feet were still numb, her soaring, witless hopes still numb. The sky outside, so gray and numb.

"You'll scorch your stockings like that."

Marguerite inched closer to the fender.

"Fine, then!" Inez pushed the quilt down to her shoulders. "Are you sulking? Are you going to pack it in after one false start? *You're* the one who dragged us here. *You're* the one who said won't it be splendid, we'll have such a grand time, carving our fates and conquering the stars. I never wanted to come, and now look at us in this freezing hard place, far from home, and I just—I just want—"

"What?" Marguerite asked quietly, sitting up again. "What do you want?"

Inez glanced away, swiped at her eyes. "I'm so cold. All the time, I'm so cold. How does anyone stand it here?"

"I take it your latest lesson with Fräulein Wietrowetz did not go well."

"It was dazzling, *naturellement*." She leaned her cheek against the back of her hand and gave a despairing laugh. "As usual. I so look forward to our sessions. She thinks I'm a country chit reaching for glory by way of the Jolivet coattails."

"Sounds familiar."

"She believes I am a waste of her time."

Marguerite sent her a sharp look. "Did she say that?"

"She didn't have to. I felt it from her. I felt it positively emanating from her soul. She longs to be back in Berlin at her *Hochschule*, with her *talented* students and—and *strudel*—"

Marguerite pressed a hand to her mouth to cover her smile. She forgot sometimes how young her sister was, still only sixteen, and a coddled sixteen at that. But no doubt Winter Queen had coddled them all. Certainly it had been easier there to stand out, to blaze, to bend the rules and be applauded for it. Perhaps it was Inez's passionate heart that made her seem older, or her musical gifts that could shame virtuosi thrice her age. Yet in this moment, she was very much a frustrated adolescent, chafing against this new London life, against the ironclad will of their parents.

Inez glared at her, tugging the eiderdown high again. "I don't expect you to understand."

"But I do, darling." Marguerite slid off her chair, knelt before her sister. "Or at least, I'm trying to. I know it's been something of a rough start for us here. But we're not waving the white flag yet. It occurs to me that, so far, we haven't had much of a chance to be scandalous. Here we are, in the big, bad city, and still decent as seraphim. Imagine how disappointed Maman will be."

Inez shook her head. "I don't wish to be scandalous."

"Only a little scandalous. Just the tiniest touch of scandal. I have an idea about that. I think we'll start tomorrow."

"I don't want—"

"In the meanwhile, though, I have another idea. Nothing shocking, per se, but..."

Inez's gaze angled to hers, her brows scrunched with doubt.

"How about a fresh start for us both?" Marguerite sat back on her heels; the fire's heat on her left side was finally beginning to smart. "How about from now on, we each become someone else?"

"What on earth do you mean?"

Marguerite stood, slapped out her skirts, and spread her arms. "I was informed today that my name is too foreign. You'd think I'd come straight from the Tower of Babel, the way they mangled it. So from now on, for the sake of the stage and my future adoring fans, I am going to be Rita, not Marguerite. Rita Jolivet. English enough, don't you think?"

Inez stared up at her, her eyes wide. "It's...well, yes. It's English enough, I suppose." She tried it out slowly. "*Rita*. It's bold. I like it."

"Good. So do I. All right, then. Your turn."

"I'm fine with Inez."

"No, sorry." Marguerite pulled her upright with both hands; the striped quilt rumpled into a pink-and-white mound between them. "A new name, if you please. A good London name. A good English name for when you perform for the king at the Royal Albert Hall."

Inez shook her head again. Marguerite could practically see her spirit shrinking at the thought.

"Very well, I'll name you. How about Nezzie?"

"What? No!"

"Inezabeth?"

"You're ridiculous."

"Well, then, come on. Give me something."

"Leigh," Inez said after a moment. Firelight glinted off her lashes, cast gold across the blue of her irises. "I've always admired it, ever since we were little. Leigh Jolivet. Simple enough, but... flowing."

"Perfect."

"But only for the violin. For my music. Otherwise, I'm still just me."

A knock sounded on the door. It eased open to reveal the housemaid bearing a heavy silver tray.

"Oh, the tea," Marguerite said and gestured to a side table. "Over there will be fine, Della."

"There came a message for you, miss, to the scullery door. Some scrapper came by. I've put it with the cups."

"Thank you," she managed, hardly hesitating, although her heart began to pound and the top of her head suddenly ached, as if all the blood in her body had flooded to her crown, making her dizzy.

Inez gave her a significant look, waiting for the maid to leave, then crossed to the tray and lifted the envelope between two fingers.

"You've gone rather pale. Shall I?"

Marguerite nodded, speechless. All these years, all her life, all this waiting and dreaming, and here it was in front of her in the shape of a small, snow-battered envelope, her fate decided.

All at once, she didn't want to know. If it was a rejection, if she wasn't good enough, fair enough, strong enough—she didn't want to know. She was a coward who wanted to keep dreaming, for better or worse.

But Inez was already breaking the seal, tugging free the sheet of paper inside. "*Regarding the Catharine's* Good Girls Stay Home. *Miss Marguerite Jolivet is cast as 'Bessie Johnson.' Rehearsals begin Monday next, noon precisely. Salary negotiable. Have your agent contact for details. Confirm at once.*" She looked up, dismayed. "Are you supposed to have an agent?"

Marguerite braced a hand against the black walnut mantelpiece, light-headed and stunned and caught in the strangest sensation of vertigo. She felt afloat. Flying above herself.

Everything, once again, was numb, but in the best possible way.

"I don't know," she answered at last and flattened both palms atop her head. "Do you think I should find one?"

"Yes? Yes. Probably." Inez frowned at the note, then carried it over to the secrétaire, pulling out the chair. "But for now I'll just write them back, shall I, telling them that *Rita* Jolivet accepts."

THE NEXT AFTERNOON, flush with success, Rita took them both to purchase the pistols.

She'd first glimpsed them a fortnight ago in a storefront along Piccadilly, shining with wicked purpose on the other side of the front window. The shop itself was a small, nondescript place wedged between a haberdashery and one of the many ubiquitous booksellers that choked the road. But for a hard beam of sun that pierced the glass, glancing across the weapons on display, she might have walked right by.

JOS. CHRISTIAN & SON read the lettering painted across the glass. FINE FIREARMS, PRACTICAL MUNITIONS & MILITARY ANTIQUITIES.

"Yes, miss. These two? Right you are, miss. Allow me to re-move them from the case."

The salesman—gray-bearded and bespectacled; the senior Mr. Christian, she presumed—presented the matched pair with gloved hands, placing them reverently on a black velvet cloth spread along the main counter.

The shop was even smaller inside than she'd imagined, but every inch seemed to bristle with weaponry: assorted rifles and pistols and swords fixed to the walls, crossbows marching in rows up the corners to the ceiling. A grouping of scimitars, most tarnished with age, had been arranged along the far wall in the shape of a starburst. A mounted ram's head anchored its center, its mouth grimly set, glass eyes staring.

Inez was staring back at the ram with an air of dismay, her hands clasped against her stomach. Rita focused on the pistols laid before her.

"Browning," the proprietor said, running a finger along the engraved sides, the gleaming mother-of-pearl grips. "Belgium-made these are, best of the best, and prime examples of 'em, too. Notice the slide mechanism, very modern indeed. We have our share of Pistolet Brownings here in the Old Smoke, but you don't see many like these, what with the pearl han-dles and all. And the etching, eh? We tend to find the more practical sort over here, don't we? But these are pretty as a penny, miss. Rare fit for a lady such as yourself or your friend here. Semi-automatic, never used, not even a year out of the factory yet."

Rita lifted the nearest one, turned to direct it at the window, and squinted along the barrel. Inez tore her gaze from the ram, took a nervous step back.

"Mar—Rita, are you sure?"

"It's hefty, certainly, but not unwieldly. These will do."

"Done some shooting, miss?" asked the man, respectful.

And Rita, who had never even touched a gun before this moment, said, "Oh, we're country chits, both of us. You know how it is. Stag, moorcock, the usual."

"I do, I do indeed." He leaned closer and lowered his voice. "I might mention that the American president himself owns a pair of these. Custom-made, pearly and all."

"Really, sir, I'm quite sold. You needn't butter me up." He bowed. She waited until he straightened to meet her eyes, then added sweetly, "Could you personalize them?"

"Miss?"

"The etching, the scrollwork. It's very attractive, but could you add a little something to it, along the barrels or somewhere? Our names, I mean?"

"Oh! Yes, of course! Nothing easier. My boy has a master hand, trained with the best. Handles commissions like this all the time."

"Splendid. Have you some paper? I'll write them down for you."

THEY EMERGED FROM the shop into the day, blinking at the shoveled mounds of snow edging the pavements, miniature mountains that had begun to melt under the sun before hardening again, their crests streaked with soot. Black dagger shadows stretched past them to score the road; a pair of motorcars puttered by, trailing exhaust, and the sisters paused to watch them pass.

"The Old Smoke," Inez said thoughtfully. "It's what he called it, the city. It makes sense to me."

"I suppose so. Let's walk a bit while there's still some daylight."

Piccadilly was rowdy, crammed with commerce. Horse trams clattered along the icy cobbles, hansoms, a few more motorcars, and even a brave landau, roof lowered, revealing a laughing set of young men. A footman in deep green livery walked toward them with a trio of waddling corgis on leashes. The dogs snuffled at their skirts as they passed, tails wagging, and Inez finally smiled.

"Tell me. How does owning pistols make us scandalous?"

Rita tipped her head, considering it. "Why, we'll wear them on our hips, like the cowboys do. We're in the Smoke now, after all. And in the Smoke, it never hurts to have a little something extra on your side."

Inez made a faint sound of amusement. She raised her arm and aimed her index finger at the filmy haze of roofs and spires that crowded the horizon.

"Bang!" she said, pretending to shoot.

Bull's-eye.

Chapter 4

And then, reality galloped apace and caught up with us. Ha.

I know your grand theatrical debut didn't go as planned, but what a wild, mad gift it turned out to be anyway. When the Fates decide to catch you up in their grip, there's no avoiding it, I guess.

For weeks, I watched you coming and going at odd hours, practicing your lines in mirrors, refining your character. Throwing yourself into rehearsals, all for that mindless bit of candyfloss that didn't nearly deserve you or your gifts. And you never complained. You never showed any anger or dismay or trepidation. I would have, in your shoes.

If I hadn't run lines with you so many times, I might have been shocked by how things ended up. But I did. So I wasn't.

My sister, my twin heart, I will write this down in strong India ink and pray you never, ever forget it: You were always a shooting star, meant to streak fire across the heavens. Even when we were going over your lines, those boorish old things, I could see the magic blazing in you, incandescent. It was only a matter of time before you burned away everything mediocre around you.

JANUARY, 1902
LONDON, ENGLAND

It didn't take long for the delirious promise of the Catharine to disintegrate into a harsher truth. Three days at most.
Three days of rehearsal, and the unheated air, and the other
actors either ignoring Rita or else addressing her with exagger-
ated, upper-crust enunciation, as if she could not understand
them otherwise.

Three days. Discreet inspection of the ornamentations revealed that much of the gilt was flaking, and the plaster murals
decorating the ceiling and walls had been repaired so
frequently, and so carelessly, that great patches of color no
longer matched. A towering figure of Aphrodite on the western wall wore a perilously draped tunic now three different
shades of cantaloupe, and Adonis, his hand in hers, had two
different colored eyes, one green, one gray. The red velveteen
seats were worn shiny along the seams, and once, when an errant limelight dashed light across the closed curtains, a
punchboard of moth holes was revealed, countless dazzling
dots chewed through the cloth. Everyone caught unaware
backstage was blinded for minutes.

But the worst was the play. Or perhaps it was Ansel Lurie,
director of the play. Or, most likely, it was both of those things.
Thin-haired and slumping into middle age, Lurie had come
into modest fame a decade earlier, mainly by directing plays
exactly like this one: vacuous, broadly painted, barely saved
by the vaudevillian titillation of a plot verging on bawdy. It
was clear to Rita that he deplored the limitations of his reputa-
tion. Lurie was a titmouse that dreamed of being a hawk; he
spoke of Shakespeare and Molière and Kyd as if he had
known the men personally. She'd realized quickly that he had
hired her for the sharpness of her wit along with her looks,
and that deep down he likely despised her, the girl who'd lied

to him, who'd used her connections to pry her way into his realm and then turned out to be the best of the lot anyway.

The very first thing he'd said to her, that Monday when she'd shown up for their initial rehearsal, joy and excitement bubbling through her, was, "Listen, Miss New. I have rules, and you're going to follow them. I expect you to be prompt, to learn your lines, and to shut your gob when I tell you to, instantly and at once. Oh, and I'm not going to bother to learn how to pronounce your bloody name."

"Yes, you will," Rita had replied calmly, the only possible response.

And so he had, although it had taken over a month. Neither of them had mentioned it again.

Yet the only time her director ever praised her work was when he could contrast it to one of her fellow players. *No, no! Do it as Miss Jolivet does! Listen to her! Watch her face, her movements, how she always reacts! Are you an idiot? Be more like* her. *Great God, it's her first sodding play, and she's waltzing circles around you all!*

Which hardly endeared her to the rest of the cast.

Callie Slater, the gray-eyed blonde who had shunned her at the audition, was now playing her bosom friend, Verna. The other lead, Josie, was played by an actress named Mayme with beautiful auburn tresses and a cockney accent so thick that it had even Rita wincing, although she tried not to show it. Onstage, Bessie and Verna and Josie bantered and embraced and showed off their cleavage and ankles, giggling at the antics of their suitors. Offstage, both Callie and Mayme treated Rita with an icy hostility that no amount of friendly overtures would thaw.

She was still someone's bit of fluff, uninvited, unwelcome.

The women shared a single small dressing room in the upper reaches of the theatre's attic. The men shared a larger chamber in the basement, although Rita didn't envy them the space, as the walls down there were dank with moisture and the ceiling a patchwork of black mold. At least the attic trapped whatever precious heat there was in the building, scant as it was.

As the weeks wound on, little things of hers began to go missing. A pencil from her reticule. The middle button from her shirtwaist, hanging unprotected as the rehearsals inched closer to opening night and they all had to be in costume. A porcelain pot of kohl, brand-new, plus the brush. A tortoise-shell hair comb, plain and unremarkable except that it had been a birthday gift from Alfred when she'd turned sixteen, and that was when Rita decided she'd had enough.

The next afternoon, the afternoon of the final dress re-hearsal, she brought a silver flask with her, discreetly tucked in her purse. It wasn't really silver, only pewter with a wooden stopper, but there could be no mistaking the brandy inside it.

"Bessie!" yelled Lurie from the audience, his tone threaded with impatience. "Show them again what you just did, stage left and cross up, then down right again. People, pay atten-tion! There are musical cues, just *follow* them! Blood of Christ, how many times must I say it?"

It was the night before the opening, and Lurie's temper was a storm inside him, a jittery squall, one he let loose on the en-tire cast at any slight infraction. Not just the cast and five-man band, but the crew as well, which was always a risk. Offend the stage manager enough, and perhaps the footlights might fail. Berate the props mistress enough and the cold, shellacked goose needed for Act Two might mysteriously vanish. Cos-tumes might no longer fit, belts lost, hats misplaced.

Ansel Lurie always seemed to contain his temper just short of having anyone walk out. However, tonight he seemed espe-cially irate.

In a way, Rita didn't blame him. The play wasn't quite in
shambles, but it was certainly rough around the edges. All the
ladies knew their lines, but the gentlemen were less certain.
The actor playing Bessie's beau, Alonzo, sandy-haired and si-
newy, tended to chew his way through his lines, with frequent
uncomfortable pauses. His real name was Frank Monroe. He
was impossibly comely and impossibly unsuited for the stage.
Offstage, he would barely acknowledge her, but the moment
he forgot what he was supposed to say or do onstage, he'd
turn to Rita helplessly, puppy-eyed, and she'd have to impro-
vise something to prod him along.

Tomorrow night the show was to open. Posters had been
plastered across town; newspaper advertisements had been
prominently placed. Both featured excerpts from the reviews
of the show's New York run.

*A saucy romp for all! Laughs aplenty! Go on, boys, bring along
your best gals and prepare for an evening of cheeky delight!*

And, added just for the British premiere: *Come and let the
three prettiest lasses in London entertain you!*

"Alonzo," snarled Lurie, walking down the center aisle to
brace his hands along the edge of the stage, "Alonzo, don't
just gawk at her! You're supposed to go to your knee here, remember? The big proposal! Oh, God, man, remember?"

"Yes," said Frank, sounding aggrieved. "Yes, sir, Mr. Lurie.
It's not my fault, though. Bessie didn't give me the right cue.
She dropped her last line, and how am I supposed—"

"I certainly didn't," cut in Rita.

"She didn't," the director agreed. "We all heard her. I need
you to bloody *listen*—Verna, what's wrong with you?"

Rita turned to see Callie, done up in a wild froth of jonquil
petticoats and lace, standing still as a statue, her face gleaming
with sweat. She hugged her arms over her chest and shook her
head at the director.

"Are you ill?"

She shook her head again, her mouth a thin, tight line.

"Oh dear," said Rita, going to her. She placed a hand on the other girl's arm. "You're looking a bit off the mark, dearie. Was it something you ate? Or . . . drank?"

Beneath the burning lights, they locked eyes. Rita smiled.

"Oh," groaned Mayme suddenly, farther upstage. She bent over and vomited her lunch across the boards.

Everyone except Rita cried out, especially when Callie jerked away and tried to stagger offstage, but didn't quite make it before retching too.

"WHAT WAS IT?" Inez asked much later that night, well after midnight, both of them nestled by the fire, Inez in her eiderdown, Rita in warm flannel, clean from her bath. The moon shone cold and distant through the windows. A block or so away, a pair of dogs called the watch, short barks, long yelps. "What did you give them? Nothing dangerous, I trust."

"No, nothing dangerous, just something from our nursery days that Mrs. Corbyn was good enough to procure for me. Castor oil."

"Oh . . ."

"Just a touch. Still, you'd think they would have tasted it, wouldn't you?"

"Perhaps they're unaccustomed to the flavor of brandy."

"Plebeians," sneered Rita, who was her mother's daughter, and stretched out her legs. "Neither of *us* would have fallen for it."

"Neither of us steal, though."

"No. We don't."

"But . . . perhaps you might forgive them now? Now that they know that you know."

"Perhaps." She narrowed her eyes at the fire. "Let's see how tomorrow goes. If they doom the show and sink my first chance at everything, I might use rat poison next time."

FOR OPENING NIGHT, the theatre was freshly cleaned, the floors mopped, the stage swept, all the wooden armrests and backs of the seats dusted. Every work light was checked and checked again.

The solitary chandelier had been freed from its linens. It hung like a crystalline flower, remote and sparkling, above the house seats, far more sophisticated than the building deserved, Rita thought.

A fine bit of sparkle, the assistant stage manager had informed her, catching her admiring it. It had been imported from India thirty years past by the father of the Catharine's owner, packed up and whisked abroad right before the fall of the East India Trading Company. It seemed an unlikely story at best, but there was no doubt the chandelier was delicate and detailed, and far more interesting than the faux-Greek murals or faux-Jacobian plasterwork. It wasn't a stretch to imagine it glowing in some British nabob's ballroom in Delhi, throwing sparks across the guests.

London, Rita had begun to realize, was an enigma of a place, even more so than the countryside, or New York, or the sleepy vineyards of France. London had ghosts upon ghosts, history stacked upon history, layered like a cake, and nothing could ever be truly discounted as truth or lie. London was both, and would always be both. How absurd that she had wasted all of her youth somewhere else, in some soft quiet land, when surely she was always meant to bask in this heart of radiance, in the flaring, prismed rainbows of cut crystal, ready to take her bow.

"All right, everyone, gather up," commanded Ansel Lurie, and the people backstage made an uneven circle around him, confined by the limits of the area and the prop furniture waiting for Act Two shoved against the walls.

The audience was arriving, taking their seats. Rita's whole family should be out there; once she swore she heard Alfred break into his particular snorting laughter. But otherwise everything beyond the curtains became a dull rush of sound, coughing and conversation, the dry rustling of playbills and clothing.

"It's been a road," her director said, his palms pressed together before his heart, "and it's been a journey, and like it or not, we're bloody well in the quicksand now." He paused as a few people chuckled. "Tonight, we rise. Tonight we are the art as well as the artists, and I want you all to remember that. The art and the artists. It's a full house, God bless 'em, so go out there and give the people what they've paid for."

"Oy, our girl Mayme always gives 'em what they pay for, don't you, luv?"

"Sod off, Harv."

"That's it, you lot," Lurie said. "Break a leg."

The gathering stirred, a few offering half-hearted applause. Lurie bowed his head in acknowledgment before striding off, heels clicking, tugging at his waistcoat.

Rita turned her head to follow his retreat into the darkness, her arms crossed over her chest.

Tonight, we rise. We are the art as well as the artists.

Short as it was, clipped as it was, it was a good speech. In any case, it was by far the most encouraging thing Ansel Lurie had ever said to his cast. Too bad the rotter had saved it until just before curtain.

"Places," called the stage manager in a low voice, and Rita smoothed out her gown, inches away from the limelight that was ready to capture her in brilliance, moments away from the glorious rest of her days.

"... WHICH BRINGS US *to the revival of the Catharine with its winter showpiece* Good Girls Stay Home. *This reviewer acknowledges the fact that it is always a challenge to bring a play 'across the pond,' one that certain rough-and-tumble Yankee audiences enjoyed, but*

*which might not suit the more refined palate of we Brits. It might even
be said that to attempt the feat at all deserves a measure of praise.*

*"However, faint praise may prove worse than none. In this instance,
your reviewer must withhold his accolades of nearly any sort.* Good
Girls Stay Home *lays bare the worst of both worlds, crass American
writing combined with crass British acting, and almost all of it misses
the mark by a mile."*

Papa looked up from the article he'd been reading aloud, allowing the pages of the newspaper to fall forward along the
fold. "I believe I'll stop there."

"No." Rita raised her head, bleary-eyed. She'd been prop-
ping her face in her hands over her plate of greasy sausage and
tomatoes. Bars of sunlight along the walls singed her vision;
she kept having to close her eyes against it. "No, don't stop,
please. It can't say anything worse than what I already know.
I need to hear it all."

It was eight-thirty in the morning in Bloomsbury, and an
early breakfast for her, at least. The sulfur stink of eggs and
black pudding turned her stomach; the hot coffee burned all
the way down her throat. It might have had something to do
with the bottle of Bordeaux she'd pilfered from the pantry late
last night, after finally arriving home from the play. The stupid, stupid, disaster of a play—

Rita poked her fork against a slice of tomato, miserable.
Why hadn't she just stayed at Winter Queen, where she be-
longed? Why had she even tried to break free? Living in a
dream was surely better than enduring stark reality.

"I liked it," piped up Alfred, at the other end of the table. He
hoisted a forkful of fried egg, yolk dripping down the tines;
Rita had to look away, concentrating on the wall again. "I
thought it was funny. Especially when that bloke tripped and
fell when he went to propose to Marguerite, and that other
girl laughed, and Marguerite said, *Dearest Alonzo, perhaps you'll
discover your dignity in Act Three*—"

"Alfred," warned Inez from across the table, and he shoved his fork into his mouth, silently chewing.

"Indeed," said Pauline, after a moment. "If only young boys could compose the audience every night." She reached for a slice of toast from the rack. "Charles, dear, won't you keep reading the review?"

"Oh? Er, I'd much rather—"

"Only perhaps skip to the end. Ahem. The . . . second-to-last paragraph, as I recall?"

"What?" Charles shot a look at his wife and then at Rita, still slumped in her chair. "Right, then." He flipped open the paper again, rattled the pages a bit, and gave a slight cough. "Ah. Here we go. *"If one might mention a single saving grace of this farce, a lone spark in the void, as it were, it would be the debut performance of Miss Rita Jolivet, the charming young actress in the role of Bessie, a stereotypical, flippant sweetheart. Yet it is clear that Miss Jolivet's talents are far from flippant and far from stereotypical. Her presence onstage brought beauty, focus, and delight, despite the shambles around her.*

"We wish Good Girls Stay Home *a speedy, merciful demise. In the same breath, we hope to see Miss Jolivet testing her mettle again under a far worthier London script and sky."*

Rita sat up slowly, blinking. Her mind was looping, spinning; she still tasted Bordeaux on the back of her tongue, and surely she'd heard wrong. "What, does it really say that?"

"It does."

"I *told* you," said Inez.

"No, *I* told you," said Pauline.

Rita turned to her mother, suspicious. "Did you pay them to write that?"

"Je vous le jure, I did not. It's *The Illustrated Sporting and Dramatic News,* love; they're rather incorruptible. Now, if it had been one of those street rags . . ."

"There's a sketch," Papa said and half-rose to offer the paper to Rita. "Not bad, considering."

She opened the pages. There *was* a sketch, a hasty thing, with rough black crosshatching depicting the stage, the set, and a trio of actresses frozen in poses. The actress center stage stood with her arms spread wide, her face upturned; the other two figures remained almost cringing in shadow. But that center girl, with her long dark curls and winning smile, with a halo of white framing her from crown to toe, as if she literally shone—there was no question who it was meant to be.

Rita began to laugh, even though it made her head ache. She pressed her fingertips to her temple and said, "As if any of them needed an excuse to despise me more."

"Only the bitter earthbound," said Maman, buttering her toast, "despise a rising star."

Chapter 5

After that, the world spun more and more quickly. Your play. My lessons. Our mother's social whirl. I recall the evening we both collided straight-on with our futures, at that soirée at Mrs. Cornwallis-West's home. I'd turned seventeen and almost didn't attend because Maman was so appalled at the state of my fingernails.

I was practicing so many hours then, hellbent on Fräulein Wietrowetz's approval, perfecting every note. I was playing and playing until my neck and shoulders pinched with agony and my fingers cramped.

Poor Maman! Before we left for the party, she made me promise that when I removed my gloves for supper, I'd eat strictly with my right hand, to hide the calluses on my left.

MARCH, 1902
LONDON, ENGLAND

The rigid expectations of high society were gradually becoming easier for Inez to manage. She hadn't overcome her bashfulness in the midst of the unfamiliar; she still grew tongue-tied at the most mundane of questions. She felt stiff and shamed in the elegant, tight gowns her mother insisted she wear, as if she were some sort of imposter princess, and all anyone had to do was squint hard enough against her shiny diamonds and pearls to glimpse the raw country girl underneath.

She had to remind herself not to scratch at her scalp when a bejeweled clip pulled at her hair and not shove away a wayward feather from an aigrette when it tickled her ear. But Inez was nothing if not resourceful in her efforts to remain unseen and had learned certain tricks to work around the rules.

Smile when greeting her hosts while lightly clasping hands, then look down.

Smile at anyone she was introduced to while lightly clasping hands, then look down.

Murmur *Yes*, or *No*, or *How kind*, or *Do you think so?* to anyone persisting in pursuing a conversation.

Keep looking down.

Retreat to a wall whenever possible. A chair set against a wall was ideal.

In this way, Inez preserved her sanity and learned that a good many London mansions made liberal use of parquet flooring.

The residence of Mrs. George Cornwallis-West was no exception. Once upon a time, she had been Miss Jennie Jerome, and then Lady Randolph Churchill. She'd had a famous first husband and an even more famous son—and now a scandalously young second husband, to boot—but what Inez liked most about Mrs. Cornwallis-West was that she was American. When Inez had offered her *smile-shake hands-look down* routine as they were first introduced, Mrs. Cornwallis-West had wrapped both her satin-gloved hands around Inez's, drew her near, and whispered, "Don't worry. It's a jovial enough group, and none of us bite. But there's a little alcove over there if you want it, just right behind that screen."

Inez had been so startled she'd broken her own rule and looked up again. Her hostess met her eyes and nodded, still smiling, then released Inez's hands to move on to the next guest in line as if nothing extraordinary had happened at all.

She would later learn that Maman had warned Mrs. Cornwallis-West about her younger daughter's daunting shyness, and that Jennie, well accustomed to the freezing cold shoulder of British disapproval, had taken pity on her enough to supply Inez with the screen and the alcove and a solitary chair beside a potted date. An oasis from the splendor and glamour of the evening, hidden in plain sight.

It would not hide Inez from the fated events of the party itself, as it turned out. But a false sense of security was better than none. At least, so it seemed at the time.

She did manage to dine with mostly her right hand, keeping her left on her lap atop her napkin and gloves, fingers curled. Mrs. Cornwallis-West's table had been dressed in cool blue damask and enormous silver centerpieces of hothouse roses and hydrangea with petals of pink and peach and purple, shiny leaves. Each arrangement had been studded with small, lime-colored pears; Inez could catch their summer perfume even over the first course, cream of barley soup.

The centerpieces were, in fact, so lush and extravagant that it was impossible to see the person seated opposite her across the table, which was a relief. But she was still expected to maintain polite conversation with the two gentlemen flanking her. Happily, Rita was only a seat away to her right, entrancing everyone in her easy way, drawing every eye nearby, so Inez only had to worry about the man on her left. She'd glanced at him briefly as they were introduced—as was her way—and really all she remembered about him was that he was brown-haired and handsome, likely in his late twenties, and his name was George Something. He had the breezy, casual air of the outdoors clinging to him, the mark of someone who didn't

spend all his days toiling inside. An importer, maybe? A dip-
lomat? Younger son of a lord? She'd met over thirty people so
far tonight and honestly couldn't recall a single solid fact
about this one beyond his first name, and only that because
the farrier's son in Medmenham was also named George, and
he liked to whistle at her whenever he chanced across her
walking alone.

She tried her first spoonful of the soup. The steam rose up,
filled her nose with the aroma of barley before her tongue
tasted it, followed by a slow wafting of pear.

George Something had his head cocked and appeared to
be listening to Rita, allowing his own soup to cool. Behind
them stood a footman at attention, waiting to refill water or
wine. Across were those pears and flowers, and when she
allowed herself a longer glance, there was Mr. Something,
faintly smiling. His eyes cut to hers, and instantly Inez
dropped her gaze.

He leaned nearer. "Your sister is quite the entertainer."

His voice was pleasingly honeyed, surprising for a man so
young.

"She's an excellent storyteller." Inez dunked her spoon into
the soup.

"I understand she's captured the fickle attention of the West
End. Good for her."

"She's very talented," Inez said loyally.

"I'm sure. And you, Miss Jolivet? Have you any talents?"

"Perhaps," she said, and hesitated. "I hope so, at least."

A pause; he tried the soup. Rita released a light, musical
laugh, and half the table laughed with her. Mr. Something
spoke again.

"Did you know we have a genuine palm reader with us here
tonight?"

Inez was surprised. "No. Do we?"

"Mademoiselle Thenaud." His eyes were a soft smoky green, a fine contrast to his tanned skin and dark hair. "Just across over there, past the saltcellar, to the left. Gray ringlets, the rubied tiara." He returned to his soup. "She was Victoria's personal soothsayer, as a matter of fact. But she doesn't merely read palms, of course. She's also an actress. I've met her before once or twice, but I understand that Lady Churchill—pardon me, Mrs. Cornwallis-West—is a devoted follower." Another sip of soup, another sidelong look. "You should seek her out after supper. Perhaps she'll tell your fortune."

"Oh, I—I wouldn't really care for that, I think."

George Something turned his head to smile at her, nothing faint this time, a real smile that crinkled the edges of his eyes and revealed a dimple in his right cheek. "Perfectly understandable. Sometimes it's best to leave the future alone, isn't it?"

"I guess so."

"If you don't mind, I might venture a guess as to your talents, Miss Jolivet."

"No, really—"

"You are an artist," Mr. Something said. "A musician. The… cello? No. Nor the harp. Too traditional for such a radiant soul." He rubbed a finger along his chin, then smiled again. "The violin. You are a master of the violin."

Inez forgot herself enough to actually laugh. "A master? Hardly. I'm barely an amateur."

"Now, that is a lie. I've been informed by no less than King Edward himself that you're a genuine virtuosa. He said your skills are enough to make grown men fall to their knees in wonder, and women to take up arms to conquer nations. I fear he's quite smitten with you. Good thing he's already wed."

Inez blinked at him, momentarily speechless. "*Who* are you?"

"Just the fellow lucky enough to be seated beside you at supper."

"You knew all along that I play the violin."

"I confess I did."

She shook her head, bemused. "Why pretend you didn't?"

He leaned close again; she caught a hint of lemon and lavender beneath the constant fragrance of the pears. "Would you believe I was trying to impress you with my own soothsaying skills?"

"That's—"

"Sadly asinine, I know. I apologize. I'm not usually so clumsy in the face of radiance. Allow me to say merely that I hope someday I'll be the lucky fellow who gets to hear you play, Miss Jolivet."

She stared up at him, mired in that green-smoke gaze, in that attractive smile that was improbably, impossibly, aimed just at her. That felt like warmth and admiration and genuine interest, and sparked a hot, uncomfortable blooming in her chest.

"Well, maybe," she replied, stilted, as the servants shifted around them to clear the course and her heart pounded *Never, ever, not ever.*

HIS NAME WAS George Vernon. After the ladies retired to the drawing room to leave the gentlemen to their cigars and port, she'd sidled up to Rita to ask.

"A bit of a Renaissance man, from what I understand. He's originally from America and grew up to become a nice, boring banker for years, from a respectable enough family and all— the Butlers, I think? Somewhere in Virginia, if I remember right. Anyway, decent money. Vernon is his stage name. Just like us, he's reinvented himself, and now he's a concert singer." Rita sipped at a tiny glass of sherry. "A bloody good one, too, I heard. Why? Are you smitten?"

The teasing tone told Inez her sister wasn't being serious, but still that heat blazed in her chest. Inez ducked her head.

"Wait." Rita caught her by the arm, looked her up and down. "Are you?"

"Don't be silly; we've only just met. He was kind to me, that's all."

"Was he? Good. I like him a little better, even though he's a feckless singer."

"You said he was bloody good—"

"Oh, it's not an insult. I think all professional singers are feckless. It's what makes them so interesting."

"My pets." Pauline approached, regal in dove-gray silk and an overskirt of black netting, diamonds and opals around both wrists and her throat. "Tell me how we're faring."

"Splendid," Rita said, just as Inez mumbled, "Fine."

Maman tapped Rita affectionately on the forearm with her fan, then turned to Inez. "You seemed not entirely miserable at dinner. Your companion—who is he?"

"Mr. George Vernon," Rita supplied. "A concert singer."

"Mr. Vernon certainly seemed engaged in your conversation. Is he a pleasant gentleman?"

"Good golly," Inez burst out, defensive, and quickly lowered her voice. "I just met him! I hardly know him! He—he was perfectly fine. Perfectly adequate."

Pauline arched an eyebrow at Rita. "I believe that's the nicest thing I've ever heard her say about a suitor."

"It is," Rita agreed.

Inez burned with mortification. "He is not a suitor!"

Maman bent to press a perfumed kiss against her daughter's cheek. "As you say, my darling. Our hostess has been pleading with me to liberate some notes from her terrible antique pianoforte. I think I'll just have a bit more champagne before obliging her."

She drifted off without another look.

"How am I a member of this family?" Inez wondered beneath her breath.

"By virtue of blood and sinew and providence. You got every ounce of the genteel Jolivet grace. The rest of us are feral, messy beasts, but you love us."

Inez brought a hand to her cheek, just where her mother's kiss had landed. Even through her glove, her face felt too warm from the heat of the room and the fire and her rushing pulse.

Unlike Maman, Rita, at least, seemed disposed to linger. She swirled the last of the sherry in her glass; the liquid rose up and up, but never quite crested the edge.

"Only," she began, sober suddenly, very quiet, "listen, sissy..."

"Yes?"

The other ladies revolved gracefully around them in jewels and sequins and velvet, so unhurried it was as if they moved underwater, meeting, chatting, breaking apart.

"I heard a rumor about Mr. Vernon. That all those things I mentioned to you before, his being a banker and a singer, his background, it's all true. But also all a pretext for something else."

"What? What do you mean?"

"A pretext for government work. *Secret* government work."

Inez couldn't help it; she started to laugh. After everything else that had happened tonight, it was too ridiculous. "Oh, really! You're saying he's a spy."

"I'm saying nothing of the sort. I'm saying others are saying it. Look around you. Aren't we all rather prime? Aren't we all rather entangled in the beau monde? What's a concert singer from an unknown family doing here? Or, for that matter, a former boring old banker?"

"Or an actress, or a violinist," Inez retorted.

"Hmm." Rita tipped the last of the sherry into her mouth. "Well, it's only a rumor. I would have kept it under my hat, but I saw how you were looking at him, and he at you."

What a curse it was to be so fair; Inez felt her cheeks prickling. "And how was that?"

"Like you'd both just accidentally discovered the reflection of Narcissus staring back at you from the stream. Do me a favor, and don't fall in love with him."

Inez took her own tiny glass of sherry from a passing footman, grateful for the chance to angle away. "Love! That is the last thing you have to worry about with me."

No DOUBT MRS. Cornwallis-West had been correct when she'd told Inez it was a jovial group, but after an hour of standing, and then sitting, and then standing again, trying to blend in with the walls as everyone around her laughed and drank and conversed and the evening wound on, Inez was exhausted. She had very little small talk to offer beyond commenting on the weather or the elegance of the mansion; she had none at all to offer about fashion or childrearing or royal gossip, as most of the other ladies seemed to enjoy. Occasionally, she found Mr. Vernon watching her from across the chamber, but even though he would nod his head to her, he never approached. Which somehow made her feel even more uncomfortable.

When at last Pauline moved to the pianoforte to play, Inez seized the opportunity to retreat to the alcove. It stood at the western edge of the drawing room, some carved-out, architectural whimsy that was meant to hold a statue, perhaps, or an important piece of furniture. Tonight it held only her, keeping her near enough to eavesdrop on the party, but hidden enough to sit down with a sigh and close her eyes.

Her feet throbbed. She wore sleek new satin slippers with paper-thin soles that had seemed to fit this afternoon, but now felt at least a size too small. After a quick survey of her surroundings—there was only the date tree and the Chinese screen, embroidered peacocks with shimmering feathers floating across the folded silk panels—Inez bent forward, hooked a finger behind the heels, and eased off both slippers.

She sat back again. From rooms unseen, a series of time-pieces began to chime, at first the pretty, tinkling melodies of bracket clocks or mantle clocks, soon joined by the more serious bass of a longcase.

Midnight. Inez bent her head and lifted her hand to massage the back of her neck, trying not to disturb the pins in her hair. Surely the champagne was done by now, the coffee and conversations done. Surely it was time to head home soon.

"Don't look now," said a familiar, masculine voice, "but your sister has fallen under the spell of two of the most interesting people here."

Her head snapped up. Mr. Vernon leaned a shoulder against the wall nearby, just beyond the screen. From her position she could see only part of him, shadowed and lean, his face in profile. He was surveying the drawing room, all the places she could not see. She half-rose, remembered her discarded slippers and stocking feet, and sank back again.

Mr. Vernon brought a coup of champagne to his lips. The cabochon in his cufflink flashed a brief topaz glow, a cat's eye in the dark.

"Who?" Inez finally asked.

"Mademoiselle Thenaud and her good friend, Mr. Charles Frohman. Do you know him? No? He's a theatrical impresario from America. A very big deal, as they say over there. If you catch his fancy, he can pluck you straight up from nothing and land you in the heart of Broadway."

"Oh."

"I think it's fair to say your sister has caught his fancy."

Inez bristled. "Rita's not like that."

Now he glanced her, his lips curved. "Neither is he, believe me. I'm speaking strictly in the professional sense."

"Oh," she said again and decided to stand anyway. As she moved toward the edge of the screen, he moved back, arms crossed, keeping a proper distance between them.

She peered around the screen.

Rita was seated in a high-backed salon chair drawn close to two others, not far from the fireplace. The palm reader sat in the center, tiara glinting, and on the other side of her was an ample, fortyish man with plump cheeks and slicked-back hair who was laughing at something. Mademoiselle Thenaud held Rita's gloveless hand in her own, Rita's palm cupped upward. The fortuneteller was drawing her index finger across it. Rita's expression was engrossed.

Mr. Vernon murmured, "I suppose your sister's not much afraid of the future."

"She's not afraid of anything."

"Are you sure you don't want to go over there and join them? I can always carry your shoes for you."

"Please," Inez sighed, giving up and turning to face him, "I'm already so embarrassed. Don't make it worse."

He studied her; she had the sense that she had caught him off guard somehow, had done something unexpected, though she couldn't imagine what.

He bowed his head. "Miss Jolivet, I beg your pardon. I give you my word that I would never deliberately embarrass you."

She found, to her great astonishment, that she could not look away from him. She wanted to; she knew she should. Even with three feet between them, he was too close, too warm, too real. Lemon and lavender. His eyes, his voice, this moment, small and fine and intimate. For the first time in a long while, Inez didn't feel like a stranger in her own skin, trapped in a life and a world that was not her own. She felt seen. She felt recognized.

And those two facts together felt suddenly, beautifully dangerous.

She very nearly touched a hand to his sleeve, to complete their unlikely connection, but instead only confessed, "I don't know how to talk to you. I've never known anyone like you before."

"Ah! You're fortunate, then. I'm not a complicated fellow. I don't require quips or tittle-tattle or social niceties. My rough edges barely rub along with this group. But you're the virtuosa who's enchanted the king. That's good enough for me."

Inez looked back at Rita, who was leaning forward around the palm reader to say something to Mr. Frohman, who was nodding in response. But Mademoiselle Thenaud herself had lifted her head to observe Inez—Inez and Mr. Vernon standing there together, in their secluded corner of the room—and beneath her tiara of sparkling rubies, her lips were mirthless and her face stiff as stone.

Chapter 6

I wonder what Queen Victoria's palm reader said to you that night, those years ago.

I wonder what she would have said to me, if I'd been courageous enough to ask.

APRIL, 1902
LONDON, ENGLAND

There are angels around you. There are demons, too, but the angels are stronger. See this line here? It's your heart, strong but broken twice. This one? Your fate. Also strong and deep. You'll enjoy good fortune, great success. There is . . . there is something here in your lifeline I can't quite read. A—a violence. An interruption. An act not of your own will, but still one that slices straight through you.

You will survive it. The angels will ensure it.

Rita didn't believe in angels. She'd seen enough of the antics of men to know that if there were such things as angels, guardian angels, they didn't feel like helping out all that often. Still, for months, years even, after Mademoiselle Thenaud's murmured predictions about angels and demons and acts of violence—her head bent over Rita's naked palm at that party, her index finger cool against Rita's warm skin—sometimes she caught herself wondering.

She'd never seen an angel. She'd encountered some demons, though.

Even as a child, even before her menses had come and her breasts had grown and her little-girl softness had melted into firm adolescence, Rita came across men who took pleasure in hunting her. A subtle stalking, yes: she was still a child of privilege, born of parents who had power, who knew people of even greater power still.

But after a certain age, certain men always followed her. Certain men could be counted upon to show up wherever she went in Medmenham, to the greengrocer's or the ribbon shop or the butcher. Certain men felt free to leer at her, to come close enough to brush against her arm or her skirts, to press their palms against the small of her back, as if to herd her, to push her where they wanted her to go, as if they were sheepdogs and she was the sheep.

These men told her in false, flattering voices that she was so fair, as if she didn't already know. That her smile was so fetching. Her figure so sweet. Her teeth were white as sugar, her hands were tender as swans. They hovered over her and whined about her dark eyes demolishing them, her sultry gaze that demanded *more, more,* her cherry lips that wanted *more,* and well, she should just stop pretending, shouldn't she? Stop teasing them, because she *knew* she wanted more, just as they did . . .

Was she sixteen already? Already? Soon she'd be a wife, a solid country wife. What about a little fun before that? What else was there going to be for her, ever—even a conceited, half-foreign bitch like her, the eldest Jolivet girl who kept pushing their hands away?

There was a great deal more, as it turned out. A universe more, far away from those men, and if there was a secret angel in her life, someone beyond the circle of her own blessed family, it didn't take long for Rita to figure out who it was.

CHARLES FROHMAN DID not take her to Broadway. At least, not right away. Charles would, of course, be the man credited for eventually leading her there, but before any of that—before her American debut in one of his plays that would lead to international accolades, and her picture on posters, and the interviews, and all the silent motion-picture offers to come—before *that* was the layout in *The Sketch.*

Which had also been arranged by Charles.

He refused to allow her to call him Mr. Frohman. "We're going to be good friends," he told her not long after they'd been introduced at the supper party, but before Mademoiselle Thenaud and her unsettling predictions. "Friends call me Charles. The people who work for me call me Mr. Frohman."

"I'd like to be the friend who works for you," Rita said candidly, which made him laugh.

"My dear, let us watch and see how the planets align."

He'd read the review of *Good Girls,* that infamous review with that infamous illustration of Rita, a small goddess practically floating off the page. What's more, he'd made it a point to quietly go and see the show before its unceremonious closing, to judge for himself if Miss Rita Jolivet was truly the crackerjack prodigy she seemed.

He'd never told her what he thought of her performance, and she never asked. But as he'd sought her out at the former Lady Churchill's party, and as he'd invited her to his suite at the Savoy Hotel three times since, apparently she was skilled enough to hold his interest.

His *professional* interest, Rita emphasized to her mother, so Pauline wouldn't harbor any unlikely ideas.

"I understand he has a special friend back in the States," she'd added.

"Male or female?" Pauline asked.

"I don't know. Does it matter?"

"Not even a little."

Once a year, Charles Frohman, renowned theatrical manager and producer, traveled from his permanent suite at the Knickerbocker Hotel in New York to his other at the Savoy in London, scouting for fresh shows, for fresh talent, for any overlooked spark of beauty and ambition that he might bring back to America and shape in his favor. He had a keen eye and ruthless spirit when it came to getting what he wanted. If he needed to bribe a playwright to secure the performance rights for Broadway before, say, Toronto or Paris, he would. If he needed to poach an actor from another manager to get him in Charles's own stable, he would. He had a round, boyish face (*like a custard pie, my mother used to say*, he'd chuckle) and merry gray eyes that belied the relentless ambition that steeled his spine. He enjoyed gourmet sweets and wine, silk ascots, and diamond rings on both hands.

"What you really need right now," he'd told her over tea in his private parlor one muggy spring afternoon, "is exposure."

Rita tilted her head, waiting, a gold-rimmed Limoges plate holding a single scone and dollop of clotted cream balanced on her knees. The cream was slowly settling into a puddle; the temperature inside was nearly as warm as outside, even with all the windows open. An occasional breeze scented of the Thames trifled with the lace curtains, and the slant of sunlight cutting through them cast long, filigreed shadows across the floor and up the Egyptian-green plastered wall.

Della, the housemaid from the Bloomsbury apartment, sat discreetly in a corner chair nursing her own cup of tea, pretending not to eavesdrop as they spoke.

"Public exposure," Charles was saying. "Not just your face, but your name. You're not going to have a problem being cast again, not for the next three months at least. William Poel has already asked for an introduction."

Rita nearly dropped her plate. "William Poel? Of the Elizabethan Stage Society?"

"The very same. He's putting together his next production. *Much Ado About Nothing.*"

"Heavens—"

"If I recommend you, you'll go to the audition, and you'll be commendable enough, no doubt. But as of right now, no one around you, no one, is going look at you and have the slightest idea who you are. Do you understand me?"

"I suppose so?"

"Because the key to lasting success in this business, Rita, to genuine fame, isn't luck or even necessarily talent. It's having the public recognize you right away, having them *crave* you, more and more of you, before they ever come to see you perform, before they ever read your name on a marquee. You want them to eat you, drink you. Dream you. *You* are their ambitions for fame and glory fulfilled. *You* are the elusive key to a life of glamour. You are every single one of them in their fantasies, young and irresistible. When they're in the audience, we don't want them saying, *Now, who is this girl?* But rather, *Oh, it's her, how lucky we are, what a treat.*"

Rita frowned at her hands, cupped around the delicate porcelain plate. "It all sounds very grand. But I can't imagine how to make anyone look at me and think such things."

"Why, it's the simplest trick in the world, if not the cheapest. Most people have no notion of how easily influenced they are by what they read." The river breeze slipped by again, tilting the shadows; a pair of women somewhere outside near the windows were conversing in soft, feminine tones. Charles sat back and dabbed his napkin to his forehead. "Tell me, do you subscribe to *The Sketch?*"

"Yes."

"So does everyone else. That's where we'll begin."

THE IDEA BEHIND the photography session was to showcase Rita's beauty and versatility in the simplest, most dramatic way possible. Charles had reserved a full page in the magazine on her behalf, a layout that would feature her in a series of posed photographs demonstrating the Characteristic Dances of Various Nations.

She hadn't known the theme until she'd arrived at the studio that morning. Charles wasn't in attendance; it was just Rita and the photographer and his two assistants. (And Rita's pearl-handled pistol in her reticule, just in case. It was her first official publicity shoot, at a studio all the way across town in Cheapside. Inez had made her promise to take it along, even though it wasn't loaded . . . which was funny, since Inez never carried her own.)

When Rita had pointed out that she wasn't entirely familiar with the characteristic dances of various nations, the photographer, a burly man with a razor-thin moustache, told her it didn't matter.

"You've seen an Irish lass before, yeah? A Frenchie? All you have to do is pose like you'd think they'd pose. The girls and I will take care of the rest."

The girls were a former lady's maid, who would manage Rita's face paint and hair, and a silver-haired matron, who was in charge of a long metal rack crammed with costumes in rainbows of colors.

It was the costumer's job to pair the tall Welsh hat with the correct knitted shawl, the zingara's tambourine with the proper hair ribbons, the geisha's kimono with the yellow silk chrysanthemum to be tucked in the sash at her waist.

"How many dances are we photographing?" Rita asked, surveying the bulging rack with trepidation.

"As many was we need to. We're booked for the day, miss. *That* many."

IN THE END, it wasn't so many dances after all, barely a sampling of nations, but it still devoured hours and hours, eight hours straight with a quick break at noon for coffee and stale ham sandwiches. She became a Welsh girl for the camera, a French girl, a Spanish girl. A gypsy, a zingara, a British sailor. An American cowgirl. She lifted her tambourine or her fan and sometimes kicked up a foot, holding whatever pose she had to for as long as she had to, muscles aching as the photographer adjusted the lighting and muttered instructions to his girls, who sometimes darted forward for some small adjustment—the drape of an apron, the position of a hair comb—before the shutter clicked and the flash powder burned.

For the cowgirl, Rita showed them her pistol, and even though no one could quite believe that Americans danced with their guns in hand, everyone agreed it would look perfect in the shot.

The geisha costume, however, defeated her. It wrapped around her so snugly Rita could hardly bend at the waist, much less do anything with her feet. In the end, she knelt on the floor before a lacquered screen, sat back on her heels with her arms slightly open and smiled tenderly at the camera, as if it were a long-absent lover who had finally returned home.

"Good God," muttered the photographer, peering at her from behind the lens. "Yes. That look. Do that one again."

And she did. It was easy.

THE LAYOUT IN *The Sketch* was published in July, accompanied by a peppy little article about Miss Jolivet, how fresh and exciting she was, and how she was sweeping London by storm, which was a wild exaggeration. Yet, by then, she *had* been cast in William Poel's austere version of *Much Ado About Nothing*.

She was Hero, the young, innocent heroine battered by fortune and her fiancé's fickle faith. So, months after she'd stood on the stage of the Catharine and boldly lied about playing the same part, her lie had lifted up on the wings of faith and transformed into truth.

That was how Inez had put it, in her soft and earnest way: *wings of faith, transformed into truth.* Rita preferred to think about how Ansel Lurie was likely squirming with rage, wherever he was.

Lurie was now far behind her, along with his embarrassing farce. Mr. William Poel was all that Ansel Lurie had hoped to be but could never be, and William Poel had grand ideas about how to stage the Bard. (Some said odd ideas, modern ideas, as if the notion of change offended their very souls.) Poel eschewed overly fussy sets and ornate, glittery costumes. He demanded an open stage, minimal props, and outstanding acting. On Rita's first day of rehearsal, at the smoldering crack of dawn at St. George's Hall, he shook her hand and told her that even though she was young and new, she must not fall behind. The company would move like a locomotive through the acts, he said, pushing all detritus out of the way like dying sparks along the rails.

He had not been in jest. That morning, Rita took her chair at a long wooden table for the cast's first read-through. When Mr. Poel, at the head of the table, kept banging his fist against the tabletop, rhythmic as a train, urging, *faster, better,* everyone did as he said. She learned on the jump to speak as quickly and eloquently as she could, with as much emotion as she dared without descending into parody. Thank God, it seemed to work.

Hero was the role of a lifetime, at least for a girl her age. She wasn't going to waste it.

The truth was, though, that maybe she wasn't as clever as she hoped. Maybe she wasn't the discovery of a generation for the stage. The celebrated Mr. Poel seemed to take a special interest in her, yes, but perhaps it was because of Charles. Or perhaps it was because she was so raw and eager, so ready to be what he wanted. Mr. Poel gave her very pointed direction, his attention so focused on the details that he would comment on the placement of her hand on her hip in the wedding scene (higher; her fingers should pinch at her waist as if in pain). The half smile on her lips when being wooed (too coy; be more sincere). The degree of anguish in her brow when she realized her betrothed's betrayal (just right). Rita soaked it up like a sponge. She wasn't in love with him—she didn't even know if he had a wife, or wanted one—but she was seduced by his vision. By the purity of his dream. It felt exactly aligned with her own. She wanted to make herself the best vessel for the art that anyone could be.

Much Ado ran for months.

Then one early September afternoon, Rita's world shifted. Only a little, only enough to allow a startling, lucid glimpse of what her future might hold. It was a small moment in an ordinary day, so small that in a remarkable life, it might easily go unremarked. But it was the first of a thousand small moments just like it that would follow ever afterward. More than a thousand, perhaps even ten thousand. So she did remember it—the first time she was recognized in public.

She and Inez had gone shopping for hats and ended up taking luncheon in an intimate, elegant café in Covent Garden. They ate sole and roasted potatoes under a series of colorful murals by Alphonse Mucha, and when the waitress approached at the end of the meal with a copy of *The Sketch*, asking quietly for an autograph, Rita borrowed a pen of aquamarine ink from the gentleman at the table next to hers, signing her name beneath the pictures of the improvised dances with an elaborate, sculpted flourish.

My Best Wishes. Rita Jolivet.

When she was finished, both she and Inez paused a moment to admire it, that jeweled blue scrawl across the page, how the "a" at the end of her first name formed a tail that crisscrossed under her last name, three long loops.

"Draw a heart, there," Inez said, pointing at the bottom of the loops.

"A heart? No. That's so sappy—"

"A heart, just there. Do it. It makes it special."

So Rita bent closer and drew a careful heart where her sister had told her to, and honestly it wasn't half-bad. Certainly the waitress seemed happy enough. She thanked them with pink cheeks and carried the magazine away with the pages still open, so the ink would dry without smearing.

Rita returned the pen to its owner at the next table with a curtsy. He was older, with white hair and jowls like a bulldog, but he smiled at her easily enough as he tucked the fountain pen back into his jacket pocket.

"So you're famous, then, young lady?"

"No, not really," Rita demurred.

"She is," Inez countered. "But not as famous as she will be. Perhaps you should have her autograph too, sir."

"Perhaps I should," the man agreed, and that was how Rita came to borrow his pen a second time, and how the fashionable art nouveau café lost a single linen napkin that day, one stained with a few bold lines of bright blue ink.

Chapter 7

I suppose it doesn't matter what the palm reader would have told me, does it? I looked at George, and he looked at me, and that was that, as they say.

You asked that night if I was *smitten*. Such a small, trifling word for how it all turned out.

OCTOBER, 1902
NORFOLK, ENGLAND

Inez had been a guest at Sandringham House exactly twice before, both times with her parents when she had been a girl. The royal residence reminded her a little of Winter Queen, albeit on a much more colossal scale. Like her childhood home, the original manor house had been turned into a fairy-tale fantasy, wings added, stone trim added, parapets and gables, but also formal gardens and lakes and rockeries and cupolas. It lacked the mild, misted wilderness that hugged Winter Queen, true, but Sandringham was said to be the king's favorite place to hide from public view, and it was easy to see why.

It was a brick-and-limestone palace on nearly eight thousand sculpted acres. Far from London, far from the smoke and fumes and constant, clanging commotion of city life, it afforded the monarch and his family a rare privacy that they occasionally shared with friends or allies. Or people who hoped they might become friends or allies.

Pauline and Charles had been invited more than twice, of course. But twice was all that Inez had been afforded, until that crisp autumn of 1902. By then, she had graduated from the music lessons her mother had imposed upon her and had begun to enjoy a measure of independence. Which could have explained why she'd been summoned, all by herself, to visit the king and queen.

Fräulein Wietrowetz had returned home a month past. She'd claimed she'd taught Inez all that she could, and it was time for her to attend to her teaching post back in Berlin. Until that moment, suspended in the hazy hush of the drawing room of the Bloomsbury apartment, the city alive outside the windows but the rooms inside so quiet and still, Inez hadn't fully realized how bound she was to this other woman. How desperate she was for her approval.

Miss Wietrowetz had ended their final lesson with a firm handshake and a wish for her pupil to keep practicing five hours a day. That was it, that was all. No comments on Inez's talent, or lack of it. No promises of future visits. She seemed almost desperate to leave.

On her way to Victoria station, however, the Fräulein had unexpectedly stopped by the apartment one last time, her bags stacked on the hansom that waited at the curb. She'd rung the bell and embraced Inez on the front steps, whispering in German, *Never accept less than you deserve. You are a prodigy, a gift from God. Walk the path He has given you.*

Inez had been so startled she'd only tightened her grip around her teacher's sturdy middle. Never once, in all her months of tutelage, had she suspected that the Fräulein thought her anything more than a dilettante.

"*Wirklich?*" she'd asked, because Inez knew German, at least a schoolgirl's version of it, and thought that maybe she'd misunderstood.

"Yes," Gabriele Wietrowetz had replied in English. And then she'd smiled. "You have the capacity for greatness, Inez Jolivet, such a rare thing. Use it well. I'm happy to have known you." Her gloved fingers clenched over Inez's own. "No doubt I'll read about you in the periodicals soon. God bless."

A flustered *ma'am!* was all Inez was able to manage in response, but it was enough. Her teacher turned and descended the steps back to her carriage, bombazine skirts in hand. Inez watched the cab driver flick his whip, the poor horse clattering into action, and the hansom wheeled down the lane, gone forevermore.

Her last tutor—as it turned out, the very last tutor of her life—gone forevermore.

So perhaps she was ready for her recital at Sandringham that bright honied autumn. Perhaps not. Either way, it didn't matter, as Edward himself had summoned her to his weekend house party, her gift, her violin, her music to transport his guests.

The invitation had arrived on a stiff ivory card etched in silver. The dates, the place, and that her presence was cordially requested, along with perhaps a small, informal solo recital to be performed at the pleasure of their majesties.

Both Maman and Papa were in Provence, tending to society there, and their vines. Inez had wired them at once in a panic, asking what to do. The reply had come barely an hour later: DONT BE ABSURD YOU MUST GO STOP TAKE THE ROSE SATIN FROM WORTH STOP YOU WILL DAZZLE STOP BULLESY EXCLAMATION MARK

Rita was caught up in her excellent world of Shakespeare, and Alfred was away at Eton. It would be just Inez performing alone in Sandringham's conservatory, or some drawing room, or a grandiose parlor, hoping to impress the king and queen and all their friends.

From London all the way to Wolferton station, a pampered guest aboard the royal train, she was afraid she might vomit. She refused all offers of wine or biscuits or tea from the steward and distracted herself by gazing fiercely out the windows, at the rushing of meadows and downs, blocky orchards of apple trees stippled with red fruit. Birches and spindles and chestnuts sped by, their leaves waving goodbye in a blaze of scarlet and orange. The October sky spread to infinity above it all, blue as the ocean.

It helped a little, at least until the train pulled into the station. Then she and Della, the maid, were bundled into a glossy black Daimler, Inez in the back, Della in the front, the chauffer promising Miss Jolivet that her luggage would follow. Her violin, in its case, remained with her. She never surrendered her instrument, not to anyone.

The auto's door closed with a solid *thunk*, heavy and slightly ominous. She was cushioned in tufted leather, surrounded by smoked glass and polished walnut trim. When the chauffer climbed into the front beside the maid, Inez leaned forward a bit, hoping to glimpse the road ahead between their shoulders. The darkened glass of the back windows dulled the world to gray, like an eclipse.

But the front of the Daimler was mostly open, so she was able to breathe in the fresh country air, tinged very faintly with salt from the cold North Sea. The auto rumbled to life, a low growly purr. They angled out the station and down a paved lane that soon turned to dirt.

Norfolk was still wildly green, even so late in the season, although the changing trees lent a shimmer of gold along the fields. At one point, they passed a long hawthorn hedge and a bouquet of pheasants burst free from it, a flash of autumn colors lifting up to the sky. Inez followed them as long as she could, twisting in her seat to keep them in view until the road rolled on and she lost them.

The estate was only a few miles from the train station; she would have appreciated a bit more time in the motorcar to compose her nerves, but almost before she knew it, they were approaching the graceful limestone arches of the *porte cochère*. The Daimler slowed, stopped, and Inez had to remind herself to wait for the approaching footman to open the door for her. She took her case in her right hand and accepted his proffered arm with her left, stepping onto meticulously raked gravel.

A giant, unlit glass lantern hung just inside the *porte cochère*, round as a globe and supported by heavy iron braces. In the shaded gloom of the entranceway, it seemed to shift between cloudy and clear, like an uncertain crystal ball.

"Miss Jolivet," said a new man in black tie, standing beneath the lantern. The butler, she assumed, although he didn't look familiar. "Welcome to Sandringham House."

"Thank you," she said, and then cleared her throat because her voice sounded so thin. "How kind," she said, more firm.

"This way, please."

Inez threw a look over her shoulder in time to see the footman leading Della away, presumably toward the servants' entrance.

She tightened her grip on her case and followed the butler into the saloon.

The chill of it hit her first, that distinctive, minerally wall of air that still lingered in her memory, the scent of atoms encased in old brick and wood and stone. The saloon itself stretched almost large as a yacht. It served as the reception room and main living room, covered in plasterwork and paintings and antique Spanish tapestries. Clusters of chairs and tables stood in lonely isolation, islands of polished stone and gilt floating amid the crimson-and-sage rugs that spread from wall to wall.

She recalled it vaguely from her girlhood. She thought the chamber would have seemed a little smaller to her now, now that she was grown, but it didn't. The ceiling, with its engravings and elaborate Jacobean fretwork, loomed so high above her it might have been real angels in the fresco of cherubim and pastel clouds above her head.

A woman in jet silk appeared, utterly unadorned, her hair slicked into a hard bun.

"Miss Jolivet. I'm Mrs. Matthews, the chatelaine. Their majesties regret that they are unable to welcome you in person, but most of the weekend guests arrived yesterday for the first shoot this morning. They won't be back until later this afternoon. If you like, I can show you to your room for a rest before supper."

"Yes, thank you."

"This way, please," the woman said, in cadence and tone sounding exactly like the butler.

Inez had no hope of memorizing the way to her room; she only followed silently down corridors decorated with sprays of axes and swords and spears and—more distressingly—the decapitated heads of animals, rams and boars and stags. It was like the gun shop in Piccadilly, only if Mr. Christian had decorated a palace instead of a cramped store.

The housekeeper opened a white-lacquered door and stood aside so that Inez could enter first. It wasn't one of the two bed-chambers she'd been assigned before, but that wasn't surprising. She wasn't even sure how many rooms Sandringham had, but it had to be over a hundred. This one was smaller than her previous accommodations (or was she just bigger?), but styled in the typical carved woodwork and flourishes that embellished the rest of the House. Glimmers of cut-crystal from sconces and lamps winked at her from the corners of the suite.

"I trust you'll be comfortable here, miss."

"I'm sure."

"Your maid should be up directly. Supper is at eight. You'll hear the gong, but I can send a footman to guide you down to the dining room, at least for tonight, if you like?"

"Thank you."

The housekeeper turned to go, one hand on the brass knob. "If that will be all?"

"No! Wait. That is—I wonder if you could tell me when I'm expected to play."

The woman paused. "Play, miss?"

"Yes." Inez hefted up her case. "My violin. The king requested it."

Mrs. Matthews dropped her gaze to the case, then raised it again, her face unreadable. "I'm afraid I have no information about that, miss."

"I only—I wonder if it's tonight, or tomorrow? I need time to prepare."

"I'll look into it for you, if you like."

"That would be so kind—"

"Good afternoon, miss."

"Good afternoon," Inez echoed softly, as the door clicked shut.

ABOUT AN HOUR later, well after Inez was blissfully immersed in a hot bath, the housekeeper sent a note to her chamber. It explained that Miss Jolivet was not expected to perform for the king's guests this evening, or any other. Far from it. Miss Jolivet was a respected visitor. If she *chose* to honor the king and queen with her music, it would be considered her gift to the House.

That said, after such an arduous day of shooting, perhaps the next day might be best for such a recital.

So there it was. Time for a bath tonight, time for a dinner. Tomorrow would be her testing point.

Then Della had arrived, full of excited chatter about every-thing she'd heard and learned downstairs.

Weekend shoots at the palace were tremendous social events, apparently. King Edward looked forward all year to the season, to the degree that he had even changed time itself: all the clocks in Sandringham were set thirty minutes ahead, to maximize the hours the winter sun would shine above his royal head and across his royal, doomed birds.

Members of the shooting party were beginning to trickle back by the time Della had left to come upstairs. Apparently, they'd bagged so many pheasants and partridges, the caver-nous game larder was already a quarter full.

"I expect you'll be dining on naught but bird the whole while here, miss," Della said, meeting Inez's eyes in the dress-ing table mirror as she arranged her hair.

"And birdshot," Inez predicted, fastening her earbobs.

Night had fallen, and the windows showed only obsidian glass and stars. The light inside the bedroom chamber was silky gold, flickering. Shadows moved silently across the chintz curtains and the thick pile of the rugs.

The maid's hands paused; she shook her head. "I never in my life thought I'd come here, not for any reason."

"And I never thought I'd be invited back."

"Fancy! The king's home itself! So grand, it is!"

"I'm glad you're enjoying it."

"Oh, I am, I am! Wait until I tell Mrs. Corbyn all about it!"

"And the cook. She's your auntie, isn't she?"

"Yes, miss."

"I'll report any and all birdshot to you, so you can let her know how they manage things here."

Della stifled a laugh. From somewhere below them, a dinner gong sounded, low and long, like a heartbeat slowly fading.

"There," the maid said, taking a step back. "You're ready."

Inez closed her eyes, resisted the urge to crush her hands into fists. "I hope so."

SUPPER PASSED IN a haze. There was wine, and there was china emblazoned with the royal coat of arms, a bright splash of red and blue and gold in the center of each piece. There was laughter and candlelight and mirrored plateaus reflecting the ceiling in slicks of light. It was *service à la russe*, with place cards and a calligraphed menu beside each setting, every course detailed. It was polished silver epergnes dripping with flowers and ivy and fresh fruit so vivid and perfect it might have all been wax.

Inez considered the fat orange practically hanging over her glass of Chablis. She nearly lifted a hand to poke it, but didn't.

Her previous two visits had her eating in the royal nursery with her siblings, where the most stressful part of the meal was keeping neat and still under the watchful eyes of a trio of nannies. Those meals, she recalled, had been mostly bread and butter pudding, some sliced cheese, chicken salad with boiled potatoes, or a hash of minced lamb.

Nothing like this. Likely there was nothing in the world like this, a weekend gathering of some of the most important people in the realm, slowly chewing their way through course after course of fragrant delicacies, local dishes, Continental dishes. Not a humble smear of chicken salad in sight.

Their majesties had greeted her very graciously when she'd returned to the saloon before the meal, making her curtsies. They acted as if she were a dear, bosom friend who had at last come to call, which spun her into an even quieter sort of misery, so afraid of saying or doing the wrong thing in the face of their regal kindness.

She remembered enough of her manners not to linger before them after their hellos, so she smiled and angled away, managing to find a saffron satin chair mercifully positioned in a corner. She settled there, pretending to be entranced by the tapestry of Zeus and Diana beside her as everyone else chatted and sipped brandy or champagne, until they were all called in to the dining room.

Which brought her to that too-perfect orange, and the menu, and the bone china encircled with plump, even dots of gold, none of them chipped or broken off, everything flawless.

The gentleman to her left was sunburnt and sweating. After his initial nod to her, his name muttered (she'd already lost it in the echoing splendor of the room, the swell of conversation all around them), he focused entirely on his oysters.

To her right was a blond man with a long nose and an unkind mouth, who had read her place card from the side of his eye and offered a brief, introductory comment on his great success at the shoot today, ten brace, to which she had no response beyond *How nice for you.*

He nodded and paused, his lips puckered, then also began to concentrate on the oysters, dabbing each one with a precise little spoonful of horseradish.

To be fair, the oysters were excellent.

Inez had surveyed the table once, twice, and seen no one she recognized. She frowned at her plate and had the unsettling thought that maybe she wasn't even really here, maybe this was just a dream, or a nightmare. Why else would plain Inez Jolivet be dining at the king and queen's private palace all alone, all apart, without even her parents or her sister to buffer her? It was ludicrous. It was madness. Two days ago, she'd been eating gingerbread with her bare fingers in her bedroom without a napkin, staring out the window at the clouds and thinking lazily about decrescendos, crumbs sprinkled across her lap.

That was who she was. That was her life. Not this.

But the evening wound on. Eventually, she was able to make her excuses and fly away for the night, back to her pretty guest room, where Della had brushed out her hair and Inez

handed her, with a sly grin of triumph, the small lead ball
she'd fished from her roasted pheasant three hours before and
hidden inside her glove since.

It left the barest red dent in her palm.

THE SECOND SHOOT began just after breakfast. Inez was not included. She wouldn't have wanted to go anyway, and she
supposed this was another little gift from Maman, who in all
likelihood had informed the household about her younger
daughter's disinclination for the hunt. It left her free, along
with a handful of other leftover ladies, to enjoy a leisurely afternoon tea and then a stroll through the gardens.

The sun burned a white-hot button above them. The sky
shone nearly cloudless, only a few glorious puffs lingering
above the palace, as if snared in place by the crenulated chimney stacks. Inez walked not-quite-behind the cluster of women,
most of them gossiping in low, civilized voices. As soon as she
could manage it, she slowed, slowed... and then turned the
corner around a sculpted hedge to lose them entirely.

No one seemed to notice. She heard their footsteps pressing
on, their tidbits about Lord This or Lady That gradually fading.

She took a deep breath, smelling rich loam and dying
leaves, and felt her shoulders begin to relax for the first time
in hours.

The hedge enclosed a small labyrinth composed of rhodo-
dendrons and climbing vines on black iron trellises. Nothing
was in bloom, but the path was gentle, and the rustling of
leaves around her reminded her of home. A coal tit eyed her
from its perch atop one of the trellises as she passed. Well beyond the maze, a swan called out, answered by another, harsh
and happy notes that echoed across the grounds.

The sun felt warm on her head and face and shoulders, a
bit blinding along the taupe silk folds of her gown. If she
wasn't careful, she'd end up as red-nosed as her dinner com-

panion last night. Still she traced the path, discovering in the heart of the labyrinth a life-sized bronze of Diana again, posed mid-run with one foot fixed to her pedestal, the other kicked back, a hart behind her, her bow in hand.

Inez circled it, trailing her fingers along the curve of the bow, down the back of one metal leg. She marveled at the perfection of the piece and then wondered why she marveled, since the entire estate seemed devoted to perfection.

Diana's gaze was turned outward, her lips smiling. Sunlight glanced along her figure in lean lines, the bronze dark, the gleam fiery. The coal tit darted close and landed atop a new trellis nearby, keeping Inez in sight.

"Is this your home, then?" she asked it. "I think it must be. I'll go now. You needn't worry about me."

She traced her way back to the opening in the hedge. After wandering aimlessly along a few more paths, she found herself at the green edge of a lawn that led back to the House, to an open pair of French doors she hadn't seen before. She paused, glanced around, but there was no one else nearby, not even the little bird, and it appeared she was no longer anywhere near the main entrance. So she crossed the grass to the doors.

The sudden plunge from daylight into shelter had her pausing again, blinking.

This must be—well, she didn't know what. A ballroom? Something splendid, something painted in ivory and marbled in pink and gray, but with so much gilt, so much golden scrollwork and carved garlands climbing up the walls and along the ceiling and dripping down to the floor itself . . . she'd never seen so much gold in one room before.

And it was hushed, and empty. The flesh along her arms began to crawl; Inez had the unmistakable feeling that she should not be intruding here. She moved quickly to the nearest door, finding herself in a wide hallway—still unfamiliar—which she followed at a slower pace, telling herself she was doing nothing wrong, no one had warned her against exploring the House, no one had restricted her to her room. She was *allowed*. She was fine.

She passed five footmen and a maid, none of whom would meet her eyes. After a few minutes, she began to realize that she was well and truly lost, and was going to have to accost the next servant she saw for directions, no matter how much she didn't want to—

But then she found the saloon. Thank heavens, that huge hollow space where a few of her fellow guests sat chatting in the saffron satin chairs, turning toward her curiously as she entered, turning away again.

Inez composed herself. She tucked a loosened curl of hair behind her ear. There was a minstrels' gallery in here, high above her. She'd noted it yesterday when she'd first arrived and wondered if that was where she'd be expected to perform. If so, she needed to see it. Acoustics, temperature, the light. The more prepared she was for all the variables, the better.

She ran a nervous hand once more along her coiffure, which seemed to be mostly holding up. She headed toward the steep stairs that led up, up to the gallery. Skirts lifted, her short train brushed the limestone steps behind her with a rhythmic *swish, swish*.

It wasn't much of a space, just a long rectangular balcony hemmed with carved wooden panels barely as high as her hips. There was a lone candelabra in a corner, no candles in the sockets. The ceiling here was coved and loomed very close, so any sound would bounce downward. It *might* work, if she figured out the best place to stand . . .

She was leaning over the railing, examining the space below, when someone walked directly beneath her and tipped up his face.

"Hullo," George Vernon said, his hands poked into his pockets. He smiled. "Look how high up you are."

"Oh! Mr. Vernon! Er, hello."

"What are you up to?"

"Only looking. Only . . ." But she ran out of words to explain herself. What on earth was he doing here? She hadn't seen him since they'd met at Mrs. Cornwallis-West's soirée months ago, and Rita had said he wasn't fancy enough but was probably a spy, and Inez didn't even care, because of the way he smiled at her then, just like now, right now—

"Shall I join you?" he asked. He disappeared into the stairwell before she could answer yes or no.

Inez raised a hand to her hair again, quickly lowered it. Then he was there, practically bouncing free of the old-fashioned open doorway.

"Miss Jolivet. Delightful to see you again."

"And you." She studied him more closely; he was wearing a gray pin-striped lounge suit with a navy tie, nothing appropriate for roaming out of doors. "Have you just arrived?"

"My party encountered some scheduling conflicts, I'm afraid, now thankfully resolved. We've been here an hour or so." He looked around them. "Are you planning a concert?"

"No, not a concert. I only—I'm to play a bit, you see. And I thought it might be up here, so I wanted to take a look at it. Get to know it."

"Very wise." He faced her fully, ducking his head a little against the low ceiling. "I admire an artist who learns her ground. But I fear you won't be serenading us from up here."

"What?" she said, instead of *Us?*, which is what her tongue wanted to say.

"I heard a rumor that their majesties hoped to hear your violin in the splendiferous grace of the White Drawing Room."

Inez felt a tingling begin along her spine that might have been fear, or anticipation, or both.

"Please, sir," she said. "What room is that?"

"You know, I'm not certain. But between you and me, based on the looks of this place, I'd wager it's far more *cuivre doré* than white." He stepped closer. His eyes were that same slaty green as before, the same dark lashes, the same slight smile. The tingling turned into disquiet as he leaned his head to hers and lowered his voice. "And I'm no *sir*, not by a long shot. You must call me George."

THE WHITE DRAWING Room turned out to be the ivory-and-gold chamber she'd stumbled across before, even more magnificent when lit by the sconces on the walls and the huge crystal chandelier that held no fewer than sixty tapers. The chandelier was tiered, thick with droplets and pendants and hanging so low that if she passed beneath it and raised her hand, Inez might easily have sent the bottom ring of crystal daggers chiming through her fingers.

Dinner was concluded; Mr. Vernon had not been seated beside her. In fact, he hadn't been there at all, which was odd, and (she had to admit to herself) disappointing. He'd mentioned he'd arrived with some group, but she hadn't noted anyone new at the table from the night before. There was the king still at the head of the table, the queen at the foot, and their merry band of fellow bird hunters all around, nearly everyone talking animatedly about the day's success.

Her two table companions had settled in much as they had for their last dinner, ignoring Inez to concentrate on the *consommé tortue*, the *filet de perdrix et foie gras*, the *geléees noyeau aux pêches*.

Which was fine with her. She'd barely tasted any of it, so filled as she was with dread for what was to come.

She wore the gown of rose satin from the House of Worth, as her mother had commanded. Thank goodness she had; it was the only dress she owned that was as sophisticated as her surroundings. The rigid folds of it dragged at her, heavier than she liked, but if it slowed her steps and made her seem more deliberate in this space, made her more *right*, so much the better.

Monsieur Worth had embroidered the skirts with star-bursts of silver diamantés and beading, and edged the bodice with a puff of sheer, metallic chiffon. The tiny paste jewels caught the light and scattered it in sprays whenever she moved.

As soon as the queen rose to end the meal, Inez had re-treated upstairs to fetch her instrument. By the time she returned downstairs (now guided by a footman in livery and a powdered wig; how embarrassing it would be to become lost in the warren of hallways and be late), nearly everyone had meandered into the White Drawing Room, standing and con-versing in clusters with drinks in hand. A few were beginning to take their seats in the rows of chairs arranged before the marble hearth at the end of the room.

George Vernon was nowhere in sight, despite his lofty use of *us* this afternoon.

The very first row of her audience consisted of just four scarlet satin chairs even larger, even grander, than the ones ar-rayed behind them. No doubt their majesties would occupy two of those, but who could the other two be for?

The king stood by the fire with one leg bent, in deep discus-sion with a trio of black-coated men. He caught sight of Inez lingering at the entrance, flicked away his companions with an easy left hand and beckoned her to him with his right. The men bowed and walked off as she approached.

She managed a credible curtsy without touching her skirts, since she was holding the violin and bow.

Edward smiled down at her, gray-haired, portly. He looked exactly like the official portrait of him hung in the parlor in Bloomsbury, one that had come with the lease. "How pleased we are to have you here, my dear."

"It is my pleasure, sir."

He was so familiar to her. Beyond portraits, beyond his face in the papers, she'd known him for years. From a distance at least, sometimes less so. One of his stays at Winter Queen had fallen on her ninth birthday, and he'd brought her a tissue-wrapped gift himself, cascading with ribbons. It had been a china doll, with a painted porcelain face and a plush body, and she had loved it at once. She'd hugged him then, hardly aware of how improper it was, but the king of England—at the time Prince Albert—had only laughed and smoothed a hand down her hair, and said he was glad she liked the dolly.

In her mind, he flipped from king to kindly uncle, back and forth, like that paper card trick of a bird in a cage, or a bird free, depending on how fast you twirled the strings on either end.

Right now, he definitely seemed more king than not.

"We're awaiting a few more guests. I hope you don't mind."

"Of course not."

"Shouldn't be long, I wouldn't think. They've been travel-ing for days, but I told them you were too special to miss."

"Oh," she said and swallowed the lump of trepidation in her throat. "I'm honored."

He paused, his gaze drawn to something beyond her shoulder, and sighed. "You must excuse me. I see the prime minister headed this way. He's been determined to corner me all day. I might as well indulge him now, as he'll have to stop talking once you begin. If not, I do hope you'll play loudly enough to drown him out. Consider it a royal request."

"Sir," she said and managed her awkward curtsy again.

She retreated to the far end of the hearth as Edward's guests settled and sparkled, observing her as she stood there and stared nervously down at her skirts.

She wished she had something to hold in her hands besides her violin and bow. She wished she had a glass of water, or

that she could stand somewhere else, *be* somewhere else, anywhere else—

"I'm informed you go by Leigh now, for when you perform."

She looked up. Mr. Vernon stood before her in proper
evening attire, black jacket, white tie, a cream waistcoat and
mother-of-pearl studs.

"No," she replied, relieved to see him, sharply relieved, as if
she'd just found her one friend amid a crowd of strangers. "I
mean, yes. It was just something my sister and I were discussing. How did you know?"

His dimple flashed with his smile. "I hear things. Also, if
I'm honest, your sister mentioned it an interview in the *Times*
a few weeks past. Didn't you read it?"

"Rita gives interviews all the time now. I can't keep up."

"Sometimes we adopt new names for the very best of reasons, don't we? I like Leigh. But I think I like your real name
better."

Her lips parted; she couldn't decide if she should remind
him he didn't have permission to use *either* name or not, but
he was looking at her so warmly. She felt that strange, tremu-
lous connection between them rise up once more, a fantasy
surely, a wishful hope, but it felt so true.

She pressed the lower bout of her violin hard against her
side, denting her skirts. "Mr. Vernon. You say the most extraordinary things."

"George," he reminded her. His eyes held hers, smoke and
green. "Do I? Perhaps you bring out the extraordinary in me,
Inez."

She fought her smile. "And you're very forward."

"Forward is the best direction to keep moving."

A stir took the room behind them, not quite gasps, not
quite sibilation, but a sense of both, a hush that was not a
hush that rose and expanded and settled again, lost against
the priceless rugs and tapestries and the ceiling.

George turned his head and straightened, his smile widening. "At last, they're here. Shall I introduce you?"

Inez looked toward the entrance of the room. The tsar and tsarina of Russia were approaching in slow, stately steps, trailed by an entourage of stiffly decorated lords and ladies. King Edward and Queen Alexandra rose from their chairs.

"You know them?" Inez murmured, shocked.

"I do. I'm part of the official delegation, in fact, at least for now." He glanced back at her, grinned at her expression. "Lovely little Inez. You're going to find that I'm full of surprises."

Secret government work, Rita had said that cool spring night, not long ago.

George Vernon, dark-haired, green-eyed, so handsome, so in control, took her by the elbow as if he had every right, drawing her away from the hearth and out into the full brilliance of the drawing room.

SHE PLAYED FOR them, all of them. She played her best, piece after piece, Mozart and Vivaldi and something of her own, a dreamy, stormy partita she called "Map of the Sea."

Inez received a standing ovation and accepted it with a bow at the waist, not a curtsy, her hair falling down in curls around her face, damp with perspiration.

Months later, in a far less public moment, George would inform her that her music had moved the tsarina to tears, which the lady had carefully concealed behind her lace handkerchief.

Chapter 8

He sent flowers after that. Daffodils. Tulips. Lilacs and hyacinths. Flamboyant spring blooms in the midst of barren winter. Then came the picture postcards, remember those? A few at first, then one a fortnight until we met again. They'd been franked from all over, each with a waggish little message for me: *The view is fine, the croissants are better* (for one of the Eiffel Tower). *One must not actually drink the water here* (for one of Bath). *I made friends with this good dog* (for one of a dachshund holding a frothy mug of beer in Munich).

I think the farthest was from Calcutta. It had a drawing of a tiger wearing a crown, and he wrote: *For a true queen.*

MARCH, 1903
LONDON, ENGLAND

There had never come a chaperone to the Bloomsbury lease. In time, Pauline had stopped mentioning it, and Rita had pressed Inez to quietly go along.

"We're doing well enough, just the two of us," she'd argued. "Neither of us are simpletons. We don't require a nanny any longer, do we?"

"Not a nanny," Inez had replied, tentative. "Yet don't you think, for the sake of—"

"Right. We're smart and we're capable. We've got Mrs. Corbyn, don't we? And Della, and the cook. We're a house full of grown women. What good would one more do us?"

"I suppose—"

"Just don't mention it to Maman again, that's all. None of it, the chaperone or what's proper, or any of it. I honestly think she's hoping we won't. Let the notion of it simply, I don't know, settle away into the mists of the past."

Inez had only shaken her head.

"The past," Rita had said again, firmly, holding her eyes. "Where it belongs."

Eventually, Inez had capitulated. Even she had to agree that Maman seemed to hold a particular pride in her daughters' semi-independence, sophisticated and contained as it was, two pretty young birds in their pretty cage. And it wasn't *that* unusual to maintain a houseful of womenfolk in the city without men. Was it?

No catastrophes overtook them, no social shame tainted them because they thrived alone.

Not yet, anyway.

Much Ado About Nothing wrapped up its scheduled run quite neatly, a great shiny gift to its ingénue actress wrapped a spectacular bow, but not before the accolades and sold-out houses and subsequent mentions of Rita's name—*that gel, that jaunty gel with the hair and the lips, what a job she did, what a face, what a voice*—rose and rose, until it seemed there wasn't a theatre manager in London who had not heard of her, and not an agent who hadn't handed her his card, either backstage after a performance or else on the street. Or at lunch with her sister. Or outside the apartment, as if they were stalking her now, which she supposed some of them must have been doing, because how else would they have discovered where she lived?

But she was firmly devoted to Charles Frohman, because Charles was firmly devoted to her, and she was not a girl who trifled with loyalties. Rita knew better than that.

A week before the final performance, as she was heading to the dressing room to get into costume, William Poel appeared at her side and touched a hand to her elbow.

"Come with me," he said, serious.

She followed him to his office, a space so compact it seemed more suited to a storage room than the retreat of a fabled director and producer. But he'd managed to fit in a desk, two lamps, and two chairs. The desk was littered with papers, invoices and loose script pages and hand-scribbled notes. An ashtray piled with smashed cigarettes was near to overflowing. A mug of cold coffee sat atop what looked to be a typed letter from the Empire Theater in New York. The mug had clearly been there a while, based on the series of watery brown rings staining the paper beneath it.

"Sit," Mr. Poel commanded, taking his own chair behind the desk.

Rita did. He'd left the door cracked; for a moment, they only regarded each other across the messy expanse of the desk, unspeaking. People bustled back and forth in the hallway beyond, quick footfalls striking floorboards. The stage manager called out, *Forty minutes, people! Forty minutes till curtain,* as two of the crew tromped by, urgently discussing a faulty footlight.

The walls in here were covered in posters, most of them autographed, every one of them from Poel's productions. There was scarcely an inch of plaster to be seen between them. If anyone needed to be reminded of William Poel's extraordinary success with his shows, these walls said it all.

He wasn't a young man, caught somewhere in his fifties, with striking, patrician features and a shock of salt-and-pepper hair that resisted his pomade. His eyes were deep-set, sharp. In the back of her mind, he always reminded her of an eagle, and sitting here now, with the silence expanding between them, Rita remembered her comparison of Ansel Lurie to a titmouse. It almost made her smile. Almost.

She forced herself to not fidget under his examination, keeping her hands and shoulders relaxed, her expression mildly curious. But her mind was racing; she tried to think of anything she'd done wrong, a flubbed line, a break in character, a late entrance, and couldn't.

"You've done a credible job," he said abruptly, leaning back in his swivel chair. The springs at its base creaked in complaint. "Better than I'd expected, if I may be frank."

"Aren't you always frank?" she replied, rather bold, but it won her a brief smile.

"I'm putting together something new. *Romeo and Juliet*, a traveling production. Still settling on the timing of it all, but the plan is to take it across the kingdom. Only the larger cities, of course, ones with universities or the like. It might take as long as a year. You're eighteen, aren't you?"

"Yes," she said, her heart beginning to smack against the bones of her chest.

"No husband, no children?"

"No."

"A sweetheart?"

"No." He looked skeptical, so she added honestly, "I've had no time for one."

"And your parents?"

"Very liberal. At least in their support of me."

"Is there anything to tie you to London for the next year or so?"

"No," she said a third time, a little too intense, and then smoothed her tone. "Nothing."

"Excellent. I'll have you read as soon as I've gotten a better notion of the rest of the cast. In the meanwhile, I need you to keep this conversation between us. I don't want any discord sewn backstage. Am I clear?"

"Yes, sir. I only..."

He'd been in the midst of rising. At her words, he eased down again, and again the springs protested.

"Yes, Miss Jolivet?"

"Forgive me," she said, and went on in a rush. "I only wonder which part you had in mind for me? Of course, I'm thrilled with any part, any at all. But..."

He raised his eyebrows. "You're wondering if I'm considering you for Juliet?"

She looked at him straight on, nodded.

In many ways, he was still a mystery to her, a stranger, even after all these months. She knew him as a director, but that was it. They'd never interacted socially or in any other manner beyond this small, perfect bubble, this theatre, this whirlwind production. Until five minutes ago, she hadn't even known how he took his coffee. (Black, as it turned out.)

"Miss Jolivet, rest assured I wouldn't have pulled you in here for the role of a *jeune fille* standing in the background." He came to his feet; so did she. "If there was ever an actress I've met meant to play Juliet Capulet, it is you."

He extended his palm to her, the tips of his fingers stained with nicotine. With her heart still smacking so hard she thought she might be trembling from the force of it, they shook hands.

"A YEAR?" INEZ said that evening in the parlor. She looked up from the postcard she'd been reading and re-reading, tracing her thumb over the inked lettering. "You'll be gone an entire year?"

"Or so. It's not clear yet. But these traveling productions usually do take a lot of time, you know. You have to gather up a cast and crew, the set, all the costumes and props. Lumber and hammers and lights and—and I don't know what. A million little details to be stitched together for the performances and then picked apart again as the caravan moves on to the next town. And then you start it all over."

"But who'll look out for you? Who'll take care of you?"

"Who does it now?" Rita laughed. "It's *Juliet*. The most—oh, the most shattering ingénue role ever written. I'm not going to pass it up, no matter what comes. Even if I have to drag old Corbyn along with me!"

"Hush," Inez cautioned, glancing at the door.

"If anything, we need to start thinking about who'll take care of *you*. You can't go back to Winter Queen. You've grown wings since then."

She spoke swiftly, flippantly, attempting a distraction, but as she said the words, Rita realized it was true. Her sister was not only a shade taller than she had been this time last year and several shades more beautiful, she carried a sort of glow within her now, an ethereal, muted radiance Rita hadn't noticed before. Or maybe she had, but it had evolved so slowly, and Rita's world rotated so quickly, anything muted or ethereal was faded against the glare of the stage lights she bathed in every night.

Inez's eyes seemed bluer, her complexion more alabaster. Even her hair had changed, no longer the color of light honey but more an ambered gold, rippling in heavy curls.

We should get her portrait taken, Rita thought, the actress in her taking over. *Publish it in the social sheets like the American debutantes do. Caption it "A Perfect English Rose."*

Inez's eyes lowered. She tapped a finger against the postcard, then placed it on top of the blanket chest by her chair, next to a vase of red-and-white streaked tulips. "No, I won't be going back. Not anytime soon."

"Is it your Mr. Vernon?"

The pale cheeks took on a becoming flush. "He's not *my* Mr. Vernon. And no. I haven't even seen him since Sandringham."

"But you've heard from him. He's certainly diligent about sending flowers and those postcards, cryptic as they are. Well-traveled for a singer, isn't he?"

"I suppose he's very much in demand."

"By the *tsar* of *Russia*," Rita drawled.

"Stop it, sissy, I mean it. No doubt he's just very well connected. It's not unheard of for a person of singular talent to be adopted by the elite. We, of all people, know that."

And this was also new: the brittle edge to her voice that warned Rita she wasn't joking, that the teasing had gone further than warranted and as far as it ever should, lest something more serious be damaged between them. Something permanent.

Whatever he was, wherever he was, Mr. Vernon had clearly made an impression. Stamped himself right on her sister's tender young heart.

Rita yielded a hand in surrender, and Inez blew out a breath.

"Anyway, the reason I'm not going home is because my social calendar is beginning to fill up."

"Is it?"

"Well, as far as I'm concerned, it is. I've been asked to five more *parties de plaisir*, including one hosted by the Duke of Connaught at Bagshot Park, and three bloody damned balls."

Rita gave a blink, and Inez lifted her chin. "That's right. I swore. I've decided I'm swearing now, when the occasion warrants it."

"And . . . these balls warrant it?"

"When they consume my life, yes! Apparently, the king's invitation was as good as opening a floodgate. Balls, weekend retreats, teas. A letter from Maman arrived this morning—I put it on your pillow in your room—to let us know they're returning in a week's time. She's threatening to drag us both back to Paris for more clothes. I think she expects you to join us for these jolly frolics, at least some of them."

"Lord, no."

"Now you know how I feel," Inez said darkly. "I don't know how you'll convince them to let you fly free for a whole year. Even you aren't that silver-tongued."

Rita clicked her fingernails against the wooden arm of her chair. "We'll see about that."

IT TURNED OUT that she had to do hardly any convincing, silvered or otherwise. Papa objected, of course; he was almost obligated to, wasn't he? But it was barely an echo of the scene that had birthed this one, back in Winter Queen's humid conservatory when Marguerite had informed her family of her intention to become an actress.

This time Charles had protested: *a year?* And she'd told him why that had to be, how the whole company would travel like circus folk across the king's land, a cohesive band of them, a solid, safe mass.

He'd said, *no chaperone?* And she'd assured him the company would supply one, which was probably not an untruth, but anyway she was a citizen of the Old Smoke now, practically wizened, and knew how to look after herself.

And then she'd gone to him, knelt before him in his chair and taken his hands in hers and pleaded, *Please*, and *Juliet*, and a few more impassioned sentences that all added up to: *A role like this may never land in my lap again.*

The last time she'd gone to her knees before him, had grabbed his hands and actually pleaded was when she'd been twelve and she'd begged him for a pony and cart of her own. She'd gotten the pony, but not the cart, and that was enough, as it turned out. She'd spent years afterward braiding Mathilde's mane and tail, currying her, whispering her ambitions into soft equine ears in exchange for apples and sugar cubes.

And now Mathilde resided, plump and happy and retired, back at Winter Queen, while Rita was ready to soar on, even farther away than London. Out into the yonder.

Pauline understood. She sat calmly and listened without speaking, only watching, but once again with that slight, satisfied curve to her lips. The entire conversation unfolded so tamely that no one even bothered to switch to French.

"Let her go," Pauline had said finally. "This is who she is. This is what we've hoped for her."

"I've hoped for rather more than *this*," Papa had grumbled, by which Rita understood he meant a husband, a family, stability.

"But this," Rita said, rising again and leaning over him to buss him on the cheek, "is what *I've* hoped for. All my life, this."

Stability was for houses and bridges, solid things that needed solid earth beneath them to remain upright. The stalwart masses who toiled and wed and reproduced as they should, never getting lost in the Milky Way above their heads, never hoping for more than what they'd been given, what was within ready reach.

Rita had always stood at the hazardous precipice of *more*. She had always looked up and hoped.

Fame and freedom. Freedom and fame. The very notion of them entwined fizzed through her blood, surged hard and fast through her entire body, head-to-toes delicious, finer than champagne.

THE TOUR KICKED off in Brighton, in a May so mild and pleasant after months of winter and a very soggy April, that the birds seemed to never stop celebrating it, and the wildflowers lining the roads bloomed in thick vivid clusters. Yellow horseshoe vetch and magenta corncockles, lacy white cow parsley, and—as they got closer to the sea—pink papery clusters of thrift, clinging tenaciously to rocky ledges.

Rita couldn't say if they were traveling as the circus folk did, as she'd never actually seen a circus, but maybe. For the most part, they were a caravan of horse-drawn wagons and carriages, plodding but constant. William Poel typically led the way in his motorcar, a red Phelps runabout he'd had imported all the way from Massachusetts. It was a two-seater, three if the person in the middle was small, and even so, it was a squeeze. Rita would occasionally ride with him, one hand clutching the top of the seat, the other on her hat. It was noisy and dusty and impossible to converse unless they shouted. She finally begged off by telling him she needed to save her voice for the shows, which was true. But even more true was the fact that she preferred the slower, more peaceful pace of the Cleveland Bays. Sometimes she'd travel atop one of the wagons instead of inside a carriage, and that was finest of all.

The breeze on her cheeks, the warmth of the sun along her shoulders. The placid horses, their flanks shining. The steady, hollow clop of their hooves.

In Brighton, they stayed in a splendidly shabby Victorian hotel overlooking a long strand of beach, the English Channel an iron sweep beyond it sliced with foam. France lay at the other edge of those rough waters; the whole of Europe lay at the other edge. The wind rattling the hotel room windows carried the constant scent of fish and brine, and of taffy candy from the vendors on the sand.

For this, their first official performance, in the first official town for their first official tour, the stage was set out of doors, in a grassy park surrounded by low-slung Georgian shops selling everything from seashells to fried cod to bathing costumes. The park featured a sunken amphitheater, with tiers of cement seating surrounding it in a half-circle, row after row carved into the slanted earth.

"As the Greeks did it," Mr. Poel said approvingly, as the salt air whistled by and flipped up his tie.

Two tents had been staked past the back rise of the amphitheater, one for the gentlemen actors, one for the ladies. There was no water closet available, only a chamber pot in each tent hidden behind a leather screen. The precariously secured flap for the entrance was mere feet away, and the wind never stopped tugging at its ties. By the end of the evening, everything inside—the pot and the screen, the mirrors and folding tables and chairs—would be dusted with grit.

Ellen Terry, the actress playing Lady Capulet, looked at the pot and sighed.

"How much one doesn't miss the good old days before proper plumbing."

Rita had to laugh. "At least we don't have to share it with the boys."

"Amen to that! Good God, can you imagine? With these drafts and their aim, nothing would stay dry."

Rita liked Ellen, a famed veteran of Shakespeare, who had kind eyes and a wry wit, and who had welcomed her into the troupe with a handshake that had turned into an embrace. Everyone here had been so nice, so easy to befriend, even the crew. Even the young man playing Romeo, who was just as sandy-haired and handsome as Frank Monroe had been, but with ten times more talent and none of the arrogance. He'd made it simple for her to inhabit the soul of Juliet. To fall in love with him, and kiss him, and die for him, night after night. In time, it felt as natural as breathing.

The play opened late in the afternoon, before the shops closed and so before the tourists departed, as the park had no gaslights and the wind was too untrustworthy for lanterns. Mr. Poel, familiar with both the town and the amphitheater (and apparently the capricious wind) had planned it all out.

"We should wrap up just at the first blush of sundown. Still enough light to see, and the colors in the sky will be our lanterns and scrim."

And so it was. They opened to a full crowd, some of them locals, most heavy-eyed tourists already weary from the sun-drenched day. A sprinkling of university students, surreptitiously passing flasks back and forth between them. The pubs would stay open later than any of the shops, eager for the business after the show, and the students knew it. The flasks were quickly drained.

Rita waited at the edge of the stage for her entrance, in full view of the audience but frozen in tableau. She used the precious few minutes she stood there, unmoving, to watch the patrons. Their faces. Who was awake and interested, who was already drifting off.

She was going to bring them along with her, every one of them, on Juliet's tragic, twisting journey. She would not leave a single soul behind, whether they liked it or not. But right now, still waiting for her cue, Rita remained motionless, her head lifted, her hands clasped modestly together. Her velvet skirts rippled; the tassels on her sleeves bobbed. She'd forsaken her usual stiff headdress for a more simple jeweled net, gleaming with false gems, and so at least her hair was contained, if not her costume.

She listened. She waited.

The nurse and Lady Capulet, discussing Juliet's age.

The nurse calling *lamb*, calling *ladybird*, summoning her charge as if she might be years away, not rooms.

And then her cue.

Rita dropped her pose, took up her skirts. She rushed to the heart of the stage, obedient, smiling, youthful and joyous. Entirely unaware of her fate.

How now, who calls?

Your mother.

Madam, I am here. What is your will?

WHEN RITA HAD told the great producer Mr. William Poel that she had no sweetheart, she hadn't been lying. There was no man in her life who particularly tugged at her heartstrings, although she'd received a couple of not-so-subtle propositions during *Much Ado*. One from a fellow cast member (an older roué playing her character's father, thankfully not included in this tour) and the other from a member of the crew, a comely fellow her age named Freddy who had a cheeky smile and a talent for carpentry, for building things.

Houses. Bridges, perhaps. But more practically for the tour, a movable, puzzle-piece set and the large, ungainly flats that would stand behind it.

She'd declined both of them as diplomatically as she could. She'd made certain to avoid the roué whenever possible and practiced her charm from a distance on Freddy Stern, not wanting to alienate him.

But other than that, she survived alone. She thrived alone.

The tour wound on, Brighton to Southampton, on to Exeter, Plymouth, Bristol. Sometimes it felt peculiar, this deliberate slow march across the land, never staying in one town more than a fortnight or so. But mostly it was fine. More than fine, because she was enthralled with the wonders of this vagabond acting life, even when the hotels were so threadbare there was no hot water, or all the food from the kitchen came boiled and served with cabbage, or there weren't enough rooms to let, so she would share with Ellen, who snored.

Within a little under two months, Rita had settled into the rhythm of it. She knew who of their group would stay up late at the pubs, drinking more than they should; who told the best jokes; who told the worst. Who could be counted on to share a bite of bread and cheese on the road, or a nip of gin.

Surprisingly, the lack of reliable laundry service would turn out to be their most vexing problem. Eventually, the costumes began to reek, and their everyday clothing began to reek. The actors began to shy away from close contact onstage. Even Rita and her Romeo suffered through it, holding back grimaces as they kissed. Most of the inns they frequented had at least a local girl who could do the basic wash, but the costumes were another story entirely. Elizabethan layers of velvets and braiding and feathers and starched lace collars—nothing ordinary, nothing plain. The costume designer was supposed to have tended to it all, but she'd gotten word that her daughter had come down with the pox. She'd abandoned them for Glasgow a bare eight weeks into the tour.

They'd endured nineteen performances without her. Nineteen performances under hot lights. Nineteen evenings of moving and sweating and making the scenes run like that locomotive, making the dialogue swift and believable. Poel had had scant luck finding a qualified replacement on such short notice.

A London tailor agreed to join them in Plymouth, a connection of a connection, but took an unflinching look at the work ahead of him and quit within the day.

"I think I know who can save us," Rita had finally said to her director, desperate for a reprieve. Her entire world smelled of the great unwashed, and it was sour and awful.

"Yes?"

"There's a good salary for the position?"

Mr. Poel pinched two fingers to the bridge of his nose. "Miss Jolivet, at this point, I would hand over my own salary to fill the position. In gold doubloons, if necessary."

Rita wired her mother.

NEED COSTUME HELP STOP EXPERT TO CLEAN IRON MEND STOP MUST STAY THE ENTIRE TOUR STOP CANNONT STAND THE SMELL STOP WHAT TO DO QUERY COMPANY CAN PAY STOP

The remarkable Jolivet wheels and cogs turned, efficient as ever. In less than five days' time, Pauline directed a pair of widowed cousins from Cornwall, a seamstress and a laundress, to the troupe. Both of their husbands had been roustabouts for Mr. Magellan's Magickal Circus. They were well accustomed to a vagabond life.

William Poel thanked Mrs. Jolivet most kindly. He sent tiger lilies to Pauline and handed, in person, a binding contract and a generous cash bonus to the cousins, who eventually used the funds to help purchase a retirement cottage in Trythogga, a cozy, shingled place with roses and lavender and a resident cat to chase the mice.

RITA WAS FULLY Juliet, falling desperately in love and marrying and dying, then dying again, before a fresh applauding audience every night. How amazing that she could traverse the kingdom with friends (all right, friendly acquaintances), seeing places she'd never seen before. Stepping on grass she'd never pressed a foot against before, leaving a mark, fleeting as it was. Breathing in the fragrance of trees and shrubs that she'd never encountered before, that she didn't know the names of and could not guess.

It wasn't long before she realized that many of England's more populated towns resembled each other to an extraordinary degree, especially in the antiquated quarters, places that had existed since the Romans had first invaded and chiseled out their long, straight roads, established their bathhouses and their forts and temples amid the native druids and wolves.

The wolves were gone now, the druids mostly too. Yet surviving still were the many cobbled medieval roads that traced those Roman town lines, with deeply trenched funnels down their middles, ready to slough away rainwater and waste, to keep the city clean. Thatched and patched buildings of all sorts loomed over those old pungent lanes, blocking out the sky. Some stood braced by timbers, but many were simply bowing back to the earth. Rita would sometimes walk beneath them, marveling at people's faith in a few stilt poles to keep time from having its way.

Every quaint country church seemed fronted by a grave-
yard spilling with lopsided headstones, lichen crawling green
and rust along the granite and bricks.

Every tea shop seemed to sell the same scones and Eccles
cakes and pork pies. The same rigid ritual of tea, cake, tally,
get out.

Every theatre they visited seemed afflicted with drafts tinged
with the aroma of linseed oil and face powder and oranges—
although the oranges were probably Rita's imagination, a leftover fantasy from the Bard's time, when the common people
stood crowded against the proscenium to watch the show, dig-
ging into the fruit with their bare fingers, dropping the peels to
the straw-covered floor.

And the ghost lights, of course.

All the theatres on the tour had a ghost light burning, some
small oil lamp usually, a slender pale flame flickering from the
center of the empty stage, a brave stab at the dark.

"Oh, don't you know?" Ellen had said, when Rita had asked
her about it after noticing the first one. "It's the ghost light.
You have to keep it lit when the theatre's empty, no matter
what. It's bad luck otherwise."

That was early on, a bare month into the tour. The company was staying in a small but picturesque inn on High Street
in Southampton. Every room was taken; a few disgruntled
crewmembers were forced to bunk in the stables. For the next
two weeks, she and Ellen would share a plain, white-plastered
chamber fitted with two simple beds and a fireplace that
slowly leaked smoke whenever lit, because the chimney didn't
quite draw properly.

That first night, heated bricks had been tucked between the
bedsheets; chamber pots had been tucked beneath the beds.
They'd already settled in, sated from a dinner of lamb stew
and a few glasses of red wine from the pub below, drowsing in

the fading light of the fire. Rita's feet hurt from the slightly too small slippers Juliet had to wear.

"Bad luck?" Rita had said, half-asleep, her toes aching. "From angry ghosts?"

"Or the lonely ones," Ellen answered from her side of the room. "Which can be just as unlucky, as it happens. Every theatre has a ghost." She turned her head against her pillow, her braid a tawny slash across the paler case. "You smile, love, but it's a fact. The lights appease them, keep them calm, or restful, or whatever they prefer." She paused on a yawn. "*Remembered*, usually. That's what I think. Unforgotten. An unhappy ghost can doom a whole production, everyone knows that."

"Really?"

"Really."

She'd never once seen a ghost light burning at the Catharine. Perhaps that explained a few things.

Minutes passed. The shadows in the room melted together, stretched from charcoal into black. The last ticking log in the fireplace fell apart with a sigh.

Ellen said sleepily, "We all hope to be remembered, even the dead."

AT STRATFORD-UPON-AVON, THE entire company lingered an extra day in honor of the Bard. They gathered after the evening's performance at the Toad and Goose, a fine establishment almost right upon the river—or so swore Freddy Stern, a local son determined to get them there—but down only just a few crooked alleyways first.

SHAKSPAIRE STAYED HERE, declared the sign swinging above the entrance, the paint peeling away in curls.

It might have been true. The tavern looked old enough, with its rough thatched roof and worn wattle. Framed prints of sheep and geese and dogs climbed up and down the walls (along with a few toads); most of the windows were frosted, several panes cracked. The bar was long and carved with leaves, the top polished but uneven in spots, as if generations of keeps had rubbed their rags too long in one place, over and over.

The troupe took over the entire bar and most of the tables, there were that many of them. Rita sat with Ellen and two other actresses, all of them careful with their pints because the floor was uneven and the table wobbled. They ordered shepherd's pie and bangers and mash, steak and chips and potted shrimp.

Rita had the steak and chips, which was so hot and delicious that after weeks of cold, greasy fare, she felt her eyes sting with pleasure. Someone propped their elbow on the tabletop and the entire surface tilted, dashing ale across the wood. Rita lifted her glass and took a hefty swallow as the other women laughed and grabbed for their napkins.

She lowered her glass. Freddy sat at the bar. He grinned at her, still cheeky. With the warmth of the ale sliding through her, with the fragrance of good beer and good food filling her nose, expanding through her chest, Rita decided to grin back at him.

Chapter 9

The wooing. The wedding. I'm so glad you were there, even if it did make certain people cross.

JUNE, 1903
LONDON, ENGLAND

He arrived, unannounced, on a soft Sunday afternoon. Inez had been practicing in her room, lost in some song she'd never noticed before, the melody of it drifting through her open window as inspiration sometimes did. Maybe from the clouds, maybe from the sun, or the trees. Unannounced, but welcome.

Normally, she'd practice in the parlor, but lately she'd begun to feel as if she was too much a distraction to the staff. A week ago, she'd overheard Mrs. Corbyn rebuking Della for lingering outside the parlor door while Inez had been pacing her way through Handel's opening aria from *Xerxes*.

She was a child of peace, not strife. She never wanted anyone to get into trouble, certainly not over her playing,

and so had retreated to the smaller, stuffier space of her bedchamber for practice.

Hence, the window being open.

Hence, hearing the motorcar tearing up to the curb, even
past her song.

The motorcar was very loud. She tried to ignore it, but its
engine grumbled and growled right beneath her sill. At last, irritated, Inez set down her violin and moved to the window.
She leaned past the frame to gaze down at the street, waving
a hand in front of her to disperse the petrol fumes.

It was a bright yellow roadster just below her, long and very
shiny. The engine cut off. A man in a tan duster leapt out from
behind the driver's seat, his coattails flaring, his hair gleaming.
He strode up the steps to her front door and beyond her view.

Inez pulled back, her fingers to her mouth. She looked
blankly around the room, her same old ordinary room, her
same old floral-print duvet on the bed, ceramic jug and basin,
crocheted doilies draped along the rosewood bureau and chest
and nightstands.

Her violin and bow atop the duvet, settling plush against
the down.

The vanity mirror showed her a silvery hint of girl, summer
shadows all around, since she'd lit no lamp to add to the heat.
She rushed to it, bent down, and took a closer look.

Yes, all right, her hair was still mostly smooth and her eyebrows were fine and there were no smudges on her face. No
stains down her bodice from the oxtail soup she'd had for
lunch about an hour ago. She cupped a hand over her mouth
and exhaled, and couldn't smell the soup. So.

So.

A light tapping at her door.

"Miss? There's a gentleman here for you. A Mr. Vernon?"

"Yes," Inez said, drawing away from the mirror. She brushed
a palm down her skirts, wishing she was wearing something

more flattering than her lavender-sprigged muslin, as light as it was. "Very good, Della. I'll be down directly."

She descended the stairs slowly, deliberately, determined to reveal nothing by the squeak of the steps. He was waiting by the bay window in the parlor, the place she sometimes sat to watch people and horses and birds flit by.

"Mr. Vernon," she said, and he turned with a smile.

"Inez. Would you care to come for a ride with me?"

He spoke as easily as if they'd just parted yesterday, as if they'd long planned to meet today, right now, in this room. As if there had not been months and months of flowers and post-cards with queer, foreign stamps and whimsical messages. She'd never even had the chance to ask him how he knew where she lived.

"Yes," she said. "Let me get my hat."

IT WAS A fine day for a drive, with clear sunlight and hardly any breeze, except for the wind generated by the auto itself, zig-zagging roofless along London's congested streets. He drove quickly, a little too quickly for Inez's taste, but she said noth-ing, just clamped a hand on the crown of her hat and watched, wide-eyed, as the buildings and parks and carriages flit by.

He'd lent her a spare duster to cover her dress and sug-gested a scarf to tie down her hat, but the one she'd grabbed was a thin, pretty gossamer shot with gold threads. Even knotted tight beneath her chin, Inez worried it stood no chance against the wind.

"Where are we going?" she shouted over the noise, as the roadster swerved around a one-horse shay, the driver's whip biting through the air like a curvy black snake.

"A concert," he yelled back cheerfully. "One at the Lyra. I think you'll like it."

"I'm not dressed for a concert!"

"Don't worry. I know the management."

"That's not the point!"

"You're ravishing." He shot her a smoky look, his hair mussed, bright light sliding across his cheekbones and the line of his jaw. "As ever. Trust me, you'll outshine every other lady around."

He drew the roadster around the back of the concert hall, where a flattened stretch of macadam held half a dozen parked automobiles. She shrugged out of the duster and untied the scarf, letting it dangle between her fingers. As she was trying to figure out what to do with her hat—a picture hat, fashionable and wide-brimmed; she could hardly wear it inside—he plucked it from her fingers and opened up the boot of the auto, tossing it in, followed by the scarf. She couldn't help but notice the boot had no lock.

"But—" she began. The hat was new, plum straw topped with pink taffeta roses, hardly worn. She was very fond of it.

"No one will steal it. Trust me," he said again.

He offered his arm. With a single, unhappy look back at the roadster, she tucked her hand through the crook of his elbow, allowing him to lead her to the rear entrance of the hall.

"George!" someone called out. He lifted his free hand in response without pausing, guiding her along a maze of barely lit corridors. It was much cooler inside than outside; gooseflesh crawled up her arms and down her neck. She could hear the orchestra warming up from somewhere nearby, men's voices talking about scaffolding and trimming the lights.

"Here we are," he said. They crept down a short flight of steps, pushed aside some curtains, and entered the auditorium itself, already filling with patrons. He escorted her to an empty pair of seats in the front row, released her arm, and gave a short bow.

Seats 19 and 20, her mind noticed, winding into a slow building dread, fixating on small details: 19 and 20, exactly in the middle of the row.

Inez sat down nervously, discomfited by her simple day dress, the locks of hair torn loose from her pins, when everyone else around them looked so sleek and polished.

Everyone here was so obviously prepared for a concert, when all Inez had prepared for was an afternoon by herself in her bedchamber.

She tried to smooth back her messy chignon, but it didn't help. She needed a mirror. She needed a comb and pins and probably a lady's maid at this point. It had been a rough drive.

"Hang on a bit," George said in his nonchalant way. He hadn't yet taken his own seat. "I just need to pop backstage a moment to freshen up."

"Oh," she said, rising. "May I come? If I could just borrow a mirror—"

"You're ravishing," he said again firmly, holding up a palm to stop her in place. "I swear it. Inez, or Leigh, I'll be back soon."

He was gone, swallowed by the curtains concealing the edge of the stage.

Inez sank back into seat 19. The orchestra was already in place, their chairs arranged around the conductor's podium. She watched the musicians tuning their instruments, practicing their notes, the strings, the brass, the woodwinds and percussion, her eyes instinctively following the movements of the first-chair violin, the concertmaster. How, even though he was a slight man, he seemed bigger somehow than the rest of the group, more important.

She frowned at him, thinking, *Focus!* If she could just focus enough on the concertmaster, forget where she was, *how* she was—

The house lights lowered. The audience gave a faint smattering of applause. Inez looked around for George, but he still hadn't returned. Then the conductor entered with quick hard strides, and the applause swelled.

She didn't even have a program. She had no idea who the conductor was, as he didn't look familiar, or even the name of the orchestra. She tried to peek at the program on the lap of the lady next to her, but it was turned facedown. All she could read of it was an advertisement on the back, framed in black lines: PEARSON'S BEST CLOTHES WRINGER! STAY FRESH WITH THE BEST! DOUBLE WHEELS, DOUBLE COGS!

She rubbed her hands up her arms, fighting the cold. What was she doing here? Was George playing some sort of joke on her? How was she going to get home if he'd abandoned her here? She wasn't even certain she had enough money in her reticule for a cab.

But then he was there, a silhouette looming before her, dropping down beside her into number 20's blue leather seat.

"Apologies," he whispered, leaning his head to hers as the conductor began his opening remarks. "I tried to hurry, but it's miles of corridors back there. I had to trot in the end. I wouldn't want to miss any of this."

"Gracious," she whispered back, amazed, taking him in. "You've changed entirely."

And he had. Gone was the duster and lounge suit he'd worn beneath it; gone was the wind-mussed hair. He now wore a tailcoat with black silk lapels, white tie over a stiff linen collar. His hair was neatly brushed and oiled. His shoes shone polished ebony in the dark.

Inez clenched her hands against her armrests. "George! What on earth is happening?"

"...give you our celebrated tenor, Mr. George Vernon," the conductor was saying grandly, gesturing toward the side curtains off to the left.

George pried free of her right hand and pressed a quick kiss to the back of it. He sprang from his seat and climbed the stairs up to the stage, as the conductor looked around, surprised, and the audience was once again stirred into applause.

She listened, rapt, as he sang. The chilled air faded away; the people around her faded away. Even the undeniable prowess of the concertmaster, which ordinarily Inez would study and memorize to try to pick apart every detail in her mind later on—even that was nothing compared to him. To George Vernon and his pure, heartrending voice, song after song.

She would not recollect most of what he sang, not the titles, not the melodies, only that he did sing, and it was so beautiful and flawless that she felt something inside herself, some inner turmoil she'd scarcely fathomed or put a name to—that slow smothering dread, in fact—fall still. Become arrested. Suspended by him. Made weightless through him.

By the time he was done, she had a neckache from her first-row seat just below the stage, one she wouldn't even notice until hours later, after he'd dropped her off at the flat.

When George offered his final bow, every member of the audience was on their feet, applauding. Roses were being tossed just past Inez, the first to stand, clapping madly. Loose petals settled like red snowfall all along the apron of the stage.

He insisted upon taking her to dinner afterward.

"It's a cozy place," he'd assured her, when she'd tried once again to point out she wasn't wearing anything smart enough. "No one will mind."

But as soon as they were seated at their table, she'd excused herself to the ladies' lavatory to try to do what she could with her appearance.

Good gracious. Was that her in the looking glass? Was that her with her hair in messy coils around her face, her cheeks flushed, her eyes so vivid?

She hardly recognized herself. She looked young and exuberant. She looked foolishly happy. She looked like some insipid country milkmaid, star-dazzled by her first taste of the town.

Inez tried scowling at her reflection, attempting decorum, but it was no use. Her heart was still beating in time to his voice. Her weightless worries were flying dim and far away, and it felt like . . . it felt like . . .

Don't be ridiculous. This isn't love. This is infatuation. You are infatuated, that's all. Who wouldn't be at this point?

Inez splashed water on her face. She pinned back what she could of her hair and tried to brush out the wrinkles in her skirts. When she rejoined him at their table, none of the other patrons even glanced her way.

Only George did, rising to pull out her chair. It was an Italian eatery on Oxford Street she'd never noticed before, although surely she'd passed by it. They'd taken a table by a window, in open view of the road outside. Night was falling, and the sky beyond the pitched roofs and sawtoothed treetops was stained a thin, translucent blue, chased with clouds. A solitary votive burned in a small purple glass bowl between them; the window doubled the flame, twin lights dancing.

A server walked by carrying a tray of something garlicky and sizzling, and Inez's stomach gave an audible rumble.

Her face heated. She was more milkmaid now than ever. "I beg your pardon."

"It did smell rather splendid, didn't it? That's the *scampi in umido*. I recommend it."

"It's been a while since luncheon, is all."

He looked at her affectionately, and her heart did a peculiar hard flip. "Dear girl. I kidnapped you, didn't I, and didn't even think to feed you until now. I apologize."

"No," she said, leaning forward. "It's been . . . oh, it's been the most astonishing day."

"Has it? I'm glad." He lifted a finger for the server, who appeared at once, a gentleman perhaps in his fifties, with very black hair and a surprisingly gray moustache. "Valerio, my friend," George said. "How is your Ginevra getting on?"

"Very well, Mr. Vernon. She's finished her studies and is a nurse in the East Midlands, nearly six months now, out in Leicester. We're proud as could be."

"Naturally you are, you and Beatrice both! Congratulations."

"Thank you, sir. May I bring some wine, sir, or chilled Prosecco?"

"A bottle of your Nebbiolo, if you please."

"Of course. And menus?"

"Yes, thank you."

The man bowed and moved off.

"How easily you do that," she said.

"What, now?"

"I don't know, just..." Inez tried to find the right word. "Charm people. Transfix them. Put everyone at ease. I think it's a gift."

George lowered his eyes, brown lashes masking green. The flame rising from the glass bowl flicked and twisted. "A good one, do you imagine?"

"It could be," she answered, thoughtful. "I suppose so, yes, as long as your intentions are honorable. My sister thinks you're a spy."

His lips lifted, not quite a smile. "Does she?"

"But after today, I believe I can safely inform her that you are indeed a singer. A *celebrated tenor*."

He raised his eyes again, did not look away. Between the light from the candle and the sky outside, he was contoured in dusk and gold, lit from beside and below. "I could be both, though. You never know."

She opened her mouth, closed it again. The server named Valerio reappeared with the wine and two crimson cut-glass goblets on a tray, plus paper menus so recently printed that a thumbprint of ink smudged the bottom of hers. She waited until he left before replying.

"I honestly can't tell if you're in earnest."

George released her from his gaze, turning his attention to the menu, angling the written descriptions of the dishes toward the meager votive. "I was speaking hypothetically, of course. The fact of the matter is, you might as well know that I *am* two opposites at once. A walking contradiction, if you will. Singing is my passion—one of my passions," he amended. "Less sensationally, I am also an agent for certain kinds of imports and exports, depending on market forces. Supply and demand."

"You sell things?"

"No," he said, abandoning the menu to the tabletop. He moved to pour the wine, monitoring the thin aubergine splash filling their glasses, finishing off both pours with a deft twist of his wrist. "I make things available for selling or buying. I connect people with others who might need their products, or their money. Or their information. I am the grease on the wheel. The whisper in the ear, the hand guiding the pen drawing up the contract."

"So . . . a mastermind."

He laughed, that real laugh, hushed but genuine. He lifted his glass to her. Light sparked every shade of red on the carvings along its surface, tracing lozenges and whorls. "Your word, not mine. But it's quite flattering, so thank you."

Inez tapped the rim of her goblet against his. They both drank. It was her first taste of Nebbiolo; it slipped warm and tart across her tongue.

"But how fascinating to travel so far and wide. To see so many different places, meet so many different kinds of people."

"And wade through so many different layers of bureaucracy, from so many different governments," he added dryly.

"Oh?"

"It can be a delicate dance, balancing the politics of it all. The diplomatic affronts, perceived or real. The personalities. Half the crowned heads of Europe are either siblings or cousins, so you have all the usual petty family jealousies play-ing out on an international scale."

"But you're good at that dance." She didn't make it a question.

"I try. It helps to make friends as you go."

"Have you many friends, then, in all these countries?"

A pause. "*Friends* is perhaps not quite accurate. More spe-cifically, I have people who owe me favors. And people for whom I can grant favors in return."

"Mastermind," she said again, and his faint smile returned. "Were you really off traveling the world all these months since Sandringham? With the postcards, I mean?"

He nodded. "Did you like them?"

"Immensely."

"I'm glad if they pleased you. Trifles, I know, but I didn't want you to forget me."

"An impossible task."

"Is it indeed?" He bowed his head again, his long fingers ad-justing the fork beside his plate, then the knife. His voice came to her muted, almost drowned beneath the ringing steel echo of a landau bouncing by. "From anyone else, I would doubt. But from you, Inez Jolivet, the artist who is sometimes Leigh, I'm simply grateful."

BY THE END of the meal, he'd admitted that, although he had posted most of the cards to her himself, there were occasions when he'd relied on fellow professionals—that was the term he used, *fellow professionals*, not colleagues or coworkers or teammates—around the world to send her one or two when he was unavailable for the task.

Another enigmatic word: *unavailable*.

He'd written every one of them himself, he assured her, all in his own hand; every silly sentence in the message box was his own creation. But when she'd pressed him about if he'd actually been in Moscow, or Munich, or Barcelona, he only shrugged as if embarrassed, and said he couldn't recall. He traveled so much, so often, by stage and train and steamship, the lines on the maps tended to blur in his memory. Some mornings he awoke and for minutes couldn't recall where he was, what city or country, he'd galloped through so many.

That's what he said.

But Inez wondered. George Vernon didn't seem a man who let *any* relevant fact sneak away from him.

She ordered the *scampi in umido*, and so did he. As George broke into the warm boule of bread served with it, sending a spray of crumbs across the tablecloth, Inez asked if he himself had sent the one from Calcutta. The one with the tiger and crown.

"Oh, *that* one," he said, passing her a slice. "Yes, absolutely I did."

"It was my favorite," she said.

"Mine too."

They asked Valerio for a second bottle of wine, and toasted to that.

By the time he drove her home, it was full night. The feathery clouds of before had bunched and thickened and now hung a dark pearly gray above them, their bellies illumed by London's legions of streetlights.

The roadster pulled up to the flat. George set the brake and killed the engine. A lamp had been left burning in the parlor window, thin marigold light brushing the curtains.

"Well," she said, looking at her lap, looking up at him. "Thank you for this. Thank you for today."

"Thank *you*," he replied, serious, "for allowing me the pleasure of kidnapping you."

She laughed a little, still feeling the heat of the wine buzzing through her, the heat of his look even warmer, even better.

"I came willingly, so it was hardly a kidnapping. More like—an unexpected adventure."

"Might I tempt you into adventuring with me again, Inez?"

"Gladly."

"Tomorrow, then. I'll be here at noon."

"Another concert?"

"No, no, that's all done, at least for the next few months. A picnic, I think. My cook packs an excellent basket. Sandwiches and chutney, apple tarts. The most respectable courting food imaginable. It wouldn't hurt to follow *some* of the rules, in case anyone asks about this disreputable fellow calling on you. You can tell your mama in all honesty that we're as prim and virtuous as the Pilgrims. Some of the time, at least."

"*Are* we courting?" she asked, audacious with wine.

He slanted her a sideways look. "It is my ardent ambition."

Mrs. Corbyn met her at the door.

"Good evening, miss. You left so quickly this afternoon I wasn't certain when you'd be back, but I've had your dinner kept warm for you. If you like, I can have the girl bring it to the table now."

Inez was not imagining the undertone of disapproval in her housekeeper's voice, she thought, but nothing could dim the happiness spreading through her.

"No need. I dined with Mr. Vernon. Why don't you have it?"

Mrs. Corbyn forgot herself enough to raise an eyebrow. "The staff has already had our supper. Shall I tell the cook to save your plate for tomorrow?"

"If you like. I'm going up now. I'll see you in the morning."

"Yes, miss."

"Oh, and Mr. Vernon will be calling again tomorrow afternoon. We're going on a picnic."

"Very well. What time shall I inform Della she is to chaperone?"

"No need," Inez said again. She placed a hand on the railing, one foot upon the bottom step, then turned around.

"Mrs. Corbyn, I feel I should warn you that Mr. Vernon will be calling often from now on. I'm going to marry him, you see, so he'll be here more and more. Chaperones are superfluous at this point."

At last, she'd broken through the housekeeper's iron façade. Inez turned back and began climbing the stairs, smiling to herself at the confounded look on the other woman's face.

THEY WOULD DEBATE for hours the notion of love at first sight. George, for all his worldly ways, was a firm believer in it. Inez, the idealist, was more dubious. But neither could deny the strange and marvelous connection that had overtaken them both, rendering them both as helpless as babes, as George liked to say to anyone who was foolish enough to inquire how'd they'd met—

I was merely infatuated, Inez would cut in.

—helpless as babes, he insisted. Helpless to stop what was to come.

He was probably right. He was nearly always right, Inez was discovering, but instead of being irritated by this fact, she found it comforting. George Vernon was handsome, he was cosmopolitan, he was intelligent and he was right. He consorted with kings and knew the names of the staff at his favorite restaurants, and those of their children. He'd sent her postcards so that she would not forget him, even when they were continents apart.

A bright new horizon spread before them. All their years to come spread before them, and sometimes Inez felt so suffused with joy she no longer recognized herself.

RITA WAS NOT so sanguine. Her tour was taking a weeklong midsummer break, and she'd arrived back in London even more glamorous, even more tempestuous and beguiling than when she'd left. She filled the flat with a thrill of excitement, like a whirlwind whipping near enough to touch. Like lightning striking too close.

The parlor where she and Inez had spent so many hours plotting and laughing and arguing seemed too small and ordinary now to contain her. The entire apartment seemed too small. But here they were again anyway, the two of them together, with daylight slipping rectangles of luminance across the rug, and the delftware teapot and cups Della had brought gleaming white-and-blue on the table between them.

Rita had draped herself along the chaise longue, heels kicked off, the pleated chiffon layers of her canary gown spread around her like translucent wings, spilling over the cushions in dramatic folds. She rested her head back against a gray satin pillow and watched Inez through the fans of her lashes.

"Are you really sure, darling?"

"With every atom of me," Inez swore, and meant it. "Every single one."

"It only seems very sudden."

"Not to me."

Rita turned her head, rubbed her cheek lazily against the smooth satin, like a cat. "Two months of pitching woo. It's not that long."

"It's been more than two months. More like eight, with all the cards and flowers."

"And has Mr. Vernon been a perfect gentleman during your time together?"

"Absolutely!"

"That's too bad," she said, and laughed when Inez tossed a pillow at her, barely missing the teapot. "I only meant, sometimes a little naughtiness can lead to all sorts of fun."

"What are you on about?"

"Nothing." She sat up. "Please tell me that he's kissed you, at least."

Inez buried her face in her hands.

"He has, hasn't he? Smashing. You can tell a lot about a fellow by how he kisses."

"I know you're only trying to shock me. It won't work."

"Then why are you blushing? You're pink as a flamingo."

Inez flung down her hands. "Yes, we've kissed. More than once, and it was—it was astounding. Transformative. I—I never knew I could feel such things."

Rita's teasing expression sobered. Her gaze lowered; she began to rearrange the bunched chiffon, smoothing it flat against the cushions.

"No," said Inez, recognizing the look on her face. "No, don't try to deflate this, or make it less than it is. Don't doubt my heart."

"I don't doubt your heart. I merely—"

"No."

"Have you considered it all the way through, is all. Where will you live? *How* will you live? Will you travel with him around the world, willy-nilly into the hinterlands of Russia or North Africa, or—or the jungles of the equator? That doesn't sound like you at all. You like being at home."

"I will be at home. Because I am at home in his heart."

Rita sighed and shifted. If she actually carried any lightning with her, Inez imagined it would be crackling along her fingertips right now.

"What about Maman and Papa? I can't imagine they have nothing to say about this."

"George is on his way to Provence right now. He's going to do all properly, he says. Ask Papa for my hand in person."

"Commendable. Are they actually expecting him?"

"I wired yesterday."

"Well, then." Another sigh. "It seems like you have it all figured out."

"I hope so," Inez said, fervent. She rose and crossed to her sister, sat down on the floor before her and put her head in her lap. Rita's fingers lifted, lowered, ran lightly over her hair, the barest touch, then came to rest against her nape.

"A concert singer," her sister said, musing.

"And an importer's agent. Not a spy."

"Hmm. I told you not to fall in love with him, remember? Back at the party? I told you, and you went and did it anyway."

"Perhaps some of your wild rubbed off on me."

"Oh no," Rita laughed, "I'm not taking the blame for this. You fell head over heels all by yourself."

"I did," Inez murmured in agreement, closing her eyes. "Head over heels."

That was exactly how it felt. A turning tumble, the earth and stars spinning above and below at once, and she could hardly catch her breath.

She never caught her breath.

THE WEDDING TOOK place inside the Orangery at Kew Gardens, only a few miles from Winter Queen, on a brisk November afternoon that was already tilting into twilight. They said their vows beneath a canopy of flowering vines, looping tangles of pink and vermillion blooms that lent the humid air a tropical sweetness. Outside the high, arched windows, crystalline clouds raced across the blue, and the branches of the cedars growing near the building twitched and bobbed. To the east, the world was fading into violet.

Candles had been lit, dozens of snowy white beeswax tapers. There were lords and ladies in attendance, and George's American relatives (his parents at least, subdued but smiling), and the Jolivets' far more boisterous French relatives, and an emissary from the king himself. The hall was filled to the brim with elegant, pastel people chattering in all sorts of languages: German, Serbian, Dutch and Afrikaans, Italian and Arabic and Hindi. A few languages she couldn't recognize at all, but they sounded as splendid as the rest, poetic and powerful.

(Inez tried not to wonder who among this rarified crowd owed her soon-to-be husband certain favors, and vice versa.)

The tsar and tsarina of Russia had sent their congratulations to George via messenger, along with a gift for his bride: a diamond brooch in the shape of a swan, with ruby eyes and outstretched wings. The center stone had to weigh at least seven carats.

Rita stood as maid of honor. She mentioned she'd had do some fast talking (silver-tongued, indeed) to win another week away from the tour, but fortunately, she was missing only three performances. Her understudy, a Yorkshire lass who was normally one of Lady Capulet's ladies-in-waiting, almost wept with happiness when Rita had told her she was leaving on a temporary holiday.

"But I can't linger, as much as I'd like to. Poel threatened to replace me permanently if I'm not back by Friday."

"He never would," Inez protested, appalled.

"No," Rita had said, pulling her into a light embrace. "Don't worry, sissy. He never would."

How fortunate Inez was to have all of her family surrounding her on this blessed day, this glorious day, blustery cold outside and perfectly temperate inside, and George sliding the simple gold ring on her finger and then she doing the same for him. And everyone in the Orangery applauding, just as they would after Inez would play her violin or George would sing.

Only now it was a celebration of them both, together. For their legal union, and no one had to sing or play. They simply had to appreciate the sorcery of this moment, gold and flowers and twilight, as all of her dreams were manifesting.

"I love you," she said up to him at the altar, before everyone bearing witness. "And I promise to keep falling in love with you every single day."

"Then I am the luckiest man in the world," he'd responded. "And with you at my side, I always will be."

Mr. and Mrs. George Ley Vernon.

Inez rose up on her toes for his kiss, her first kiss as his wife, and his lips were warm and tender, and her heart was a dove, flying from her chest.

His hands closed around her waist, drawing her closer.

What a beautiful moment. A beautiful day, with the most beautiful life ahead of them.

Part 2

Chapter 10

How happy we were. How swiftly the years winged away from us, one after another. We traveled so much, lived so much. Sometimes in my memory I can hardly separate one city from another; I confuse Lisbon with Budapest, or Florence with Milan.

Other times I recall moments, fragments of moments, with such vivid clarity, it's as if I'm living them again, my heart beating, my voice speaking, my blood pumping, just as it happened back then.

Standing beside him at the edge of Lake Como, squinting out at the dark waters, trying to finish our gelato before it melted, orange and sticky, down our fingers.

Saint Petersburg in the winter, when, in the lobby of our chic hotel, he presented me with a fur hat with flaps around the ears, and the flaps were so long I looked like a cocker spaniel. Neither of us could stop laughing. The staff thought us quite drunk.

Athens, at the Parthenon, when he whispered to me beneath the stars that I was surely more beautiful than Athena, and I smacked him on the arm and told him to hush, because it was never a good idea to make the gods jealous.

Taking my bow at the Met after my debut performance. Stealing a glance at him, standing in the wings, as I rose. He held an

enormous bouquet of pink roses in his arms, the biggest bouquet
I'd ever seen. Autumn Damasks, they're called, so richly perfumed
their fragrance ended up saturating the entire apartment. I made
a sachet from their petals.

If you look, it's still beneath my pillow.

JUNE, 1914
NAPLES, ITALY

A bank of sapphire clouds was unfurling along the southern edge of the Bay of Naples, great boiling plumes that
devoured the line between sky and sea, blending all to blue. A
breeze skated the bay waters, fitful, pushed by the clouds. To
the east loomed the heavy cone of Mount Vesuvius, green
and slate and amethyst, ringed by a haze along its base, one
that stretched long arms all the way down into the city, making silvery shapes of the medieval cathedrals and castles and
cream-and-ocher buildings that lined the piazzas and winding
stone roads.

"An enchanted view," said Charles Frohman, standing at
the edge of Rita's rooftop terrace, holding a glass of dry white
wine. "An ancient city. I can understand how you'd not want
to leave."

"It's ancient, all right," she said, pouring her own glass from
the carafe on the table in the middle of the terrace. "Cathe-
rine de' Medici is said to have danced with her Henry in the
grand hall below us, and I can well believe it. The roof leaks
and the plumbing barely functions and there are cracks in the
floors deep enough to lose a silver dollar. Don't drop any
loose change."

He laughed, looking back at her with one foot braced
against the rim of the low wall lining the edge. "Even so . . ."

"Yes, I know. Even so."

Even so, Rita's Italian flat stood within kissing distance of the bay, right above Via Partenope, crowded with donkeys and autos and yachtsmen, dandified fellows with too much money and likely not enough wives, on their way to and from the slips cradling their sleek, waterbound homes. On clear days, the horizon stretched nearly to infinity. If she stared at it long enough, the corners of her vision would prickle and dissolve until she lost sight of everything but that blue.

Rita took up her glass, joined Charles at the edge. It was a pleasant afternoon despite the mist, an idyllic warm Italian summer, and the air carried the scent of rosemary and citrus and a coming rain. She'd lived here for nearly a year. She knew from experience that the rain might tease and tease along the horizon, but would likely only roll in across the waves much later, carried along by the dusk.

Her skirts plastered against her legs, flicked forward again. By the doorway to the apartment's interior, a pair of terracotta planters held clusters of white-and-yellow daisies, their sweet faces nodding.

"It suits me," she said. "For now."

"You're well cocooned."

"Cocooned from what?"

"Everything beyond. Beyond this mist, beyond this country. Politics and posturing."

"Believe me, Charles, there's no escaping politics, even here. The papers go on and on about it. The French seethe over the German annexation of Alsace-Lorraine. The Serbians despise the Austrians over Bosnia. Wilhelm versus Edward, and the ungodly amounts of money they're both burning through in their race to control the seas and straits."

"*E la bella Italia*, caught in the middle of it all, everyone holding their breath. You're a butterfly in a bottle."

"Hardly that! As I said, I do read the papers—I'm not a complete naïf—and I'm out and about nearly every day. The photoplays are shot one after another with barely any pause, you know. Even so, I follow the news. I care about what's happening. Here *and* abroad."

He turned his head, gave her an appraising look.

In the years that had passed between them, he as mentor, she as acolyte, the celebrated Charles Frohman appeared nearly the same as the first time they'd met, back at the Cornwallis-West party. Back when he'd first sought her out in the crowd and said, so very casually, *Ah, Miss Jolivet, how'd-you-do. I saw your play, you know.*

Round face, keen eyes. Perhaps a little less hair that had gone a little more gray. He'd changed her life back then. She hadn't fully realized the extent of it, the power of the force behind his will to bend her path, but he had. She might have been a star plucked from the heavens, destined to simply drop to the earth. In fact, maybe she still was. But how bright he'd made her trail. How brilliantly she shone because of him and all that he'd envisioned for her.

"I'm glad you've come," she said, softening her tone, drawing him away from the roof's edge. "I've missed you. Lucky for me you're on holiday for a bit."

"Not a holiday. A mission."

"A mission! How mysterious."

They returned to the tiled table, set their wine upon a surface painted with plump lemons and nightingales. There was bread and cheese laid out by Rita's very efficient maid, prosciutto and grapes and a shallow bowl of bright green olive oil dusted with herbs for dipping. The woven runner beneath the bread basket shivered along its edges, the breeze tugging.

"Tell me." Charles smoothed his hands along the table. Nails clipped, neat, tidy, exactly as she would expect. "How *are* your photoplays coming along?"

"Well, I hope."

"You're sorely missed back in London, I'm told. And certainly back on Broadway. I haven't had another hit like *Kismet* since you left."

"You're very kind."

"Don't be coy, darling. I'm asking about your schedule."

She sat up, taken aback. "I'm not being coy. *Fata Morgana* is wrapped, and as far as I know, the director was pleased. *Zvani* is nearly done, only a few reshoots planned. I have *Cuore ed arte* coming up next week. So, again, I'm not coy, Charles. I really do think it's going well." She gave a small shrug. "The Ambrosio Company likes me."

"We all like you."

"Thank you, but they like me in their films. Honestly? It's a relief to get away from the routine of putting on a show every night. My Italian isn't what it should be, I know, but I'm getting better by the day. And it hardly matters for the sake of the moving picture, since the title cards will be in English for most of the audiences, anyway."

He studied her, unblinking, and Rita felt a flush of shame. "Don't get me wrong, I love the theatre, and I know you put me there. I loved Poel and Shakespeare. I loved being in *Kismet*, and the rest. I loved the Knickerbocker, and I loved the applause, and the crowds whenever I tried to duck out the back of the building. You put me on Broadway and shone the light on me, Charles. You, and you alone. But these photoplays. My time here. This is something else."

"The Italian silver screen," he whispered dramatically, looking up, wiping a hand across the sky between them. The diamonds in his rings twinkled. "Better than Hollywood!"

"Maybe not better," she said, nettled. "But something. Something new and—well, and mine."

"What if I could make Hollywood yours, too?" He chose a slice of focaccia from its basket, dredged it in the shimmer of olive oil. "Come, now. Italy is a beautiful dream, another stepping stone along your path, but is there really anything besides the dream to keep you here?"

Rita hesitated, then plucked free a red grape from its cluster. "Possibly one thing."

"One thing. One person, do you mean?"

She shrugged once more, deliberate, then bit into the grape, a burst of cool sweetness.

"I see. But is this person more important than Cecil B. DeMille?" Rita looked up sharply, and Charles smiled. "Yes, him. Director General of the Lasky Feature Play Company. You might recall he was once one of my actors. Right now he's in California preparing to make a motion picture I think uniquely suited to your talents, a four-reel feature to be called *The Unafraid*. I've already mentioned your name for the lead. A brave young heiress who unwittingly falls in love with two noble brothers, one good, one evil." He leaned forward, dropping his voice back into that dramatic whisper. "Who will prevail?"

Who, indeed.

JUST OVER A year ago, Rita had found herself one of the most popular leading ladies on Broadway, drowning in accolades and fawning fans, and she was cold and alone and exhausted.

Frohman's *Kismet* had propelled her to a level of fame she had never imagined. She played Marsinah, a beggar's daughter in a fantastical Far Eastern realm, a girl swathed in diaphanous scarves and sequins, in love with a prince in disguise. It was a typical story, yes, certainly one that had been told before in more ways than could be tallied, but the dialogue was crisp and modern and the actors dedicated. It ran at the Knickerbocker Theater forever and a day, it seemed—although in truth, it was six months—with every show sold out, even the matinees. Her dressing room brimmed with flowers; love notes from men she'd never met sat in stacks on her cosmetics table; love notes from women she'd never met sat alongside them. Leaving the theatre after a show meant waiting and waiting until the mobs cleared out, and even then there'd remain a gauntlet of people hoping for autographs, hoping to touch her hand or shoulder, hoping to catch her eye and have her notice them, bless them, make them special. A few of the fresher-faced girls would cry when she smiled at them.

There had been a time when such a thing would have charmed her. At the least, it would have gratified her, because Rita had worked all her adult life at being irresistible, and those tears from her followers were an undeniable sign that she was succeeding. But as the months wound on, and then the years, her smile grew more and more false, and the bouquets didn't smell as fragrant, and the love notes grew tedious. Everyone seemed to write the same thing.

Forgive my presumption, I admire you so.

May we meet?

Will you write back?

May I call on you?

Will you advise me?

I want to be just like you . . .

It worried her. It worried her all the way through the chambers of her heart, that instead of sparkling and rising in joy at her growing success, she was instead being drained by it. She could act and dance and sing on stage, she could give witty interviews offstage, could sign her name on proffered programs or cards with panache. Rita could fool everyone but herself. She arrived at the theatre each afternoon alone. She left each evening alone. She dined alone on the meals prepared for her. She went to bed alone and rose alone and then started the whole routine over again.

After *Kismet* came *Where Ignorance Is Bliss* at the Lyceum, and then, God help her, *A Thousand Years Ago* at the Schubert, which shot her so far ahead of her ambitions that she nearly couldn't comprehend it.

There was still satisfaction in doing her job well, so well that the critics couldn't imagine anyone else playing Turandot, the tormented princess who shunned suitor after suitor, sentencing to death those who answered her riddles incorrectly, until finally her hero arrived. Another fantastical Eastern fable, with more scarves and sequins, but also a wig of long black hair down to her knees, tangled with flowers, as if the princess in question spent her days dragging her locks through meadows in full bloom.

It didn't matter. The show was a smashing, smashing success. The love notes multiplied, and she began to give away the overwhelming onslaught of roses and lilies and carnations, spreading them around the cast. She took her bow each night center stage, her raven hair brushing the floorboards, and made sure to throw kisses at the audience at the end of her third bow.

It was mad and loud and empty. She felt so empty.

One night, she'd waited longer than usual to steal away after the performance. It was well after eleven, a cool evening beneath a sable sky. A handful of people waited even this late, so Rita plastered on her smile and pulled out her pen, keeping an eye on the chauffeured motorcar awaiting her at the curb, saying *Thank you; you're so kind; I'm so pleased you enjoyed it; I'm so sorry, I really must run*, all the usual babble, but then she was past them at last, her hand reaching for the back door of the motor. (She never waited for her chauffer to jump out and open the door for her; it saved valuable getaway time to simply do it herself.)

Someone grabbed her arm. She spun about, startled. In all her years of performing, none of her fans had gone so far as to force her to a halt.

A young woman stood before her, blond and petite, her eyes smiling, her lips smiling, and it took Rita nearly three entire seconds to recognize her sister.

"*Mon Dieu*," she laughed as they hugged. "Hello, hello! I thought you were in Cairo until next week!"

"George's business concluded early, so we decided to just come home. The *Mauretania* docked last night."

"You should have telephoned! I could have gotten you tickets to the show!"

"Don't worry about that. I knew you'd be sold out. We can do it another time."

"Where *is* your husband?"

"At the flat. Will you drop by? There's someone I hope you'll meet."

Rita threw a glance at her lingering audience, then opened the door and pulled Inez in after her, shifting across the squabs. "Oh, I don't know," she said, after the door closed. "It's late, I'm tired. And you know I'm not interested in meeting anyone right now, I barely have time to—"

"Please? You needn't stay long, just for a cocktail. It's that we've met the most marvelous fellow—well, George met him in Naples a few months ago. I met him just today, and he's only in town until tomorrow morning. He's Italian," she added, lowering her voice. "An Italian count, as a matter of fact. Quite dashing."

"Inez . . ."

"Only a half hour! Fifteen minutes! We told him all about you, and he's so interested."

"You *told* him about—"

"I know you're not looking for a beau, Rita. Giuseppe has connections to the photoplay companies over there. In Italy, I mean. He says they're hunting for fresh talent."

Rita sat back, folding her arms over her chest. Finally, she said, "How did you get here? Did George give in and purchase a motorcar for the city?"

"No, I took a cab."

"No maid with you?"

Inez sent her a heavy look. "It's been ages since I've bothered to worry about a maid at my heels."

Rita sighed. "Right. Well, we'll get you home, at least." She
tapped the glass pane between them and her driver. "Mrs. Vernon's place on West Eleventh Street, please."

"Yes, ma'am."

"And after that," Rita said, turning to her sister with a
frown, "we'll see."

AFTER THAT, WAS Count Giuseppe de Cippico.

If she had gone straight home that night instead of giving
in to her sister's pretty pleas, would she have met him anyway?
Would she have somehow ended up in Italy, in the shadow of
Vesuvius, caught in her tinseled world of elaborate sets and
hot lights and motion-picture cameras that captured her face
and movements in silver nitrate, which then cast back her
image on wide, enormous screens?

Would she have ever touched his warm skin, admired his
dark eyes, drowsed happily to his voice, that accent, late late
in the night, when they were both so relaxed and sated that
sleep was the only answer, and yet still his low voice seduced
her, *Buonanotte, mia amata, buonanotte?*

She didn't know. She was grateful she never had to find out.

INEZ AND GEORGE's penthouse in Greenwich Village was
only blocks from Rita's own on Fifth Avenue. It wasn't quite
a coincidence, but neither was it fully planned; the sisters
simply gravitated toward each other, just as they always had.
In a city the size of New York, it would be far too easy to become lost in the busy grid of streets and avenues, to drift
apart. As it was, the Vernons traveled so frequently that it
seemed to Rita they hardly saw each other anyway. Time
had shifted their roles, and these days it was Inez who sent
postcards to Rita, silly ones, lovely ones, each with a note as-

suring her that all was well, wherever Mr. and Mrs. Vernon roamed, and almost always with a word in the local language that somehow struck Inez as useful, or profound, or just interesting. Which was how Rita now knew that *pan* was the word for bread in Spanish *and* Japanese. That *habibti* meant beloved. That ordering a cup of coffee in Barcelona would get you an intensely bitter espresso and asking for a *coco natural* in Manzanillo would not get you a fizzy soda drink, but instead a fresh green coconut with the top lopped off by machete.

That whispering *ojalá* from the middle of a certain decrepit bridge spanning the Conejos River meant the saints would hear your wish and, if your heart was worthy, would grant it.

With each new card, Rita would imagine Inez eating the bread, drinking the espresso, laughing over the coconut. Standing on that bridge beside George, suspended between aspen-studded mountains, making her wish. The irony of it was not lost on her: that shy, retiring Inez—the girl who never wanted to leave their childhood home; who deliberately counted only birds and music and her siblings as friends—was now happily hopscotching her way across the globe.

And yes, sometimes Rita would also imagine what it might feel like, to be so utterly unified with another. To give herself so entirely to a lover. A husband. To be *safe* in that love. Would their hearts come to share the same tempo? Would their souls reflect an infinite sameness, like twin looking glasses that faced each other? Would they sleep together, dine together, plan their future together, travel, sex, children, dreams... and still it wouldn't be enough, still their craving for one another would never be satisfied?

Rita had never known a love like that. She'd never wanted to. Life was too full, too fast, too rich to pause for a man, any man. And honestly? That love, that all-consuming sort of love sounded exhausting.

Yet since her marriage, there was no denying that Inez had bloomed; Inez seemed nothing but joyful. Rita wasn't jealous of her, exactly. But in her more silent hours... those solitary, repetitive hours of eating breakfast alone, preparing for bed alone, day after day...

She couldn't help but wonder if there was something wrong with her. If she was simply too selfish to surrender to another so completely.

She'd stuck the postcard of that Colorado bridge into the frame of her vanity mirror, pleased with the wild green and gold of the mountains, the deep cerulean of the river. Sometimes, when her eye would catch on it, she'd think about what she'd wish for, should she ever find herself there.

Worthy or not, Rita was fairly certain her heart had no right to any more wishes. She had wealth and fame and her looks still, such as they were. She had talent, and perhaps a bit too much pride in that talent, but also the tenacity to constantly work on her craft, and surely it was all right to be a little proud of that. She was tired more than she liked these days, but that was to be expected, the price of her profession.

She was alone, but not lonely. No, not that.

GEORGE AND HIS aristocratic guest were in the parlor, if the hushed conversation and laughter Rita overheard from the foyer were any clue. The apartment was spotless and the flowers in the vases fresh; there was no indication that its occupants had been gone for the past two months to Greece and Turkey and Egypt. She handed off her coat and hat and gloves to the maid, turned to Inez, and warned for the third time, "I can't stay long."

Inez only smiled, taking her by the arm, leading her forward.

The parlor lights were low, only a few table lamps burning. The Algerian alabaster pendant chandelier, carved with pacing tigers, hung ghostly from the gloom masking the ceiling.

Two men sat in wingchairs before the fire. When they noticed the sisters in the doorway, both came to their feet.

George Rita knew, of course, even in this half-light, tall and smiling, the tumbler of bourbon in his hand lit to caramel by the fire. The other man, the count, was just a little taller, no drink, with hair that seemed as inky as the night around them, a square jaw and eyes shadowed by long black lashes.

George was introducing them, and the count extended his hand, and their handshake was firm and impersonal. Even so, Rita felt *something*, a small thrill along her spine, a hint of vertigo as she looked into his eyes, infinite and dark. His smile, not so impersonal as the clasping of their hands had indicated, but slight and knowing, as if they'd met before, or he knew some secret about her that Rita might not have yet realized herself. In any case, she knew to keep her own expression politely interested, nothing more. This count had information she wanted, perhaps business connections she could use. It was never wise to entangle her livelihood with personal gratification. She'd learned that lesson years ago.

"A pleasure," she said, as their hands released.

"An honor," the count replied, still smiling, "to meet the Pearl of Broadway at last."

She gave a little laugh. "That's a new one."

"Pardon me?"

"The 'Pearl of Broadway.'"

"The Shining Star," Inez cut in, sidling up to George, touching her lips to his cheek.

"The Magnificent Moon!" George offered.

"No, the Pearl," insisted the count. "Or at least, that's how the Italian newspapers describe her. Miss Rita Jolivet, the mystic new sensation. *Una perla afosa.*"

"*Afosa?*" Inez repeated.

His smile grew more abashed; he looked away from Rita, then back. "Forgive me if I'm too forward. It means sultry. A sultry pearl. We Italians tend to embrace the poetry of our language."

"Ah," Rita said, flummoxed. She felt, astonishingly, her cheeks begin to heat. She was suddenly glad it was so late, that the room was so layered in night.

Count de Cippico inclined his head. "So indeed, Miss Jolivet, both the honor and the pleasure are mine."

"Come," George said, waving the sisters to the chairs, drawing two more near. "Let's all sit and talk about our dreams, shall we? There's no better time for it than the sorcery of midnight, surrounded by friends old and new."

"Who's the poet now?" Inez teased.

But Rita was looking at the count, and the count was looking back at her, and it struck her that George was right. It was a splendid time to dream.

Chapter 11

Do you remember where you were when you learned of the assassination? Of course you do. Everyone in the world surely must. A moment like that, a moment when the firm and known path of history pivots, disintegrates, shattering lives...it embeds in our memory like a needle of glass, forever stinging, never dislodged.

I was here, in Manhattan, perusing the early papers alone over coffee and poached eggs. I remember very specifically that the eggs were too runny, and there was a chimney swift perched on the balcony rail just by my chair, a cheerful fellow chittering to another I couldn't see. Two weeks before that mild morning, George had left on a trip I was not allowed to join.

Not allowed. He'd told me kindly, but firmly. Certainly it wasn't the first time he'd traveled without me since our union, but, oh, my heart.

As soon as I read that headline, *ARCHDUKE FERDINAND AND DUCHESS SOPHIE OF AUSTRIA MURDERED IN COLD BLOOD, MANY OTHERS INJURED*, my fingers went numb. I dropped the paper to the table. All I could think was, *Please, God, don't let him be in Sarajevo.*

It turns out that he wasn't. But in the end, it hardly mattered.

Lives shattered. So many, many lives, blown to pieces after those first royal two. I can't stop thinking about it.

JULY, 1914
NAPLES, ITALY

Rita stood beneath the thick and spreading boughs of a holm oak, dusty leaves tossing sinuous shadows around her, over her, dappling her hair and face and shoulders, the flowing robes of her embroidered tunic. Before her lay a meadow ruffled with rye grass, dry and golden, and about forty extras in far plainer tunics, all of them facing her, all of them squinting and sweating beneath the ferocious sun.

Rita lifted one arm, curved and graceful, as high as her chest, palm up, fingers cupped.

"I have come to your land not for war, but love!"

She spoke in French, since it was closer to Italian than English. As she'd mentioned to Charles, it hardly mattered, since the title cards were going to read what they were going to read in whatever language suited the audience, but she thought maybe the cast and crew could understand her a little better, at least.

She dropped her arm, unbuckled the heavy, wide belt that held her sword and scabbard, then let that drop too, right at her feet. The oversized brass buckle barely missed her toes.

"I come because my heart, my weak and foolish woman's heart, has decided my destiny for me! I bend my armies to its will, and agree to wed your emperor!"

She bowed her head, the ringlets of her wig falling long over her shoulders and down her chest. It was the signal for the crowd before her to cheer, which they did. Rita looked up again before the tin diadem pinned to the wig could slide forward, as it had twice in rehearsal.

Raising both arms chest high again, she angled slightly to the right, making certain the camera, five feet away, could capture her face, her darkly painted lips, her darkly kohled eyes and eyebrows. She bowed her head one final time, briefly, modestly, and that was when a little bird—she would find out later it was a chaffinch—flew in front of her, so close that the wake of its passage stirred the coils of her hair. As she straightened, the bird returned to land on her outstretched left arm, right there on her arm, a weight so precious and slight she felt only a pinprick of talons against her bare skin.

For a second, no one did anything. Then the extras closest to her began to exclaim, and Rita's polished smile turned into a grin, and when the bird flew off again, startled, she waved farewell to it.

"*Mio Dio,*" the director laughed from his chair behind the cameraman. He brought his hands together in a brisk clap. "*Perfetto!*"

"So, you have a secret gift," Giuseppe said as he handed her a glass of tea from the jug in the hamper between them. It was no longer cold, not in this heat, but still blessedly cool. She took the glass and held it between her palms, knowing it was going to warm up faster that way but not caring. If she could have pressed it to her forehead without ruining her makeup, she would have.

"A gift you've never confided," he went on, bringing his own glass to hers; they clinked rims. "You, Margherita, are a bird charmer."

As one of the main financial backers of the production company, the Count de Cippico was allowed on set whenever he wished. And usually when Rita was filming, he wished it. It was flattering, really. Giuseppe was both a businessman and an aristocrat, a man who certainly had more important places to be than, for example, a field of scruffy rye grass in the middle of a hot Wednesday afternoon. But she didn't mind him coming and watching. He was more a silent presence than not; he never offered notes; he never interfered. It was possible her directors and crews were a trace more courteous when he was around than they would have been otherwise, which she also appreciated.

They sat in low folding chairs beneath a blue-striped umbrella so wide the shade easily blanketed them both. The extras were less fortunate, taking their meal break in whatever comfort they could find beneath the trees, with stern admonitions from the assistant director to not trample the grass.

"Yes, I speak bird," Rita said lightly, after a long drink of tea. "And dog and cat. A little horse. Some shark, even."

"Shark! Where did you learn that?"

"The depths of the sea. I go there at night, after you're asleep."

"I knew you were more siren than not. How could it be otherwise, possessing such beauty?"

She eased back in the canvas chair, feeling the change in him, from blithe to purposeful, wondering how best to respond. He'd been circling closer to her recently, mentioning plans for the weeks ahead, the months ahead. Next year, New Year's, the Festival of Saint This-or-That. Mentioning his estate in Mentone, which she had been judicious enough to avoid for nearly a year, except for a single visit two months past, when she'd been placed in the quarters of the countess. (There was no countess now, though, was there, so she supposed they were the quarters of whatever future countess would come.) Rooms cocooned in satin and crystal and gilt; colorful glass drops melting from the light fixtures. Exquisite marble floors and walls everywhere she looked, marble the color of frost, or blood, or blushing roses.

For the entire five days of that visit, she'd done her best to dodge the expectations of Giuseppe and his staff, everyone so welcoming and deferential. When one of the footman had slipped up and quietly greeted her, "*Contessa*," as she'd passed in a hallway, Rita hadn't looked around, hadn't paused. She'd acted as if she hadn't heard him.

She was not ready to hear that word. Not yet.

SHE HAD EXPERIENCE with matrimony, brief as it was. Alfred Charles Stern, who preferred to be called Freddy, he of the cheeky smiles and smoldering looks, that lad so familiar with all the dank and smelly corners of Stratford-upon-Avon, back when she'd been with Poel's traveling company. She'd been young and curious then; what teenaged girl, a sheltered girl suddenly set free, wouldn't be? Innocent, in her way, but certainly intoxicated with the newfound liberation of her life on the tour. As months passed, months of Freddy's secret smiles and admiring glances, Rita found herself wondering more and more what it would be like to linger over the taste of a boy's lips. To feel the touch of someone who kindled her blood. The only romantic kisses she'd ever known were stage kisses, chaste and quick. But when she imagined kissing Freddy, when she imagined his hands on her body, nothing about her felt chaste.

One evening after a show in Durham, Rita had been hurrying alone back to the hotel from the theatre, listening to cathedral bells tolling across a lilac sky. It was a short distance to walk; Poel always booked accommodations as close to their performance venues as possible. But because of a rip in her costume, and the seamstress cousins backstage who'd delighted in recounting the entirety of a letter they'd just received from a great-niece, Rita had missed joining the main company heading to dinner.

The new stagehand had followed her, stealthy as a stoat. She realized later that he must have been waiting for her just outside the dock doors, his dirty clothes, his dirty face, blending with the dusk. He'd been with the company for less than a week, bloodshot eyes, greasy hair. She'd taken note of him vaguely in the days before, in the same way a rabbit might take note of the stale scent of a predator hanging in the air, but that was all. The problem was, there were always plenty of predators around. His was just another scent.

In that tricky descending light, he'd come up from behind so quickly, snatched her by the waist so roughly, that she'd barely had time to cry out. Then they were in an alleyway littered with rubbish, and his filthy hand was over her mouth, pressed against her teeth, while the other groped at her skirts. Rita had wrenched away as hard as she could, now managing a full scream. She even got in a quick blow to his face before he hit her back, sending her spinning.

But then Freddy was there, sudden and fleet. He and his two mates were also late to dinner, also hurrying, when they'd heard her scream.

Three to one. The stagehand fled into the night, several teeth missing, his arm broken. Freddy had helped Rita gently to her feet and kept his arm about her shoulders to support her all the walk back.

That was that, really. Three to one, but for Rita, out of that vicious moment in the shadows emerged this single, attractive young man who looked more like a hero to her now than her Romeo ever had.

Freddy's voice had been cajoling and soft; his lips were salty and soft. His breath was usually spiced with liquor, and the callouses on his hands felt like rough excitement against her own smooth skin. In retrospect, their connection had been entirely physical, from the moment in the alleyway to the ultimate consummation in his bed, weeks later: sweaty and unbridled and raw.

Their marriage had lasted three months, nine days. There were no loud fights, no massive discord between them beyond that of two people born into very different stations in life, on two very different trajectories, who unexpectedly found themselves bewilderingly, legally bound.

They'd wed in Gretna Green, a quick and slippery civil ceremony spawned of a haste that only lust and pregnancy could summon. Rita hadn't even bothered to inform her family of the marriage yet. (In point of fact, she never would.)

Then the lust began to fade. Within a fortnight, it was clear that the pregnancy turned out to be a false alarm.

She awoke one morning in a cheap hotel room, one just like all the others on the tour. She opened her eyes and turned her head to take in Freddy's face pressed against the pillow beside hers, the stubble on his cheeks, his mouth agape. A strand of saliva dangled in a thread from the corner of his lips to darken the linens.

In sleep, the comeliness she'd admired melted away into folds of flesh, his chin and jowls already going to fat. A clear bottle of gin still sat, mostly empty, on the nightstand beside him.

He smelled of stale smoke and that gin and pungent something else, something like turpentine. His hair was dirty. His nailbeds were rimmed with grime.

She sat up carefully, ran both hands down her face. She drew her knees to her chest and realized she had to do whatever it took to break free of him.

So, she broke free. An annulment, nearly as quick as the wedding had been, with Charles providing the name of a discreet barrister. A generous lump-sum payment to her unprotesting groom. (A *bribe*, Freddy had called it, but without venom; they both knew it was more money than he'd likely see again. She'd told him to invest it, but, knowing him, it had probably gone to booze and cigarettes.)

It was years ago now, ages ago. Even so, Rita would never forget the dismay that had swelled through her that morning, relentless as an ocean wave, as she'd looked down at her sleeping, slovenly husband and thought, *Oh, no. No, no, no. Not this.*

BUT THAT WAS then. She'd fixed her mistake, and now, right now, the Italian meadow before her flashed gold on gold beneath a searing turquoise sky. The feathered grass swayed and whispered; the solitary old oaks clattered their leaves. Also right now, her beau, a man about as far from Freddy Stern as Rita could imagine, was looking back at her with warm, patient eyes and a half smile that was somehow a thousandfold comelier than her former husband's.

Giuseppe wanted to marry her. It was as plain as the moon. But she just . . . couldn't. Not yet, maybe not ever, no matter how honorable his intentions. No matter how much she enjoyed his company, his laughter, his kindness. No matter the hampers stuffed with bread and oranges and charcuterie, with jugs of tea and limoncello, that he brought with him each time he appeared for one of her shoots, because he knew she'd be hungry and thirsty after a long day on the set.

Or the other four hampers he always brought for the crew.

Or how he took her hand when she stood alone, no one else looking. How he laughed at her jokes, no matter how foolish. How he murmured into her ear at night—in perfumed, silken chambers, nothing like those terrible cheap hotels— that she was a goddess, a dream, a spirit of power and mirth walking the earth, grace at her heels, wisdom ahead.

That man, *that* man wanted to wed her.

Great God. What sort of fool would turn him down?

She didn't like to consider herself a fool, but even Rita had to admit her reluctance was illogical at best. Count de Cippico was no country lad who lived by the labor of his back and hands, no stagehand, no carpenter. He was a nobleman, worldly and wealthy . . . which also meant he wasn't likely to be bribed into an annulment if she changed her mind about him.

For over half a year, their names had been linked in the social sheets here and abroad, especially in America (according to Inez, who regularly sent clippings). Half a year of innuendo and speculation, *Yes they will, no they won't.*

The count would not be put off forever. No man would.

She studied him from beneath her lashes. There was such confidence in the angle of his jaw, the shape of his lips. Those slumberous eyes. On another man, it might read as arrogance, but on him it looked...right. She'd kissed those lips more times than she could count. Stroked his face, smooth-shaven or rough, and every inch of him still delighted her. But as their eyes met now, the realization that overwhelmed her was purely this:

I want him, but I don't want to need him.

Rita dropped her gaze, sipping her tea. It seemed best to keep the conversation lighthearted. Distract him, if she could. Amuse him. Giuseppe liked it when she turned playful, so after a moment, she tipped back her head and slanted him a lazy smile, hoping her lipstick hadn't smeared.

"Sharks aside, sirens are famously fickle, or even deadly. I would never turn either way with you."

"I never believed you would."

"And they resort to magic to snare their lovers. Have I ensorcelled you, my Count de Cippico? Or—"

"You know you have," he interrupted, his tone soft and serious. "You must know."

"This isn't sorcery. It's serendipity. One of the most wonderful things in the world."

Giuseppe lifted an eyebrow. "Forgive me. I am unfamiliar with this word."

"A delicious chance. A happy fluke, a fabulous one that allowed our paths to cross. So that we may laugh and play and enjoy our time together."

"I would say we've certainly done that."

"We have indeed."

He frowned out at the grass, then back to her. "Rita," he said, his tone shifting again, even more solemn.

No, she thought, her heart beginning to beat hollow in her chest. *Don't ask me here. Don't ask now.*

He said, "I've been considering Mr. Frohman's offer to you, the one that would take you back to America."

"Oh?"

"I think you should accept it."

She stared at him, genuinely surprised. "You do?"

He bent to place his drink on the ground, then took her hand in his. His fingertips felt cool from the glass. "The world is sliding into a precarious place. I know you know this. Austria's archduke and his wife are slaughtered, and there are parties—governments—howling for blood, for justice, as if there could be such a thing to bring about peace at this point. There will be a war, I have no doubt, and I think very soon. It will start here, in Europe, and hopefully it will end here. It would be best if you were safe."

"I know tempers are boiling, but nothing else has happened yet. Perhaps diplomacy will win."

"It won't. There are too many angry men in power, too many old, disputed lines on maps. The kaiser is rumored to be unfit. The French and British distrust the Germans, and the Germans distrust everyone. My own king stands frozen amid the madness. There's talk that the Russians are already mobilizing. If it's true, all the other nations will soon follow, because they'll have no choice." He sighed. "If you could go to America, even for a while, I think I might rest better at night."

"Well, but—" Rita bit her lip, then dropped her voice. "What of you, Giuseppe? You can't seriously ask me to just sail away and leave you here. Not if what you say is true."

"I could come with you. At first. For a short time. But I have obligations here. I have family; I have estates. I have people who depend upon me, generations who depend upon me, as they did my father and grandfather."

"Yes," she said slowly, remembering his palace in Mentone again, the splendor of the chambers. The warm Mediterranean light sluicing through the windows, turning all the crystal and colored-glass drops into fire. That footman who had ducked his head at the sight of her in the hallway and called her a countess.

A group of women gathered beneath one of the oaks broke into ripples of delighted laughter, drawing her gaze. A cloud of birds, more of those chaffinches, fluttered up from the branches above them, spiraling into flight.

"Yes," Rita said again. "I understand, of course. You must take care of your people."

"It would be my greatest honor to also take care of you."

She was still observing the women beneath the tree, five of them costumed as peasants, two with arms looped around the other like sisters or best friends; it took a moment for his words to sink in. Her heart heard him first, began that hard, hollow knocking against her breastbone again. Then her mind caught up, her breath caught up. She turned in the flimsy canvas chair and found him watching her with that patience, that kindness she'd found in him and no other man.

"Oh, Giuseppe." She took his hand, lacing her fingers through his. "If ever I was worthy of you, I would be so lucky. But I'm ... I'm a butterfly. I'm a swallow. Every instinct tells me to fly and fly, from one home to the next. I have to keep moving, even across countries. I don't know how to stay still."

"I've known you still, beloved. Late at night, in my arms, I've known you still."

"Then maybe it's you who's ensorcelled me," she said with a sad smile. "The point is, I'm selfish. I love my life, I'm greedy for it, every bit of it. And yes, very honestly, I love you in it. But I can't trap either of us into something that might make us miserable. Not when what we have right now is so magnificent."

His lips parted to speak. She lifted her free hand to stop him. "And, *and*, if I am to take Charles up on his offer, that means I'm leaving yet again, no doubt for months. If there's a war—if you're here and I'm there..." She shook her head, her throat closing.

What if I leave and the war comes and he dies? What if I marry him and the war comes and he dies? What if the world tilts into chaos and I don't marry him, and I never see him again?

How would she bear it, any of it?

Giuseppe tightened his fingers around hers. "Margherita, let me take on this burden between us, this distance. Let me be the one who reminds you of who we are together, even when we're apart. I do not begrudge you Hollywood. As much as I would prefer you at my side, I would grieve to steal this opportunity from you. So, I will wait." He smiled at her dubious look, then pressed a kiss to her knuckles. "I will, I promise. For how long, I cannot say. Until you realize you're as greedy for me as you are for this splendid life."

Across the meadow, the assistant director was summoning all the actors back to their places. The peasant extras rose one by one, shaking out their tunics, stooping to place their cups and plates back into their baskets.

Rita stood as the makeup girl rushed up, no older than sixteen but surprisingly skilled, brushes and pots in hand. Rita's lipstick was reapplied, her kohl redrawn, her face and neck and chest dusted with powder.

"*Bene*," the girl pronounced, when she was satisfied. She offered a bashful smile to the count before dashing away again.

Rita straightened her wig and began walking back to her tree. But then she turned. Giuseppe sat in silence, still caught in the shade of the umbrella, the mess of their meal at his feet. Prosciutto and salami, sliced cheese, hunks of bread. Orange rinds curling and drying on pastel porcelain plates.

"I like it when you call me Margherita," she said.

His smile deepened. "I like it too. It makes you more mine."

THE AIR TURNED sorrowful. She had no other, better way to describe it: sorrowful, weighted. As if just the idea of war saturated it, molecule by molecule, turning it thick as syrup. Hard to breathe. Even with the fresh wind blowing off the bay, Rita kept tasting metal on her tongue, something like rain but not rain, never the relief of rain.

Two days after her conversation with Giuseppe in the meadow, the week before her current film wrapped, Rita sent Charles Frohman a telegram, delivered express, care of his suite at the Knickerbocker Hotel, Manhattan, New York.

GLADLY ACCEPT THE UNAFRAID STOP LET ME KNOW DATES AND DETAILS STOP

Two days after that, Austria-Hungary rose up in fury, declaring war on Serbia.

Political wheels turned, diplomats argued, old wounds resurfaced, full of pus and rage. One week later, Germany, France, Russia, and Great Britain each issued their own declarations.

And Europe split apart, sliding into hell, just as Giuseppe had predicted.

Chapter 12

Until the day the world ended, that 28th of July, I don't think I truly understood the fragility of it all. How tenuous and beautiful were the invisible connections that bound us all together—families, citizens, nations, hearts. How easily they could be severed.

Just the stroke of a pen, really. Just a signature on a piece of paper declaring *Yes, war, yes*.

I hope the men who did this, those powerful and vainglorious men, rot in hell.

I hope they rot there forever.

DECEMBER, 1914
LOS ANGELES, CALIFORNIA

The foamy tongue of the wave lapped over her feet in a thousand sizzling bubbles before vanishing against the sand. The Pacific Ocean was cobalt and glitter, although, if Rita was being honest, not as warm as she'd thought it would be.

Inez stood at her side, feet planted in the surf like Rita's, hands planted on her hips like Rita's, her blond braid swaying with the wind. They stood in silence, in similar but not-quite-matching black bathing costumes, both of them gazing out at the horizon.

It was their first time in California, although Rita had been here over a month already, shooting Cecil B. DeMille's romantic thriller. Inez had arrived just yesterday, after long hours and hours aboard trains, ready for a two-week respite in this sun-soaked land. The first thing she asked to see was the beach.

"Santa Monica," Cecil had advised, when Rita had telephoned him to ask about the best one to visit. The shooting schedule was so intense she'd barely glimpsed anything beyond the sleepy hills and vales of Hollywood and Burbank, but even Cecil allowed Sundays off. "Or more specifically, Ocean Park. The streetcars won't get you all the way there, though. I'll send an auto. No, don't," he interrupted, as she started to thank him. "The call for Monday is six in the morning. The last thing I need is for you to take the wrong line and end up in goddamned Reseda."

So here they were, two young women from far, far away, enjoying the tug and surge of the newly acquainted Pacific along their ankles, allowing it to rock them both in its timeless rhythm thanks to the generosity, or unvarnished practicality, of the famed Mr. DeMille.

Cutters and sloops with sharp white sails glided by. Yachts, thicker and heavier, moved far more slowly in regal rows. Seagulls and brown pelicans squawked and soared, kiting beneath silvery clouds.

A pack of golden-skinned children splashed nearby, slapping palms in some game of their own invention, darting in and out of the waves. Well beyond them, the Municipal Pier stretched its long, concrete pilings far out into the water, so far Rita could hardly make out the end of it, its wooden-planked top swarming with people. From this distance, the pier looked sprinkled with ants, scores of bodies coming and going.

"It's not quite the Thames, is it?" said Inez.

"Not quite."

"It smells nicer, for one thing."

"Bluer," said Rita, after a moment.

Inez flicked a hand toward the water. "More rich people. I don't think I've ever seen so many yachts in one place before, not even in Monte Carlo. Where are they all going?"

"Here and there and anywhere. I don't believe *going* is the point. Just seeing and being seen aboard one's floating mansion, I imagine."

The surf rushed and retreated, rushed and retreated; the sand gradually crept higher, engulfing their feet. Neither of them said aloud what both were surely thinking, which was how serene it was here, how idyllic, how far from the reality of boiling blood and guns and regiments of eager young men that were now everything and all back home.

"How is your count?" Inez asked.

Rita smiled. "Still handsome, still wonderful. A letter a week, which I appreciate. How is your husband?"

"Still handsome, still wonderful. I don't get a letter a week, though. I'm envious of you."

Rita looked at her. Inez had her eyes closed, her chin lifted. The sun sculpted her profile in bright lines, tipped her brown lashes translucent. "Do you know where he is now?"

"No. It's been . . . difficult, occasionally. Especially after . . ." Her left hand lifted, passed briefly over her womb before falling to her side again.

The wind changed direction, tossed Rita's hair into her face. She pushed it back. "I'm sorry I wasn't there with you in New York when it happened."

"It's all right. You have your obligations here. To be honest, I hardly knew I was *enceinte* before I wasn't. And this was the fourth time. I guess—I guess I'm more used to it now."

"Next time. You'll have all the luck in the world next time."

"Yes." Inez opened her eyes and smiled, but her lashes were now moist. "Next time."

A trio of sandpipers dashed near, almost close enough to touch. They pecked at the sand, chasing clam bubbles as the foam pulled back into the glass sea.

"I did receive a letter from Maman," Inez said. "I'm sure you get the same news from her as I do, but apparently Alfred is itching to enlist. There's a whole group of them from Medmenham who plan to sign up together next August, as soon as they all come of age. They want to be in a pals battalion together."

"What does Maman think?"

"She didn't say, but how could she not be beside herself? You know Alfred, though. Once he gets an idea in his head, he doesn't let go of it."

Rita gave a laugh. "Remember when he was so determined to get to Antarctica? And he thought if he could sneak away to the docks in London, he could find a ship to take him?"

"Thank heavens Father caught him trying to hide the sugar pot in his school satchel, the one he meant to sell for his fare. Who knows how far that pot would have gotten him?"

"Well, it was only silver plate. He didn't have the sense to nick the solid sterling one, so probably no farther than a knock on the head for his troubles."

They both laughed then, softly beneath the wind; the children splashed and screeched. A small, perfect cowrie shell tumbled by the sisters' toes with the next gushing wave, smooth and glossy, cream and hazel and brown. Inez bent and scooped it up before it was sucked away again. She didn't lift it to the light to examine it, as Rita would have, but only kept it between her fingers and thumb, rubbing it over and over, like a solitary bead from a rosary.

"Perhaps the war will be over by August anyway. Apparently back home they're saying it will only take months to defeat the kaiser. The papers and government officials, I mean. They've said it from the beginning."

"Perhaps," Rita said, without pointing out that the war had already chewed through six brutal months and millions of souls, with no clear end in sight.

Inez turned to her. "I think you should marry him. Your devoted count. Honestly, Rita, marry him and be happy."

Rita had a brief and unwelcome flash of Freddy, his face from that night in the alleyway, one eye already swelling shut as he smiled down at her and helped her to her feet. Even then, he smelled of gin and ambition, and she'd found it so stupidly wonderful.

"I might." She lifted a leg, extending it in front of her long and straight like a ballerina, marveling at the fact of her bare shin and ankle in public daylight. She flexed her toes, and wet sand dribbled back to the earth. "Someday," she added, and went back to balancing on both feet.

"Don't wait for someday. Don't wait for a dream to become real. Take the reality and make it your dream."

"You've turned into a philosopher, I see."

"No. I'm just sort of standing apart now, if that makes sense."

Rita sent her a quizzical look.

"I'm a wife," Inez said, earnest, "and I adore being a wife. Someday, God willing, I'll be a mother too. But when George is gone, I feel almost like I'm not around anymore. Almost like I'm a creature born of his glow. I can thrive there, but nowhere else. Even on the trains, even on my way here, I would catch my own reflection in the windows, with all the prairies and mountains rushing by, and I was a ghost against them. I was less."

"You're not a ghost," Rita countered, more harshly than she intended. "You are real and alive for all of us, not just him, trains or glow or whatnot. You always have been."

"Oh, gosh, I'm saying it all wrong. Don't get upset. I don't think I'm nothing without George. I'm simply so much better with him than without, that's all. And that's love, isn't it? He's my heart and hope. When he's away, especially when I don't know where he is or how he is, it's—it's as if I can't quite take a full breath any longer. I need him beside me to inhale, exhale, and without him, I can't quite remember how to do any of it. Or at least I can't until I know he's safe." She beamed up at Rita. "That's what I hope for you, too, with Giuseppe. That you find that pure, deeply moored love that pumps your heart and fills your lungs, and you exist for each other."

"Good gracious," she said, truly appalled. "No, thank you!"

Inez laughed, unoffended, facing the ocean again. Rita only stared at her, replaying her words in her mind, trying to find the flaw in her reasoning—because to exist only for another was certainly flawed, wasn't it; it would be a weakness, and who would hope for that? Strength was what carried anyone forward. Especially a woman. Especially a woman ensnared by love, whatever that was.

But all she saw was her beloved little sister, her cheeks and chin and nose already turning pink, her hair tangled with sunshine. Her body slightly too thin, too frail to be fashionable.

It's been so long since we've seen each other, she thought. *It's been too long, and she's changed so much. Sage and breakable at once. When did that happen?*

Inez finally stopped rubbing the shell, gave it a bounce in her palm. "Everything's so vibrant and alive here, even this close to Christmas. Is it always like this? Palm trees and green grass and blossoms, all year long?"

"I think so," Rita said, glad for a tamer topic. "It reminds me of Italy, actually. Or parts of Spain."

"Yes, you're right." Inez lifted the hand without the shell to shield her eyes, taking in the dark blue waves. "It reminds me of God, and faith. That no matter what else happens, what else is taken from us ... what other troubles mankind may invent, near or far, surely this will remain. The sun, the sky. This wide ocean and the blessed air."

And us, Rita added silently, studying her sister, her somber grace, her delicate beauty, undimmed even beneath the Southern California sun. *Surely, Lord, save this, save us, her and me. Or just her, only her and our family and Giuseppe, and whatever else is good in the world.*

Amen.

THE NEWSPAPERS STILL routinely referred to her as an ingénue, as in, *lovely Miss Rita Jolivet, ingénue of Broadway,* but more and more the words *moving-picture actress* were beginning to appear beside her name. Charles Frohman was busy working his usual behind-the-scenes magic on her behalf; gossip sheets dropped pieces of her life into the open maw of the public's appetite for anything shiny and tinseled and larger than life.

Ingénue Rita Jolivet, a moving-picture actress of royal French descent, is testing her skills here in the good ole U.S. of A., courtesy of Mr. C. B. DeMille, director of Brewster's Millions, *that runaway success ...*

Popular moving-picture actress Rita Jolivet has been snapped up by the Lasky Feature Play Company. Expect to see her on your hometown silver screen sometime next spring, where she'll be playing heiress Delight Warren in a spectacular new romance ...

Actress Rita Jolivet has been a busy bee! Not only has this bewitching young lady been seen of late in the company of her delectable costar House Peters, it's rumored she keeps her own Italian nobleman on a gilded leash, at her beck and call ...

Say Adieu to the War Blues! Sultry pearl Rita Jolivet (Rita supposed they'd unearthed that little gem when following up on the tittle-tattle about Giuseppe), *Lasky's beguiling new photoplay actress, has been a welcome sight in town along with her sister, famed violinist Leigh Vernon, fresh from her smashing success at the Met* (New York, *darlings, for those of you not in the know). These glamor-*

*ous gals have lent our humble hills some serious sparkle! Mrs. Vernon
is said to be a favorite of Tsar Nicholas himself, who supposedly gifted
her a diamond the size of a quail's egg upon her marriage . . .*

"WHEN DOES IT stop?" Inez tossed the broadsheet to the glass-
and-granite table that separated the hotel suite's dining area
from its reading and writing area.

"It never stops." Rita lifted her cup of coffee to her lips, her
feet propped on the pouf in front of her chair. Inez, seated at
the table, began to pick apart a blueberry muffin with her
fingers. "Nor do we want it to."

The hotel was nestled in the hills above the city proper,
plain on the outside, splendid on the inside, well known for
its discretion regarding its distinguished guests. Maids and
page boys were always pleasant and smiling, no matter the
task; the servers in the madly expensive café and restaurant
were never tipped—too bourgeois—yet would do practically
anything to satisfy their customers, even if it meant ordering
some special meal from a rival establishment and presenting
it under glass. The air always smelled of irises, from the many
vases lining the halls, and the view from the windows showed
the living city sprawling below, streets and buildings and
houses forever. At night, the land glinted with electric lights,
like countless silent fireflies hovering just above the earth.

Rita had been given a two-bedroom suite, but Inez was the
first person to use the second bedroom. Maman and Papa remained ensconced at Winter Queen, no doubt attempting to
dissuade their son from doing anything rash, and Giuseppe
hadn't yet had the chance to wrap up any of his affairs for a
visit. Crossing the Atlantic had become an increasingly peril-
ous notion these days, anyway. The Germans were holding
back attacking neutral-flagged ships (including American and
Italian ones, since neither country had entered the war), but
it seemed everything else was fair game for the U-boats.

As the subject of salacious articles herself, Rita was the last person to lend automatic credence to the pressmen's stories, but paper after paper described the *Unterseeboote* in uniformly ominous terms: sleek, highly advanced, dark and deadly. For years, Kaiser Wilhelm had lavished funds on his navy, his favorite pet project, and his fleet of submarines were physical proof of the success of his ambitions. They were iron sharks beneath the water, always moving, always hunting.

Los Angeles, with its golden people and golden beaches and hills, seemed a dreamy universe apart from dark things. Only the papers reflected the faraway truth. Ships torpedoed, trenches filled with mud and men, battle lines shifting. There were days Rita couldn't bear to glance at anything beyond the headlines. California dazzled her eyes, and the movie busied her body and mind.

Maybe it would be different once she returned to Manhattan. Maybe the East Coast, sharing that vast Atlantic with the shores of Great Britain and Europe, felt the bite of war more keenly.

It was the second Sunday of Inez's visit. Last night they'd stayed up too late playing poker with House, his wife, Mae, and Alvin, the movie's sharp-eyed cinematographer, who'd cleaned them all out. (Despite what the gossip sheets implied, Rita's relationship with House Peters was as platonic as could be; anyone could see he was devoted to his pretty wife.) The evening had ended in clouds of cigarette smoke and laughter and too much champagne, so instead of rushing to the beach or museums or anywhere else this morning, Rita and Inez had slept and slept, rising only when the brunch tray Rita had ordered the night before arrived.

She stirred another spoonful of sugar into her coffee. "The moment the press begins to lose interest in us, either of us, the public loses interest in us."

"The sooner the better, as far as I'm concerned. Regarding the gossip columns, at least."

"Fine, then. Nor do *I* want it to stop."

"Even when they print such things about Giuseppe?"

"Giuseppe wholeheartedly supports my career. He's aware of Charles's wily publicity campaign, the teasing leaks of information that link us together. He promised to come to New York for the premiere of *The Unafraid* in April, and then everyone will know we're a couple. We'll be deliriously, openly in love. Americans adore an aristocratic romance, and ours will complement the movie quite nicely."

Inez dropped her forehead into the palm of her hand with a groan. "That is not what I meant when I said I hoped you'd love him."

"I know. But this is what love feels like for me, and I like it. He likes it. We're both happy enough, so where's the harm?"

Inez returned to the remains of her muffin, pushing crumbs across the plate with her thumb, not meeting Rita's eyes.

"What?" Rita said, alert.

"Nothing. I'm glad you're happy."

"Yes, I can tell. You sound immensely glad. If you have something more to say, say it."

Inez plucked a fresh muffin from the basket on the table—this one cranberry—and began breaking it apart too.

"Sissy..."

"All right. I'm not supposed to tell you, but he bought you a ring."

Rita's mouth went dry. *A ring*, she wanted to say, but couldn't, because her bravado had dried up too. *So? He's wealthy, he's devoted, he's already given me jewels, brooches and necklaces and bangles. Also, what kind of a ring?*

Inez abandoned the muffin, shoved both the plate and the basket away with impatient hands. "He wrote to ask me what your favorite gemstone was, and whether I thought you'd like platinum better or gold. I told him emeralds and platinum. So I imagine he's bringing a nice, fancy emerald ring to New York with him, set in platinum, probably sprinkled with a few diamonds for good measure, because it will be, after all, an engagement ring. For this romance of yours that the papers will adore."

Disaster. Elation. She was swooping up and down inside, excited and scared and worried and yes, even a little bit angry, because he said he'd wait for her, wait for *her* to decide, and now he wasn't. He was taking matters into his own hands, carving their path forward by himself, and she still wasn't ready to hear that word. *Contessa.*

Wife.

Inez narrowed her eyes at her from across the table. "It's supposed to be a surprise."

"I don't like surprises."

"You love surprises."

"Only the proper kind. Ones of my choosing."

"Then how could it be—never mind. The point is, he's coming with a ring. So, I suppose, act surprised, whatever else you do." A pause. Then: "Are you going to say yes?"

"Honestly," Rita answered slowly, "I don't know."

Outside the pristine glass windows shone a sky so blue it was nearly painful to behold, and a slope of vivid manicured lawn that ended in a long hedge of bush anemone, thick with white flowers. Just in Rita's view, a rabbit sat very still in the shadow of the hedge, small and brown and brave.

"I'm going to think about it," she said. The rabbit took a single hop forward, briefly lit with sun, then leapt back to the shadows again. "Just as I have been for months. I promise I have been."

Inez stood, came to press her hand to Rita's shoulder.

"Did I get the ring right, at least?"

Rita reached up, covered her sister's hand with her own. "Heart of my heart, soul of my soul, of course you did. How wise he was to ask you."

"I rather thought so, too."

ALVIN THE CINEMATOGRAPHER, he of the very sharp eye, had taken one look at Inez as they were introduced on poker night, clapped a hand over his heart, and exclaimed, "Those peepers! I'm slain!"

It was Alvin who convinced Cecil to cast her as an extra, for just a single day of shooting—all right, two, probably; she was promised the time would fly by—and it was Rita who convinced Inez to accept. Right before she left sunny California to head back to snowy New York, Inez was hustled to the movie set, a convincingly gothic interior of a Montenegrin castle, painted backdrops of jagged mountain peaks visible through the windows. A solitary staircase climbed up one wall before ending abruptly, and a bit dangerously, beyond the camera's view, three stories high among the light rafters.

A half hour after Inez went into Costumes, she emerged as a maid in a long gray dress only slightly too large, a square apron, a frilled cap covering a falling mess of curls.

She sat beside Rita as the makeup artist transformed her face, a pale cream foundation to even everything out, and then her eyes and cheekbones and brows and lips returned, redrawn with kohl and rouge and tinted powders. She seemed both fascinated and appalled by what was happening, staring at herself in the mirror with round eyes.

"I don't know..." she began at least three times, and each time Rita would laugh and tell her it was so simple, so fun, so easy. All she had to do was curtsy to Rita and House (playing the Montenegrin prince who kidnaps Rita's American heiress) when they passed and stare after them with something like curiosity, or longing.

And then do the same thing when handing a bouquet of flowers to the prince to give to the heiress.

And again when the prince bends his knee to propose, with the maid caught breathless in the background.

"This is what Alvin meant by your eyes," Rita told her. "Your beautiful, expressive eyes. Literal pools of light, I swear. The camera's going to love you. Maybe we'll have to start filming photoplays together from now on."

"Oh, no! This is it! You're a madwoman! I'm a madwoman to even consider this."

But of course, even through the takes and retakes, the hours spent waiting for the perfect light adjustment, the perfect camera angle to be decided, the perfect edit or addition to the script, it *was* fun. House and all the other actors were so kind to the sister of their star, so patient. Cecil told her exactly where to stand, where to look, and for how long. At one point, after their third take of the proposal scene, the famed director wove his way around the set furniture to Inez, leaned close and whispered something into her ear that had her dissolving into laughter.

That was what Rita would always remember about their last good day together, what she would cherish: her sister in that maid's outfit and cap, holding her arms together over her stomach, bent nearly double with mirth. She laughed so hard she cried, and the makeup artist had to come and retouch everything around her eyes. But Cecil's ploy worked, and after that, Inez's stiffness melted away, her uncertainty, her cumbersome shyness.

Just as Rita had predicted, Inez shone on film. She was luminous, always so luminous, even in the background.

Chapter 13

I was so sorry to miss the premiere, I truly was. I did read about it, though, back in England. We all did, Maman and Papa and Alfred and I. *The Sketch* had a photograph of you and Giuseppe walking arm in arm into the theatre. You were stunning in spangles, looking straight at the camera with a smile, but the count was looking at only you, rapt.

Through some quirk of the camera or the lens (I'm not sure what), the sparkles from the circlet of diamonds in your hair were captured as well, but they were refracted, forming this most astonishing circle of lights around your head. It looked as though you wore a crown of stars. Perhaps that was why that particular image was printed everywhere.

You looked celestial.

And amid all those distracting lights and famous faces, the photographers begging for your attention, it was so obvious from even that single shot that, for Giuseppe, you were all that mattered. Crown or no, you were his queen.

APRIL, 1915
MANHATTAN, NEW YORK

New York *was* a darker place now in nearly every way, talk of the war threading its way through even the most mundane conversations. *Here's your coffee and change, Joe, and, say, did you hear about them Huns and that poison gas they're using now? Not just tear gas anymore but chlorine gas, for chrissakes, chlorine. Melts your lungs right in your chest, drowns you right then and there in your own juices . . .*

Spies were rumored to be listening around corners. Diplomats from opposing nations took their meals in the same exclusive restaurants, eyeing each other across the tables while offering sarcastic toasts and sneers. The United States remained officially neutral, though the fact that she openly supplied munitions to the Allies chafed the Central Powers beyond measure. Germany was said to have covert operatives stationed all along the coast, and especially in New York, with orders to sabotage any ship carrying soldiers or arms. Even ordering a bratwurst from a street cart was cause for suspicion now: slow, measuring looks from passersby, ears primed for a whisper of any language other than English. Did they add mustard or ketchup to their meal? Because only a Hun would use mustard . . .

One by one, the historic German carts and butcheries and beer gardens run by generations of immigrants or their descendants were either closing down or changing their names. Herr Schmidt was now Mr. Smith. Jägers Metzgerei became Hunter's Fine Meats. Löwes Biergarten was now the Lion's Den.

No one trusted anyone else these days; no one was *truly* neutral, *truly* safe . . . although, as Rita lazed in a ribbon of lemony light that fell through her open bedroom window, listening to the call of a mourning dove on the sill, she imagined she'd be forgiven for thinking thoughts of peace.

Giuseppe was still asleep, a faint blue-dusky shadow of beard defining his lips and jaw, one arm flung above his head against the pillow. He was tired, this lovely tanned nobleman who had arrived at the smoky confusion of New York's piers only hours ago, not much before dawn.

She'd sent her auto for him, down to Cunard's Pier 54, because the liner was late and who knew how quickly he'd be able to procure a taximeter cab at the ungodly hour of three-thirty in the morning all the way at the west end of Fourteenth, if at all. She'd waited up until he'd arrived, putting a serious dent in a pot of coffee she'd brewed herself, since her cook had retired long past.

Then he was here, slightly more disheveled than usual, even more handsome and precious than usual, because he'd come all this way for her, just for her, braving the U-boats and who knew what else, rogue waves, icebergs, the cold spring storms that could swirl across the North Atlantic with the whip-crack ferocity of a toddler's tantrum, screaming along the waves.

She'd argued with him, via telegram, not to take a Cunard steamer, or a White Star steamer, or any steamer that was British-flagged. But he'd replied that as he was already in London for business, there was no time to travel to another departure point, and all the American liners were full. He'd booked a ticket for the *Lusitania*, and everything was going to be fine. She was the swiftest passenger ship afloat these days, in addition to being the most famous and foremost. The Germans wouldn't dare target her, but even if they did, her top speed was twenty-five knots, twice as fast needed to outrun a U-boat. Rita needn't worry. He'd ended the last telegram with: BE WITH YOU SOON MY MARGHERITA, and there was nothing she could do after that. There was nothing she could do before it, either, but at least she'd tried.

Now here he was in the flesh, the tempting toned flesh, his face peaceful, close to angelic, really, if she considered it. A dusky tanned angel fallen here into her bed, and he lost none of his beauty in repose. She sat up carefully and drew her knees to her chest, much like she'd done as a younger woman years past, examining the very first man she'd ever kissed and embraced and tumbled with into the delirium of wedlock. There was none of the disappointment she'd felt back then, taking in the drooling mess of Freddy Stern. There was only Count Giuseppe de Cippico, here and now, scented of ship and sea and salt, a hint of lavender from the sprigs Rita's housekeeper sprinkled across the stored linens.

She wondered if somewhere in his luggage there was a small, square box holding an emerald and platinum ring, sized just for her finger, then pushed the thought from her mind. Tonight was the premiere. That was all she needed to think about. That was enough.

But still she followed his heartbeat, the pulse in his throat, the slow rise and fall of his chest. She watched him until the ribbon of light shifted, sliding off the bed to warm the floor, and the dove flew off in a soft, musical murmur of wings, hurrying toward a different world.

HE DID NOT ask her to marry him. All damned day long, he didn't ask her. She was primed for it, waiting, and as the hours passed, her nerves grew more taut, but he was nothing but easy smiles and teasing banter, wondering which cufflinks he should wear tonight, which shoes. He'd never been to an American movie premiere before, only Italian ones.

"I can't imagine it's all that different," Rita had said.

"But it is. It's your photoplay debut in this country, a major film, and you're the star. So of course it's different." He turned to his valet, switching to Italian. "I think the gold knot cufflinks, yes? They photograph better than the moonstone."

"Sì, conte."

It was four o'clock now, less than an hour before they had to leave. She was leaning a shoulder against the doorframe to his room, already dressed in a bespoke Lucile gown of indigo crêpe de chine trimmed with peacock feathers and sequins, a slender cut that hugged her figure and ended in a long, tiered train. Her hair was laced with diamonds, her face highlighted with a hint of cosmetics. Her wrists were dabbed with a Parisian perfume her mother had given her last Christmas, one with notes of violets and tuberose and phlox. It reminded her of Winter Queen, as no doubt Pauline intended.

The valet moved to the leather jewelry case (no ring box in view, not that Rita could see), finding the correct cufflinks, returning the moonstone ones to their sliding drawer. The count lifted his arms, straightened his cuffs, and his man inserted the links, fastening them with delicate care. If the valet had an opinion about his employer crossing the ocean to share an apartment with an unmarried woman, he was smart enough to keep it to himself. Besides, she'd gone through the social niceties of ordering the spare room freshened up for her lover, even if he only used it to dress.

The undressing, *naturellement*, was done in her own chamber.

There was an art to donning evening clothes, one Rita understood very well, but it came to her in that moment, observing the count and his servant complete their rituals, that she'd hardly ever watched a man dress. There had been Freddy, of course, but he was cut from a markedly different fabric than Giuseppe: shirts of worn flannel or linsey-woolsey, scratchy woolen jumpers, moleskin trousers and leather work gloves stained with grease. Everything donned quickly, efficiently, arms crammed through sleeves already rolled up, head popping through neck openings only partially unbuttoned. Messy hair and a boyish grin if he caught her looking. On their wedding day, he'd traded his usual flat cap for a billycock she hadn't even known he'd owned, but that was about it. At least he'd forgone the work gloves, normally stuffed in a back pocket.

But here was Giuseppe, and it was like watching a man—a man, not a boy—from another realm, another time and place compared to Freddy. Every movement was deliberate, graceful; every item of attire properly cleaned, bleached, starched, buttoned, brushed.

A silk dress shirt. Cotton piqué waistcoat. Gold studs, narrow white bow tie, black tailcoat. A black silk scarf (her Christmas gift to him) and custom white kid gloves so fine they could be worn only once before stretching out. He had pair after pair of them, ordered from the best shop in Rome.

She felt almost sedate, watching him. Not sedate, perhaps... more like content. Goodness knew she had every reason to feel content with him, especially after this morning, after he'd finally opened his eyes and turned to her in the mess of the sheets and reached for her—but there was something so intimate about this small, private ceremony unfolding before her, in her guest room. Small moments, small details: his top hat ready and waiting on the dresser. His walking stick propped against the kingwood footboard of the bed. The quilted satin smoking jacket, still on its hanger in the open portmanteau, that no doubt he'd wear later on tonight, after the film, after the parties, after they'd returned home.

There was a kind of satisfaction in witnessing the minutiae of his life, the everyday seconds that built and built to become the scaffolding of his world. Motions and thoughts, signatures of who he was, how he preferred to live, routines becoming habits, habits that stretched into a lifetime.

She was thinking about that now, Rita had to admit. His lifetime. Her lifetime, with him. She was, she was, there was no denying it.

But I don't want to need him.

AT FIVE-THIRTY PRECISELY, the silver Winton limousine Cecil had sent for them rolled to a dignified halt at the curb of the theatre. One of the studio assistants standing at attention nearby leapt to open the door. Giuseppe climbed out first, smiling at the sudden bursts of light from the news photographers. He turned his back to them to offer his hand to Rita, who accepted it as gracefully as she could while still keeping the layers of her gown over her ankles. Then they were smiling together, strolling along a long runner of crimson that would show up as matte black in all the photographs, her left arm tucked in his, her right hand lifted, waving, but slow enough and low enough so that nothing in the printed images would turn out blurred near her face.

She watched the movie with an acute focus she'd never found before, not even when attending the premiers of her photoplays back in Italy. She watched herself on the screen, scrutinizing every gesture, every look, every quirk of her lips, every arch of an eyebrow, and still she couldn't tell if any of it was any good. At the time, cushioned in the warm embrace of the City of Angels, Rita had felt confident in her role, secure in Cecil's direction and her own instincts, but now...

She sat in the middle row of the seats, Giuseppe to her left, Cecil to her right. Two places away from Charles. Whenever the audience reacted to a certain scene—laughing, sighing, gasping—she checked their faces, these men of hers, to see if Cecil was as pleased as everyone else, or Charles as absorbed. If Giuseppe was chuckling.

Only Cecil seemed as focused as she, his expression never betraying an inkling of emotion. The only time she saw his face change was when the final title card appeared, an elegant, cursive *The End*, and the screen went blank and the house lights resumed, and he came to his feet amid the deafening applause, offering a brief bow to the audience.

Then he smiled.

"WHERE'S YOUR HEAVENLY sister?" Alvin demanded later that
night at the cast party at the Astor Gallery in the Waldorf-
Astoria.

"Back in England, visiting our parents." Rita offered a nod
to a trio of Lasky starlets staring at her from across the
chamber with eyes that might have held envy, or admiration,
or both; she couldn't tell from this distance. "And careful
there," she added, turning back to the cinematographer. "She's
a married lady, you know."

He lifted his cocktail glass in salute. "Well, then, tell her
from me when *that* doesn't work out, I'm very available..."

They laughed and toasted each other, her Rob Roy slipping
fragrant just over the rim of her glass, sprinkling her fingers.

It was a great party, a swell party to celebrate *The Unafraid*,
filled with stars and starlets, with producers and directors and
writers and wives, a few high-rolling finance types, mostly un-
deremployed scions of wealthy families, scattered throughout.
(*Someone has to front the cash*, Charles had told her, when she'd
asked about the pack of laughing, red-cheeked young men at
the bar, drinking glass after glass. *It makes them feel important,
and trust me, their wallets aren't even dented.*)

The room was long and lined with seven floor-to-ceiling windows on one side and even more French doors on the other side,
tipped with gilded metal braces and elaborate plaster wreaths,
murals above each of gods and men, the twelve months and
four seasons depicted in pastels of blue and cream and gray and
green. The middle set of windows opened up like the French
doors to a wide balcony overlooking Thirty-Fourth Street.
They were open now, so beneath the laughter and chatter and
the music of the string quartet stationed in the main gallery,
there came the constant low hubbub of automobiles hemming
and hawing along, the iron clatter of horse's hooves, men and
women's voices, all lifted skyward by a breezed scented of ex-

haust and spring and tarry macadam. Every now and then a motorcar backfired, *pow!*, like a gunshot ricocheting through the streets, but no one in the gallery flinched.

Giuseppe stood on that balcony, sipping his own Rob Roy while listening with a furrowed brow to one of the finance scions, she thought, a rusty-haired fellow who was talking with his hands (no drink in them, at least) in grand, sweeping gestures. The fellow paused for a breath, and the count said something Rita couldn't hear, but it set off the scion once more, his voice rising, his hands moving to sculpt the conversation as a conductor might an orchestra's concerto, never still.

Rita watched Giuseppe. The hard set of his lips, the tension held in his shoulders. He lowered his eyes as he brought the cocktail back up to his mouth, and she had the feeling that the conversation had turned for him, whatever the topic was. That he could use rescuing. Even as she finished the thought, as she took that first step toward the balcony, another man walked by—staggered by, almost—coming up to the conductor scion and interrupting everything, talking and pointing back toward the band of others still at the bar. The scion nodded, made some excuse to Giuseppe, and headed her way with his comrade.

Rita kept walking. The pair of them nearly bumped into her, but the conductor managed to juke left in time, with a hasty *Pardon me, miss!*, followed instantly by the widening of his eyes as he glanced at her face.

"Oh!" he said, stopping entirely. "Excuse me! Miss Jolivet! An honor! A real honor, I swear!"

"Thank you," she replied, also stopping, since both men were mostly blocking her way.

"That was some moving picture, wasn't it? You did some job!"

"Some job," echoed the other man, with a very faint slurring of the first word, so it sounded like *sshhom.*

"Thank you," she said again. "How kind of you."

"It makes me glad just to be a part of it, you know? I mean, I'm not much, just the man behind the scenes, but I guess I played my part too, you know?"

"I do," she said gravely. "None of it would have happened without you."

"Aw," he said, and actually blushed. His companion pawed at his arm. "Well, look, it was swell running into you—"

"Almost," she corrected him, smiling.

The conductor barked a laugh. "Sure, almost! It's been swell to meet you. I'm sure we'll cross paths again soon."

"No doubt."

He winked at her—*winked*, whoever he was—and vanished back into the jaws of the party.

Rita glided out to the balcony, taking a deep breath of the tainted air. She smiled up at Giuseppe, touched a hand to his lapel as he bent down to brush his lips against her cheek.

She resisted the urge to close her eyes and rest that cheek against his tailcoat alongside her hand; all at once, her body buzzed with fatigue. She hadn't even known she was this tired until she was near him again, feeling his heat, imagining his arms around her. The solid strength of him, easily taking her weight.

She imagined they were home already, in her bed. She imagined them in Naples, or in that perfect Mediterranean paradise called Mentone, in the tiled and airy rooms of his ancestral palazzo, everything warm and perfect and golden. Colored-glass chandeliers; an emerald ring on her hand; her place right beside him, hand in hand, arm in arm, the pair of them linked and permanent.

And bound, her mind whispered. *Bound and caged.*

Instead of all of that, any of that, Rita gathered her strength and eased away from him, straightening one of the peacock feathers along her bodice that had bent just enough to tickle her collarbone.

"What were you two talking about out here? He certainly seemed animated enough about it."

"The war."

"Oh, the war," she sighed, and moved to lean against the stone railing of the balcony, almost sitting atop it. "Even here, even now?"

"Always, I think. Or—I hope not always. But yes, that's the way it feels. It's like a toxin already consumed, already racing through our veins. Inescapable, even tonight. The young man, a Mr. Belmont, I believe, is all for compulsory conscription in the Allied nations, so he says. He's convinced it will end the conflict sooner." Giuseppe paused, downed the last of his drink. "I suspect he's never fired a gun in his life, except perhaps to shoot clay birds."

She bowed her head and contemplated her hands in her lap, her own empty glass, the way the folds of her gown sifted and fell with the breeze. The subtle twinkle of spangles against indigo silk, as if she were a fragment of the night, dusted with stars. She stood and placed her glass on a wrought-iron table, turned to him, and lifted her hands.

"Shall we dance?"

He glanced around them. "Out here?"

"Sì, conte. It's the perfect place to escape toxins. A moonlit sky, no one else nearby."

"There are about a hundred and fifty other people nearby."

"But not out here with us, not right now. Right now, it's just you and me and that big fat moon shining down on us. Shadows and silver, and the music. Can you hear it? My plan is to spin you into a corner until you're dizzy, and steal kisses until neither of us can breathe."

He accepted her hands in his, pulled her closer. "Darling Margherita, you don't have to steal them. Don't you know? Every single kiss of mine already belongs to you."

So THEY DID dance, just the two of them, to the tune of *If I Had You*, just audible beneath the chatter inside the gallery and the stop-and-start snarl of traffic outside of it. A photographer's flash sent a sudden hot burst of light over them both, but Rita happened to be facing the photographer in the doorway and got the worst of it.

She stumbled a little. The photographer—one of Lasky's hired hands, no doubt—called out *Grand shot, thanks!* before retreating back into the gallery.

The blind spot in her vision was a great blue void. Giuseppe led her back to the iron table, guiding her into one of the chairs.

When she looked up again, the spot was dissolving, and he was kneeling before her.

Her heart actually skipped a beat, went ka-*thunk* inside her chest, hard and unpleasant. She realized he was still holding her hand and then couldn't stop staring down at this tender vision of the two of them joined: his darker skin against hers, his longer fingers over hers, their palms lightly touching.

Rita felt, remarkably, the return of that breath of anger in her that had first stirred to life in California, when Inez had told her about the ring.

He'd promised her he'd wait for her. Back in Naples, he'd promised her he'd wait.

"My pearl. My heart. *La mia bellissima ragazza*—"

"Giuseppe—"

"No, please. Allow me to finish." His fingers tightened. "I was going to do this later tonight, without all this"—he tipped his head toward the party—"to distract you. But you look so beautiful, and I am so proud. So proud to have you on my arm."

Her voice came cooler than she meant it to. "We agreed, I thought. We agreed to proceed slowly."

The dark slash of his brows raised, then lowered; a faint pinch appeared between them. "It's been nearly a year. Is that not slow?"

"Well, slower," she said, sitting up against the hard metal back of the chair.

He studied her, his expression caught between puzzlement and hurt, and for some reason, that made her even more angry.

"Look. I adore what we have. I thought I was clear about that."

"You were."

"Well, then! Why does anything have to change?"

"Because *I* have changed. The world has changed. You've changed too, even if you don't wish to admit it."

She opened her mouth to reply, but before she could, another flash of light burst over them, white-hot.

Damn it. The photographer, maybe the same one as before, tipped an imaginary hat from the doorway and melted off.

Rita the actress, Rita the star, understood instantly how it would appear, what the whole world would think had just been captured in that flare of light. In that one image that could and would be published anywhere. Everywhere.

They both came to their feet. She pivoted a step toward the gallery, intent on the photographer, but Giuseppe still had her by the hand.

"Are you afraid?" he asked, almost incredulous.

"I'm not afraid. It's simply that it's not the time or the place for this. I thought we had a very reasonable agreement. An adult agreement."

"Yes, we are adults. So we cannot continue to carry on as children."

"Children!"

"Adolescents. Infatuated, with nothing but pleasure before them. No future in mind."

"I have plenty of future in mind," she said, smiling through this mean and mulish ire inside of her, because it was still a party, wasn't it, and there were still loads of people watching, a couple or two spilling in now from the gallery, curious, and that bloody photographer out there somewhere. She lowered her voice. "My future right now will be to go find that man with the camera and tell him not to publish that shot. After that, we can go home and maybe *then* have a reasonable conversation. Maybe then I can remind you of everything we said before."

He looked down his nose at her, now every inch the aristocrat. "I remember everything we said before."

"Good," she snapped. She snatched back her hand and walked away.

"*Solo gli sconsiderati non considerano il futuro,*" she heard him call after her, in his velvet low baritone.

Only the reckless fail to consider the future.

But she didn't turn around, because her heart was still beating so hard, and her face was burning with rage or shame or both.

THERE WAS NO reasonable conversation later that night or any other night of his visit. There was only the two of them and a very stiff silence, awkward and awful, even as they returned to the flat, undressed, and climbed into the same bed. It wasn't the first time they didn't make love after a long day, but it was the first time, ever, that he didn't roll to his side to hold her, his breath in her hair, his arms warm. They slept as mummies entombed side by side, arms and legs rigid, never touching.

In the morning, Rita awoke before he did, but stayed as she was, staring up at the ceiling.

Her eyes were dry, and her heart returned to its normal rhythm. When she turned her head to see him, silken hair tousled, soft asleep, still with that faint pinch between his brows, all she felt was regret.

I'm sorry, was what she said as she drew her hand down his arm, causing his lashes to flutter, from sleep to watchful awake.

I'm sorry, she said again, scooting closer to him, stroking his cheek. Stubble already like sandpaper, bluish gray, very fine.

Sorry, she whispered, as he lifted that same arm to her, his palm cupping her shoulder, pulling her closer, and that lovely familiar heat rose between them.

His lips were plush and tasted of morning and forgiveness, although for the rest of his visit he never uttered the words *Marry me*, or *Will you*, or anything like it, and neither did she.

THE COUNT STAYED a week and a half, a glorious ten days, two hundred and forty hours. Many of those long, languid hours— she had no idea how many, actually—were spent entangled in her bed, the two of them celebrating the beauty of their physical relationship (*why does anything have to change?*), the electric thrill of touch and taste and friction that built and built into release. They dined in bed, they drank in bed (champagne, mostly, followed by glass after glass of water). They ignored the universe beyond her penthouse; they ignored the newspapers and the ugly, seething fact of war churning just across the ocean.

They ignored the words left unsaid between them.

For ten days, it was just them, only them. Moonlight, sunlight, starlight, and the two of them living in this temporary grace, bathed in it all.

Rita chose, deliberately, to be as delighted with the Count de Cippico in these short days as her heart would allow, because soon he'd be gone again, back to Italy, while she would return to California for her next photoplay. Fate and nature and their careers were pushing them apart, at least for now. They'd meet again in two months. Maybe three. He would come here or she would go there, but either way, they promised each other no more than three months.

Already it seemed too long to her. Already it seemed fool-ish to spend so much time apart. Sometimes, wandering around the flat in her robe (or less), she'd catch a glimpse of her own reflection in a mirror—or a window, or the glass pane of some framed picture—and think almost helplessly, *What are you doing? What are your hopes, after all this? What more can he give?*

The morning of his departure, Rita went with him to the docks. Giuseppe had capitulated to her pleas and was sailing on an American steamer headed straight for Cherbourg. She'd accompanied him onboard to his suite and kissed him goodbye with all the passion in her heart, thinking, *This is surely agony. This is surely bliss.*

This is surely love.

But all they'd said to each other was goodbye.

Amid the jostling throngs on the pier, she stood and twirled her handkerchief in the air as the steamer eased back-ward into the muddy waters of the Hudson, guided by tugs. If he was there at one of the railings, waving back at her, she couldn't pick him out.

The tugs veered away. Slowly, like an elephant lumbering down a long road, the liner slipped toward the horizon, the wharves of Hoboken hazy, fantastical shapes in the distance.

Rita waved until her arm ached. Only when the ship was a dot in the haze did she stop, turning back toward the city and dry land, cramming her handkerchief into her purse.

SIX DAYS LATER, a sharp knocking on her front door jolted her from the script she was reading in the study, her next project for Charles and Lasky, a film they wanted to be even bigger than *The Unafraid*. She pushed the pages aside on her desk, waiting for the maid to come to her and tell her who it was.

Not a who, as it turned out. A what, a telegram, a folded sheet of paper neatly tucked into a thin yellow envelope, and even before she opened it, even before she knew anything, Rita's skin crawled with alarm.

It was from Inez, still at Winter Queen:

ALFRED ENLISTED WITHOUT SAYING STOP DEPLOYING TO FRONT IN A WEEK STOP EVERYONE PROUD SAD MAD STOP COME SAY FARE-WELL QUERY

Part 3

---◦◦◦◦◦---

Chapter 14

---◦◦◦◦◦---

I forgot to ask you if you saw that warning notice from the German Embassy, the one published in the newspapers the morning of your departure. I have to think you didn't.

I wish I could tell you that I'm sorry I sent that telegram. That, in retrospect, I should have told you to stay in New York, that there wasn't time for a goodbye. I wish my heart was sorry. But I'm telling the truth in these pages, and the truth is, I'm glad you were aboard the *Lusitania* too, horrific as it was.

I'm glad he wasn't alone, surrounded by strangers.

SATURDAY, MAY 1, 1915
MANHATTAN, NEW YORK

To say the Cunard Pier was crowded that drizzly spring morning would be an amusing understatement. It teemed with people; it was surging and alive with people: passengers and crew and Cunard Company personnel, Secret Service men, private detectives, journalists, photographers, sightseers, film crews, pickpockets, spies. Nearly every one of them was focused on the colossal black-and-white ship docked at 54; nearly every one of them was talking about the notice printed in over half a dozen New York papers that very morning, the morning the Lusitania was scheduled to depart for Liverpool.

The Imperial German Embassy, the notice read, wished to remind travelers that there was a state of war between Germany and Great Britian (it was unclear if the Germans had misspelled *Britain* deliberately or not, but there it was), and anyone choosing to sail on a British-flagged ship, or one of any of her allies, was hereby politely warned that such ships were liable to destruction in the war-zone waters surrounding the British Isles.

In several papers, the warning appeared directly next to Cunard's own advertisement for the *Lusy*. The message was not subtle.

Rita, in fact, *had* seen the warning that morning over a very early breakfast of bagels and lox and freshly chopped dill. She was sleepy still, fatigued, having spent half the night wrestling with the decision of which liner to take to England. Ellen Terry, the former Lady Capulet to her Juliet, had spent nearly twenty minutes on the telephone with Rita the evening before, trying to convince Rita to join her on the American Line's *New York*, but the ship was scheduled to get in at least a day later than the *Lusitania*, maybe more, and Rita sincerely didn't know if she had an entire day to spare if she hoped to see Alfred in time.

"Surely, if it's just one day..." Ellen had coaxed, her rich voice crackling with static over the line. "Think of the fun we could have if we sailed together, darling!"

But Rita wasn't thinking of fun. She was thinking of her little brother, his golden hair, his serious smile, his undaunted ambitions. She was thinking of the stories she'd read and heard about young men just like him, brave brothers and sons *just like him*, over three million of them already dead in trenches and scattered along fields, honeycombed with bullets or blown into chunks of meat or choking on sulfur-green gas.

She was thinking, *What if he never comes back? What if I miss him by just a day, just an hour or a stupid damned minute, all because I took the safer route, the slower ship, when nothing about Alfred has ever been slow or safe?*

So Rita was still chewing her bagel and scanning headlines when she came across the warning halfway down page five of the *New York World*, framed in black. *NOTICE!* it began, and she did. She put down the bagel, picked up the paper, and read the whole thing twice, her gaze lingering on the typo; was it some sort of insult? And then, just beneath it, Cunard's advertisement listing the schedule of the *Lusitania.*

She glanced at the Sèvres mantel clock above the fireplace; it was nearly eight. The Cunard advert informed her that the *Lusitania*, the fastest and most luxurious passenger ship in the world, winner of the coveted Blue Riband for crossing the Atlantic in under five days, would depart for England this morning at ten o'clock.

She ate the last bite of bread, took a hard swallow of coffee, and rang for her maid. Now that her mind was made up, she'd have to hurry.

BUT GOODNESS, THE pier was crowded. It seemed like half of the city had shown up to gawk at the liner, at the passengers who were bold enough or foolish enough to decide that the German warning was nothing but bombast and bluster. Yes, the *Lusy* was British-flagged. But she also routinely carried Americans across the sea, usually wealthy Americans, important ones, Rockefellers and Roosevelts and Astors. It would be the most foolish decision of all to torpedo her and risk the wrath of the United States by killing her citizens. Everyone knew the last thing the kaiser wanted was to draw America into the war.

By the time Rita had booked her ticket and secured a porter to direct her trunks to the escalator that reached from the dock to the baggage hold inside the liner, the clouds had more or less thinned into a gauzy layer of gray, and the rain that had sprinkled down since early that morning had dried like tears already forgotten. A cool sky arched above the chaos below, dotted with seabirds, with the temperature more reminiscent of March than May. It was five minutes to ten, she had cut the timing *that* close, and as Rita struggled through the knots of people, she was truly worried she wouldn't reach the gangplank in time.

A man in a brown homburg turned a camera her way, lifting it for a shot; instinctively she paused and smiled at the lens. *Always look beautiful, always look professional, friendly, even when people are shoving you and stepping on your toes and yelling in your ears.*

But far more of the cameras were aimed up at the razor-sharp lines of the ship herself, accompanied by hefty doses of gallows humor.

"Did you get it, Eli?"

"Sure did. Last snap of the *Lusitania!*"

"It'll be worth a fortune by next week!"

"Har!"

THREE YEARS EARLIER, almost exactly, on a gloomy and rainy night, the RMS *Carpathia* had glided slowly and expertly up to this very same pier, surrounded by uninvited tugboats, surrounded by shouting pressmen, with thousands of people ashore pressed shoulder to shoulder, eagerly awaiting her arrival. Rita had seen pictures of it—well, everyone had; the whole world had—so many pictures in the papers back then, showing the near-hysterical crowds, showing the worn and exhausted survivors of the RMS *Titanic* disaster disembarking from the ship.

She recalled two of the images quite clearly, and whenever the memory of them happened to resurrect in her thoughts,

Rita always felt an uncomfortable welling dread, subtle but definitely there, creeping along her nervous system, because she had crossed the Atlantic so many times before without incident, because she had been so lucky so many times, but luck could always run out.

The first was of *Titanic*'s junior wireless officer, who had to be carried off the steamer because, even though he was alive, one ankle was badly twisted and his other foot was dead, unusable, blackened flesh wrapped in bandages. A brave young officer with a grimace on his face, who, by his own admission, had likely killed a man in the great liner's final moments because the man was trying to steal his comrade's lifebelt.

The other was of the winsome Mrs. Astor, infamous bride and now suddenly teenaged widow of John Jacob Astor IV, obviously pregnant, obviously in shock, her face white as snow and her lips parted as she was being escorted away. Eventually it was revealed that she'd been a heroine in her own right, helping to row her lifeboat for hours, giving away her fur coat and shawl to third-class passengers who had nothing but cotton on their backs. But in the picture that Rita remembered, Madeleine Astor was caught too near the hungry crowd, and there were hands reaching for her from that seething, shadowy mass, so many hands trying to touch her, grab her, tear at her as she stared back at them with wide, startled eyes.

Now here Rita was on the same pier, maybe even struggling along the same path as Mrs. Astor once did, who knew. She thought there were surely as many people packing the wharf and grandstands now as there were in those photographs capturing the rough and ragged end of the *Titanic* survivors' journey. Press everywhere, cameras everywhere, even motion-picture cameras. But the passengers heading toward the *Lusitania* were neither rough nor ragged. Their journey was ahead of them, not behind.

"Of course it's safe, madam." A Cunard man in a Harris tweed jacket was speaking in a plummy, reassuring voice to an elderly woman in a fox stole and a hat trembling with silk petunias. "There isn't a U-boat in the world that can catch up with this ship. She's the greyhound of the seas, you know."

The gentleman standing next to the lady spoke up. "And there will be a Royal Navy escort, Mother, through Great Britain's waters. Is that not so, sir?"

"Absolutely. We have the guarantee of the Admiralty itself. Once she reaches our waters, *Lusitania* will be escorted by no less than two destroyers all the way to Liverpool Harbour."

"Only two?" the woman said, as her flowers bobbed nervously.

"Two more than even necessary, I assure you. You'll be safe as houses aboard our ship, madam."

Rita repeated that under her breath, *safe as houses.* Naturally they would be. Because they'd be traveling on the fastest steamer to be found, winner of that international Blue Riband that Cunard had plucked straight from the previous winner, a German liner. Plus those destroyers awaiting them, bristling with arms, with eagle-eyed sailors ready to blow up a U-boat a mile off.

The Cunard man was right; he had to be. There was no genuine peril, just nerves, just rumors. Just that ruddy notice in the papers, a slap of German bravado, no doubt meant to rattle everyone's bones.

The man was still speaking, but his eyes were scanning the mob. "I fear the time is getting on, though. May I conduct you to the saloon-class line? Just this way, if you please."

Rita followed them, keeping a wary eye on that gangplank. According to her corsage watch, ten o'clock had come and gone and she'd heard no *All ashore!* gongs ringing out. Droves of people still milled about, groups of families or friends laughing, pointing at the ship, her impressive four funnels and steep, towering sides that loomed seven stories above them. The colorful alphabet flags strung from her masts that snapped in the breeze.

Instead of the usual red-and-black Cunard bands, the funnels were now painted entirely black, along with most of the rest of the ship. Only the topsides remained white. Even the enormous gold lettering along the stern, LUSITANIA, LIVERPOOL, was covered in black paint.

Fat plumes of smoke puffed lazily from three of those four funnels, rolling up toward the clouds. No one seemed in any particular hurry to board the ship, and the ship seemed in no particular hurry to leave.

Trailing behind the lady in the hat, Rita began inching her way up the gangplank, toward the open doors of the Shelter Deck, her valise and suitcase in hand. She hadn't bothered bringing her maid, not on such short notice. She'd be assigned a stewardess for her stateroom anyway, so no sense in upending anyone else's life but her own for this trip.

The wind gusted, tearing at her hat and hems. Stories below her, the murky waters of the Hudson River splashed and hissed against wooden pilings and the bottom of the ship.

Safe as houses. They had to be, because the *Lusy* was her key to reaching Alfred in time, and, by God, she *was* going to reach him in time.

ONCE ABOARD—ONCE PAST the youngish, russet-haired officer who welcomed her and checked his paperwork and informed her very courteously that the grand staircase was just over there, Miss *Jaw-liv-it,* one level down for cabin D-15, and the electric lifts were just there as well, if she preferred—Rita took a deep, relieved breath. She'd never been on the *Lusitania* before, but she had traveled more than once on the *Mauretania,* her sister ship, now commandeered by the Royal Navy. The layout was familiar. She didn't need the officer's gesture toward the stairs or the pair of elevators with their elaborate filigreed

grills, which had clusters of passengers waiting before them anyway, every bench nearby occupied. She'd take the stairs.

It seemed the interior of the ship was hardly less crowded
than the pier. People were schooling like fish, masses of them
pooling here and there, clogging doorways and hallways, discussing the Italian walnut paneling, the gold-leaf trim work,
the dense jade carpeting and fluted columns, the double-tiered
dining saloon and stained-glass ceilings. It was all so familiar
that Rita found herself relaxing into the promise of the *Lusitania*'s elegance, of its assurance of wealth and stability, where
nothing untoward could possibly occur. Nothing could pierce
this bubble of luxury, because every inch of it had been designed and constructed to safeguard some of the most powerful people in the world.

And for a while, six days (more or less), Rita would be safe-
guarded amongst them.

The grand staircase was a sweeping span of hand-carved
banisters and balusters inset with panels of sinuous iron scrollwork that turned and turned, hugging the elevators humming
up and down the hollow core of its center. It cut from the top
of the steamer all the way down to the bottom level of cabins,
but she only had to descend a single level to reach the Upper
Deck, where D-15 was located, slightly forward, not far from
the walls shielding the second funnel vent but very far from
the propellers.

She always booked a stateroom amidships, the better to
manage the roll. Yet because she'd taken so long to decide
upon the *Lusitania*, tossing and turning in her bed last night,
she'd had to accept whatever first-class cabin was still available at the last minute. D-15 was in the middle of the ship, at
least, but it was an inside room. A solitary bed, nightstand,
wardrobe, basin, chair and sofa. No portholes. No ocean view,
no fresh air. She had no one to blame but herself.

Even so, the cabin echoed the same bountiful opulence as the rest of the saloon-class section of the liner. The bed was brass with a sea-green satin duvet and crisp clean linens. The walls were papered in moiré silk the pinky-coral color of seashells; narrow strips of gilded crown molding traced the outlines of the ceiling. The sconces were brass again with silk shades, and the sofa was upholstered in teal jacquard, dark yellow tassels dangling from the cushion corners like miniature lions' tails. The wardrobe was tall and polished to a sheen; a discreet sign fixed to the wall beside it mentioned that her Boddy's Patented Life Jacket was stored on its uppermost shelf.

A vase of fresh flowers sat upon the nightstand, cut-crystal and peonies in extravagant bloom taking up half the surface.

She set down her suitcase and valise with a sigh. No view, no cold briny air, but it would do. Honestly, she longed for a nap, and she had to admit that the bed looked plush and inviting. There was still so much to do, however, unpacking her essentials, taking her spare jewelry to the purser's office, wherever that was. Securing a table in the dining saloon. Wondering if, before all that, she should send for at least one of her two trunks, since the suitcase had been filled with great haste only an hour and a half before by her maid, and Rita honestly didn't know what was in it. At least the trunks had been packed and locked last night.

Probably she should send for her trunks. One of them. Both? Where would they fit?

Someone knocked on the door. A stewardess in a black dress and white apron waited for Rita's *Come in*, then slipped inside. She looked to be in her early twenties, not much younger than Rita herself, with flaxen hair (much like Rita's costar back in London so many years ago, back in that terrible, terrible show), but also soft brown eyes and a friendly smile.

The maid dipped a curtsy. "Good morning, Miss Jolivet. I'm Eleanor. I'll be taking care of you for the voyage. Do you have everything you need?"

Rita was mildly surprised to hear the girl pronounce her surname correctly, in the French style. She wondered where she'd learned it.

"Hello, Eleanor, happy to meet you. I was just thinking about unpacking. I was in such a rush this morning, and I'm not certain what all I have here with me. I'm afraid I might need my trunks from storage."

"Of course," said the stewardess. "I can send word at once."

"Well, let's see what we have here first. Perhaps I'm fine for a day or so."

"Yes, miss."

Rita checked the gold watch pinned to her bodice. "It's almost 10:30. Do you have any idea why we haven't departed yet?"

"Yes, miss. We're taking on passengers and crew from the *Cameronia*, and they're still coming aboard."

"The *Cameronia*? Why? Is something amiss with their ship?"

"Only that it seems the Admiralty needs it more than the Anchor Line do. They requisitioned it for the troops this morning, miss, just like that." She snapped her fingers. "No warning at all for those paying passengers, all set to sail."

"Gracious!"

Eleanor moved to the suitcase, hefted it to the foot of the bed, and thumbed open the locks. "I'm sure they'll finish boarding soon, and we'll be on our way."

Rita watched, unsettled, as the maid began to unpack, opening the wardrobe and its drawers, hanging and folding and sorting again, as slowly the empty spaces filled with Rita's pale dangling lingerie, laden with ribbons and lace, gossamer as ghosts.

She glanced at her watch again. "I thought I'd pop down to the purser's while I can. Or maybe it's up? I'm not sure yet."

"It's up two flights, miss, just to the Promenade Deck. I can take care of sorting all of this for you while you're gone, if you like. Then when you get back, you can see what's what."

"You're a treasure. Thank you."

Rita adjusted her hat, found her jewelry case in the valise, and moved to the door. As her fingers closed over the latch, Eleanor spoke again, her voice coming shyer than the brisk, professional tone she'd used before. More uncertain.

"Miss Jolivet? I—I'm so sorry, but I just have to ask. Please don't be offended. I swear, all the other girls begged me to ask."

Rita turned. "Yes?"

Eleanor's cheeks were rosy as apples. She was pressed against the bed, her hands squeezed along her middle, her expression clearly torn.

"Yes?" Rita tried again, very gentle.

She blurted, "Is House Peters really as handsome as he is in all the moving pictures?"

Rita eased open the door, smiling at this familiar territory. "Even more so, believe me. And he smells like spearmint and leather, like a cowboy, like a man. It's quite delicious. Almost makes you swoon. I had to hold my breath against it every time we kissed."

"Oh," whispered the stewardess, both hands now clasped atop her heart, as if to keep that beating muscle firmly trapped inside the confines of her chest.

THE PURSER'S BUREAU resembled nothing more than an oval-shaped teller's cage at a fine uptown bank, with metalwork grills and smiling workers behind them, handing out receipts for whatever was to be deposited in the ship's safe: gold, jewels, cash, stock certificates, bonds. Anything rare or precious or valuable. And on a ship like this, with passengers like this, *valuable* included a great many items. So Rita was waiting in line once more, drowsing on her feet, when a voice to her left spoke softly in her ear.

"Miss Jolivet, may I have your autograph?"

She started and turned, and there was Charles Frohman, dear old Charles, smiling at her with his wise gray eyes, dressed in an outdoors overcoat and hat and leaning on a walking stick she'd never seen before, ebony with an ivory wolf's head.

"Why, Charles! How marvelous! Are you sailing, too? Or are you here to see someone off?"

"I'm sailing. You know I go over about this time of year."

"What luck! I had no idea you'd be here. How glad I am to see you." She stepped forward, kissed his cheek. The people in line shuffled around her, and Rita found her place again. "Where are you situated?"

"One of the Parlour Suites."

"Well, frankly, I'm envious. I'm in the tiniest little room. Gorgeous, of course, but an inside cabin."

"Oh," he said easily, "you won't be there all that much, anyway. I'm gathering up quite the glittering group for my amusement, and you'll certainly be a part of it."

The line crept forward, and they crept with it.

"In fact," he went on, tapping the tip of his cane twice against the floor, "I can't even fib and say it's a surprise to find you aboard, as it happens we are both invited to the Captain's Dinner at his table tomorrow night. I saw your name on the list."

"We are?"

"We are." He gave a nod to the wooden case in her hands. "So perhaps don't hand over all of those diamonds quite yet. You'll want to sparkle."

ONE OF THE most tedious and necessary chores of beginning a transatlantic voyage was heading to the main dining saloon as quickly as possible after boarding to try to arrange for a prime table for the journey. One might quietly reserve a table at any point during the day, for the right price, but there was no guarantee that that table would remain reserved by the evening if some other, flusher passenger came along (or merely one with a more recognizable name), someone who offered an even greater cash bribe to the head steward. Discretion was guaranteed aboard the best ocean liners; table reservations were not.

Rita had planned to go after her visit to the Purser's Bureau, even though she knew, as a lady traveling alone, she was probably going to be assigned to either a large group table or else one composed of similarly solitary women, usually paid companions or widows or the unwed daughters of men of industry. She had ten dollars in her reticule and the determination not to be stuck in the back of the saloon, next to the swinging doors leading to the service entrance.

But Charles Frohman, producer of hits, unearther of stars, surprised her yet again.

"Don't be ridiculous, you're at my table. I've already taken care of it. You, me, a smattering of other luscious people, authors and singers and playwrights, everyone divine. Why would you want to dine with anyone else? We've got Alfred Vanderbilt, too, in case you're curious. He's always up for a scintillating conversation, especially if you want to talk about racehorses. Nice chap, actually. You two might hit it off."

"I know hardly anything about racehorses."

"Even so, I can promise you possess all the right attributes"—he glanced meaningfully at her figure—"to hold his interest."

They shared a chuckle. Vanderbilt was known to be good-looking, soft-spoken, obscenely rich, and extremely married. Still in his thirties, he enjoyed travel, nearly as much as he enjoyed keeping a mistress in every port.

They began to wind their way back to Charles's suite, so he could rest. She'd pressed him about that cane, but all he'd said was that he'd taken a tumble on his porch steps a few weeks back in New York and had injured his knee. It was nothing, he insisted, it was over, but as they walked, his limp grew more and more pronounced.

"Are you sure about the table?" Rita asked. "I hate to impose."

"I'm as sure as can be." He opened the door and, golly, beyond his shoulder she glimpsed a parlor, a real parlor with real windows, not round portholes, oxblood velvet curtains and a fireplace, already lit. His personal phonograph set up on the coffee table, records in paper sleeves neatly filed in a wire holder nearby.

Charles hobbled over the threshold, tipped his hat, and gave a nod. "You're one of my most favorite people, Rita Jolivet," he said, holding her eyes. "I don't know that I've ever told you that. You make me laugh. You make me think. You make me remember what it was like to be hotblooded and young and formidable. So I owe you for all that, I think. I owe you for the reminder that life still holds marvels."

Rita murmured his name, touched.

"See you around," her old friend said, and smiled down at the floor as he closed the door.

ELEVEN O'CLOCK. ELEVEN-FIFTEEN. Eleven-twenty. Rita wanted to be outside when the liner left the pier; she wanted to be in the crowd that waved and cheered and watched the land they were leaving behind fade into a distant ocean haze. Normally, it was one of her favorite moments of a sea voyage, the undeniable treat of interacting with happy strangers, hundreds or thousands of strangers, everyone excited about the same thing, everyone joyous. But today wasn't normal; there was no use pretending it was. The *Lusy* was still idling in place, belching coal smoke, and there were still far more people on board than could possibly be passengers.

She wondered about that some. She wondered that there hadn't been any sort of extra security measures apparent when she'd embarked, considering that dire notice in the morning papers. Perhaps a phalanx of police officers or Cunard officers inspecting identification cards or passports or whatnot. It seemed to her that it wouldn't have been difficult for a malcontent to blend in even with the first-class crowd, much less second or steerage.

But that was what war did to you, she thought. It made suspicions bloom, your skin itch with paranoia. It made you search unfamiliar faces for any hint of something Other, something off.

Just after eleven-thirty, the gongs sounded at last, leading to a rush of goodbyes, of kisses and hugs and tears. Rita waded through that rush all the way up to a spare bit of railing along the starboard side of the Boat Deck, wedging into place between a man with an unlit cigar clenched between his teeth and a lady in a netted hat and an impressive ruby ring worn over her glove. Like Rita, the woman gripped the railing with both hands. Whenever she shifted, the ruby flickered in the cool, steely light.

The gangplank was slowly raised. A ripple of excitement took the crowds on the pier and the ones aboard, yet the steamer remained where she was.

Men below her began shouting in harsh voices, giving orders for the gangplank to be lowered again. When it was, a solitary young woman hurried off the ship, one last straggler, who, Rita would later discover through the ship's lively gossip chain, was in fact the niece of the captain, William Turner. He'd been giving her a tour, and apparently neither of them realized the gangplank had already been raised.

But the young lady was now gone, consumed by the swarm on the quay. Rita could feel the slight vibration beneath her feet that meant the propellers were beginning to turn. Gradually, carefully, the Lusitania backed out of her slip, unmoored. Everyone watching on land and water began to cheer.

The railing shivered. That ruby broke daylight into tiny, blood-red shards.

Three tugboats bobbed close, closer, guiding the much more massive vessel safely into the flow of the Hudson.

Rita found her handkerchief. She began waving it at the people on the pier, who waved back with enthusiasm, kerchiefs and hats and American flags. Confetti was flung, bright paper bits that winked through the air before sifting back down to rest on shoulders and heads and dust the water. To Rita's right, a chorus of male voices rose up, expertly singing "The Star-Spangled Banner." It was a thrilling adieu.

Lusitania's foghorn blared, shattering the air: three long, farewell blasts.

"A late start, but nothing irredeemable," muttered the man next to her, around his cigar. She looked up to see if he was addressing her, but he was talking to the fellow on the other side of him. "No doubt Turner'll make up the loss along the way."

"He bloody well better," replied the other man. "I've got meetings in London. I've got Juno waiting, and Venus after her. I didn't book a greyhound so we might take our bloody time."

As KIND AS Charles was to include her at his table, Rita realized she was too tired tonight to attend the formal meal service. She sent her regrets, had Eleanor bring a tray of bread and cheese and fresh fruit to her room, and ate it all while reading yet another script, one Cecil had sent along at the last moment after he'd caught wind she was scrambling to leave for England.

Close to midnight—how did it get so late?—she stood and stretched and thought about visiting the Ladies' so she could finally retire. She looked around her windowless room, unhappy once more with the lack of air, the lack of sky. So instead of retreating to the washroom, she shrugged on her coat and found her gloves.

The ship was still buzzing with activity, even this late. As she climbed the stairs to the first-class lounge and music room, she passed men and women talking, laughing softly, not too loud because it was late and perhaps it wasn't quite as seemly as it should be, having such a good time during, well, these times. But the lounge itself, with its overstuffed satinwood chairs and settees, with its green marble fireplaces that burned real wood and the barrel-domed, stained-glass skylight—the lounge itself still held a surprising number of well-heeled passengers playing cards or simply conversing over drinks. A grand piano waited off to the side of the chamber, lid closed, silent now but ready for the concerts that would be performed every evening after the dinner service. A wooden box on a stand accepted cash donations—cash only, please—to the Red Cross.

It took her a moment to register that there was no obvious exit to the outside from here, so she turned around, back to the staircase lobby, and found the handsome double doors she'd missed before that led to the deck, the promise of fresh air just beyond them.

She went port this time instead of starboard, just for a change. She found a bench and settled into it, letting the wind scrub her face.

Salt. Dampness. A clouded sky lacking moon or stars. Darkness barely thinned by the light shining behind beveled glass windows, golden and subdued.

Water sluicing by far below, a tinny, rushing sound, like a distant waterfall.

She closed her eyes and allowed the night to seep through her, cold as it was, misted as it was.

Rita thought of Giuseppe, so recently returned to Italy, of the world he was confronting there, politics and alliances shifting so rapidly, atrocities raging just beyond borders. She thought of Alfred, her impetuous brave brother, and of her parents. How distraught Maman must be, and Papa too, although he was less likely to show it. At least Inez was with them. Her tranquil ways might smooth the waters.

None of them knew she was on her way. There had been no time to send a cable before the *Lusitania* had sailed. It hadn't even occurred to her in those frantic last minutes, and so none of them knew. Tomorrow she'd return to the Purser's Bureau and send a wireless to remedy that. She was going to have to catch train after train from Liverpool to reach Winter Queen, but maybe an auto could at least meet her at the Medmenham station.

Someone paced by in slow, measured steps. The blue-acrid aroma of burning tobacco wafted against her face and was gone.

Rita opened her eyes.

A man with a cigarette stood at the railing about ten yards aft, one foot propped up on a lower rail, the tails of his coat flapping. He touched the cigarette to his lips and a brief orange glow brightened his cupped fingers and taut jaw. His hair was pulling free of its pomade, stirring with the wind.

She frowned at him. She knew him, didn't she? A fellow actor, maybe, from one of her plays?

He flicked the cigarette over the railing in a spiral of dull falling sparks, turned and saw her. His face broke into a smile.

"Marguerite," Inez's husband said. "How splendid to see you again."

Chapter 15

I envy you those peaceful days aboard the ship. I don't like to admit it, but I do. I would have switched places with you in a heartbeat if I could have.

Even the ending. Even that.

Especially that.

SUNDAY, MAY 2, 1915
ABOARD *LUSITANIA*

They met for luncheon at the Verandah Café.

It seemed every modern liner now sported some version of the concept: a bright, verdant space jammed with potted plants and hanging plants and crawling plants, so much living greenery in the middle of a salty sea. Porthole windows every-where, too many of them open now, Rita thought, because there was a distinct chill to the air circulating through the chamber, just an edge beyond what could be called refreshing.

Coffee, tea, wine. Light meals, mostly hors d'oeuvres, grilled meats, sandwiches and soups. Ice creams and tartlets for dessert.

The *Lusitania*'s rendering of the restaurant had even more foliage than she'd ever seen aboard a ship, ivy and bay trees and palm trees and baskets of pretty rainbowed blossoms, all of it framed against white trellises, wicker seats, and hardwood flooring. It really was like an elegant bistro one might come across fronting the Seine or the Thames, only with the distinct tang of open ocean instead of inland river.

A gray day shone through those windows, blustery; the sea was chopped with white. Rita's wine sloshed in her glass, and her stomach sloshed with it. So, actually, she appreciated that sharp air.

The room was busy, with several people waiting near the doors. Every table was occupied or else being cleared, but with the smooth bearing of a man accustomed to exclusive, busy restaurants, George had only handed a folded pound note to the steward taking their names, along with a murmured *How good of you to make room for us*, and straightaway they had a spot by the forward windows. From their seats, they were able to observe other passengers moving along the saloon promenade, a determined yet elegant parade of spring fashions braving the rolling pitch of the ship and patches of fog that rose and fell, shrouding everything in mist.

A trio of young ladies had arranged themselves around the table just behind them, leaning in close over the tablecloth to whisper in soft, scandalized tones about someone named Nellie, or Mellie.

"Whenever did you take up smoking?" Rita asked, selecting a roll from the bread basket, tearing it apart with her fingers. She'd slept in late and skipped breakfast this morning, on top of missing a full meal last night. She was rested, wide-awake, and starving. An iced butter bowl next to the bread brimmed with curled pats; she stabbed one with the tip of her knife. "Or have you always? I'm sorry, I don't recall."

"No, not always," George answered, his regret obvious. "Only since I gave up performing, professionally, at least. About five years past." He crushed the cigarette in his left hand into the ashtray at his elbow. "It's a dreadful habit, I know. I try not to do it around Inez."

"I can think of worse. We really haven't seen each other very much, have we? Even living in such close proximity in New York."

"We really haven't. It's good we have the chance now to change that."

She was buttering her roll, concentrating on the turn of her blade against tender white insides. "Inez knows you're coming?"

"She does."

"Our parents?"

"Naturally. I'd never dream of descending upon your Maman without warning. I'm American enough already for her. I don't need to offer any further proof of my bad manners."

Rita laughed, looking up at him. "Excellent choice. She'd smile and welcome you with open arms—"

"But her eyes," George sighed. "Those dark, brilliant eyes. They'd shrink me into a puddle of shame."

"Exactly as they loved you anyway."

"Yes. Exactly as they loved me anyway."

The ship pitched. She put down the bread, picked up her wine. "That reminds me. I need to send a message today to Winter Queen. I forgot to tell anyone I was coming, if you can believe it."

"Bad luck there, I'm afraid. Passengers are no longer allowed to send wireless messages during the voyage. We can only receive them."

"Really?" she said, dismayed.

"Really. Security measures. Orders from the Admiralty, I believe. But I can't imagine Pauline won't be delighted to see you under any circumstances."

Their server arrived carrying a silver tray. He bent carefully to place Rita's *potage à la fermière*, then George's lamb croquettes, on the table.

Rita dipped a spoon in her soup, coiling with steam and already threatening to spill over the rim of the bowl, in concert with the ship.

"You know about Alfred, I take it."

"Yes." George shook his head. She noticed he looked paler than she was used to seeing him. More weary. Lines bracketed his mouth. She knew he was older than her sister, but for the first time since they'd met, he looked it.

His fingers tapped an absent tattoo against the tabletop. "I'd hoped, like everyone else, that if he just waited a while longer . . . If he'd just waited to be conscripted instead of volunteering, who knows how matters might have turned by then."

"Waiting," Rita said, "has never been Alfred's strong suit. He was already chafing at the bit. Honestly, I'm relieved he didn't run off months ago while he was still underage. He'd have had no qualms about lying about it. Likely the only reason he didn't is that Maman and Papa would have raised holy hell at the highest levels. Every recruiter across the nation would've been on alert."

The girls behind them broke into bouts of laughter, one of them almost instantly commanding, *Shush! Shush!* as the other two kept giggling.

George didn't speak again until they quieted. "I'm afraid conscription is likely to come sooner than later, anyway."

"Do you think so?"

"I do. Despite the outward optimism of the Allied governments, we're nowhere near the bitter end. We're not even close to a tipping point. The bloodshed has spread like a cancer across the globe. It's as if the entire world was waiting to erupt. Chile and the battle off Más a Tierra, the mutiny in Singapore. The goddamned Ottomans—pardon me!—the Ottomans and the Suez Canal." He looked bleakly at the remains of his cigarette, then picked up his fork. "Sorry. Sorry for that. I don't mean to . . ."

"It's all right."

"After this stopover at Winter Queen, I'm taking Inez to Russia with me."

She paused over her soup. "What? You are?"

"I have business there, urgent business. We can stay in Moscow under royal protection, in the Grand Kremlin Palace, for as long as we want. The Central Powers don't stand a chance of penetrating that far, not for a good while, if ever. Bonaparte couldn't conquer Russia, and I'm betting the Germans can't, either." He glanced around them, dropped his voice. "The air raids are growing more and more brazen. The dirigibles and aeroplanes navigate by the ribbon of the Thames because it's so visible from above, even at night. Winter Queen's too close to it, much too close. Too easily seen, too easily bombed. I'd take your entire family with me, if I thought any of you would go."

"No—I mean, no thank you. If Alfred's sent off to the front, nothing on earth will dislodge my parents from England."

"That's what I thought."

"Besides, I've already begged and begged all three of them to come stay with me in New York, at least until it's all over. Honestly, that's where Inez should be, too."

"She will be, after this one last trip. Hopefully, we both will be. But even the United States won't be immune forever."

She pursed her lips, waiting. In all the years she'd known him, and despite all of her sister's protestations, Rita had never stopped believing that George Vernon was far more a government man than importer's agent.

He leaned closer, those gray-green eyes intent. "President Wilson is committed to neutrality. Every source I have confirms it. It would take something catastrophic to shift him." He sat back, his expression stark. "Only, Marguerite... catastrophes have become our everyday currency. Churchill himself is counting on it, I assure you. Why do you think the *Lusitania*, fast as she is, is still a civilian vessel?"

He lifted a hand to the chamber, a brief, eloquent gesture that said, *Look at this place, this ship, this world. Look how vulnerable it all is.*

AFTER THEY FINISHED their meal, they joined the parade of strollers along the Boat Deck, coat collars turned up, Rita's hands tucked deep into her pockets. She'd left her ermine muff back in Manhattan; she'd had no notion it would be this chilly in May.

The fog consumed them in moments, clinging and clammy. But then it tore away again, as if the *Lusitania* was a bird in flight, slicing her way up and down across the sky, right through a cloud, only to surge free to the other side. For a few minutes, the sky was a blazing pearl and the ship merely damp and gleaming with moisture, the wooden deck, the metal walls and rivets, droplets of clear water beading and dripping from brass-rimmed portholes.

"We ought to figure out where to meet," George said to her, matter-of-fact. "Just in case."

"Just in case?" she echoed, although she knew exactly what he meant.

He moved to the railing. Rita followed him, mimicked him, her back braced against sturdy bars of hard metal. The ocean behind them pitched and splashed.

He searched the deck a moment, the rows of cowrie-shaped lifeboats hanging from their davits, the canvas collapsibles tucked under them, as the other passengers walked heavily nearby.

"There. That's our best bet." He pointed to the doors leading inside to the entrance hall containing the grand staircase and elevators. "A Deck, amidships, just outside. Just past those doors. It'll be important to get outside as quickly as you can. Don't linger inside, even if it feels safer, because it won't be. We'll say this side for now, port, but if it's impossible for some reason, or underwater, head to the same set of doors on the starboard side, and we'll meet there instead."

"All right," she said softly.

"Grab your lifebelt before, if you can. There'll be a scramble for the lifeboats. If I'm not there within five minutes of your arrival, get in one and don't get out of it, no matter what anyone tells you. Only get out if they point a gun at you."

"Well," she said lightly, "I brought my own. If someone points a gun at me, they're in for rather a surprise."

He didn't smile, as she hoped he might. "The pearly pistol? Like Inez's?"

"Years ago she made me promise to take it with me whenever I travel into the unknown."

"Did she? Rather surprising, since she won't even touch hers."

"To be honest, she was never keen on the idea of owning a gun, but at this point, I consider mine something of a lucky charm."

"Good," he said, serious. "Good."

"Listen, can we bring Charles Frohman into this? This plan of ours? He's got a bad knee and might need help into a boat."

"He's aboard too? Of course."

"I'll tell him."

From the bow of the ship, the fog was sweeping toward them again, a wall of gray, shadows moving through it, indistinct. She turned around and faced the Atlantic, keeping it in sight as long as she could before it was erased, too.

George covered her gloved hand with his own, his palm pressing hers against the rail. She couldn't feel the wet through her glove, only the cold.

HER INVITATION TO the captain's table arrived that afternoon, delivered to her door by a smartly uniformed officer in a navy jacket and gold braid who took off his cap and handed her the card with a brief incline of his head.

Miss Marguerite L. Jolivet is cordially invited to share this evening's meal at the table of Captain William T. Turner, main dining saloon, seven o'clock, répondez s'il vous plaît . . .

"I would be delighted," she told the officer, who nodded again and thanked her before replacing his cap and leaving.

ELEANOR ARRIVED AT six to help her dress. Rita had had to send for her trunks after all, having found nothing quite fine enough in the suitcase, only a couple of tailor-made day dresses and various underthings. But in the second trunk—what a squeeze to get it in the cabin!—she discovered that her maid back home had been thinking ahead to more formal evenings. In that trunk were the gowns of silk and satin and delicate lace, slippers and heels, everything carefully stored, wrapped in tissue paper and scented with sachets filled with dried lilac.

She chose a Parisian concoction of mulberry taffeta and black tulle, a collar of diamonds, black satin gloves. A pair of crescent-moon diamond clips in her hair, done up in curls. Charles wanted her to sparkle this evening, and she didn't plan to disappoint.

"You're very good at this," Rita observed, following the stewardess's deft movements in the mirror fixed above the marble basin, how her fingers shaped the curls just exactly, pinning them in place.

"Thank you, miss. I've been practicing. I plan to be a proper lady's maid after this. After my contract with Cunard is up."

A touch of cosmetics that Rita applied herself, just a suggestion of powder and lip rouge, faint kohl around the eyes, and she was done. She stood, tugging up her gloves, then turned to face her stewardess.

"What do you think? Will I do for the Captain's Dinner?"

Eleanor stepped back, her eyes shining. "You look just as glamorous as in your moving pictures, I swear. You look a real star."

CAPTAIN TURNER WAS, by all accounts, a gruff soul, tanned and craggy, with sharp pale eyes and a decided dearth of humor. More than accomplished at his job when it came to any aspect of his ship or crew—indeed, he was known to be the best captain employed by the Cunard Line—William Turner was far less polished when it came to interacting with his paying customers.

For a single evening of the voyage, Turner maintained the tradition of dining with a select number of first-class passengers in the main saloon, because it was tradition, and he was a man who respected both ceremony and convention. But the fact that he usually took his meals alone in his quarters spoke volumes about his preferences.

It was up to Staff Captain Jock Anderson, second in command, younger and much more jovial, to provide the charm at the table. He told wry, amusing anecdotes of life at sea and of unusual customs at exotic ports. He knew how to flatter the ladies and gentlemen alike, asking all the right questions and always paying close attention to the answers.

"And you, sir," he said, with a friendly look toward Alfred Vanderbilt, brown-haired and dapper in his white tie and tails, a dainty pink carnation, his signature boutonnière, a small flourish of color against his lapel. "What inspires you to travel to England, if I may inquire?"

Vanderbilt smiled. Rita, seated next to him, saw at once how easy it would be to succumb to such a smile, modest yet sincere.

"The war," he said simply. "Actually, the war, and the International Horse Show Association. There's a board meeting coming up, and I'm the director. But mainly I'm going to finalize arrangements for a donation to the Red Cross, a fleet of automobiles. Ambulances, armored lorries and touring cars, anything that could be of use."

"How noble of you," said the pretty redhead sitting across from him, completely without irony. Josephine Brandell, another of Charles Frohman's fosterlings, on her way to fame.

Rita knew her, or knew of her. As a teen, the girl had landed a few minor roles in Broadway musicals, but eventually, at Charles's prodding, found her footing as an opera singer. When they'd shaken hands as they were introduced, Josephine had mentioned that she'd seen Miss Jolivet in *When Knights Were Bold* (*You were magnetic!*), and Rita had replied that she'd seen Miss Brandell in *The Belle of Brittany* (*You sing so beautifully!*). Then Rita had said *Please call me Rita* just as Josephine said *Please call me Jenny*, and they'd both laughed.

"Oh, no, Miss Brandell," Vanderbilt said now. "Thank you, but it's not noble, not really. I'm just thinking ahead. Any little contribution, any little anything to help out, to shorten the conflict. War benefits only power mongers and madmen, and you can't count on either of those sort for mercy in the end. It's the rest of us who must manage the ruin of it all. If I can send autos now to stop a shortage later, to save lives, I don't know why I wouldn't."

"Hear, hear," said Anderson, raising his glass.

"I must agree with Jenny," Rita said, raising hers as well. "It *is* noble of you, as well as pragmatic."

At the head of the table, Captain Turner was slicing his *tournedos à la bordelaise*. He spoke without looking up. "It is the lack of foresight regarding the practicalities of war that sinks nations. A lack of automobiles leads to the lack of reliable supply chains. The lack of supply chains leads to disadvantaged soldiers. Disadvantaged soldiers lead to defeat."

"And yet," pointed out a man with a pageboy haircut, a Mr. Hubbard, dabbing his mouth with his napkin, "it is an *American* supplying the autos."

The staff captain jumped in. "Ah, but we British are nothing if not practical. If Mr. Vanderbilt finds himself burdened with an excess of autos, why then, it behooves us to take them off his hands!"

Beneath the strains of the five-piece orchestra, a round of laughter took the table.

The *Lusy*'s first-class dining saloon was advertised as the most unique and beautiful restaurant afloat, and Rita thought it likely true. Certainly she'd never seen anything fancier aboard a ship, or even in a hotel. The dining area was double-tiered, taking up two levels, with a wide oval well in the middle topped by a gilt-and-plaster dome stretching to a third level high above, everything supported by an array of white marble columns crowned with more gold.

The captain's table was in the center of the lower chamber, right beneath the dome. If she looked straight up (she did so only once, very subtly; she was not *that* gauche), Rita had a dizzying view of the frescoes of cherubs and clouds decorating it, the ornate friezes of garlands and medallions, and the carved, grinning faces ringing the rim along the base that she thought might be gods or mythical beasts.

The lower part of the restaurant was the larger space, with mahogany walls inset with mirrors, leaded-glass windows throughout. It offered the traditional prix fixe menu, but in the smaller chamber upstairs, one could order off the sumptuous à la carte menu. Rita didn't know if the captain and his guests were being served from the same menu as the other tables around them or not, but the food was undeniably plentiful and exquisite.

Those tournedos of beef in that rich, red wine sauce. Fresh oysters on beds of chipped ice. Caramelized shallots and carrots with tarragon. *Sole meunière,* soused salmon, Virginia ham, jacket potatoes, roasted chicken and duckling. Beef ribs, sea bass, mutton chops. New peas, green corn, boiled rice.

She could scarcely finish one dish before another was placed before her. They were on only the fifth course, and she was already picking at her food because she was so full. She began to smile apologetically at her waiter when he had to take away her plates still half full.

He was an older gentleman, deferential, who only looked back at her with a mournful expression that said, *Yes, of course, what is there to do?*

The saloon could seat over four hundred, although she noticed that tonight not every table was occupied. Perhaps it had something to do with turbulent seas. The staff captain assured everyone they were in for calmer weather soon, possibly as early as tomorrow morning.

"Excellent news," commented Charles, as the orchestra began a new piece, one of Dvořák's lilting nocturnes. "Some blue sky would be most welcome."

"The better to see them coming," Mr. Hubbard said.

Captain Turner shot him a glance, returned to his meal.

The long-bearded gentleman at Rita's other elbow, a Mr. Kessler (as he shook her hand he introduced himself as "The Champagne King," but she wasn't sure if the sobriquet represented his high-end frolics or else his business) lifted a forkful of peas and said, conversationally, "I was told that *Lusitania*'s cat abandoned ship just before we departed. A pity! I like cats. Seems like every good ship should have one. What was its name?"

Turner's face went blank, his knife and fork paused over his plate.

"Dowie," Staff Captain Anderson supplied. "Our feline mascot. Yes, I suppose she decided to live out her ninth life amid the bright lights of New York City. It was shame to lose her. She was an excellent mouser." He caught himself. "Not that *Lusitania* has any mice!"

"Perhaps they all left with the cat," said Vanderbilt, and for some reason, everyone laughed.

But Mr. Hubbard—an author, Rita remembered now, some controversial author—was not finished. "Mr. Vanderbilt, sir. I heard a rumor that you received a telegram after you boarded yesterday."

"I received a stack of them, sir. Seems I'm a fairly popular fellow, Lord knows why."

"Yes," Hubbard went on, cutting off the chuckles, "but this one surely sticks in your memory. It warned you that the *Lusitania* was doomed. To get off at once before she departed. I believe it was signed 'Morte'?"

For a moment, there was only shocked silence at the table. Around them, other conversations ebbed and flowed, punctuated with laughter, with the clinking of silverware against china plates. That nocturne, rising into a sweet crescendo. Then Jenny whispered, "Oh, my," and the captain released an impatient breath.

Alfred Vanderbilt had barely tilted his head, like a hunting dog noting a soundless whistle. The saloon's padded chairs swiveled but were bolted firmly to the deck; he couldn't physically push his back, although it appeared he wanted to. Instead, he only sat there and regarded the other man with a flat expression.

"You seem to know a great deal about it."

"Only rumors."

"It was a joke, merely. And a poor one at that."

"Rumors serve no one but fools," growled the captain. He replaced his utensils to the table, the four rows of gold wire lace on his cuffs gleaming; four rows of gold denoting his outstanding leadership, his outstanding service to the line. He picked up his water goblet and glared at each of them in turn.

Behind him, a waiter in white gloves deftly removed his empty plate, signaling to another server behind him to begin the next course.

"Look around you, sir," said Captain Turner to Mr. Hubbard. "Look at all these good people who chose to sail with us, rumors be damned. The fact is, this ship can't be caught by a U-boat. It hasn't yet, and it never will. The Huns have nothing on us, and well they know it."

Chapter 16

I've come to recognize there is a sort of divinity in the everyday, in the mundane.

His shaving kit. His favorite necktie. His gray woolen Chesterfield, still hanging in the closet, still scented of him.

That band of gold we took from his finger. Such a simple ring, so plain, a little scratched. Yet it bounded all my hopes and dreams.

MONDAY, MAY 3, 1915
ABOARD *LUSITANIA*

The next morning dawned magenta and flame atop a much calmer ocean, just as the staff captain had predicted. The roll of the ship was very nearly unnoticeable, so Rita decided to indulge in a seawater bath.

Lusitania sported few of the more modish amenities that had overtaken some other steamers. Her passengers would find no Turkish spa onboard. No swimming pool or racquetball court. No gymnasium. None of the fashionable innovations (some critics sniffed *newfangled nonsense*) that had swept through the ocean liner industry in the short span of years since the *Lusy* had been christened. Cunard's flagship was a nimble, speedy lady. A dashing lady, without question, brimming with elegance. However, her passengers were expected to entertain themselves.

There was the Reading and Writing Room for the ladies, done up in tints of ivory and pink and pale oyster gray. Rose du Barri curtains, Colonial Adam furniture, electric desk lamps with fringed shades. Tall windows of etched glass and a glass dome above, so that, under clear skies, the room would flood with sunlight, and its occupants could bask in a heavenly glow.

The Smoking Room, for gentlemen only. They did more than smoke in there, of course. There was gin and whiskey and port as well, poker games, speculation about certain businesses or certain women or else the stock market, always reliably the stock market. All of it taking place in the dark luxury of walnut walls and pillars and deep red upholstery, under yet another stained-glass ceiling.

And a smallish library, for everyone. Everyone in saloon class, that was. Second and third had to provide their own reading materials.

But one fine feature the *Lusitania* did have was that her baths, in every class, were supplied not with freshwater but salt, straight from the sea, heated and delightful.

There was a ladies' washroom not too far from Rita's cabin, just an offshoot of a corridor away, but far enough so that, in her bathrobe, even very early or very late, anyone passing by would realize at a glance that she didn't have an en-suite stateroom.

Damned, damned last-minute cabin.

But once she was in the washroom, it was actually quite nice. Compact, of course. But marble counters and floors, polished fixtures, cut-glass sconces, much like the rest of the ship. Everything clean and glistening. The tubs themselves were partitioned into narrow, separate chambers for privacy, with heavy damask curtains that could be either tied back or fall free, concealing the entrance. Hooks for clothing, shelves for shampoo, soaps, beauty oils.

She was fortunate enough to have the whole washroom to herself. Rita chose a bathtub, untied the curtain and loosened the spigots. Water rushed into the tub clear as ice, splashing along the bottom and against the sides. She opened the hot water tap farther and veins of steam began to rise and entwine, veiling the air.

As the tub filled, she balanced a hip along its edge, already savoring the scent of salt. She tested the temperature with her fingertips and remembered, without warning but with acute clarity, the slippery caress of the Pacific along her skin, that body of water another world away. The beat of the sun searing the top of her head. How her sister's nose had burned pink on the beach that day in Ocean Park and later began to delicately peel, enough so that the makeup artist for the photoplay had to apply extra layers of paint to hide it.

Rita flicked the wet from her fingers. She shrugged out of her robe and nightdress, hung them both on the brass hooks provided, then stepped, one foot at a time, into the bath.

SHE RETURNED TO her cabin scrubbed clean, her body relaxed, warm and supple, ready for the day. Just as Eleanor finished all the careful details of Rita's toilette, her hair arranged, her dress donned, her boots buttoned, the cabin-to-cabin telephone fixed to the wall let out a short, ringing trill.

Rita picked up the receiver, stood close enough to the mouthpiece to be heard.

"D-15, yes?"

"Dear girl," said Charles, on the other end of the line, "come to my suite. We've got caviar and oysters on order, along with half a dozen bottles of excellent blanc de blancs." His voice grew distant; he must have shifted from the wall. "Is that right, Justus? Six bottles?" Louder again. "Hurry up. I have a play I want to discuss and at least two gentlemen begging for the honor of a dance with you."

"Champagne and oysters? Dancing? Charles, it's barely ten past nine."

"In America, we call it brunch. See you soon."

Far below them, in the dark and sooty bowels of the ship, down narrow corridors and stairwells that most of the passengers above never even thought of, never considered, the fires that fueled the mighty *Lusitania* burned, and the firemen and trimmers and greasers worked and worked, never ceasing, ensuring that there would always be coal shoveled into the furnaces. Covered in coal dust, breathing and eating and pissing coal dust, until even their spit was tinged black.

They were hard men, strong men. Men eager to get ahead in this world no matter what it took, mostly through brutal labor in the stokehold. Their time aboard trapped on the lowest decks was to be exchanged for a fair wage sent back home to their families, keeping food on the table for hundreds of hungry mouths.

The *Lusitania* was so famously fast because she was equipped with four massive boiler rooms instead of nearly everyone else's one or two or three, powering four steam turbines that, in turn, powered four massive propellers. Twenty-five boilers all together, equaling one hundred and ninety-two separate furnaces, all supplied with coal nonstop by these dirty, sweating men, shift after shift. On average, the ship devoured about eight hundred and forty tons of coal a day.

She was a bullet along the surface of the ocean, swift as could be.

And *that* was what gave *Lusy* her advantage over every other bullet sailing the seas. That. Those boilers. Those men.

Their resolute dreams, bought one heavy shovelful at a time, tossed into an inferno before their faces.

RITA WOULD SOMETIMES wonder, later on, why she hadn't taken better note of the golden days sliding away from her on that ship. Why she hadn't taken care to mark the hours, the dawns and dusks, the black-lacquered nights blazing with moonlight or stars. But it was always like that on a longer sea voyage, at least for her. The minutes melted away, the hours vanished, lost to the minutiae of meals and promenading and whist and conversation with people you barely knew, and would likely never see again. Naps, when there was truly nothing else to do.

Only the wind remained constant. The water below the black metal sides of the ship, sliced apart and tossed skyward by the blade of the hull, cascading back and away in powerful, sheer sheets.

It did seem to her, however, that this particular voyage was taking longer than usual. Longer than she thought it would, but then, no matter how many times Rita had crossed the Atlantic (a good many), she was no sailor. She wondered if it had anything to do with the fact that the fourth of *Lusitania*'s famous four funnels never seemed to have smoke pouring from it, no matter when she checked.

She mentioned it to George, who said he'd already noticed, and already inquired.

"The fourth boiler room has been shut down. They're trying to save on the cost of coal."

"The cost of *coal*?" Jenny repeated incredulously.

It was Wednesday afternoon, well along on their journey. The *Lusitania* was a tiny floating toy somewhere in the middle of a giant's endless blue ocean, nothing else in view, not even clouds. They were reclining in their rented deck chairs on B Deck, Rita and Jenny and George, letting the sunlight warm them, watching the sky glide by.

Rita had ensured that George was included in Charles's *glittering group*, including the dinner table. And George, in his seamless way, had blended in instantly, suddenly a performer again, a handsome fellow comrade of the stage. More than once, Rita had caught Josephine Brandell looking at him askance through her lashes, her face lightly flushed. Rita might have been a little indignant of behalf of her sister, but the truth was that George Vernon had eyes only for his wife, and Rita knew it. So let Jenny dream.

Her brother-in-law leaned back, laced his fingers over his chest. He rested his head against the wooden slats of the chair, his bowler pushed low over his forehead. In the slanting bright light, Rita noted the pale thread of a scar crossing his chin. A straight, short cut, some long-ago injury.

"Since the war," George said from beneath his bowler, "transatlantic passenger traffic has dropped off considerably. Not just for Cunard, but all the lines. This is how Cunard decided to staunch the bleeding."

Rita grimaced at the wording; he squinted at her from beneath the hat's brim.

"Pardon me. I meant to say, this is the inevitable result of hours of meetings between desperate accountants and the ponderous powers that be."

"So . . . we're not on the fastest ship, after all," Rita said.

"No, we are. Even with just the other three boiler rooms in operation, and based on the daily betting pool for our miles, I'd say we've been cruising at about an average speed of twenty knots on the open sea. The U-boats have never sunk a ship going faster than fourteen."

Jenny said, nervous, "Perhaps the captain will speed us up when we're closer to shore, though."

"No doubt."

A gaggle of children thundered past in pinafores and short pants, shrieking with laughter, none older than seven, two harried stewardesses hurrying after them. Three more stewardess followed at a much more leisurely pace, pushing perambulators.

"So many little ones aboard," Jenny observed, tendrils of hair blowing along her cheek. She pushed them back with two fingers, a stage gesture, unaware, one Rita instantly recognized: keeping the fingers together in twos or threes so they wouldn't remind the audience of cat claws or spider legs. "More than usual, I think. More than I've seen before on a crossing."

"I heard someone mention they're mostly Canadian families heading to Great Britain, not just England but Scotland and Wales. Wives with their husbands gone off to the fight, returning home with their youngsters, likely to their parents."

The children began marking out a game of hopscotch not far off, drawing chalk along the deck in wild, happy lines.

"Surely Canada is safer," Jenny fretted.

Rita shook her head. "I don't know that anywhere is safe."

"Except here," said George heartily, after a moment. "We are safe here, ladies. Blessed with food and warmth, with sun and sky. Blessed with a staunch ship and fine company. This is a charmed day."

AND HE WAS right, it *was* a charmed day. It was, in fact, the second-to-last of the charmed days.

THE CHILDREN HAD their hopscotch. The adults resorted to only slightly less rambunctious deck games to pass the hours: shuffleboard, quoits, a daily race of egg-and-spoon, followed by one of potato sacks. There was a medicine ball as well, most popular among the brawny set. Winners were awarded small tin pins of the ship, proudly worn for at least an hour or so after the victory.

Nothing could convince her to hop in a dusty burlap sack across the deck, not in her heels and fine gowns, and not with any shred of dignity. But Rita joined the egg-and-spoon race, her right hand gathering up her skirts and underskirts, her left holding the spoon and its precious cargo. Years of dance training for the stage had taught her how to move smoothly, how to keep her knees bent and her balance even while walking quickly. She lined up with the other hopefuls in their fashionable hats and coats and the steward barked, *Ready-Set-Go!* She took off at once, knowing *not* to look at the egg, to trust her gait to keep it steady and focus only on the finish line. She beat George by two feet and Jenny by six, but surprisingly it was Alfred Vanderbilt, in his trim suit and polished shoes, who nearly won, only dropping his egg right at the end, a messy splat, his cheeks red with laughter.

Rita accepted her pin of the *Lusy* with a grin, panting a little, holding it up high above her head as everyone around them clapped.

She asked Mr. Vanderbilt at dinner that night if he'd dropped his egg on purpose to let her win, and he laughed once more and said that, alas, no, he wasn't *that* much of a gentleman. He was hoping to win the pin to give to his children when he returned home.

Rita smiled, fished it from her reticule and gave it to him, agreeing that it would make a fine souvenir for his sons.

THURSDAY DAWNED AS clear and fine as the previous few days had, no chop to the ocean, no clouds. It was to be their last day in safe waters; they were now nearing the war-zone boundary fronting the Celtic Sea, closing in on Ireland's hilly southern coast. Passengers awoke to the fact that the lifeboats had been swung out early that morning to hang over the sides of the ship, many with their canvas covers removed. Swaying and creaking gently from their falls, they looked ready to drop into the ocean at any moment.

Just a precaution, they were told by passing officers and stewards, when pressed. *Standard procedure, nothing of concern.*

Rita took a stroll by herself outside after breakfast, joining a host of strangers. She noticed the change in position of the lifeboats, but everyone around her seemed more excited about searching the horizon for the destroyers that would escort them inland. A few of the gentlemen began placing wagers on exactly which ships the Admiralty would assign them, perhaps the *Moorsom* or the *Laertes*—or even one of the four superdreadnoughts, maybe the *Orion* or the *Conqueror*, the most valued warships in all the fleet. Surely the *Lusitania* and her many souls aboard deserved nothing but the best.

But that horizon remained flat and empty. Rita searched for ships, for sirens, and only managed to strain her eyes.

THAT AFTERNOON, CHARLES invited everyone he knew, and some he didn't, to his suite for a soirée, calling it a *So Long, It's Been Swell!* party. It had to be during the day because that evening, after dinner, all the elegant people would put down their napkins and put on their gloves and traipse from D or C Deck up to A, to the first-class lounge, for the traditional voyage fundraiser benefiting the Seamen's Charities: a passenger talent concert, volunteers needed.

Staff Captain Anderson, dropping by the party, smilingly and charmingly backed Rita into a corner as Charles's phonograph filled the suite with ragtime.

"Won't you grace us with a little something tonight, Miss Jolivet," he entreated her. "A bit of Shakespeare or something? Even something modern, if you like! A speech from one of your photoplays! That would be splendid, I'm sure."

"Oh," she hedged, "I don't think so. Would it really be fair to everyone else?"

"Fair?"

"What if there's some ambitious young lady out there hoping to perform her own Juliet tonight, or Delight Warren? I'd never want to outshine someone like that. Not for this, such a worthy cause."

"I fear Miss Jolivet's talents are trademarked and copyrighted," Charles declared, coming up to pass her a cocktail, liquid amber on ice with a single spiral of orange peel dangling from the rim. "By me, I might add. Let her sit in the audience for a change and enjoy the shining performances of our other friends."

The staff captain forced a smile. "By all means. I must admit, Miss Brandell told me nearly the same thing."

"Disappointing, to be sure." Charles took him by the arm, leading him amiably away from Rita, still with that limp. "But if it helps take some of the sting out of it, I promise all three of us will empty our wallets this evening for the charities, down to every last penny."

Rita watched them go. She tried the cocktail in relief—something with bourbon in it, something sweetish and a hair too strong—and before she knew it, it was half gone. She looked down at her glass in surprise; when she looked up again, George was at her elbow.

"Hullo," he said.

"Hullo. You're looking very chic." And he was, a smart suit she hadn't seen before, a fresh haircut and shave.

George gave a nod to a man standing across the room. "I was able to obtain a coveted appointment with Mr. Gadd over there, the finest barber on the seven seas."

Rita looked at the man, unremarkable but for a luxuriant nut-brown mustache that caught the light. He was engaged in ardent conversation with Mr. Kessler, the Champagne King, who kept tugging at his beard.

"I do love how Charles loves everyone."

"Americans are a democratic sort, my dear. We know in our bones that anyone can rise up from nothing to become something, with enough luck and gumption. Charles has made it his business to recognize a true talent when he comes across one. Mr. Gadd is famous enough to pick and choose his customers as he pleases. If it's a game of democracy versus aristocracy, in his case, democracy has won. He'll turn away princes and all the Four Hundred if he's already promised his appointments to his peers. Charles was canny to invite him. No doubt it'll shoot him to the top of the list on the voyage home."

"Well, as I said, you look quite fetching. Better watch out for Miss Brandell. She's already half in love with you."

"My heart," George said, "cannot be ensnared, as it no longer resides in my chest, but rather your sister's."

Rita tried not to laugh, she really did, but in the end she had to give in. "Sorry! I'm sorry! It's the booze, I swear. I have such a gruesome turn of mind these days!"

He ran a hand along his chin. "I guess it wasn't as graceful out loud as it sounded in my head. But you know what I mean."

"I do." She leaned close, feeling the heat of the bourbon thrumming through her veins. "You know, Inez once said something quite like it to me, right before you wed. She said—oh, what was it exactly? She said that she was *at home* in your heart."

He flashed a smile. "Did she indeed? She's always been a better bard than I."

And with that smile, abashed and direct at once, Rita sobered some. She gazed at him and thought, *They're really in love.*

And then, with a pang she couldn't help: *How lucky they are.*

How lucky they are to have found their perfect union, a love that asks no questions and demands no answers, but only is.

At home in his heart. What would that even feel like?

Across the parlor, someone changed the record; the conversation around them peaked and fell. Someone dropped a glass, a sharp shatter against the floor, and everyone laughed.

Rita drained the last of her cocktail, set it on a side table.

"Let's dance, shall we? 'Maple Leaf Rag' is perfect for the Turkey Trot, and I'm rather good at it. You can teach it to Inez."

"Brave girl! I'll try not to trot on your toes."

THE LOUNGE WAS filled to nearly overflowing. Several late-comers had to make do with standing behind the rows of chairs that had been arranged in a semicircle to face the make-shift stage. It wasn't truly a stage, of course, just a cleared area of carpeting in the middle of the chamber, with a table for props and that grand piano at the edge.

Rita and Jenny found seats near the back to minimize the risk of being called up to perform. Vanderbilt sat with them, along with Charles, George, and an absurdly good-looking British military captain whom George introduced as Alick Scott, on his way from the Straits Settlements, by way of Japan, to volunteer for the home forces.

Rita wasn't the only one struck by his features. She noticed with some relief that Jenny couldn't seem to look away from him. George noticed as well; they exchanged sly smiles.

There was no ambitious lady willing to perform either Juliet or Delight, as it turned out, but there were plenty of acts, most of them amateurish, a few polished, all heartfelt. A Scots-man dressed as Bonnie Prince Charlie, kilt and all, told jokes that had his comrades hooting with laughter, although his brogue was so thick Rita could hardly follow anything he said. A matron took her place at the piano and gamely accompanied her teenaged daughter, who sang "Jolly Good Luck to the Girl Who Loves a Soldier," managing to hit nearly every note.

You should go over there and sing, Rita whispered to George.

After you go over there and soliloquy, he whispered back.

A young man in spectacles recited a poem he had written about his horse. Another picked out a delicate song on the mandolin. Mr. Hubbard read a passage from his latest book in a low, sonorous voice, his intonation so rhythmic and pre-dictable Rita's eyelids began to sag.

I'll pay you five pounds to sing, she whispered.

I'll pay you ten to start clapping now, to shut him up, he whispered back.

A pair of women from second class were circulating through the audience, quietly selling embossed programs for ten cents apiece, all proceeds going to the charities. Alfred Vanderbilt, at the end of their row, smiled up at the pretty blonde shyly offering him one, pulled out his wallet, and handed her a five dollar bill, no change. Rita thought the lady might faint at his feet in admiration.

The final performance before intermission was the Royal Gwent Male Voice Singers singing "The Star-Spangled Banner," just as they had when the *Lusitania* had departed New York. They took their bows to enthusiastic applause.

As people began to rise from their seats, ready for a break, for a drink at least, Captain Turner appeared in his navy jacket and splendid gold braid, walking up the middle of the room to stand beside the grand piano. The audience hesitated, voices quieting, slowly sinking back into their chairs. The captain rested a hand on the frame of the piano as he waited for their full attention.

"As you know," he began, not even bothering to project his voice—but then he didn't need to, did he, because every single person before him was watching him, nervously alert—"soon we will be entering the so-called war-zone waters. We have received wireless warnings of submarine activity ahead—"

At this, the audience began a collective murmur, but Turner spoke over it, still not raising his voice, so the murmuring swiftly collapsed.

"—however, there is nothing to fear. Upon entering these waters, we will be safely under the escort of the Royal Navy. Tomorrow morning, we shall carry on full steam ahead to Liverpool. You're in good hands, I assure you."

He began to leave, stopped, and turned back to them. The murmuring that had risen once more subsequently died once more.

"You'll notice our running lights are dark tonight, and all skylights and windows and portholes are being covered. You will not remove any of the coverings for any reason. All doors leading to the outside decks are to remain closed. If you see one open, close it. If you see window curtains open, close them. Finally, I must remind the gentlemen not to smoke outside for the duration of the night, lest the light from your matches or cigars or cigarettes be visible to enemy eyes. Thank you, and good evening."

AND THAT, as the saying went, was a tough act to follow. The fundraiser did continue, with the audience that returned to it fortified by at least a glass of wine or gin or lemonade, but the mood had changed. The previous sense of levity felt unnatural now; after each act, the applause came more sparse. By the time the ship's orchestra ended the evening with "God Save the King," followed by "America," everyone seemed in a hurry to get away.

Rita and George said their good nights to Charles and Jenny and Mr. Vanderbilt. Captain Scott offered them a cheerful salute before heading off himself.

"Strange times," George said, as they passed a couple quietly arguing about whether it would be better to sleep in their cabin or in one of the public rooms, fully dressed.

"Yes," Rita agreed. The bare beginning of a headache was starting to uncurl along her left temple. She rubbed at it absently.

The couple were not the only ones with the thought of remaining near the lifeboats. All around them in the lounge, people were claiming settees, pushing chairs together to form makeshift beds. Stewards began fanning through the chamber with armloads of pillows and blankets, distributing them to any who asked. A few of the passengers were audibly debating if they should bed down in the lifeboats, just in case.

Just in case.

Rita looked forward to her actual bed, with its thick feather mattress and satin comforter. Even so, as she watched the men and women in their diamond-and-silk evening best remove their gloves and shoes, settling like weary nomads in whatever nook or cranny they could find, she turned to her brother-in-law and asked, "Do you think it safe to go back down to our staterooms?"

"Yes. Come with me. I'll show you something."

He led her outside, both of them making certain the double doors were quickly opened, quickly shut.

There were others there already—none of them smoking—some pacing the deck in muffled footfalls, some lingering near the lifeboats, eyeing them, maybe wondering the best way to climb in. The world had gone misted again, bepearled, as great walls of fog rolled in, thinning and thickening.

Through it all, the *Lusitania* sliced confidently ahead, spume in her wake.

"I spoke with the staff captain during intermission. We're expected to pass through this Scotch mist for most of the night. Eventually they'll have to sound the foghorn for it, but even so, U-boats can't spot us in this. Even if they can hear our engines, they won't waste a torpedo on a ship they can't see."

Rita wiped the moisture from her cheeks, wrapped her arms around her torso. The fog was cold, slimy cold, chilling her marrow.

"We should go back in," George said. In the murk, she caught only a suggestion of his features, his shadowy hair and the planes of his face, his shadowy eyes. "It's getting late, anyway. Tell you what, tomorrow we'll wave a hearty hello to the emerald coast of Éire as we pass by."

"I've never been," she said, as he opened the door and they both hurried through. "To Ireland, I mean."

"It's enchanting. People say that all the time, trying to anchor a feeling to a place, trying to digest it in a neat word, but

Ireland truly is. Olden. Magical. Someday, after all of this madness is over, we'll visit, Inez and you and me. Giuseppe too, if
we can pry him away from his Italian Arcadia. You'll love it."

"Yes," Rita said. She blinked as her eyes adjusted to the dim
interior of the entrance hall, the grand potted palms in their
huge jardinières, the slick tiled floor, the low-burning electric
lights. Even this late, the elevators hummed, carrying restless
souls up and down the heart of the ship.

She rubbed her temple again, trying to massage away the
pain, but it was only spreading.

"Yes," she repeated. "Of course. Let's all go."

Part 4

Chapter 17

It will not astonish you to learn that conversation aboard the *Saint Paul* primarily concerned the *Lusitania*. It seemed every corner I turned had people clustered together, eating or drinking or smoking or playing cards, all of them talking about what happened, chewing to pieces every juicy detail like morsels of steak. Fact or rumor, it hardly mattered. I heard a few survivors were aboard as well, returning to America on our American-flagged steamer, but if there were, I never encountered them. I imagine they remained in their cabins for the duration. That's what I would have done. What I wanted to do, but my unquiet thoughts would not allow it.

Passengers discussed the torpedo, of course. The breathtaking speed of the ship's demise. The temperature of the water with all those people churning in it; how quickly one might die of exposure at 50° Fahrenheit versus 55°.

The medical facilities aboard. How Cunard offered them, gratis to everyone, even those in steerage, and how so many pregnant third-class women took advantage of it—those were their exact words, *took advantage of it*—by attempting to time their delivery dates to coincide with the week's voyage. So that their babies might be born in a clean room, in a clean bed, with a real doctor and nurse attending.

The first-class ladies enjoying this particular conversation over their tea did not use the word *babies*, however. They said *litters*.

I stopped short my pacing; it felt as if the very air had been siphoned from my lungs. I could only stare at them, their à la mode gowns, their cultured pearls, their discreet sneers.

I remembered that story we heard in Queenstown about the man who witnessed a woman in labor in the ocean after the sinking, a woman still without a name. How she was tossed amid the wreckage, deck chairs and bodies and dogs, screaming for help even as she was giving birth. But he couldn't reach her through the suction and debris. No one could reach her.

In my mind's eye, I see it so vividly. A scarlet bloom spreading around her like poppy petals against green waters. Her dead infant squeezing from her body. Her ashen face as she finally went under.

Oh God, was all I could think, staring at those smug, smiling ladies. I wanted to go over to their table and smash in their heads with the teapot.

Oh God, that poor woman. That poor, poor baby.

FRIDAY, MAY 7, 1915
ABOARD *LUSITANIA*

Rita couldn't sleep. Her headache worsened through the night, a slow, relentless throbbing.

She rolled over in the dark, punched her pillow to fluff it and settled back again. She tried to distract herself with pleasant thoughts. Her family's faces when she showed up at Winter Queen beside George. Or maybe she'd hide just behind him, popping out—*Surprise!*—and how happy everyone would be. How good it would feel to be among them again, even temporarily. The laughter, the hugs, the cheerful loud chaos. Her old room, no doubt still with its antique Tudor bed smelling of beeswax, and the butterscotch silk wallpaper painted with wagtails.

But her imagination could only take her so far. Hours passed; she had no idea how many or what time it might be. The cabin held her close in its small, velveteen dark. She had the regrettably gratifying realization that even the staterooms with portholes were now equally dark and airless, since they were all hidden from the night. No silvery starlight, no briny breeze for anyone now.

She wondered how the people in the lounge were faring. If they were as uncomfortable as she, tossing and turning on sofa cushions.

At one point, exasperated, Rita got up and flicked on the lights so she could check the time. About a quarter to six.

She rubbed her eyes and turned off the lights again, clambered back into the bed. She stared up into the blank nothing of the room, fighting a sigh, then sighed anyway.

The minutes ticked by. She dug her fingers into the sheets, relaxed them. At this rate, she was going to have to skip breakfast entirely and head straight to luncheon. Hell, maybe dinner, if she could ever, *ever* get some sleep.

And, ah . . . just as she was finally beginning to sink into that floating moment between dreams and awake, that tender space soft as cotton wool—the foghorn bellowed.

It might have been worse. Had she had an exterior room, it would have assuredly been worse. Even so, the sudden blast screamed along her nerves, sent a painful jolt straight through her heart, leaving her gasping.

Rita brought her hands to her ears, praying that was the last of it.

It wasn't. The foghorn went off once a minute after that, every single minute, for the next five hours.

She tried sleeping on her side with a pillow covering her ear. She tried sleeping under the covers, with the pillow on top of

those. She tried clenching and then relaxing all the muscles in
her body, from the crown of her head to the tips of her toes,
concentrating on relaxing.

Blaaaast! Silence. *Blaaaast!*

Nothing helped. It occurred to her that if Captain Turner
had decided to deliberately reveal their position as they
steamed along, he could not have chosen a better method.

Eventually, in a dozy blur, she realized the blares from the
horn had ceased. Rita opened her eyes, actively listening now,
counting out the seconds. One minute, another. At a full three
minutes of silence, she turned over again, readjusted the duvet,
and slipped into blessed sleep.

THE BREAKFAST HOUR passed, and Rita didn't stir. She got up
for luncheon, though, because her stomach insisted, even
though her eyes were still gritty and her mouth parched.

Eleanor poured her a glass of water from the basin. Rita sat
up and drank it with her eyes closed, wishing for coffee instead.
When Eleanor asked which dress to lay out, Rita yawned and
said it didn't matter, the stewardess could choose.

A small decision, an unthinking offer. One that would turn
out to matter a great deal, in fact, and very soon.

Eleanor sorted happily through the hangers in the wardrobe. She turned around with a day dress of dusty peach
marocain crêpe draped over her arms, organza sleeves and
cuffs and a long, pleated overskirt. It was delicate, feminine,
perfect for spring.

But Rita was late to sleep, and late to rise and dress, and so
late to lunch, but that was all right. She gave her name and was
shown to a small, unoccupied table for two that she had to herself, toward the bow, just beneath an open porthole. A lapis
sky burned beyond it, unblemished, no hint of mist or clouds.

The room was about two-thirds filled, no one she knew.
Likely George and Charles and the rest had already finished

both breakfast and luncheon, and had moved on to their afternoon entertainments.

When the server arrived, she ordered Norwegian anchovies on toasted rye, grilled filet mignon, chipped potatoes, and the mayonnaise of fresh lobster. Apricot soufflé for dessert.

"And coffee, please," she added, then held up a finger as the man nodded and began to move away. "Wait, sorry. No. Never mind the coffee. A glass of Bordeaux, thank you, and some water."

"Of course, madam. Items ordered from the grill require an extra fifteen minutes or so, if you don't mind."

Despite her fatigue, she smiled. "The more time to enjoy my wine on this fine day."

"Very good, madam."

The table was draped in bleached linen, with a small bud vase of black-hearted anemones framed with fern that trembled almost imperceptibly with the vibration of the vessel. The water inside the vase gently slanted and fell. Slanted and fell.

Somewhere right outside the dining saloon, the string orchestra was playing Vivaldi's "Autumn" from *The Four Seasons.*

The waiter returned with her wine and water. She tried the wine first; it tasted almost sweet along her tongue, but that was probably because she was still so thirsty. And ravenous. She was enveloped in the aroma of hot food, smoked ham and flaky pies, fish and charred meat. Despite what she'd told her server, even fifteen minutes of anticipating her lunch sounded too long.

She took another sip of wine, then moved to the water.

"Germans," a man two tables away was saying, his voice lifting just enough on that one word to prick her ears. "Three or four, what I heard. Hiding below decks in a steward's closet, if you can believe it. Cowering in there all day, just waiting for nighttime to slink out and do what you will."

"Bloody Huns," breathed his companion.

"Aye. Don't speak a word of English, but they sure as hell all had Brownies on them, didn't they? Cameras *and* knives, yeah?"

"Yeah?"

"Fund 'em the first day on a routine check for stowaways. The first day. Captain locked 'em in the brig straight away. Tried to keep it all hush-hush."

There was a pause. Both men looked young, no older than twenty, with the burly, muscular builds of athletes, maybe football players. They wore cashmere sweaters and brown serge trousers, and spoke with a blunt, clipped accent Rita couldn't quite identify. Perhaps something northern, far north.

Fund 'em, she repeated silently to the vase of flowers, trying to place it. *Fund 'em.*

"We got a brig?" the companion asked, sounding doubtful.

"Well, we've got *something* down below, don't we? Maybe another locked closet or a storage room. Meat locker. Ship's got a translator too, but I reckon they wouldn't tell him nothing, just sat there like beaten dogs. Dodgy as hell."

"They'll get it sorted ashore."

"Let 'em rot in the box a while, I say. See how life behind bars loosens their tongues."

Another pause. Rita studied the reflection of the ceiling in her wineglass, white trim and plaster dancing across a circle of dark red.

"Still..." said the companion.

"Yeah?"

"If the Huns smuggled their own aboard to spy, it ain't likely, is it, that they'll come after us. I mean, they wouldn't torpedo their own, would they?"

"I'll tell you what I think, mate. I think we're *all* fodder to 'em," said the first fellow, and let out a belch.

SHE TOOK THE time to enjoy her meal, the rosy anchovies, the grilled filet mignon as thick as her fist. The Bordeaux lost its unexpected sweetness as she ate but not its creaminess, a perfect companion to the beef and lobster and fried potatoes.

The wild sky at her shoulder beamed down at her, honed the shadows along the tablecloth into sharp gray-and-bright. Rita appreciated the air the porthole allowed in, even as she wondered if it should, in fact, be open at all.

If a torpedo hit them—

If the liner should be hit, and tip—

She glanced around, curious now. Nearly every porthole down the wall was open. It seemed the same across the saloon, but the wall over there was far from her, the entire width of the ship, and she couldn't be certain.

Likely they were open because the Royal Navy was escorting them now. The *Lusitania* would be safe under the care of the Admiralty, her best destroyers, so what would it matter if the clean air flowed in and freshened the room?

She finished her meal, savoring the last bite of soufflé, the last swallow of her second glass of Bordeaux, then sat a few minutes longer, listening to the orchestra playing "The Blue Danube" as warm air skimmed her face and neck. She noticed again the water in the bud vase. Its mild, predictable tilting.

Beneath the mahogany paneling and gilded trim, the beveled mirrors and damask adorning this chamber—beneath this wide, domed, fairyland of a saloon—there was a modern and very real vessel still burning coal, still steaming along, transporting Rita and another two thousand or so souls across the globe.

A miracle of sorts, when she considered it, that iron could float.

Rita replaced her napkin on the table, stood up, and began to make her way back to the main doors. All down the exterior walls, that blue, blue sky was captured again and again by the portholes, unobscured by glass, a little too blinding to look at long.

———

SHE RETURNED TO her cabin, a short walk from the saloon. She closed the door and perched on the edge of the bed, feeling sleepy again, thinking it might be nice to take a short nap, only a half hour or so. Then she could ring Charles or George and see what everyone else was up to.

She was bending down to unbutton her boots when the explosion came, a hard hollow WHUUUMP! that stabbed her eardrums and shook the room, toppling the vase of peonies and her water glass from the nightstand. Both cracked against the floor, liquid streaking across the carpet, and at once the world tilted, a hard lean to starboard that dumped her from the bed and cleared the basin of all her cosmetics and perfume bottles in a clatter.

Her ears were ringing, a hard, high whine.

Oh, God. Had they actually been hit? Had they actually—

A second explosion, thunderous but slightly more muffled. The floors and walls and ceiling shuddered; the doors to the wardrobe popped open.

As she was staring at that, shocked, all her clothing swaying wildly on their hangers, George's voice—his strong, beautiful voice—rang through her.

Get outside as quickly as you can.

Rita scrambled to her feet, staggering, and made it to the door. She yanked it open and peered down the hall, expecting smoke or cinders, expecting screaming and blood, but there was only a young lady down the corridor gawking back at her from her own doorway, hugging her life jacket.

"Is it a U-boat?" she asked, her voice shaking.

"That, or a loose mine. You should go up, quickly."

Grab your lifebelt before, if you can.

Rita didn't wait to see if the girl followed her advice. She turned around, fighting the ship's pronounced list to reach the wardrobe, but the top shelf was too high for her. She grabbed the brass railing of the bed, heaved herself up to stand on the covers, fighting to stay upright. With her left hand braced against the wall, she reached inside the wardrobe with her right, groping along the shelf until she found the life jacket.

It was heavy, thickly padded, tapes dangling from every which way, nothing like the lifebelts she'd seen on other voyages, stiff vests made of canvas and cork. She sat down carefully, slid from the bed, and the duvet slid with her, creasing into a pile around her ankles. She lifted up the jacket and shoved her arms through what she hoped were the proper openings; she'd worry about tying the tapes later.

The glass stopper from one of the perfume bottles had come loose. Her mother's Christmas gift to her, that scent that evoked phlox and Winter Queen, saturated the chamber.

There'll be a scramble for the lifeboats.

The ship was alive now, alive and dying, metallic ticks and groans sounding from all over, from everywhere, as the list increased. The lights began to flicker. Still holding on to the bed, Rita took in the strange, askew shambles of her cabin, trying to think of what else to grab.

Only get out if they point a gun at you.

Her pistol. Her reticule.

Another muffled explosion rocked the floor.

She found them both, and ran.

THREE FLIGHTS OF stairs from D Deck to A. Three flights jammed with people, children and babies wailing, a few of the ladies fainting, everyone forced to climb over the scattered dirt and thick fronds of the fallen palms that had decorated each landing, their large pots either shattered or else rolling on their sides as passengers tripped and struggled to get past them.

Rita managed her way up the grand staircase by holding tight to the banister, pulling herself along hand over hand against the list, which now seemed not only starboard but forward as well, as if the liner was sinking by the nose. Just beside her loomed the darkened, open shaft that held the electric elevators, only their cables visible now, the cages stranded far below. Voices rose up from the bottom of that shaft, a slow rising commotion. She would realize later that it came from people trapped in the lifts, trapped without power between landings. But that would be later. Right now, the commotion was all around her: people calling out names, asking each other what had happened, was it truly a torpedo, had the Germans really done it, had anyone seen, was anyone killed?

One flight. Two. *Lusitania* shuddered and moaned.

She's going down. It's not real, and it can't be true, but she's going down—

Rita's breathing grew ragged and her heart was pounding so loudly in her ears that she no longer really heard the racket around her, but she could feel it. The air was dense, cloying, tasting of metal and panic, and *that* was bloody real. A man shoved by, his meaty hand clamping her by the shoulder for leverage as he went. She lost her grip on the banister and knocked back into another man, who caught her with a grunted *Steady on!* but held on to her until she could find the railing again.

She thanked him without looking back, breathless, and kept climbing.

By the time she reached the Boat Deck, the tilt had begun to level out. Rita was able to nearly sprint up the final few steps, her hair coming loose, her arms aching. But there was a mass of passengers blocking her way to the deck outside, dawdling in the entranceway, standing around like dazed sheep. She pushed through them, turning and squeezing, until she reached the doors.

Great black clouds of smoke smeared the sky. The ocean was still speeding past, still *blazing* past. Astonishingly, the ship was plowing ahead as if nothing had happened. She glanced around frantically for George. In the confusion of it all, she hadn't even noticed which side of the ship she'd exited, and now she couldn't remember, was it supposed to be starboard or port? Port, yes, that was right, and there he was, right where he said he'd be, standing calmly with Charles—thank goodness!—and Captain Scott. George spotted her and immediately came forward to take her by the hand.

"There you are! Well done. Come over here with us, out of the way. Did you bring any other lifebelts?" None of them was wearing one.

"No, I—I think there was only this one in my room. Or if there were others, I couldn't reach them." She held her hair back from her face. She looked, bewildered, out at the glass sea, flat calm, a green bump of land in the distance. "Where are the warships? Where is our escort?"

Charles, a lit cigar in his hand, said impassively, "They never arrived."

Her mouth opened; no sound emerged.

Never arrived. The promised safety of the Royal Navy, the assurances of the government, of the Cunard Line. Never arrived.

Deckhands were working feverishly around the lifeboats, yelling orders that were almost impossible to hear under a low, dull roar of steam escaping from somewhere, something, some crucial ruptured line or pipe that was never meant to be ruptured. She counted barely a dozen of them; they were far outnumbered by the passengers and having scant luck keeping them at bay. A few were already trying to push their way aboard the crafts, even before they were ready to be lowered from the davits.

She turned back to George. "Was it a torpedo?"

Captain Scott answered. "Yes. Got us starboard, not far back from the bridge. I talked to at least five people who saw it coming at us, a streak of silver across the water. Two more told me they saw the periscope of the U-boat just before." He scowled at the crewmen, still struggling with the lifeboats' blocks and tackles. "I'm going to go look for more jackets. I'll be back as quick as I can."

He was gone before anyone could reply.

The starboard cant was returning. The lifeboats were gradually centering more and more over the deck, instead of out beyond it. The wind rushed by.

"They're not going to have any luck there," George noted quietly. Rita looked up at him, the lines carving his face more pronounced than ever in the hard direct light. "At this rate, when they try to lower them, they'll just scrape along the hull of the ship. The rivets will shred them apart."

"Should we try starboard, then? When Mr. Scott returns, I mean?"

"Doubt it will help. We're going too fast. I suppose they can't reverse the engines, or they would have done it by now. Lowering a boat at this speed will likely cause it to capsize as soon as it touches the water. But even if we slow, those starboard boats are likely hanging too far off the side by now to board."

She shook her head. "So... we just..."

"We just stay here. We watch and see."

"We're getting farther and farther from land."

Neither man responded; they didn't need to. The green-and-gold promise of Ireland's shore was obviously, gradually receding. Along with the engines, the rudder must have been incapacitated too.

Staff Captain Anderson was making his way through the crowd, arms lifted, braid glinting under the sun, shouting that everything was *fine*, it was all *fine*, the ship would *not* sink, of course she wouldn't sink. Everyone must remain calm.

A surge of people from steerage trampled past him, dragging children of all ages along by the hand or wrist as they hurried toward the lifeboats. Stokers coated in coal dust wove between them all like living shades moving through the chaos.

"Here," George said briskly. He turned Rita by the shoulders to face him. "Let me fix this jacket for you."

"Is it not right? I was in something of a hurry when I put it on."

He smiled. "It's backward, which will do you no good at all. These jackets are designed in such a way to keep your head up and your front as much out of the water as possible, almost as if you could float on your back. But you must have it on the right way 'round, or you'll be in for an unpleasant surprise."

She shrugged out of it, put it on again the correct way, and as George was fastening her tapes Captain Scott returned with three more.

"Here we are. Took a bit of searching, but I found these. Mr. Frohman, sir, may I help you into yours?"

Charles waved his cigar in the air. "I don't need one. Give it to someone else."

"*Charles*," Rita protested. He looked her, pushed out his lower lip, then nodded.

"All right. If I must."

Rita stood back to give them room, clutching the third life jacket to her chest. George quickly donned his as the captain assisted Charles.

The commotion around them was growing more frenzied. People were running, stumbling, knocking into each other. Dogs were barking and snarling, at least a dozen of them skittering about unleashed. The deckhands had achieved some success with one of the boats; the rush to fill it was like watching wasps swarm. Within moments, it was packed with women and children and unhappy infants.

An extra set of crewmen began to yell at everyone else to get back, *get back*, while the other sailors were handling the ropes.

A man in his shirtsleeves darted up to Rita and wrenched the life jacket from her hands, hard enough to send her to her knees.

"*Figlio di puttana*," she shouted after him as he ran off, in her loudest, reach-the-back-of-theatre voice. "You ruddy *bastard!*"

"I'll go back down," Captain Scott said, as he and George helped her to her feet. "Don't worry. I'll find another."

"No, you can't," she argued, stupidly close to tears. "Don't go. There's no time." She began to pull at her tapes. "Take mine instead."

"I'll find another," he repeated, patient, and disappeared into the bedlam.

The filled lifeboat started at last to jerk lower, swinging wildly as it went. The ladies aboard began to cry out, echoed by the little ones, but still the boat lurched down, down—

One of the crewmen lost his hold on his rope. The stern plunged, a sickening dip, and everyone in the boat was thrown screaming into the sea.

Rita was staring at where it had been—just seconds ago, where that boat had been, all those people—horrified, both hands pressed over her mouth. She realized she was breathing in short, choking sobs around her fingers.

Charles limped close, put his arm around her shoulder.

"Come away, my sweet. Come stand back here with me and save your strength. We'll find our calm together in this storm."

They retreated to the exterior wall of the ship, George too. Rita closed her eyes, managing her fright. Then Captain Scott was back as well, thankfully wearing a life jacket.

"This was it," he told them, low. "There's no power anywhere, no lights, nothing. As far as I could tell, everything below the Promenade Deck is awash. I could go no farther."

"The lifeboats are no good," George replied, just as low.

"Agreed." Alick Scott rubbed a hand over his eyes. "Down by the Smoking Room, there had been one loaded and ready to go, but the rope broke, or was cut, poor bastards. It must have swung like a damned pendulum back against the wall, crushing every—" He shot a glance at Rita, cut himself short. "Let's move to the railing. It'll be easier to hold on."

The forward tilt was severe enough and the deck was slick enough that they had to hold hands to reach the rails, pulling each other along in a chain. Rita wrapped her arms gratefully around the top bar. If she leaned out, she could see below to the water, her hair whipping about her shoulders and face, her hem smacking hard against her ankles. To her right was the bow, rapidly going under. To her left, out at sea behind them, was a wake of people and foam and shattered lifeboats, brilliantly illuminated by the sun.

"We need to stay here as long as possible," George was saying, next to her. "We need to take our chances with the sea when it comes."

High above them, the funnels began a low resonance, dull and baleful, still spewing smoke. One of the guy wires broke, then another: gunshots cracking through the air, the long wires flipping and slicing.

A perambulator rolled past, too swift to catch, dashing toward the bow. A pair of chocolate Labradors chased after it, pink tongues lolling.

George turned to Rita.

"Listen, I need you to tell Inez something from me."

"No," she snapped at once, instinctive. "Anything you have say, you can tell her yourself."

"Tell her that love at first sight does exist. Tell her she is the living proof of it. Miracles are fact, as sure as she is fact." The ship lurched; they both lost their footing, caught themselves again. "Tell her that."

"No, George. You're going to tell her. You are, because, by God, we're all getting out of this, I swear we're getting out of it."

She spoke the words because she had to speak them; they were the only possible words to speak. But they rushed from her so quickly, without substance, without proof.

"Marguerite." He smiled at her, chucked her lightly under the chin. Behind him rushed blue ocean against blue sky, a dazzling May day. "I know you'll always be the strong one for her, the big sister. So remember it, please, and tell her. No matter what comes."

THE FORECASTLE WAS gone, submerged, the base of its mast tipping crazily from the water that lathered and billowed around it, rising in a rush of green. The *Lusitania* continued her endless arc out into the Celtic Sea, leaning and leaning but slowing a little. Even so, the lifeboats swung over the deck, useless, the collapsible boats beneath them still fixed in place. Nearly everyone around Rita and her little group had already abandoned the middle of the ship for the false safety of the stern, gradually rising above the ocean as the hull creaked and cracked in protest.

An elderly woman in a black gown lined with ermine hiked by, no coat, no life jacket, using her cane to pull herself along in slow, hard thumps. Captain Scott went to her, urging her to take his jacket. She never nodded or agreed, only gazed up at him blankly. She allowed him to place the jacket on her, but as soon as he was finished, she only walked away again, ignoring his pleas to join them at the railing, making her slow, thumping way aft.

All three of them offered their life jackets to him. He declined.

"I'm a good swimmer. Lived around the world. I know tropical waters, cold waters, currents and tides. We're not that far from land, so we might have a shot. But if I have to die here, so be it. No use worrying about it."

Charles took a long, last drag on his cigar. He dropped it to the deck, crushing it under his heel, a smear of ash along the fine teak. When he looked up again, their eyes met, his so kind, his dear face so familiar, his gray hair tattered with the wind.

Rita tried to smile, but her lips wouldn't obey. Tears smeared her vision.

I'm the strong one, and I'm not afraid. I am never afraid. This is the end, somehow the end, and I'm not afraid.

Charles Frohman, her mentor, her guide, then said the words that would haunt the rest of her life, words she would repeat over and over again to the press and friends and colleagues, that she would put in her movie, emblazon on posters and advertisements, making certain that no one, *no one*, would ever forget them.

"Why fear death?" he asked, and reached up to gently wipe away a tear from the corner of her eye. "It is the most beautiful adventure in life."

The ship reeled again and plunged again, *really* plunged, rousing a swell of screams from the hundreds of people crowded along the stern. A wall of water was devouring the front of the ship, frothing up from the bow.

George grabbed her hand. Rita grabbed Charles's.

It was a mountain of green seawater, an avalanche of water, rushing faster and faster, higher and higher, filled with monstrous dark shapes—splayed people, deck chairs, sharp broken things.

Rita said, *This is the end,* or tried to, but the avalanche came smashing over them. It ripped their hands apart, ripped their bodies apart, sending them spinning down and away into emerald darkness.

Chapter 18

I know you tried to hold on to him. Of course I know you did.

It's going to sound strange, and maybe you won't even believe it, but I also know exactly when it happened.

That Friday afternoon, I was in the conservatory with my violin, serenading a nest of baby birds in one of the pomegranate trees. I was playing softly, because they were only hatchlings, still pink and blind. I was lost in the music, listening to the forest notes, Mab's notes, caught in her dream. But all at once, my eyes—

My heart—

It's hard to describe.

All the light around me was doused in an instant, no warning, no quarter. The music was gone; the air was gone. I couldn't breathe. My knees buckled and my heart just . . . stopped.

It lasted only seconds, but I had to sit down, I was so dizzy. I had to put down my violin.

I haven't picked it up since.

FRIDAY, MAY 7, 1915
IN THE CELTIC SEA

The cold of it nearly caused her to inhale in shock, but Rita
managed to keep her lips pressed closed as the water dragged
her lower, her arms out, her hair dark tentacles around her
face. She was tumbling, flailing, her dress wrapped tightly
around her legs, unable to kick, unable to right herself. Tiny,
brilliant bubbles surrounded her like a celebration, trapped
air siphoning away from her clothes. She spun and spun,
caught in an eddy, and when it finally loosened, there were
spots in her eyes.

The layers of her skirts unwound, releasing more bubbles.
She kicked as hard as she could for the surface, her lungs afire,
buoyed by the life jacket, aiming for the silvery green luminance shimmering above her.

She surfaced. Sucked in a huge breath, coughing as she in-
haled saltwater as well, swinging up and down, back and forth,
as the sky rocked above her head and the sunlight blinded her.
Screams bounced along the waves, the rushing thunder of the
ship. She tore her hair from her face, trying to see where she
was, where the *Lusitania* was, was it near enough to hit her—
but before she could take another breath, the suction stole her
again, pulling her under, and everything went silent.

Just her heartbeat in her ears, a frantic drumming.

Just the gurgle and slosh of the deep water all around,
smothering.

The sea faded to olive, to black. All the bubbles were gone.
Her eyes burned, her lungs burned. She kicked and kicked, desperate, fighting for her life to reach the surface again, but she
was stories below it, fathoms below. Her skirts billowed and
thinned around her like a jellyfish, so much silk and organza,
so much extra drag. Her corset bit into her torso.

I'm not going to die here, I'm not ready to die, I won't die here, like this—

For some reason, for no reason, just luck or physics or chance, the eddy weakened. She fought her way upward again, *Please, God, let me be going up,* and when the light returned, there was a new shadow above her, almond-shaped. A lifeboat.

This time when she broke free, Rita took a deep, whooping breath. The lifeboat was overturned but still floating, so she sliced her way to it, green water, white froth.

She reached it at the same time as a man with a wide walrus moustache; he grabbed it by the bow, she the stern. They briefly locked eyes, then both turned away again, searching their surroundings.

There were people everywhere, alive and dead, wreckage everywhere, deck chairs, planks, ropes, shattered boats, barrels and oars. A pair of guinea hens in a coop next to a life buoy squawked and threw themselves against the wood, scattering feathers.

She forced herself to look at the people, no matter the blood, no matter the gore. Charles and George were nowhere in sight.

A stoker swam up beside her, startling blue eyes in a face still blackened with soot. Like her, he dug his fingers into the scalloped edges of the wood and tried to inch higher.

A woman nearby was wailing and sputtering. Rita twisted in place and saw that she was struggling to keep her head above water, despite the fact that she was in a life jacket. But it was backward, Rita realized. Just as her own had been before George fixed it.

"Here," she called hoarsely, still holding on to the overturned boat but reaching out an arm to the woman. "Swim over here."

Slowly, awkwardly, the woman did. Rita grabbed her by the sleeve and pulled her the rest of the way to the boat. Then, like everyone else around her who still could, she turned to watch the end of the *Lusitania*.

The steamer was still groaning, venting steam and smoke as her stern lifted higher above the waterline. Lifeboats dangled crookedly down her hull, white against dark. Wires and aerials fell every which way; the funnels were collapsing. Portholes were exploding open, rings of brass flung bright and blazing into the air as the pressure inside the sinking ship built. As her end rose, her four giant bronze propellers broke free of the water, liquid pouring from the blades, blinding and beautiful, ropes of diamonds falling back into the sea.

Two-thirds of the liner was underwater; she tilted so far starboard it seemed a wonder she hadn't already toppled over. Still people clung to the railings, swung from the falls.

As the stern began to disappear beneath the waves, they jumped or tumbled from the sides. More than a few struck the propellers on their way down.

Then the *Lusitania* was gone, swallowed beneath the skin of the sea.

Seconds later came a mighty underwater *BOOM*, an eruption of boiling ocean and debris that pushed people and corpses and wreckage far and wide, a tsunami of the dead and desperate rolling toward them, the water stained with blood.

Rita turned her back to it, trying to climb higher up the lifeboat. Her stocking feet slipped for purchase against the wood; both of her boots had been torn away by the suction.

IT WAS 2:28 P.M. on that lovely May day. A mere eighteen minutes since the German torpedo had sliced across the Atlantic and blown a hole as large as a house into *Lusitania*'s starboard hull, rendering moot all standard disaster protocols: the watertight doors, the lifeboats, women and children first.

Twenty-five minutes since Rita had placed her linen napkin on the dining saloon table and risen from her chair, her luncheon finished.

THE OVERTURNED LIFEBOAT still had its canvas cover attached. The stoker was working at the ropes, attempting to loosen them so they could flip the boat right-side up, as more and more people swam up or drifted up, trying to gain a handhold on the steep, curving sides. The undersea explosion had scattered everyone and everything in a wide crescent at least a half mile across, but people—the people still alive—were doing what they could to stay afloat, clinging to oars, to boxes, to narrow strips of planking.

Apparently a few lifeboats had successfully launched after all, but nearly all of them were filled, and none rowed close. They remained far away along the blue, nowhere near the swath of the dead and living bobbing in the water. None of them even tried to row close, no matter how many arms waved, how many voices begged.

Rita had managed to climb as high as she could up the craft, hooking one hand over the thick, flat base of the keel, using the other to tug along the woman with the backward jacket.

"I'm terribly sorry," the lady was saying, trying to follow her. "So sorry. I believe I've injured my shoulder."

"It's all right," Rita panted, pulling her higher. "Here, just hold on here."

"Have you seen my girls?" the lady asked. Sunlight cast gold along her dark blond hair, dripping with water. A tortoiseshell comb was still neatly fixed in her chignon. "Anna and Gwen? Have you seen them?"

"I haven't. I'm sorry. Just hold on right here, all right? Keep holding on."

The boat was being overrun. A thicket of survivors had spotted them, were splashing their way to them, pushing aside the floating rubble in their paths. Pushing aside the dead, men and women and even children, so *many* children, faceup or facedown, water lapping their heads, smoothing slick over their soft faces. Some were still in the arms of their mothers, the life jackets keeping them tragically afloat.

Hands smacked against the wooden shell, a hollow banging; bodies heaved upward. Inch by inch, the lifeboat was sinking. The stoker and a few of the other men were telling the new-comers to stop, to go back, find something else afloat, anything else, but it didn't matter. Logic had fled, drowned in the cold, and the hands kept reaching. The desperate kept flocking, yel-ling for help, praying for help. The boat rocked and rocked.

The sea hit her ankles. Rita sat up taller, began hunting for anything else nearby to seize, a barrel, anything, for when the entire contraption tipped.

Then, damn it, it happened. She *thought* it was happening, that they were being capsized. The lifeboat listed hard and began to spin, dislodging about half the people. The tortoise-shell comb lady next to her cried out, and Rita took her wrist with the half-formed notion of dragging her along with her when they spilled, dragging her to some new safety—but with a tremendous grating sound, *another boat* scraped free from under theirs.

A collapsible boat, upright, its canvas sides mostly down. But somehow it floated.

The survivors knocked loose followed it, grappling with it, some trying to clamber inside, but most clinging to the sides as it was carried away with the current.

The upturned lifeboat steadied, placid now atop the calm-ing sea.

Rita was still stationed near the keel, clinging with all her might to the side. She looked around until she located the Irish coast off her right shoulder, only a few miles away. She squinted and searched for any sign of rescue, ships, fishing smacks, smokestacks. There was nothing.

Surely they knew about the sinking, though. Surely they'd seen it, they'd heard it—

The ship's wireless operators must have had time to send out a distress call—

A woman hanging from the other side of the craft cried out, pointing away from the land, toward the open sea.

"Look there! There they are!"

Oh, God. Not rescue, and not far, not even as far as the coast: a submarine had erupted from the sea, iron gray, streaming water, its blunt nose aimed at them. It floated there in place, faceless, no men emerging, but clearly a predator observing the death throes of its prey.

"They won't shoot us again," the man with the walrus moustache said, but he sounded unconvinced. "There'd be no point to it. They won't target us again."

The stoker snorted. "You sure about that, mate?" He made a rude gesture with his hand toward the U-boat.

Figli di puttana, Rita said to them, under her breath. Perhaps they were watching, perhaps they could read lips, perhaps they spoke Italian as well as German. She hoped they did.

"*You sons of whores,*" she yelled, rising to her knees. She would have said worse, but it was the worst profanity she knew.

The U-boat maneuvered a slow circle around the wreckage. Then, silent and swift, it submerged again, not even a periscope visible among the dead.

Everything smelled of blood and salt.

THE NEXT FOUR hours took on a monstrous, hallucinogenic quality; time slowed down. They'd never managed to flip over the boat, but Rita was able to stay more or less above the waterline. Barely. The sun blazed hot but the water was so cold, and she found that at times she had to drop down and submerge

her legs or splash water on her chest and arms, because otherwise she was burning up, the top of her head scorched, her
tongue swollen.

"Have you seen my daughters?" the lady with the injured
shoulder kept muttering. "They were in the water with me. We
were together. We all jumped together. Have you seen them?"

"No," Rita always answered, stroking her good arm. "No,
but we'll keep searching."

The fact was, she wasn't really searching for Gwen and
Anna, the daughters of Marguerite, Lady Allan.

(*Why, we share the same given name,* Rita had told her, after
coaxing Lady Allan into supplying it. Rita tried to sound encouraging, cheerfully distracting; the other woman's face was
already red with fever or sun. *Isn't that something?*

Which name? Lady Allan had replied, her eyes glazed. *Which
are you, Gwen or Anna?*)

Rita wasn't searching for a pair of girls she'd never seen,
never met, could not possibly recognize, even among the float-
ing dead. She was searching for George, beloved of Inez. For
Charles, beloved of her. For Captain Scott, so gallant. For
Jenny or even Alfred Vanderbilt, or Staff Captain Anderson,
Captain Turner. Eleanor. People whose faces she knew.

There were so many dead. And so many still mumbling for
help, still pleading and sobbing, although less than had been
there an hour before. Or two.

Those without lifebelts sank into silence, one by one.
Those with lifebelts but injuries, broken limbs, smashed
bodies, bleeding heads ... those folks only settled into a whim-
pering quiet, and then quiet absolute.

The dogs had continued their distraught barking for about
a quarter of an hour after the sinking.

The hens in their coop had lasted only minutes.

As the lifeboat moved through a plume of blood flowing
from a cluster of bodies trapped in wreckage nearby, arms

wide out, heads back, mouths open—*don't look, don't look*—
Rita began to wonder about sharks.

Were there sharks off Ireland? She tried to remember her lessons, those long-ago instructions from her tutors, and couldn't.

Yes, there were sharks. No, there weren't. The water was
opaque either way, hiding any kind of monster.

She wanted to think about her beloveds. She wanted to
think about Giuseppe, wonderful Giuseppe. Her parents, her
sister and brother. But what she found herself remembering instead was that bloated, gray face from her childhood, the son of
the gardener who'd drowned in the koi pond. The horror that
had crawled through her upon finding him. The way his body
had vanished halfway into the murk but his hair still stirred, the
fish still came up and tested their mouths against him—

"Stop it," she scolded herself, but had to bend over to hide
her face in one hand. She could not waste the tears. "Just stop."

Lady Allan brushed her fingers along Rita's hair, carefully,
tenderly, all the way from her crown to her waist.

"Have you seen my daughters," she whispered, pressing close.

THE WORLD SLURRED into the unreal. She was too cold, and
she was too hot; she flashed from one to the other, only sometimes she was both. Lady Allan had stopped mumbling, her
chin to her chest, but her body still slumped against Rita's.

Seagulls spiraled above them all, white and black against
the peaceful blue, descending to alight upon the corpses and
the living, testing to see what was what. The people still alive
swiped at them feebly but the dead had no defenses, and the
gulls soon figured out the difference. They began to feast.

Porpoises danced among them, great black porpoises. Rita
thought them sharks at first, but no, they were porpoises, with
smiling beaks and shiny eyes, frolicking, spouting water, as if
their games in the sea today were like any other day, and the
entire world held their joy.

She heard singing. A celestial chorus accompanied by symphonies, by hundreds of orchestras and a long, low wailing
that slowly faded to silence.

The sky became crowded with angels.

Rita gazed up at them, awestruck. They were white and lacy
as clouds. They reached down to her and she tried to reach
back, she wanted to reach back, but her fingers were frozen into
claws along the ridges of the boat. She could not unclench them.

The angels raised their arms. They summoned a circle of
stars, right there in the middle of the day. A crown of stars
that descended to her, glorious and spinning, so glorious she
had to close her eyes and drop her head and sleep.

She had to sleep.

"Oy, she alive or dead?"

"Alive, I think. Hey, you, miss! Wake up, eh?"

Rita was on her back, flat on her back, not clinging sideways to the lifeboat like a decrepit mermaid. She was . . .

Someone slapped her cheek. She turned her head, gasping.
Her spine ached, her body ached, her eyes could hardly open,
crusted with salt. She tried to rub away the crust, and moving
her hand was like moving a sack of meat, no feeling, no heat
or cold. It was something apart from her.

"There she is!" said that same voice, encouraging. Young.
Male. Cockney? "All right, luv. You wait here, eh? You wait
here for me. I'll nip down to the galley and be back in a jiff."

Her eyelids slitted open. It seemed dark to her, almost dark,
but as she stared upward at the—

—clouds? were they angels or clouds?—

—sky streaked with colors, she realized that she was lying
on something hard and flat. Something uncomfortable that
was rocking, moving up and down, roiling her empty stomach.

Sunset flamed above her, a vault of pink and orange and
vermilion. She was on the deck of a boat, some sort of boat.

Rita tried to sit up, struggling against a blanket tucked around her. An unfamiliar woman with dark blond hair leaned over her with a frown. She had one arm in a sling.

"Don't move yet. We're on the *Katrina*."

"The..."

"Greek-flagged, but I'd be surprised. The sailors aboard seem about as Greek as I. Yours will be returning any moment now with a mug of hot tea. Ceylon, if I'm not mistaken."

Rita rubbed her meat hand against her face. Her voice came out in a croak. "Am I alive? Is this a dream?"

The woman shook her head, considering it. "I don't know."

What? she tried to say, but what little saliva there'd been in her mouth was now gone. Her tongue was a strip of leather, as foreign as her hands, and all the angels were gone as if they had never been.

"You saved me," the woman said. She took Rita's numb hand and pressed it to the side of her neck, bowing her head. Her chest began to hitch.

Rita scowled, remembering her now, remembering her loss.

"Don't cry," she managed to rasp. "Marguerite, no. Don't cry. Not yet."

THE TEA WAS scalding. She held the thick, chipped mug with both hands as slowly the feeling returned to her fingers. It was a good ship's mug, heavy and plain, in this moment more precious than the finest bone china. Finer than solid gold. The chips detracted nothing from her relief at holding it, from sipping that hot Ceylon or whatever it was. She could scarcely taste it, but by gosh, she could feel its heat.

The sailor had brought her a slice of jam tart as well, cupped in a paper napkin, messy strawberry goo smearing his fingers as he handed it to her. That wedge of shortbread and jam was the most delicious thing Rita had ever tasted and ever would again. She devoured it, down to the final crumb, then sucked the last hint of strawberry from her nailbeds. If she could have eaten the napkin, she would have.

Lady Allan had been correct. Despite its jaunty blue-and-white flag, the *Katrina* wasn't a Greek fishing vessel at all. It was the SS *Westborough*, a British merchant ship in disguise, and her crew knew the filigreed coast of Ireland and the waters off of it as sure as they knew their way home. They'd picked up as many survivors as could fit on board—maybe a few too many—and were now steaming toward Queenstown.

But they were still miles and miles away. It had taken hours to reach the wreckage of the *Lusitania*, and it would take hours more to make it to port.

The two Marguerites sat beside each other on the deck with their backs against the hull, arms and knees touching, both wrapped in blankets, both with refilled mugs of tea, a little weaker this time but still hot. A pile of life jackets slowly leaked seawater along the forecastle, although some of the survivors refused to take theirs off.

The air felt mild now, almost pleasant. The pinkish gold sky was dimming into mother-of-pearl.

Compared to the *Lusy*, the *Katrina*—the *Westborough*, Rita corrected herself—seemed to chug along at a snail's pace.

But at least they were afloat. At least they were alive.

At least someone had come for them.

In fact, broadsheets around the world in the upcoming days and weeks would print dramatic firsthand accounts from sailors and townsfolk about the plucky fleet of vessels around Queenstown and Kinsale that had raced out to help as soon as they could, as soon as word of the torpedoing of the *Lusitania* spread like wildfire around the towns and along the wirelesses. Humble local fishing boats, rusting merchant boats, tugs, trawlers, an old ferry, even a rowboat, all of them speeding as fast as they could, all of them braving the risk of more submarines, more attacks. And all of them scooping up as many survivors as they could, in every condition imaginable.

(By Saturday morning, when it was clear there were no more survivors to be found, many of those same boats would return—paid, this time, by Cunard—to scoop up the dead.)

The *Westborough* plowed through the dusk. Her deck was crammed with bedraggled people, many clutching injuries, many bleeding. A doctor moved among them, asking soft questions, applying bandages and aid when he could. They huddled together, those poor tattered souls, whispering together, moaning or sometimes weeping together.

A man with a smashed leg stretched out before him, blood and pulp, the bone jutting out, begged for opium, for rum, anything to stop the agony. Eventually, he was carried away on a blanket by a pair of sailors, and his pleas grew inaudible.

Every now and again, a round of cackling laughter would erupt from some knot of souls, edged with hysteria. It spread, contagious, from person to person, lasting minutes before dying down.

Lady Allan was leaning more and more of her weight against Rita, her eyes swollen shut, her head coming to rest on Rita's shoulder; Rita did her best to keep them both upright. A woman a few feet away was invoking the name of the Almighty in a husky voice, but she couldn't seem to complete her prayer.

Dear Lord, please... Dear Lord, please...

Numb with exhaustion, Rita wasn't sure what was left to pray about anymore, either.

Gwen. Anna. George and Charles. *Dear Lord, please, all of them safe on another boat.*

A stack of clouds hugged the skyline to the southwest, deep blue ink splintered with flashes of white. A distant storm, brushing along waters Rita would never know. Or maybe those angels saying *Hello, you're awake and alive, hello.*

HER TEA-AND-TART sailor came over and told her that, although he had looked, he hadn't discovered an extra pair of socks for her, and he'd give her his own, but they had so many holes in them she'd likely be better off without them. He offered instead to wrap her bare feet in some newspapers that he had scavenged. Rita gratefully accepted, and he knelt before her, gently lifting one foot, then the other, bundling them in the crackling paper, tying everything in place with string that he cut with a wicked-looking knife.

Across the deck, the doctor was working over a man writhing and choking in pain. With his back to Rita, she couldn't see what the doctor was doing, but when he straightened he was holding an arm in his hands. A severed arm, still dripping blood, clearly visible by the running lights. He tossed it over the side of the boat, just as someone might do a fish they'd hooked that was too small.

AFTER THE SECOND hour of Lady Allan slumped against her, Rita shifted some, trying to ease the ache in her back, then shifted again. An odd, hard stone dug into her thigh.

She ran a hand down her side, encountering the stitched pocket in her dress.

It was her pistol, her good luck charm. Her reticule and everything in it was long gone, surrendered to the Atlantic, but her pistol was still in that pocket. Throughout everything, it was still there.

To be honest, she'd forgotten all about it.

THEY REACHED QUEENSTOWN around one in the morning. Rita carefully disentangled herself from Marguerite Allan and stood to watch the approach of the wharf, a line of gaslights flickering uneasily along the quay. As the *Westborough* drew nearer, she was able to make out shadows of people standing around, staggering around, maybe even crowds of people but indistinct beyond the lights, like packs of dogs lurking in the darkness.

The press, she thought, but the worry drifted away from her, unmoored.

A bed, she thought. *Shelter. Food. Sleep.* And those were the worries that burrowed into her.

For the first time in hours, she heard babies crying, held in the arms of the people watching and waiting on the shore.

Oh, good, she thought, floaty and distant. *Good. They made it, some of them made it.*

The *Westborough's* crew wove through the crowd on the deck, preparing to dock. Rita scanned the quay, her mind sharp and blurred at the same time, searching for the person most likely to be in charge. Anyone still in a hat, perhaps. In a uniform. With an assistant, or carrying a clipboard.

Lady Allan, bereft of her daughters, needed a real bed. She needed rest. Rita could do that much, at least. She could do at least that.

The boat eased into a slip, and a mass of shadow people swept forth to meet it, held back, barely, by a line of policemen. Even though there were no camera flashes, she instinctively reached for her hair, for her combs, and encountered only a wavy, heavy mess, thickened with salt. She began to quickly separate it into thirds to braid it. When it was done she pinched her cheeks and lips, forcing the blood back to her face.

She bent and whispered into Lady Allan's ear, *Stay here, I'll come for you soon,* then took her blanket and made her way toward the gangplank, her newspaper shoes rustling. She spotted a man with a clipboard—*amen!*—pacing the dock below her, gesturing to the people around him, flipping through his paperwork, pointing this way and that.

A Cunard man, then. Or the mayor. Or the chief of police. Whoever he was, that's who she needed.

She pushed back her braid so it fell along her spine and squared her shoulders, wearing her blanket like a stole. Others aboard began to come awake, rising and shambling toward her. She straightened the ruined pleats of her gown, waiting for the sailor guarding the lowered gangplank to gesture her way.

He did, a quick curl of his fingers.

She wasn't the first one off, but she was the first woman. Instantly the people ashore began to push forward, calling out names in hopeful, cracked voices, so many names. So many voices. Rita listened intently even as she headed toward the clipboard man, but no one was calling for her. No one sounded like George or Charles.

She tried to ignore them, the ragged figures still pushing toward the boat, men and women jostling, some clutching those crying children. She paid a bit more attention to a group of Royal Navy sailors in uniform holding stretchers, but kept her focus on that man with the paperwork, his hair ginger or blond or pale brown under the gaslights, his moustache neat. He wore a tailored suit and a stickpin in his tie that winked at her as she approached, a small diamond eye in the head of a fox.

"Please, sir," she said, in her most Buckingham Palace voice, and went as far to touch her fingertips to the tweed of his sleeve. "I've a lady with me injured and half dead, in dire need of aid and shelter. Can you help?"

She brought a hand to her forehead, ready to feign light-headedness, but to her dismay she didn't need to feign it. The quayside rocked beneath her papered feet, and it took a moment for the land to right itself again.

"I'm sorry," Rita said in her normal voice, and meant it. She lowered her hand; her eyes began to tear. She swallowed, still tasting salt in her throat. "I'm sorry."

The man gazed at her as if she were a little lost lamb who'd returned home badly shorn, a combination of pity and distress.

"I can help," he said. "Tell me your name, miss, and hers. We'll get you sorted."

QUEEN'S HOTEL WAS the best in town, or so she was informed, and also one of the last that wasn't already stuffed to the gills with the *Lusitania*'s anguished survivors. Even so, Rita could see at once that *best* was a subjective word in this case, as the room they were assigned was small and narrow and smelled of mold, and the sheets on the two beds didn't appear to have been changed since the last guests. Dust lay thick across the windowsill; when she pulled her fingers away from the sash after forcing it open to dilute that smell, her hands came away smeared in grit.

She didn't care, really. It didn't matter. It was a room. It had beds; the beds had linens and blankets, whatever their state. There was a pitcher and bowl painted with butterflies on the bureau, fresh water ready to pour.

She helped Lady Allan into the bed by the window, removing the woman's shoes, unbuttoning the back of her gown, loosening her corset. It turned out that she had a broken collarbone, according to the doctor on the *Westborough*. Marguerite Allan had thought that she'd injured it against a railing just as the *Lusitania* was beginning her final plunge. Just before she had jumped.

"Anna," she insisted weakly now from the bed, clinging to the ripped gauze of Rita's sleeve. Her eyes were pleading. "Gwen."

"I know. We'll look for them in the morning, I promise. I'll go look. There were so many other boats out there besides ours, so no doubt they were on one of them. Right now, you need to sleep. There's water for you there, in that glass. Do you see it? And I'll be just across the room."

"Yes. Yes, all right."

The hotel's kitchen had been closed by the time they arrived, with no one around to open it. Several of the other

guests—the regular ones—had assembled plates of sugared biscuits and jugs of lemonade, a few shots of whiskey, for the
survivors coming in, but that was all. The only person who
could start up the stoves in the kitchen, open the locked larders
and recall his staff was the owner, a Mr. Humbert, but no one
could locate him.

(It turned out that Otto Humbert was a German immigrant.
As soon as he'd heard about the sinking, he'd retreated to the
wine cellar of his hotel with his family to hide, justly fearing
Irish riots and reprisals.)

Rita had helped herself to two shots of whiskey and three
of the thin biscuits. Lady Allan would take none. So when
Rita peeled what was left of the newspaper from her feet and
unrolled her destroyed stockings down her calves, her stomach was growling but her blood was warmed by the liquor, and
that was something.

She left her dress and corset to dry over a chair, keeping on
her damp chemise, and pulled the blankets to her chin. She'd
turned off the electric lights but left one of the oil lamps burning low, because it felt safer than the dark.

It was a good thing she did, too, because less than an hour
later, when the doorknob rattled and two more frayed and
shivering women were shown into the room, she was able to
rise wearily and gesture to her bed before joining Lady Allan
in hers.

Chapter 19

After my spell in the conservatory, I was determined to head into town. I knew that George was on the *Lusitania* (nothing mystic or mysterious there; we had coordinated our schedules), and I knew, everyone knew, that the *Lusitania* was considered a particularly plum prize by the Huns. The London papers had devoted a great many columns to it, and to the warning that the Imperial German Embassy had advertised in New York.

So I knew that something had happened to the *Lusitania* because I knew, in my heart and bones, that something had happened to my husband. The ship must have gone down. I knew that as well, but I did not know where.

Maman had set off that morning to pay a call on our lord-lieutenant. You know her; she was still pulling every string she could to spare Alfred from the clutches of the army, or at least spare him the front. Alfred and Papa, however, were more philosophical about it all, or perhaps just more realistic. On that pretty Friday, one of their last days together, they had gone fishing.

(Alfred doesn't know about Maman's visit to the lord-lieutenant, by the way, so please don't tell him. It would upset him so.)

So I was alone at Winter Queen. I packed a bag as quickly as I could and had the auto take me into Medmenham. I took a seat inside the Ruby Rabbit, nursing a cider. It wasn't long before the first fellow burst in with the news. He worked at the telegraph office and was brimming with importance, but almost at once he was followed by what seemed a score more people who knew: The *Lusitania* had been hit, but she was still afloat. No, she had been hit and had sunk. All passengers and crew had been saved. No, nearly everyone had perished.

"Where?" I demanded of anyone, everyone. "Where was she torpedoed?"

"Ireland," I was told. It was the one fact they all agreed upon. "Off Queenstown."

I left my cider on the bar, got back into the auto, and had the chauffer take me to the train station.

SATURDAY, MAY 8, 1915
QUEENSTOWN, IRELAND

The next morning, Rita began to walk. First, however, she needed some shoes. It turned out that the hotel's head housekeeper wore the same size as she and stored her walking-to-work boots in her cubby (her actual work shoes, as she pointed out, pulling back her skirts, were black patent, much finer), so Rita promised her, *promised*, that she would purchase the lady brand-new boots as soon as she had access to her funds, and that she'd also replace the pair of handknitted socks offered with them, actually being made for the woman's grandson, nearly finished.

"Any sort of shoe you want," Rita vowed. "Boots, heels, satin dancing slippers. From any shoemaker anywhere, anywhere in the world."

The housekeeper clucked her tongue, handing everything over. She was pleasantly round-faced, pink-cheeked, strands of hair coming loose from under her cap. "Dancing slippers! As if I would! None of that, now. I know who y'are. Seen a few of them moving pictures shows with you in them, miss. I don't be doubting your word."

So when Rita ventured out of the Queen's Hotel's tastefully carved façade that Saturday morning, no later than eight, she was a striking figure in torn and salt-stained silk that wafted behind her as she moved, a long bristly braid and scuffed brown leather boots, no heel, that laced up past her ankles.

QUEENSTOWN WAS NOW packed with officials. Even more of them poured in from all corners, company men and military men, all of them hurrying along, all of them performing some vital task in an attempt to contain a tragedy that could not and would not be contained. When she asked how she might send a wire, she was directed to the post office along the harbor front, where she stood in line to send a free message, curtesy of the Cunard Line, to whomever mattered most.

The gulls cried above her as she waited, circling and dipping. Her eyes followed them, how they plunged and flapped their wings and landed clumsily on the wooden posts dotting the harbor, lifting their orange feet, clacking their orange beaks.

Hungry, she thought. She pressed the heel of her palm to the center of her forehead, trying to erase the image of them gorging on the dead. *They look hungry still; are they ever sated?*

When it came her turn, Rita was tired and thirsty again. She sorely missed breakfast or whatever passed for breakfast back at the hotel; there'd been nothing set out in the lobby or dining area when she'd left, not even lemonade. She stood at the post office window, chewing her lip, as the clerk stared at her from behind his metal bars (so like the purser's office onboard the *Lusitania*; so different!), his pencil poised over the paper slip.

"Miss?" he prompted, his mouth a downward curve. Behind her, people shifted on their feet, huffed and sighed. A few of the women were quietly sobbing.

"To Count de Cippico," Rita began. "In Naples, Italy." She paused, looked at him. "I'll spell it out for you, shall I?"

OUTSIDE THE POST office, tacked to a wooden signboard, was a handwritten list of names on three long, wind-tattered sheets of paper already grimed along the edges. The ink was smeared from countless hands pressing down, holding the sheets in place against the breeze as people scanned the names of the Known Saved.

Rita joined the subdued group gathered around it. She quickly picked out her own name on that list, Lady Allan's just below it. She pushed closer and started over, ran her finger down the first page, the second, the third. Barring Captain Turner, there was no one else she knew, not personally. If George or Charles or the two Allan girls had landed safely, their names had not been added yet.

Not yet.

QUEENSTOWN WAS A picturesque port by any measure, with attractive stone and brick and wooden structures rising along gentle, treed hills. Saint Colman's Cathedral, with its imposing spire and French Gothic parapets and arcading, towered against cerulean skies. Cork Harbour pulsed along her shores, sometimes misted, sometimes clear, but always providing commerce, travelers, fish. Before the sinking, the town was perhaps best known as *Titanic*'s final port of call.

The press would end up calling it the "Town of the Dead," and they weren't wrong. *Lusitania*'s survivors had been whisked away to wherever there was space and willing hosts: hotels and inns, private homes, the local hospital. But the boats were still returning from sea, now laden with corpses.

At first, confusion reigned. No one knew where to put the bodies, so the seamen simply placed them along the wharves. There was no morgue in town large enough to accommodate the growing numbers of the dead, sodden and stacked one atop another in the spare spaces around pilings and ropes and barrels. Limp, wet arms jutting out. Limp, wet clothing, those that still had any. Blanched faces, blood and mucus. Gulls. Flies.

Corpses were piling up by the hundreds.

Cunard began to direct the bodies to a hastily emptied shed on their quay, shielding the victims from the increasingly warm day at least.

But it wasn't enough. As the hours passed and the dead continued to be salvaged, the town hall was converted into a temporary morgue as well, and then a vacant building on the water that used to be a chandlery.

The sun slanted higher into the blue. The stench grew unavoidable, unmistakable. Unbearable. And still the bodies came in.

RITA VISITED EVERY hotel or inn she could find, walking, walking, her sore muscles protesting every step. Inside each location, she inquired about her men and Lady Allan's girls. Most of the proprietors had already started compiling the names of their unexpected guests, so it wasn't hard. It was, however, fruitless.

After her sixth disappointment, she paused by a little garden outside a bakery, her hands over her stomach. She still hadn't eaten a decent meal since her luncheon aboard the liner. On her rounds, she'd asked for, and been given, water, and then tea, and then a single boiled egg, smuggled to her by a sympathetic kitchen maid. But Rita had no money, no banker's draft, no passport. No way of proving who she was to any proper bank, unless she happened to encounter another photoplay fan.

When she looked up, she saw the Cunard man of last night, with the fox-head stickpin, hurrying along the cobbles, sunlight on his shoulders, his head low.

She sprinted after him. "Sir! Sir!"

He slowed, threw her an impatient glance, then recognized her. He stopped, pushed back his hat.

"Miss Jolivet."

"I've been—" she paused to catch her breath, and the man spoke over her, looking her up and down.

"Has no one told you about our credit arrangements with the town's outfitters?"

She shook her head. He took a notepad from his jacket pocket, scribbled something down, then tore off the page and handed it to her.

"Try this shop. They have women's items. Nothing as fine as you're used to, I'm sure, but..."

"Yes, I will, thank you."

"Tell them you're from the ship. They should be able to take care of you."

"Thank you," she said again. "But what I really need is something to eat."

He looked taken aback. "There was nothing at the hotel?"

"No."

"And...forgive me, you have no funds?"

She very nearly snapped, *I'm afraid all my diamonds went down with your ship,* but didn't.

Instead, she opened her arms, palms up, showing him her tattered gown, her bruised skin, then turned inside out her solitary pocket. No reticule, not even the pistol, which she'd left back in the hotel room.

The man frowned, dug into a different pocket. He pulled out a pound note, pressed it into her palm.

"I'm sorry," he said. "I hope this helps. I really must be off, though."

"Thank you," she said a third time, as he clipped away.

———————

CLOTHING BE DAMNED, she ate first. A traditional Irish fry-up at a pub well off the main road, bacon and sausage, a sunny egg, tomatoes and soda bread and beans, sliced mushrooms swimming in butter. Hashed potatoes, perfectly crisped. A waitress of about fifteen served the meal, still bubbling in its skillet.

Rita hunkered over her food and tried not to shovel it into her mouth as she wanted to, aware of the stares aimed at her from the local patrons. She used her knife and fork, Pauline's court manners still in force, but manners could only push back so far against trauma and deprivation. Rita never looked up, never paused, never slowed down.

When she finished, the waitress brought her a plate of oat flapjacks, drizzled with honey.

"Compliments of the owner," she said, unsmiling. She eased back on her heels, redhaired, stern. She tucked her hands behind her, her apron worn and spotless. "God bless."

Thank you had begun to sound like nothing to her ears, but Rita said it anyway, and the girl nodded, brusque, and moved off.

SHE HAD SLIGHTLY less luck at the dressmaker's shop the Cunard man had sent her to.

"Sorry, miss," said the young shop girl, wringing her hands. "We've been plucked clean since afore noon. All the ready-mades are gone, most of the underthings as well. We have some woolen stockings left, if you're interested, and garters. Some waist laces and chemisettes. There's a pongee wrapper in the back, and some fine sweater coats, knitted local. Excellent quality, very thick. Keep you warm no matter the wind."

Rita took the wrapper and two sweater coats, thinking one would probably fit around Lady Allan's shoulders, at least, even if she couldn't get her arm through the sleeve. She also took two pairs of stockings, although, to be honest, she doubted they would be as comfortable as the socks she was wearing.

She returned to the hotel to find that the kitchen had been taken over by the staff, who'd broken the locks off the larder and begun to serve herbed omelets and sautéed potatoes. Urns of hot tea sat out in the lobby.

Rita brought a plate and cup to the room for Lady Allan, who was sitting up in bed but still feverish. The other two ladies were absent, their bed neatly made; she'd never even known their names.

A local doctor had come and gone, Marguerite Allan told her, prescribing aspirin powder and rest.

"And hot food," Rita said, trying to sound cheerful. "Everything's better when you've had a good meal."

She handed her the plate, placed the teacup on the nightstand nearby, and sat down in the room's lone chair. Lady Allan's hair was loose now, her fine tortoiseshell comb gleaming on the nightstand, the row of pearls lining the top all amazingly intact. She hadn't asked about her daughters.

They sat in silence. Lady Allan kept her gaze on the plate on her lap, the carefully cooked and folded eggs slowly cooling in a smear of butter.

Rita said, "You mustn't give up hope. I'm not done looking."

The other woman nodded. She picked up her fork with her good hand and sliced off a bite of omelet. But she didn't eat it, only pushed it around the plate.

RITA WENT BACK out. She rechecked the list of Known Saved first—Josephine Brandell's name had been added; she felt a measure of relief at that—then spent another two hours searching, still fruitless. All day long, she'd deliberately avoided the wharf, because it was clear what was going on down there, what had to be happening down there, and she didn't want to see it. She'd already seen enough of the dead.

But as the air grew warmer, a putrid stink billowed and undulated over the town, up the quaint lanes, across flowerbeds, and into rooms, even with the doors and windows shut. It was carried along by the ocean breeze, and that breeze seemed to never stop.

No one knew anything of George or Charles. No adolescent girls answered to the surname Allan.

She realized, finally, she was going to have to go down to the wharf after all. She was going to have to join the long lines of people queueing up at the makeshift morgues, trying to find their loved ones among the dead.

But once on the quay, she only hung back, not joining any line yet, only watching. The Cunard pier lurked nearby. People shuffled toward it with their heads lowered, with tearstained faces. Rita was wearing her new sweater coat, belted at the waist, but still couldn't shake the chill that was creeping over her.

Sailors trudged past the queue, cradling babies as still and white as dolls in their arms. Disappeared inside.

She joined the line. As it crept forward, they passed six of *Lusitania*'s lifeboats tied up and jouncing in the water, all that had been successfully brought ashore. The rest, she supposed, were splinters along the waves, or else still roped and bound to the liner at the bottom of the sea.

She entered the shed. Immediately, she cupped her hand over her mouth and nose, and then her knitted sleeve, trying to block the smell. It was dim inside compared to the day, shadowy, so at first she couldn't discern what exactly was in front of her: a procession of shrouded bodies laid out on the floor, the sheets covering them patchy dark with seawater. Hands poked out from under the coverings, fingers curled. Long, damp locks of women's hair spread along the floor.

The line crawled along. She reached the first body, a torn scrap of paper pinned to the sheet with a rough "1" inked on it. Gingerly she took hold of the edge of the sheet and drew it back.

A young woman in rags. Her face contorted, her eyes bulging, her mouth open as if in a scream. Dried blood crusted her
lips and stained her chin. Rita looked down at her in horror.

Not them, she told herself, but her fingers wouldn't unclench
from the sheet. *Let go, look away, it's not them, any of them.*

"Miss," murmured a man behind her, waiting his turn.

Rita pulled the sheet back into place, blinking away the
flecks in her vision. When they were gone, she took a closer
look around the cavernous shed. She couldn't count how
many bodies stretched before her in the gloom, row after
row.

Over a hundred. Over a hundred, at least.

But she didn't have to bear witness to them all. She only
had to reach body Number 24, still in that first, ghastly row.

Rita pulled back the sheet. It was Charles.

She sank to her knees beside him. She pressed a hand to
his shoulder, his ruined jacket.

Unlike every other face she'd forced herself to see, his was
peaceful. Almost smiling. He looked the same as he always
did; he looked only asleep, and for a treacherous instant her
mind told her that it might be true, he was only asleep, he only
needed to wake up.

But he was cold, and he was dead. She stroked his shoulder
and then his hair, something she never would have done were
he alive. She wanted to smooth it into place the way he liked
it. He was always so tidy, he hated to be unkempt, but her
hand was trembling too badly, and the strands too stiff with
salt, resisting.

The most beautiful adventure in life, he'd told her.

"Oh, my friend," she whispered. And realized she was about
to vomit.

Rita stood up and ran back into the sunlight.

She was blinded at once and had to cover her eyes, bent
nearly double. Then, right there in the open, in front of

anyone and everyone, she went to her knees again, her poor bruised knees, hiding her face in both hands, fighting the nausea. She wasn't moaning, she wasn't weeping, but she wasn't able to stand either.

This could not be real. The sun could never feel this hot. The wind could never smell this foul. There could never be such a sacrifice of souls.

Minutes passed. People walked by her as if she wasn't there, carrying on their conversations, no one pausing. She was merely one more person locked in her grief amid so many.

At last, she was able to brace her hands against the pavement and push herself to her feet.

Someone caught her arm from behind. Someone yanked her roughly around.

A strange woman stood before her, wind-whipped, ashen. Her hair lashed gold around them both; she dropped a bag at their feet. Rita could only stare at her, bewildered and mute, so it was up to Inez to pull her sister into her arms with a cry, holding her tight.

THEY RETREATED TO the Queen's Hotel. There was nowhere else to go anyway, nowhere for the living, at least. Every available room in town was occupied, and the town was growing more crowded by the minute. They went up to Rita's room but Lady Allan was asleep, her cheeks flushed (the omelet unfinished on the nightstand), so they only left Inez's valise by the spare bed and went back to the lobby.

Those urns of tea were still there. Inez poured them both steaming cups, lumps of sugar, a splash of milk each, and carried them to the round piecrust table they'd claimed, two sagging armchairs drawn close.

Rita spent the next half hour attempting to convince her little sister to go back to the room to rest, while Rita continued her search.

She was the strong one. George knew it, and so did she. It had to be her.

"No," Inez said, and kept saying. "No. I've come all this way. I'm not hiding now. I've come to find him, and I'm going to find him."

"But you don't—"

"*No.*"

Rita got up and went to the curved walnut bar dominating the back of the room, a baroque monstrosity carved with curlicues and griffins. There was no one minding it—God knew why; if ever there was a day when anyone needed a drink—so she reached over the top and helped herself to a bottle of whatever was nearest. Whiskey, as it turned out, the same as last night.

The wall behind the bar was lined with mirrors, etched shamrocks and vines frosting their edges. She tried not to look at her reflection, but it was impossible. Too many years of wondering what she looked like, maybe, if her hair and makeup were correct, if she was glamorous enough, beautiful enough, famous enough.

Ragged was the word that best fit her now. Stricken. Red-eyed, destroyed—very nearly destroyed. She doubted that a single person she'd ever worked with would recognize her. It was a wonder the housekeeper had, but maybe Rita's face was less common than she thought. Or maybe someone had simply told the woman her name.

She returned to the piecrust table. Inez was watching her with her arms folded over her chest. She had that brittle, waspish expression that Rita was still learning to see on her, had hardly ever seen on her, but never forgotten.

Rita drained the dregs of the tea, looked pointedly at her sister's cup until Inez did the same. She pulled the cork from the bottle of whiskey and filled both cups to the brim.

"Drink it," she said, grim. "You're going to need it."

He was not in the Cunard shed. He was not in the town hall.

He was in the abandoned chandlery.

It was clear the building had been in disuse for some time. The air floated with dust, motes whirling in the dirty light falling from the dirty windows. Beyond the walls and beneath the planked floors, the faint splashing undertone of the sea came nonstop.

The interior seemed yellowed with neglect; the windowpanes were all splintered. But otherwise it was very much like the shed, lines of the dead laid out, mothers next to children, saltwater seeping along the floor. The same shrouds splotched with water or blood or worse.

Rita and Inez linked arms as they filed along. One or the other of them would pull back the sheet; both would look.

About twenty minutes in, they found him. Inez was the one with her hand on the sheet.

Rita was the one who propped her up as she started to fall, but in the end, they dropped down to the floor together, taking in the waxen and comely face of the late George Vernon, his eyes mostly closed, a deep gash along his hairline, not a drop of blood to be found.

As her sister began to shake, Rita clutched her close, waving away the flies.

---○○◇○○---

Chapter 20

---○○◇○○---

You can't imagine the waiting I endured on the way to Ireland. The eternity of seconds pressing down on my shoulders, tick-tock. Train after train. The ferry. Another train. The closer I came to Queenstown, the longer it took, because it seemed everyone was converging there; everyone had a loved one they hoped had been saved; everyone needed to know, needed to see. Especially the press.

I don't know if it was fate or fortune that had you there as well. All I know is I was so glad you *were* there, with me.

I think I could have endured it alone. I don't know, but I think so. But because of you, I didn't have to. My burden was shared.

At least the sea didn't keep him. He's not lost to the waves, to the sharks and crabs like so many others. We buried him, and I'm grateful for that small mercy.

JUNE, 1915
MEDMENHAM, ENGLAND

Giuseppe found her at Winter Queen. He arrived on a day so balmy it was as if the cold had never been, as if tragedy had never struck. Rita's telegram to him from Queenstown had been delayed, long delayed; the war had frayed the edges of all civility and certainly modern technology. She'd sent it the morning following the sinking. Count de Cippico had received it in Naples eight days later.

(At that point, Italy was already sliding irrevocably into the conflict, revoking its official alliance to Germany and Austria only days before, leaning more and more into the eager embrace of the Allied Powers.)

A further flurry of communication had established that Rita and her sister had departed Ireland by then, had made their way back to their parents and the sanctuary of their family estate.

Alfred was well gone by the time they'd arrived; the army would not wait. But he'd left letters for them both.

I'm so sorry. I love you. Your grief is mine. I will kill those rotten Hun swine every chance I get. Every bullet I fire will be in your names.

So turned the glorious world.

ONLY ONE OF Lady Allan's dead daughters was recovered, Gwen, a week after Rita and Inez had left. The body of Anna was never found. But both of the maids who'd been traveling with the Allan family showed up at the Queen's Hotel that second afternoon, everyone expressing shock and amazement that any of them were alive. Lady Allan's husband had been notified of the sinking, that she had been saved, and was on his way. There was nothing left for Rita to do, other than bend down to kiss Marguerite on the cheek as she said goodbye and whisper *God bless*, the softest and kindest words she could think to say, substitutes for the other words she was thinking but could not say.

I'm sorry I couldn't find them for you. I'm sorry your girls are probably gone. I'm sorry for your guilt, your unreasonable guilt, because your heart still beats without them. I know it haunts you, because I'm haunted too.

Lady Allan had clasped Rita's hand in hers and nodded, her eyes shimmering. Rita kissed her other cheek, gave her fingers a squeeze, and left.

Winter Queen was mostly unchanged. So far, George's dire predictions about it being bombed had not come to pass, but then, every dusk, the windows were covered in thick black cloth, and all the exterior lights were extinguished. No head-lamps for the autos, no lamplight for the carriages. No mild, candlelit glow from the waxed-paper lanterns dotting the garden trees. There was nothing anyone could do about the estate being so close to the Thames, but Charles and Pauline were diligent about obeying the blackout restrictions.

Nothing could stop the moonlight, though, its stark silver luminance, brighter than a Broadway spotlight. Even Inez, usually pagan and barefoot beneath the full moon, retreated from its glare.

When the wind was right, it was possible to hear the whine of the German aeroplanes in their raids, miles away. Worse still, and far more numerous, were the enormous, bloated Zeppelins, which made hardly any noise at all, delivering their packets of death from high above, beyond the reach of bullets fired from the ground. There were nights when the eastern edge of the sky burned orange from all the fires in and around London, like some false, hellish sunrise. Rita could not help but wonder, when it was all over, what would be left of the Old Smoke.

What, in fact, would be left of the whole world.

Yet Winter Queen's mist would still rise, beautifully reliable. At times, it came so swift and ferocious that the moon was devoured and the black cloth wasn't needed, although still applied. Within minutes, everything would be erased, the water, the sky, much like those foggy hours aboard the *Lusy*. Mab mantled her forest in thick gray, opaque, and those were the nights that Rita slept easiest.

But her lover arrived on a clear day, a buttery soft day. It was just over a week since Italy had declared war on Austria-Hungary and all the chaos that had subsequently ensued: boundaries asserted, troops mobilized, governments scrambling. Despite their exchange of telegrams, Rita wasn't expecting to see the count anytime soon—maybe weeks, maybe months, fingers crossed—and had done her best to put her worry for him, her longing for him, out of her mind and body.

When she heard the motorcar crunching along the drive, she was outside in the garden, helping with the removal of those paper lanterns, since they hadn't been lit in ages and likely wouldn't be again for some while. She was standing on the top rung of an old wooden ladder, had just removed a turquoise globe from its hook. She'd bent to hand it to a waiting maid as the sedan came into view around a break in the trees, a gleam of jet against the green and blue.

Inez, when she wasn't cloistered in her room, had resumed her childhood habit of gazing down at the koi in their pond, something Rita could not begin to fathom. If she never had to look at a lake or pond or any ocean again, it would suit her fine. But Inez had not spent long hours adrift in a northern sea, tossed and helpless amid gulls and porpoises and the dead. So.

In the years since Rita had moved away, Maman and Papa had installed a limestone bench beside the pond, so at least her sister was no longer sitting in the dirt, her hair draping down like a siren's mane over the water. The bird cherries arching above her had come into their full bloom a few weeks past, but errant blossoms still clung to the branches, and the air was still laden with their sweet almond scent. Occasionally one would flutter, detach, waft slowly down to the earth.

Inez wore solid black. They all did. It was sometimes stifling in the growing heat of the season—black silk, black muslin, black sateen—but Rita didn't mind. At times still she'd wake up in the middle of the night, shivering in the dark, so chilled

from her nightmares of the ocean it was as if she'd been
stranded in a blizzard.

As the motorcar drew nearer, she looked back at her sister.
Inez had come to her feet to face the drive, a wraith speckled
with sunlight; they exchanged a quick, troubled glance. A trio
of cherry petals clung to Inez's hair and right shoulder, ivory
dots that she didn't brush away.

Rita climbed down the ladder. She walked to the curve
where the driveway bent closest to the manor house, a wide
spread of crushed gray-and-white oyster shells fronting the entrance.

If this was about Alfred...

If it was a military car, and news about Alfred...

The sedan slowed, stopped. The rear door opened without
waiting for the driver to exit. Giuseppe stepped free of the auto.

She was moving before she was aware of it, walking, then
trotting. He turned and saw her emerging between the trunks
of the cherries and oaks and gnarled yews.

She was running, and then she was flying. He caught her
up in his arms and swung her in a circle, two people fully immersed in the remedy of each other's presence, acting younger
than their years and propriety allowed, uncaring. When their
lips met, her lashes were damp, and so were his.

Inez melted back into the shelter of the house.

"Is THERE to be a funeral?" the count asked. "I would like to pay
my respects."

They were in the west parlor, a cozier space than the grand
red salon, or the library, or the conservatory. Maman and
Papa sat with them, the four of them taking tea. After greeting
Giuseppe in the entrance hall, Inez had politely declined to
join them, citing a headache, and returned her room.

"No," Rita answered. She stirred her cup. "We had one in
Queenstown before we left. Well, what might pass for one. Inez

insisted he be buried there, in the Old Church cemetery. It's where—where—"

She lost her words, scowling at the tea.

"Where they buried the bodies no one could identify," Pauline finished for her quietly. "Three mass graves."

Giuseppe looked distressed. "George was not unidentified. Yet he was put in one of those—"

"No," Rita said, quick. "He has his own plot. We had a vicar and a prayer service, and a temporary headstone installed. We'll go back and order a better one after . . . after matters calm."

After the smell, she thought. After the grief had blown away, scrubbed away with a clean wind.

Giuseppe regarded her from under those long dark lashes, his lips drawn flat. He and George had been friends, she knew. Good friends, for years.

"It's a beautiful place," she told him. "Idyllic, *te lo prometto*. The greenest grass you'll ever see. Clouds and trees. Bells sounding from the cathedral. Birds, all kinds of birds, singing and singing."

"Perhaps. But to be so far from his home, his loved ones—"

"It's what she *wanted*." Rita's tone climbed to strident. She heard it, hated it, and dropped her spoon to her saucer with a clatter. "It's what Inez wanted, so it's what we did. She's his wife, and I was in no position to argue with her about it. Everything was so—just *so*—"

"Of course," Pauline soothed.

Rita set her jaw. "We did what we had to do. We did everything we *could* do."

The room sank into silence. Beyond the opened windows, a conversation was taking place in the garden about the lanterns, how many more to go. A dove began to coo.

"Sorry," she muttered. Giuseppe brushed his fingers along her wrist; she shot him a tight smile.

Papa sighed. He seemed much older than she remembered from her last visit. More silver in his hair, deeper wrinkles around his eyes. The backs of his hands were lightly spotted now, veined in blue. He took another salmon sandwich from the serving tray, transferred it to his already untouched plate.

"We'll all go back," he said in graveled French, "and pay our respects in person, as soon as we can."

"*En anglais*," Pauline prompted softly.

Charles looked up at them, surprised, as if he hadn't heard himself speak. In English, he said, "We'll all go back, for Inez."

ALTHOUGH COUNT DE Cippico had been at Winter Queen before as Rita's guest, she wasn't sure he knew his way around well enough to find her bedroom in the dark. Nor was she sure he'd defy convention that far anyway, not in her parents' domain. For his three previous stays, Pauline had assigned her eldest daughter's suitor a room in the wing opposite Rita's, respectable as could be. They'd slept apart for days.

So it was up to Rita to find Giuseppe that night, long after supper was finished.

Without the starlight or moonlight pouring through the windows, without the stained-glass panes stripped of their colors but still glowing, it wasn't as easy as she'd thought it would be. She was unused to this forced darkness and carried a candle with her, ready to snuff it out at a moment's notice. But Winter Queen kept her secret. No one was around this late, not even a hall boy. No one materialized from the gloom to demand *sotto voce* what she was doing, as if they wouldn't know.

She closed her hand on the scrolled knob to his room, and slowly twisted it. The tongue of the latch bolt clicked free. She glided into his chamber in her Irish pongee wrap and her bare feet, because barefoot was always the most hushed way to walk, the most clandestine. There was no light in here, either; it was too warm to light a fire, and none of the lamps were burning.

She carried the candle, dripping tears of wax, to his bed. Giuseppe was awake, no nightshirt, his arms crossed behind his head, watching her with his dark and knowing look.

She placed the candle on a bureau. He lifted the covers for her with one arm, a silent invitation. Rita slid out of the wrap and into the bed next to him, both shifting to the center of the mattress. He lowered his arm and the covers settled over them in a puff.

"You came," Giuseppe said.

"I thought you might not. So I took the initiative."

He drew a finger along her collarbone, dislodging the satin strap of her nightdress, easing it down her shoulder. "Your mother is formidable. I fear if she catches you in here, you'll be compelled to wed me after all."

"About that," she said, and his fingers paused their unhurried examination of her inner arm.

Rita took a breath. "I wanted to tell you that you've ensorcelled me, after all. I'm still greedy for my life, but even more than that, I'm greedy for you. For the life that you and I could build together."

He studied her, cocked his head. "Margherita. Is this change of heart because of what's happened? Because if so, you must know I'm still willing to wait for you. This misfortune, this great misfortune, does not need to decide us."

She sat up, tugging her strap back into place. "I promise you, I'd decided before I ever boarded that cursed ship. I decided the last day we were together in New York, on the harbor, as I watched you sail away from me. My heart was so full, and so empty. I knew I'd made a terrible mistake, just letting you leave like that. Letting you go without telling you how much I love you."

The flickering light sent copper along his raven hair, the lean curve of his jaw, the scant growth of whiskers that roughened his skin. But he didn't move, didn't speak.

"And then, on the water . . . *in* the water . . . when it was all cold and hot and dire, out there among the dead—sorry—out there, and in those awful days after, everything became so clear. I've been selfish, and I've been cowardly, and unfair to you. Unfair to us. It's the worst sort of cowardice, really, to deny the truth living in your own heart."

A sideward smile, barely there. "You? A coward? Never."

"Not anymore. And not ever again. I don't want to waste another day without you."

Finally he shifted, but it was only to duck his chin and run a hand through his hair. "Are we really doing it like this? Here and now?"

"Yes, here and now. I told you before, I like it when you call me Margherita. I want to hear you call me that for the rest of my life."

"You've stolen my . . . how do you say it? My moment. My thunder."

Before she could react, he'd rolled gracefully from the bed, walking to a leather case he'd left atop the secrétaire. He opened the case, withdrew something she couldn't see, although she certainly saw the rest of him, by heavens, nude and beautifully sculpted against the night.

This time it was she who lifted the covers for him. But Giuseppe didn't join her in bed. He went to one knee beside it, offering up the ring box to her on the flat of his palm.

"But this thunder," he said, "it's not stolen, because it was your moment, ours, all along. It belongs to us both."

He opened the box. In it was a platinum ring set with an emerald as green as that grass back in Ireland, the band studded with diamonds. He took her hand, slid it over her finger.

It was heavy, the stones throwing dramatic sparks. It was also a perfect fit.

"No more being a butterfly?" he asked her much later, after the candle had guttered out and the night fully enveloped them. They were panting still; he pulled her closer. "Or the swallow, always moving?"

"No." She slid her hand along his chest, enjoying the weight of her ring. She opened her fingers over his heart, skin to skin. "No. Now I'm a swan. Ready to live out my years beside my dearest."

THE NEXT MORNING, a letter from Alfred arrived from parts unknown, wrinkled and heavily censored in thick black strokes, but with enough sentences left intact to reassure his family that he was well, that his spirits were good, that the food wasn't as bad as they'd probably heard and his pals in the battalion were all grand chaps.

He'd ended it with: *My love to you all. See you when I see you!*

P.S. Send some socks and a wheel of Beaufort, will you? The canteen here doesn't know what's what about fine dining, and we're dying for some cheese the rats haven't tried first, ha ha.

He'd written the postscript in French, which might explain why it hadn't been censored.

GIUSEPPE WANTED TO delay the announcement of their engagement out of respect for Inez's bereavement, but Rita reminded him that her sister already knew about it, or at least had known about the possibility of it, before anyone else—except for him, of course—and if anything, telling everyone might lift her spirits.

"If you're sure," he'd said, still dubious.

"I am."

And it seemed that Rita was right. Perhaps buoyed by the relief of hearing from their son, her parents appeared genuinely pleased at the news, genteelly pleased. Papa insisted upon a champagne toast, and Maman threw a special celebratory dinner of beef bourguignon and hot, fragrant baguettes that she managed to whip up God knew how, since a year of steadily increasing food scarcity meant that butter and flour and red meat were rapidly vanishing from everyday life. (When asked how she'd pulled it off, Pauline would only laugh.)

Inez emerged from her bedroom for the champagne and bread and savory stew. She congratulated them both, admiring the ring, slanting Rita an impish smile over it when no one else was looking. For a moment, she resembled her old self, and Rita's heart lifted with hope.

YET INEZ WAS determined to sail back to New York. Nothing anyone said persuaded her to stay. She told them that she needed to return to their—to *her* penthouse apartment. She needed to begin the process of contacting her attorneys, settling George's affairs, taxes or probate or whatever needed to happen next. All of it was true, no doubt, but no one could look at her, so bloodless and whisper-thin, and imagine it a sound plan. There were law firms that could be hired from overseas, they pointed out; there were estate managers who might take care of it all from a distance. And weren't his parents still there, out in Vermont, or Virginia, or wherever it was? Maybe they could hire movers to box up their things, have professionals figure where and how to store it.

"No," she insisted. "I need to be there myself. I need to go home. I'm going."

Rita offered to join her for the voyage, but Inez dismissed that as well. She said not to worry; she was fine alone. She needed to be alone, at least for a bit.

Besides, she continued, Rita had already mentioned that the Ambrosio Company in Naples was itching for her return, and now she had an especially good reason to consider the list of films they'd offered her.

"Countess," Inez added, with that same impish smile.

"But I've got to head back to Manhattan soon anyway," Rita said sternly. "I have obligations there still. A flat to manage. A stack of screenplays from Lasky. This damned war has us all tossed like a salad, but I'll follow you as quick as I can, and then we'll sort out what to do next. I'm not going to let you just hide away. I mean it."

Inez took her hands. "I know you do. So don't fuss. Whenever you get back, I'll see you then. We're only a heartbeat apart, you and I, wherever we are."

Chapter 21

My final evening aboard the *Saint Paul*, I was outside as always, pacing the decks as always because I couldn't sleep. I hated to sleep.

I caught sight of George up ahead. He was walking away from me, but those were his broad shoulders, his brown hair. His familiar pace. It was *him*.

Oh, Marguerite. My heart leapt with such joy, such *relief*. I can't even describe to you that sensation of relief, except to say that it lit through me like a lightning bolt, my every living cell ablaze. In that instant, I knew it was all a mistake. The torpedo, the sinking. Of course, my God, how could George be dead, it wasn't possible, what a nightmarish misunderstanding. His body in the morgue, in the ground, no no. All these last few weeks, no no no.

It was all fine, everything was fine, because he was *still alive*.

I cried out his name from across the deck, breaking into a run. When the strange gentleman turned around, no doubt startled, I stumbled to a stop. Somehow, I managed to beg his pardon.

I returned to my stateroom and locked the door. I didn't come out again until after we had docked.

JULY, 1915
MANHATTAN, NEW YORK

Inez came home to the heat, from a clement British summer to a muggy Manhattan summer, and the difference was extreme. Limp hair, laboring lungs.

It was curious how her apartment was so unchanged when everything else had changed. An explosion, an earthquake of unfathomable proportions, had cratered her life, yet everything here was exactly as she had last seen it. Nothing toppled over, nothing shattered. No hint of the disaster that had occurred halfway around the world but still rippled on and on, like a tidal wave that only gained strength with distance, until it smashed into land.

She took a slow tour of the flat, remembering him in the chair by the fire, pulling her onto his lap. At the kitchen table, devouring the plate of madeleines she'd baked for him, his favorite dessert.

Their bedroom, that holy place.

The four-poster was dust-free; the duvet was perfectly smoothed and the pillows plumped. In the marbled bathroom, she found his shaving kit by the sink. His bottles of aftershave, his hairbrush and combs, all still in their neat lines. She picked up the brush, pressed her palm against the stiff bristles, then set it down and drifted outside to the balcony.

One of the main reasons they'd agreed upon the flat (after viewing so many, weeks and weeks of searching for their New York home) was this balcony, enclosed and private, offering fine views of the city even past the urns of bougainvilleas they'd ended up installing.

Inez fingered their dusty pink leaves. The plants had been watered, but without either of the Vernons in residence, the housekeeper only came by once a week.

Clearly, it hadn't been enough for the vines. The summer had scorched them dry.

Poor things, she thought. *Poor dead things. Poor dead babies. Everything dead.*

She glanced skyward. A lid of low, yellowish clouds did nothing to deflect the heat, so she went back inside to the shadows.

On HER THIRD day home, Inez awoke alone in the bed. She got up, made coffee (no fresh cream, so she drank it black, grimacing with every sip). She rinsed the dishes in the sink, then went to her closet, rummaging through it until she found the ebony satin gown she'd never planned to wear beyond that one time onstage at the Met for her debut, it was so elegant and severe. But George loved it on her. He loved it, said it suited her, showed the world who she really was, a tsarina in disguise.

She found her jewelry locked away in its heavy rosewood box. At first, she couldn't quite recall where the key was, but then she did. George's desk, in the hidden compartment cleverly concealed in the back.

Inez retrieved the key, fit it into the brass lock, and opened the box.

Such riches, really. Such beautiful, significant things. Her fingers skimmed the treasures inside, metalwork and gemstones and crisp facets that seized the light, dim as it was. She touched each piece, considering it, taking out only what she needed.

The diamond necklace he'd given her for their last anniversary.

The sapphire hair combs he'd given her for her last birthday.

The matched pair of rubied bangles he'd given her just because.

Just because I adore you, George had said, kneeling before her, smiling up at her. *So much, Mrs. Vernon. I adore you so much.*

I LOVE YOU, Inez wrote, the final words of the letter she'd been carefully composing over the past two days. She studied it a moment, examining the clarity of her handwriting—yes, good enough—then folded the pages in half and wrote her sister's name on the front. She hesitated, and then beneath it added a scrawled, *Don't be angry.*

Inez pushed back from her desk, leaving the letter where it was. In a slither of fine black satin, in a glitter of precious jewels, she returned to the closet and found the cardboard box stored way in the back, behind a stack of her husband's folded winter sweaters.

She carried the box to their bed, opened the lid. She removed the pearl-handled pistol, balancing the heft of it in her hand.

Chapter 22

I don't know if I will see him again. I don't know if I will ever get to hold my babies. All I know is that none of them are *here* with me, they will never be *here* with me, ever again.

I hope it's like the fish that go to sleep in the winter. Remember what Maman told us when we were little, asking about the koi in the pond? In the deepest cold, they simply go to sleep and dream until they wake, warm again, surrounded by their beloveds.

That's all I'm doing. I'm going to go to sleep, and dream, and hope that all of them will be with me when I wake.

I love you.

Chapter 23

JULY, 1915

MEDMENHAM, ENGLAND

They were nestled in the rear seat of the family sedan, Rita and her fiancé, knees touching, his right hand covering her left, as the car began to crunch along the drive on its way to the village train station. Giuseppe had to return to Italy; there was no choice about it. He'd lingered at Winter Queen as long as he could, but he was as caught up now in the war machine as any other patriotic Italian. There was so much work to do now, so much planning, so much girding of loins. He could not ignore his home.

Rita was still going back to the States, as she'd promised her sister, but she'd sort through all her business there as quickly as she could, and then they'd meet up again somewhere. Naples or New York or here. Anywhere, anywhere safe.

"And then, perhaps," he'd whispered in her ear last night, their last night together at Winter Queen, "a wedding ceremony."

"And then a wedding ceremony," she'd agreed, turning her head so their lips touched.

The auto was gathering speed down the drive, but still traveling slowly enough that Rita could see very well the boy on a bicycle pedaling toward them, then skirting past them along the edge of the way, his khaki shirt and trousers, black shoes and socks, a cap shoved low over his forehead. She had a crisply clear view of his flushed cheeks and the tips of his ears and his frowning eyebrows, sunlight burning along his back and shoulders. He shot a brief glance at the sedan as it passed; their eyes met.

Her blood froze. Every hair on her body stood on end.

She released the count's hand, turned around to follow the boy through the rear window as he kept pedaling toward the manor house, along a drive now lightly clouded with dust.

"Stop," she said, choked, too soft. "Stop!" she cried again, much louder, and pounded a hand on the back of the driver's seat.

"*Amore?*"

"Oh, God, stop the auto!"

The bewildered chauffeur did so. Before the sedan had even come to a full halt, Rita was yanking on the door handle, tumbling out, pelting back up the drive.

She reached the front door just as Pauline opened it, responding to the telegram boy's knock.

IT WAS THREE days before her body had been discovered. Not by the housekeeper but the landlord, who had read about the death of Mr. Vernon and thought perhaps his widow might be enticed into ending the lease early, as he could raise the rent significantly if she did.

The news made the New York papers first, a small bit of sensational information taking up a few column inches. Nothing like the sinking, of course, but connected enough to the sinking to matter. Tragic young *Lusitania* widow, despondent over the loss of her husband. Talented, lovely, rich. Suicide.

Hours later, just in time for the next morning's deadlines, the national wires picked up the story, which subsequently spread up and down the nation, from Maine to Florida to sunny California. By the time the details made it across the Atlantic (a few of the London periodicals taking note of Mrs. Vernon's British roots), nearly twenty hours had passed, and that telegram from the authorities in New York had already arrived at Winter Queen's door.

That luckless girl, the locals murmured over their tea or pints, some with genuine sympathy, some with simmering relish. *That fey, foreign girl, never was quite right in the head, was she? So quiet and peculiar. And then that terrible shock, the ship, her husband. Suppose she just couldn't bear it, her simple mind just broke.*

But anyone in Medmenham who'd ever heard Inez coax sonatas and concertos and fantasies from her violin, in her parents' parlor or performing outside in the meadows and woods—even the leathery old men at the pub—found themselves frowning into their drinks, blinking away a tear or two when no one was looking.

RITA DELIBERATELY AVOIDED the papers. She avoided reading them; she avoided giving interviews; she avoided the sun and the moon and her own inner rage, so saturated with sorrow she could no longer distinguish one emotion from the other.

More telegrams arrived, these all offering condolences, and Rita avoided those as well, even the ones from Cecil and Alvin and House. Even the one from the king.

She'd already sent her own condolence telegrams to Charles Frohman's family and to George's, not long after she'd come home from Ireland. She already knew exactly what those thin slips of paper would say, and how little they mattered because nothing they said would help.

BUT DESPITE HER efforts, two weeks later, in her Fifth Avenue penthouse, Rita came across a mention of it in the *New York World*, only because she was flipping through the tower of mail that had been growing during her absence, and she wanted to verify that there was nothing important in that mess of envelopes and magazines and newspapers before departing the United States again.

Her eyes picked out Inez's name in a headline, *Mrs. George Vernon*, above a short article. Before she could stop herself, she'd read the whole thing.

The reporter briefly mentioned her life, her skill with the violin, but lingered gleefully on the macabre: detailed descriptions of Mrs. Vernon's jewels and her expensive, formal black frock. The fact that her body had been found kneeling at the foot of her bed, as if in prayer. The pistol. The blood.

Rita flung the paper across the room in a fury, knocking over a vase and scattering the sheets through the air like frenzied, flapping wings. She pressed her knuckles to her mouth, hard enough to hurt. When she lowered her hand, teeth marks bit red into her skin.

She wiped her eyes and returned to packing.

She was taking her sister back to her husband.

IT WAS A season of loss. It was a year of loss, one that would stretch into several more years to come, as it would happen. Many years, many losses.

But this year, this loss, ate through her.

Rita couldn't remember a time when her sister wasn't glued to her side, either physically or spiritually. They'd shared the same parents, the same childhood, the same memories, the same sense of humor and tastes and the same artistic gift that allowed them each to tap into the Sacred Unknown, albeit in different ways.

But Inez had forsaken all that. Inez had left behind Rita and their family, on purpose. And now Rita had to figure out how to keep moving through the universe without her.

On the voyage back to Great Britain, she had plenty of time to ponder it all. She'd booked an American-flagged steamer, nothing so fancy as the *Lusy* had been, and nothing so dangerous either. In future years, whenever anyone would ask her the name of that liner, she honestly wouldn't remember. It wasn't about the ship, anyway, which had surely been anodyne and elegant and pleasant enough to blend in with all the others in anyone's memory. It was about Inez. Reckoning with Inez.

On this, their final voyage together, with Rita installed in a cabin high above (an exterior one with two portholes, although it was still very hard to look at the water) and her sister's casket strapped in place decks below, she took the time to imagine what she might say to Inez, if she had the chance. What needed to be said.

She composed her letter over the course of the passage in a bright reading and writing room, frequently with the ship's cat curled on her lap, a calico beauty with green eyes and a ringed tail that she whipped hard against Rita's legs whenever she tried to get up.

Inez,

I don't know that I can forgive you. I hope I can, someday. I'm trying. I'm not sure it's really fair of you to even ask me to.

I'm so mad at you. I'm so mad.

And I miss you with all of my heart. I miss your smile and your voice and your hand in mine. I miss your music. I miss the children you never had. I miss you at the wedding I'm going to have without you, because I have no choice. I miss our old lady years together, our sons and daughters growing up together, becoming best friends. I hate you, almost, for taking that away from me, from all of us, just because you could.

I wish you had told me what you were truly feeling. I wish I had been smart enough to guess. Would it have helped at all? I'll never know. You can pour your love into the ocean of another's heart, but that doesn't mean it shifts the current or changes the tide by even an inch. It's only you, pouring and pouring. Hoping for the best.

Did you ever *once* think about how what you did would affect Alfred, stationed heavens knows where, doing the best he can amid the bullets and mud? Or Maman and Papa? Was it really *so* bad we were reduced to nothing for you?

The cat is clawing at my thigh.

Maybe I'm being unfair. Probably I am. Who can ever truly plumb the depths of another's grief? I only thought, after that chandlery in Queenstown, after the terrible days that followed, wading our way through the disaster, coming out on the other side . . .

Well.

I've been thinking about everything that's happened, obsessing over it really, day after day, fact after fact falling in place like some sort of horrible game of doomsday dominos. The *Lusitania's* fourth boiler room shuttered. The Admiralty's abandonment. That U-boat's blind luck in finding us after the fog lifted, while our own very much ran out.

(I can say that here because this letter is just between you and me. I will toss these pages into the ocean before anyone else reads them, right into the deep blue Celtic Sea, my words melting away, the paper dissolving, just as I almost once did. Ironic, no?)

Anyway, my stupid obsession. The sinking, the suffering. The injustice of it all, the goddamned waste of lives. I've been thinking about how to make it *sear* for everyone. Everyone around the world, even more than it does. The war numbs us at some point; I've already seen it happening. The great sacrifices demanded of us become reasonable. The lack of food, of fuel, of connection with loved ones and hope becomes reasonable. All of this loss is so bloody reasonable.

So what I've been thinking, sissy, is this. I'm going to make a movie about it, a good one. I'll make a movie, and to ensure it's good,

I'll star in it and produce it myself. I know I've never done anything like this before, but I'm tenacious and tough and pretty certain I can do it. That way no one will ever, ever forget what happened.

No one will forget either of us.

But I'm still mad.

I love you. Forever and ever, I promise.

YEARS WOULD PASS, not many, only two, but Rita would make that movie. By then, she was Margherita, Countess de Cippico, and although she was not afraid of the water, she still couldn't be induced to like it. It took an act of will greater than she'd anticipated to submerge herself in the mighty Hudson for the filming of *Lest We Forget*, to allow herself to sink and rise and sink again beneath the liquid gray. To splash and act as if she were in danger of drowning, although she wasn't.

A model ship was constructed specifically for the sinking sequence, big enough and realistic enough that Rita could easily pick out which door would lead where, which section of the deck had hosted the games of quoits versus the egg-and-spoon races. The portholes of the washroom where she'd taken her saltwater baths.

Where she had stood in the steamer's final moments, holding hands with George and Charles, clinging tight to their last precious few seconds of life.

For the scenes representing those strange, gilded days as they'd crossed the Atlantic, the United States Navy had given them permission to film aboard one of the seized German luxury liners that had been trapped in the harbor since the beginning of the war.

Rita found a savage satisfaction in that.

IT WAS HER nightmare, reliving those days. Her redemption. *Lest We Forget* would be released around the world, but in America first, to fervid acclaim. It would place Rita Jolivet in cinema houses large and small and anything in-between, but also strand her squarely in front of the unrelenting eye of the United States government, which took note of her beauty, her charisma. Her personal and professional losses.

That same government would convince her to spend the rest of the war years selling Liberty Bonds while lecturing about the *Lusitania*, which Rita would do with great hidden anguish and unprecedented success. She outsold every other major moving-picture star, Pickford, Fairbanks, Chaplin. In October 1917, before her photoplay was even released, she would be summoned to raise an American flag over a captured U-boat, photographers crowding near. Her audience applauded so furiously that the din of traffic along the pier was drowned to nothing.

The Rita Jolivet Film Corporation produced just one film. One. But it *resonated*, that film. Drama, spectacle, propaganda, true-to-life atrocities. It struck a chord in the souls of all red-blooded patriots and played for years as the Great War dragged on.

The Countess de Cippico was determined to do her part to see the Germans defeated. She was determined to avenge her losses, those hours on the blooded sea, her murdered friends, even if she never said those words aloud, or ever would.

One hot summer day in 1917, their last day of filming aboard the German liner, she'd found a way to say what she needed to say without making a sound.

During the lunch break, while everyone else in the cast and crew was off with their sandwiches and beer and iced tea on the top deck, Rita slipped alone into the ship's first-class saloon. She found the most prominent, most expensive-looking mahogany pillar, took out a penknife, and carved her initials into it, rough and deep.

I was here, you sons of whores.
I'm still here.

Epilogue

AUGUST, 1915
QUEENSTOWN, IRELAND

The final service for Inez and George Vernon was held on a mild afternoon, all of the Jolivets gathered before the grave, even Alfred, on special furlough. George's parents, still mired in their mourning in America, had sent their best wishes but declined to venture from their home just yet.

No one had been expecting Alfred. He'd arrived at Winter Queen the very morning they were departing for Ireland, been greeted with joy, with kisses and hugs and a tearful scolding from his mother for not letting them know he was coming.

"I wasn't awfully sure it would happen," he'd said, young and blond and achingly handsome in his uniform. "I didn't want to get your hopes up."

What an upside-down world, Rita thought, even as she embraced her little brother, finally, at last, *to find goodness in denying hope.*

But it was a relief to have them all reunited, as brief as their time together would be, and as solemn as the occasion was. It was a relief to stand beneath the beaming Irish sun in the green, green Irish cemetery and see her whole family—what was left of her living family—come together to honor their beloved dead.

Giuseppe was there too, of course, and as the vicar began to speak in his lilting Irish tones she found herself leaning against her fiancé a little, maybe absorbing some of his calm strength, his strong devotion. He kept his hand on her lower back, occasionally moving it in a slow, soothing circle.

Her emerald engagement ring flared in the light. The air was scented of moss and brine but the sky was cloudless, much like that sunlit May day not long past when Rita's world had quite literally blown apart.

They stood amid a score of fresher graves like this one. Turned dirt the grass had not yet fully claimed, newly installed tombstones, different names and birthdates but every single date of death the same. May 7. May 7. May 7.

May 7, 1915.

As the vicar spoke, Rita wondered at the serenity of the land around her, even when threatened by war. At the unfathomable depths of love and loss and grief, the bottomless well of the human soul accepting it all, sometimes all at once.

Charles and Pauline had canceled the order for George's solitary headstone and commissioned a new marker instead, one for Inez and George both.

A granite Celtic cross atop a chiseled granite base. Modern, rounded script. They'd agreed as family, the count included, on what it should say.

IN TENDER MEMORY OF
INEZ AND GEORGE LEY VERNON
BOTH YOUNG, BEAUTIFUL AND GIFTED.
VICTIMS OF THE *LUSITANIA* CRIME.

Blackcaps and dunnocks trilled from the trees, swished into flight above them. Rita followed their fluid turns and swoops against the heavens, where once she'd imagined angels reaching down to her.

The vicar stopped speaking. One by one, Inez's family walked forward, each carrying a rose to toss down to the casket.

Rita went last. First a yellow rose, freshly purchased from the florist in town, but then a silk sachet filled with older but still fragrant dried petals, Autumn Damasks, that landed softly just beside her rose.

She stepped back to the grass again, her heels sinking into the spongy earth. Giuseppe returned his hand to her back, steadying her. She closed her eyes against the vibrant lawn, the azure sky and gold-lichened markers, concentrating only on that: the feel of him next to her, keeping her upright, warm and safe and certain.

Author's Note and Acknowledgments

The list of international grievances that lead to war are often long, petty, and confusing, but there was nothing confusing about the sinking of the *Lusitania*. Its deliberate destruction and the subsequent loss of life were straightforward strikes against the Allies, one that sent shock waves around the world. Even though Germany and Great Britain were openly at war, and even though the Imperial German Embassy published in the papers their very clear intention to sink the ship, the murder of so many civilians—especially so many women and children—incensed nations. Kaiser Wilhelm II was said to be surprised at the backlash; in Germany, submarine U-20's successful torpedoing of the *Lusitania* was celebrated as a glorious victory. Parties were held. Medals were struck.

Nearly 1,200 people died in the disaster, 94 of them children (including 31 infants). Over 100 of those victims were Americans, a fact the kaiser would come to keenly regret.

It wasn't long before the German propaganda machine (for lack of a better term) revved up a defense for those dire numbers: that the *Lusitania* had been outfitted with hidden, mounted guns on her decks, and so could be considered a warship; that she was carrying Canadian troops to join the fight; that she was loaded with massive amounts of contraband munitions intended for the Allies, which is why, when the torpedo hit, the explosion was so enormous and the steamer's ending so swift.

None of those allegations were true, as it happened. And none quelled the fury of the world.

The sinking of the *Lusitania* did not draw the United States immediately into the conflict, although there were plenty of voices demanding that it should do so. But it did contribute, without a doubt, to the nation officially joining the Allies by the spring of 1917. "Remember the *Lusitania*!" became the war cry of thousands of American soldiers journeying overseas to fight.

I HAD BEEN toying for a while with the notion of writing about the *Lusy*, but I admit I did not settle upon the idea of Rita as my new heroine until my fabulous team at Kensington suggested it. (Thank you!!!) What a fascinating woman. Well-bred, international, intelligent, lovely, and—in many ways—very much self-made. Although she more or less retired from acting after her marriage to Count de Cippico, her incandescent youth was famously toasted onstage and across the silver screen. She was a rapidly rising star when she boarded the *Lusitania*, and several passengers also on that historic voyage took note of her sparkling beauty and grace. She had a mischievous smile and dark, expressive eyes that bewitched more than one cinematic/theatrical reviewer. (And, if I'm being honest, more than one husband.)

Her relationship with Inez was as sweet and deep and soulful as only sisters of the heart could hope to have. Inez's unexpected suicide was a wound Rita would never fully recover from, although she was committed to using that pain to help the Allies win the war. It was one of the reasons why, at the American government's request, she went on to sell so many Liberty Bonds and agreed to speak of the sinking to audiences around the country. Yet it caused her, in her own words, "great anguish."

Still, she persevered.

Rita was a pioneer in her way, born into an ambered, genteel world, but determined to break free of its boundaries to walk her own path. She certainly succeeded. She survived the *Lusitania* and went on to live a life full of adventure and hope. There was spice in her soul, a daredevil sense of fun and audacity that would define all her days, but she also had a strong instinct for justice. She took her deeply personal suffering and *made a movie about it* to shame and condemn her enemies, because she could. I mean...damn.

Rita Jolivet was irrepressible. Even the depths of the ocean could not subdue her. I'm so glad you and I both get to know her now.

As I RESEARCHED the story, a ton of little interesting facts and moments kept popping up. I couldn't cram all of them into the narrative, because it would get too distracting, but I managed to slip in a few, including:

- Rita's "Characteristic Dances of Various Nations" layout in *The Sketch*. Although all the other representative dances/nations for the shoot took place, adding the American cowgirl to the mix was a bit of fictitious humor on my part.
- Rita really did book her ticket at the very last moment on the morning of the *Lusy*'s departure and didn't realize that George or Charles would also be aboard.

- She definitely had her gun with her on the liner and took it with her into the water.
- The warning printed in the newspapers by the Imperial German Embassy actually had that typo in it, although in some of the papers, editors caught it before it went to press.
- Alfred Vanderbilt did receive that mysterious telegram warning him to get off the ship (along with another one later on in the voyage from a woman—not his wife—saying how much she looked forward to seeing him soon).
- Dowie, the ship's loyal cat, really did vanish into the streets of New York City rather than remain aboard for that final crossing.
- There were indeed three German stowaways discovered aboard once the ship had set sail, hiding in a steward's closet. And it turned out that that particular steward, a newly hired Englishman, was a German spy himself.

What happened to the promised Royal Navy escort? A haze of history and secrecy clouds some of what actually occurred, but it seems the escort was never promised at all, only assumed. What isn't a secret is that young Winston Churchill, First Lord of the Admiralty at the time (and son of vivacious Jennie Jerome), understood very well that any American lives lost on a German-sunk ship would likely push the United States one step closer to a declaration of war against the Central Powers and hopefully end the conflict all the sooner.

Some important sources I utilized for my research, in no particular order:

- Lusitania: *An Epic Tragedy*, by Diana Preston

- *Dead Wake: The Last Crossing of the* Lusitania, by Erik Larson
- The *Lusitania* Resource: https://www.rmslusitania.info
- *The New York Times*
- FamilySearch.org
- imdb.com
- flickr.com
- https://11east14thstreet.com/2013/09/30/rita-jolivet-unsinkable/
- https://www.encyclopedia-titanica.org
- Rita's firsthand testimony as a witness at the Limitation of Liability Hearings for the *Lusitania*: https://www.titanicinquiry.org/Lusitania/lolh/testimony/cippico_margherita.php
- ArchiveGrid, for a picture of Rita hoisting an American flag over the captured U-boat *UC-5*, and various ephemera: https://researchworks.oclc.org/archivegrid/?q=%22Rita+Jolivet%22

I don't write my books in a void, although sometimes, in the hushed hours of the night, it feels that way! (At least until one of the dogs saunters into my office, hoping for attention.) I am so very fortunate to have so many good people at my side, literally and figuratively, helping me craft the best possible stories I can:

My amazing, patient editor, Wendy McCurdy, who deserves the highest praise for her guidance, her advocacy, and her always honest insights—especially when it comes to some precious word or passage I foolishly (sometimes ridiculously) beg to keep, but that she knows weakens the story. I'm so grateful for all of her help and attention.

Also, of course, my entire hardworking team at Kensington, who truly seem to love sharing their enthusiasm for their jobs and (happily) my books, plus all the important components churning behind the scenes to prop up said books: the editing, covers, publicity, promos, marketing, interviews, and I'm sure I don't even know the half of it. I'm so honored to be able to work with you all, and I mean it.

Annelise Robey and Andrea Cirillo, my fantastic agents at the Jane Rotrosen Agency, who always have my back, even after all these years! Thank you!

My great friend Bev Allen, historian and researcher extraordinaire, who manages to unearth the most fascinating, obscure little nuggets of history for me, no matter the topic, and then helpfully sends me a link, lol. I don't know how she does it, but I'm so glad she does.

And Sean. Always Sean, forever Sean.

I would also like to offer my sincere gratitude to the fine people at the New York Public Library for the Performing Arts, who sent me a scan of an actual letter that Rita wrote to drama critic Ward Morehouse in 1963 describing her final moments aboard the *Lusitania*, including Charles Frohman's last words to her. How amazing to read about her experience in her own handwriting.

Finally, my deepest gratitude to you, Dear Reader. Because nothing I mentioned before, none of the hard work or research or anything, resonates without you. We live in a beautiful, fathomless universe, connected by way of hearts and thoughts and history, ideas and reading and dreams. So thank you for coming along with me, and helping me with this journey.

Book Discussion Questions

1. Rita's childhood could be considered sheltered, even enchanted. There's no question her parents had wealth and status, moving in some of the most rarified social circles. How did her childhood prepare her for the real world? Or did it? Do you think Rita would have been a successful actress if not for the initial support of Pauline?

2. The Jolivet sisters shared a deep and abiding bond, but Rita was always the leader. Was it fair of her to drag her little sister along with her to London, just to get her own way?

3. Rita's first experience acting in live theatre was a disappointment. In real life, she would allude to it when pressed, but never openly discuss it. Even so, she didn't give up her dream. Would you have?

4. Rita enjoyed what could be called a bohemian lifestyle for her time, flouting convention if it didn't suit her. She was a famous, divorced woman who lived happily alone but had no problem inviting her lover into her home. She had a strong publicity machine at her back to smooth over any

transgressions, but should she have been more circum-
spect regarding her private life?

5. Inez defends her decision to marry George by stating
   simply: "I am at home in his heart." Do you believe she actually fell in love with him that quickly, or was becoming
   Mrs. Vernon more of a new version of herself that she
   couldn't wait to experience, especially since Rita had vanished into her own world?

6. Even as she began to fall in love with Giuseppe, Rita
   would tell herself, *I want him, but I don't want to need him.*
   Considering her past divorce and her thriving career, was
   she wise to guard her heart against the count?

7. Rita decided to take the *Lusitania* despite all the public
   warnings. Do you think she was too trusting of the official
   mantra that the ship was too fast to be torpedoed? Or was
   she justified in feeling that her need to reach her brother
   before he left for the front outweighed the risk? Would *you*
   have boarded the ship?

8. In 1918, Rita was summoned as a witness for a Limitation
   of Liability hearing for the *Lusitania*. She described her last
   moments aboard the ship and the hours after, in clear,
   calm detail, including the fact that she clung for hours to
   an upside-down boat, bearing witness to the death and destruction all around her. How do you think you would
   have fared in her place? In those frantic minutes after the
   liner went under, would you have let the panicked people
   still in the water climb up the lifeboat, even at the risk of
   capsizing it?

9. Inez was clearly devastated to lose George, her husband of
   twelve years and the love of her life. Did Rita and her
   family do enough to help her in those weeks after the sinking? Or do you think Inez was deliberately as emotionally
   hidden as she needed to be to conceal her true intentions?

Do you think her decision to end her life was entirely pre-
meditated, or was it more a last-minute act of despair?

10. Do you agree with Rita's decision to make *Lest We Forget*?
Was it cathartic for her or more of a publicity grab? Why
do you think Rita agreed to the government's request that
she travel around the country to speak about the sinking
while selling Liberty Bonds, even though it caused her anguish?

11. What do you think of Rita's deliberate, unspoken message
to her enemies: *I'm still here*?

12. "Talkies" came about in the late 1920s and changed the
way films were made forever. But before that, the silent
stars of the silver screen were considered fascinating, remote, glamorous, untouchable. And no one even knew
what they sounded like! Have you ever imagined what it
would be like to be a part of that world, a fêted star of that
era, like Rita or Mary Pickford or Rudolph Valentino?
What would your stage name be?